THE WHITE HOUSE

HOTEL

A Fictional Biography

A Novel By
Timothy Charles Pilkington

AUTHOR'S NOTE

I am not a historian and had no intention of becoming one while writing this book. Though my story contains a near-equal number of nonfictional as well as fictional people, it remains a novel. Many of the occurrences in the story are based on true events that happened to real people and thus justify the use of the term "biography." But like the man in Liberty Valance, I chose, rather than the "fact," to "print the legend" — their legend.

For
Carole and Christina
the loves of my life

TABLE OF CONTENTS

PROLOGUE

LAKE OZARK, MISSOURI
EARLY MARCH 1945

I'm in the womb. My father lies next to us. My mother sleeps contentedly, a slight smile on her face as though it holds a secret. My brother rests in a cradle next to my father. Born in January 1942, he is just three years old.

The room we are in is one of eight on the second floor of a two-story building along the highway just south of the dam. Our room, as are the others, is approximately 10 X 12, enough space to hold a double-bed and a small dressing table. Inadequate closet space is tucked in one corner. There is a bathroom down the hall.

The center room on the first floor is the entryway and includes a soda fountain with counter and stools at the very back. Five tables for two occupy the space in front of it, and a door behind leads to a commercial kitchen. To the right of the counter is a stairwell leading to restrooms. Just inside the front door to the left is a small package liquor store. It is closed, this being a Missouri Sunday.

The largest room, consuming most of the south side of the building, is the dining room. At one end is a small stage, a dance floor just down front, and a jukebox along one wall. This room, in the recent war years, has witnessed good food, good drink, dancing, and some sadness.

Beneath it all is the basement level, housing the mechanical plant, the boiler room, and coal.

Outside, one sign proclaims the building a bus stop, another a café with a fountain. Perhaps unnecessary is the signage announcing "gasoline," as there are three very prominent pumps positioned underneath a wide, covered driveway. The entire building is painted white. Dirty white — but white. A large sign attached to the roof proclaims it "The White House Hotel," but to locals, it is known simply as the Whitehouse.

PART I
THE OKIES

TULSA, OKLAHOMA
JULY 1923

It is said that if you reside in the city during hard times, with store shelves limited or empty, there is no place to go. If fortunate, though, to live on even a small plot of rural land, you can raise and grow what you need to take care of your family. But on this hot, dry, mid-summer Oklahoma day, the opposite seemed true. The drought's effects on the small farmers seemed to foreshadow what was to come in the future. For the most part, though, folks in the city were managing well and prospering, a lingering effect of the earlier oil boom. Black folks, not so much—a lingering effect of the riot.

It has always been about that—a plot of land. A place to hang your hat, raise a cow, or a cowboy. Live your life; make a living. There was, however, a time when no one seemed to want this plot of land called Oklahoma; one part, two parts, no matter. If you have the power, though, to move undesirables out of your way, as the federal government did in the early 1830s, then Oklahoma was a good place to put them — perceived, as it was, a big old barren rectangle with a handle right in the middle of… nowhere.

When the Cherokee and Creek arrived, thanks to the Indian Removal Act, they were joined by other tribes, some of whom were described as "civilized." Among them, coming by way of forced trades from first Missouri and then Kansas, were the Osage, settling in on a large parcel they "traded" for just northwest of what is now the city of Tulsa. They owned that land then, and they owned it when oil was discovered on it in the early 1900s. That oil suddenly made Oklahoma a very popular plot of land.

Tulsa, being the largest city near the oil fields, was tagged "The Oil Capital of the World" and became the hub for everything good or bad about the petroleum industry. It was this "world" into which Harold Pilkington, a child of English descent, was born in 1915. His grandparents had arrived in Indian Territory sometime around 1880 and had five children, the youngest of whom, born in 1891, they named Grant. He was Harold's father.

So, on this particular hot, dry, mid-summer day in 1923, Grant, now a tall, muscular man in his mid-thirties, is working in the backyard of his small house on Archer Street. He is fixing a tire, the vehicle jacked up nearby. His son Harold, now almost eight, stands in the rear doorway watching him as a man of similar stature and age as Grant appears, coming from around the corner of the house. He is holding a pistol as he advances toward Grant's back.

Seeing him, fearful, the boy suddenly shouts, "Daddy!"

Reacting to his son's voice, Grant turns quickly and, seeing the man, the gun in his outstretched hand, yells at him.

"Newton, you son of a bitch!"

"Grant, I..."

Before he can finish, Grant's right arm and fist explode into the man's jaw, and he lands hard on his back, the gun falling loose on the ground. Grant picks it up and lays it on his workbench.

"You don't ever pull a gun on Grant Pilkington! EVER, you hear me? Now get up."

Groggy and in obvious pain, Newton slowly gets up.

"I heard you were looking for me, and I didn't know what it was about," the man says, rubbing his jaw.

"I was, and if it were police business, I would've found you," Grant says. "I need to talk with you. It's personal."

"We're clean in Tulsa, Grant. Me and the brothers are clean."

"I know that. It ain't that." Grant pauses, looking at the man directly. "Just don't ever pull a gun on me again. Ok?"

"I wasn't gonna shoot you. In all these years, never hurt anyone. You know that."

It was mostly true. It had been reported that a single bank guard was accidentally shot in one daylight robbery and almost died. But most of the Newton brothers' work had been done at night. They were, in fact, notorious for robbing two banks in one evening.

"We're clean in Oklahoma," Newton adds.

"I know. It ain't that," Grant says. He turns to his son. "Harold, you go back in the house now. Check on Harry. Play with him." The boy obeys.

To Newton, motioning to the back stoop, "Sit down."

"You know how it is," Newton says as he sits. "Anything happens within five hundred miles; the newspapers blame us. Made me nervous when I heard you're looking for me," he says as Grant sits down beside him.

"Willis, I need your help," he says quietly.

Surprised at the direction the conversation is going, Willis Newton listens closely. Though there is mutual respect and peripheral friendship between the two, Willis has never seen Grant Pilkington ask for help from anyone. He doesn't do that. He doesn't need it.

Known as a tough veteran with the Tulsa Police Department, he is respected and, by some, feared. The man has been through and survived much, the race riot of 1921 most prominent. That, along with the oil boom and the Osage murders, brought national scrutiny to Northeast Oklahoma. Through it all, Grant Pilkington remained standing — strong, resolute, a rare breed in this turbulent tornado of a territory.

Notwithstanding the few unbroken bottles of bootleg liquor that came home with him after a speakeasy raid, he was an honest cop. The Newton brothers were some of the most notorious bank robbers in America, and though they lived in Tulsa occasionally, they stayed clean. Grant always told them: "You break the law in Tulsa, you go to jail."

"My wife left. Took off with some rich son-of-a-bitch from Springfield."

"Your wife? Virginia?" Willis asks.

"That's her. Said she didn't love me anymore. Nothing I could do about it. Just took off. Clothes, everything," Grant says.

"Your money, too?"

"None of that to take. But she didn't need it, I'm told," Grant says. "The guy's name's Taft. Got some friends on the force in Springfield. Checked him out. Honest and rich."

"If you need money, Grant, I can..." Willis is cut off.

"No! That's not... the bitch left the boys. Said they'd be better off."

"Left her kids?!" Willis shakes his head. "Who does that? What woman does that?" A pause. "You threaten her? You hit her?"

"Damnit, no! Never touched her. She said they'd be better off. And she's damn well right. I don't ever want her near 'em again."

Grant pauses. "But children need a mom. I need help."

"From me?" Willis asks, bewildered. "What in the world can I do? I don't have kids."

"Good God, Willis! No!" Grant pauses, trying to collect his thoughts. "I was thinking about your mother. Your mother still doing well down in Texas? Healthy?"

Newton, still confused, answers, "She is. Still got her spread near San Antonio. Jess and Joe are down there with her now. Breaking horses and rodeoing to help her make ends meet." He pauses. "Why?"

"I need to get the boys out of Tulsa for a while. Need some time to work things out. Some place Virginia doesn't know." Grant looks at Willis. "Would your mom take 'em for a bit?" A pause. "I'll pay, of course."

"Damn, Grant. I don't know," Willis says. "She's already raised eleven."

"She doesn't have to raise 'em. Just a short time. 'Til I figure things out." Grant pauses, giving Willis a moment to think. "They're good boys, Willis. Little Harry's almost three. His health's good. Harold is a little sickly. Had a run-in with that polio going 'round. Some lingering effects, but he's over it now. They're good boys. I can promise you that."

Willis thinks for a moment before responding. Then, finally, "Me and my three brothers were the last of the brood. Hell, after raising us, your boys will be a breeze," Willis laughs.

Grant smiles lightly. There is a pause. "I'm needing to head down her way in a few days, me and brother Doc. I'll talk to Mom then." Willis turns to look at Grant. "I'll try to work things out. Unless you hear otherwise, meet me in Dallas with the boys in ten days." Willis extends his hand to shake. "I'll be at the Palmer Hotel."

The two men rise. Grant reaches out and shakes Willis' hand.

"Palmer Hotel. Ten days."

Willis Newton turns to go. "Don't forget your pistol," Grant says.

Young Harold, Harry at his hip, watches through the rear window as Newton picks up his pistol and leaves. Their father finishes fixing the tire, places it back on the car, and enters the house. Harold watches his father carefully. The boy appears unsettled and afraid.

"Daddy, that man? Was he going to shoot you?"

"Willis Newton? No, he's okay. He's a decent man," Grant says. "You will learn that there are a lot of people you meet in life you don't ever want to turn your back on. But Willis isn't one of them."

Grant reaches into an icebox, takes out a bottle of beer, opens it, and sits down at the kitchen table. Harold sits across from him.

"Daddy, is Momma coming back?" Harold, a bit hesitant, asks.

"No, son. She's not," Grant says. "Don't ask about her again."

"Harry cries a lot, Daddy. He misses Momma."

"You gotta help look after him, Harold. You're his big brother. If he cries, hug him and tell him how much you love him. Best we can do for now," Grant adds, then takes a long pull on the beer.

TULSA, OKLAHOMA
FEBRUARY 1924

The flower shop near downtown Tulsa was appropriately named Downtown Flowers. Unlike the many prosperous businesses of "Black Wall Street" in the community of Greenwood, it had survived the devastating riot of 1921, most likely because the owners were white. The lady proprietor, Margaret Doebler, an attractive, diminutive widow in her mid-to-late thirties, had operated the shop successfully since her husband's passing from the flu pandemic of 1918. He survived the war only to be taken by an unknown, unseen enemy. Margaret managed the shop for an elderly retired couple who kept turning down offers to sell the property, partly out of concern for her.

Margaret had raised two children, both grown now. Tom, her oldest, was apprenticing as a pressman for a large local printer. Ruth, two years younger, lived with her mom while she took classes at the secretarial business school.

Two blocks down the street, Grant Pilkington emerged from Chloe's Diner carrying a brown paper bag. He was in familiar territory. This area of downtown had been his beat for many years as a rookie cop, and he now commanded a squad of beat patrolmen in the same area. He had joined the department in the years before the war as a young man, following in his brother Jim's footsteps. Jim was two inches taller than Grant at six-five and a few years his senior. The two tall young men proved a dashing pair in their uniforms as they walked their respective beats, getting much attention from the young women of the day. Jim, it seemed, had also caught the attention of the numerous oil men coming to town in those days and, by late 1919, had left the department, married, and appeared to prosper in their employ.

Now, on this day, Grant was in uniform, on duty, and had been checking with his men on their individual beats. It was midday as he arrived at the door to the flower shop, his destination, and entered.

"I brought us lunch, Margaret. Didn't want to eat alone," he said to no one in particular. Margaret came out from the back room and motioned to Grant. They settled in at a small table at the back of the shop, making small talk as they ate.

Finally, Margaret asked about Grant's boys. "They're fine. I get letters. Mrs. Newton can't read or write, so she has Harold write me a few words," Grant said. "She sent a picture."

Grant reached into his tunic pocket, took out a small photo, and handed it to Margaret. The scene was of a small surrey-like wagon hitched to a large goat. Harold was in the driver's seat, reins in one hand. Harry sat next to him, Harold's free arm around him.

"When are you going to bring them home?" Margaret asked finally. "Losing their mother like that—they need their father with them. Don't you think it's time, Grant?"

The two boys had been gone several months now, though Grant went to Texas to be with them for a time around Christmas. But now, in early 1924, he knew he needed to bring them home. His divorce had been final for some time. Virginia had not contested custody, but had she done so, Grant was prepared to fight.

"When Virginia told me she had met someone and was leaving me, wanted a divorce, I had no idea. I knew she wasn't happy and complained about money all the time. But I had no idea she was seeing some guy. Harold's polio... she wasn't up to it. We fought over what to do. Her answer to everything was to walk away."

"I heard it," Margaret said. A pause. "People talk, Grant. Word gets… rumors, they get around."

"When she told me she was leaving, she accused me of having an affair. With you. She was trying to blame the whole damn thing on me."

"There were rumors about that, too, Grant. People talk."

The night of the riot in late spring 1921, all TPD officers were on duty. A large group of Black people from the Greenwood community were concerned about the arrest of a young Black boy earlier in the day. Allegedly, the boy had assaulted a young white girl in the elevator of a downtown public building. A large group of whites had gathered near the jail. There were rumors they were going in and taking the boy out to provide him their own justice. The Black community was intent on that not happening. Large numbers of rioters, both Black and white, had been arriving from out of town all afternoon. A dynamite of irrational human emotion was about to erupt, and nothing was going to stop it.

Grant had been a few blocks away and was approaching the city jail when he noticed movement and lights on at the flower shop a block down the street. Grant started to move toward it but was stopped by Ryan Murphy, his shift sergeant.

"Pilk, Chief's ordering all personnel into the station for a lockdown. The white boys leading their bunch told him any cops found on the street during the night would be dead by morning. We're making our stand in the jail."

"I'll be there right away, Murph. Need to check on something first," he said.

"Well, make it quick, damnit! I'm heading in," Murphy yelled as he made his way through the crowd to the front door of the station.

The door to the flower shop was locked when he tried to open it, and seeing Margaret Doebler inside seemingly alone, he knocked hard on it. Seeing the familiar face of the officer, Margaret, double-barrel shotgun in hand, hurried to the front door, let him in, and locked it behind him.

"Mrs. Doebler, you shouldn't be here. You need to go home. This thing's gonna get out of control quick. It's dangerous to be here." He followed her as she moved to the back sales counter.

"Officer Pilkington, I have worked very hard to make this shop successful. It's my sole livelihood. I'll be damned if I'm going to let a bunch of lunatics threaten it." Having stated her resolve, Margaret held up the shotgun.

"But what about your family? Shouldn't you be home with them?"

"My home is five miles away from here. My adult son is home with his sister. They'll be fine," she said, holding up a baseball bat in the other hand. Before this moment, neither had ever said much more than "hello" or "good morning" to the other.

"I'll stay with you for a while," Grant said.

"I have coffee on in the back. I'm going to get you a cup."

For the rest of that night, Grant stayed with Margaret at the flower shop. From a vantage point through the shop's front window, the pair witnessed an incredible scene of destruction. The sounds of gunfire and explosions were unyielding and included incendiary bombs being dropped from small aircraft flying over the community. When Grant emerged from the shop early the next morning, all he could see for blocks was devastation. Unable to breach the jail and get to the young boy, the white mob burned the entire Black community to its foundation, killing many of the residents. His fellow officers having come out of the station, he saw his sergeant a block away and yelled to him, "Murph, what have we got here?!"

"Madness, Pilk! We have madness."

Three days after his February lunch with Margaret, Grant drove to Texas and brought his boys home to Tulsa. A week later, he asked Margaret Doebler to marry him. She said yes.

TULSA, OKLAHOMA
SUMMER, 1925

Margaret has moved into Grant's home on Archer, the boys settling into a small, shared room near the back of the house. Ruth has come to help her mother in the flower shop after completing her business school course and has taken a small apartment near downtown. Tom has married Lena, a tall, lean, handsome young lady who loves to fish, and Tom boasts that this is the main reason he did so.

The boys, Harold and Harry, warm to Margaret, but often at night, as they lie in bed talking quietly, Harry asks about their mother. Harold reassures him that Margaret is their mother, though the three have agreed that, for now, the boys will simply call her "Margaret" or "Ma'am." They had gotten along fine with Mrs. Newton down in Texas, all along calling her "Ma'am." They had fun there riding ponies, watching Jess and Joe break horses, and even getting to go to a rodeo. And Mrs. Newton was a good cook. "Ya can't raise up 'leven kids 'out knowin' how to cook," she would say.

It was great fun, and Harry adjusted and slept well, it seemed, but Harold lay in bed most nights wondering why his mother, then his father, would abandon them. He was confused and did not understand, and most mornings, his pillow was damp.

For the first few months after they married and formed this new family, Margaret found herself instinctively observing Harold and Harry at play. Harry, it seemed, played with abandon, jumping and running, not a care in the world. But Harold seemed hesitant, careful, approaching physical activity as if he might "break." She was unable to detect any phys-ical deformity other than the obvious hollowed-out section of the muscle of his upper left arm.

One night, after the boys had gone to bed, Margaret asked her new husband, Grant, "What exactly did the doctor say to you and Virginia when he told you Harold had polio?"

"It was 'Ole Doc Harmon. Downtown, there. Said he had polio, not too bad a case, and that if the loss of muscle in his left arm was the worst of it, then we were 'damn lucky.'"

"I know Dr. Harmon. That's it? That's all he said?" Margaret asked.

"Said he had no idea how to treat it," Grant said bluntly. "And nobody who'll admit it 'does either.'"

Margaret thought about what he had shared with her and knew there was truth in it. She had read about it all. Huge epidemic, especially in the teens — 1916 in New York, she remembers. Thought of her own children when she read about the mothers of the city's crowded tenements. Doctors and nurses trying everything while, the polio won a hell of a lot more battles than it lost.

"I'm not trying to be funny, Margaret, but the bottom line here is Harold has flat feet, a fact of birth, not polio. Other than the muscle in the left arm, if you measure both legs from his crotch to his instep, there's about a half-inch difference. If you watch real close, you might catch a slight limp when he walks. That, too, is from the polio."

Margaret had not noticed that. She saw no limp. It wasn't what mattered; that wasn't it. It was his hesitancy, as if he thought, "I can't. I'm sick." Too many people, she concluded, had told him over time that he was "sickly," and nobody ever thought to tell him he was "well." By God, she thought, we have to change that.

"One more thing," Grant continued, "ever since polio, he has developed a slight bow-leggedness. And it ain't from riding ponies at Newton's ranch," he added.

"Well, whatever," Margaret said, closing the discussion.

A few days later, Dr. Harmon came into the flower shop. He was a frequent customer, usually buying a bouquet to take home to his wife. Ruth and Margaret were never sure whether he loved his wife that much or carried a lot of guilt. Either way, he was a valued customer, and you didn't gossip about valued customers.

"Dr. Harmon," Margaret ventured while the doctor waited at the counter for Ruth to finish his bouquet. "You treated Harold, Grant's boy when he first got polio. I want to know if there is anything we can do now to help him come back from the effects of it. Do you remember? Can you help me?"

"Yes, I do recall Harold. He lost some muscle in one arm if I remember correctly," the doctor said.

"His left arm," Margaret said.

"If memory serves, that was about the worst of it," Dr. Harmon says. "I remember thinking at the time that he was a very lucky boy. No paralysis. That was good."

"So, what now? What can I do to help him?"

"Do exercises. He lost some muscle, but he didn't lose it all," the doctor says. "Muscles can be strengthened. Can be built back up."

"We can do that," Margaret says.

"A lot of patients, their lungs get affected, which makes their breathing labored. Not the case with Harold." The doctor pauses a moment. "But if I were doing it, I'd work to build up his wind—his lung capacity, I believe." Then, almost as an afterthought: "Sports would be good."

Ruth comes to the counter with the finished bouquet and hands it to Dr. Harmon.

"No charge today, Doctor. You saved me an office call," Margaret says with a grateful smile.

"Well, thank you, ladies. It is much appreciated," he says as he turns to go. When he gets to the front door, he pauses, remembering something. "One more thing, Margaret," he says. "Some believe using warm compresses and rubs on the muscles helps. Could be. Can't hurt." And he goes out, carrying his bouquet.

Harold responds well to the efforts being made by Margaret to strengthen his body, especially the warm rubs. He likes the attention, the closeness of it.

One day, he tells her about a boy at school who picks on the smaller boys. He doesn't like it but is afraid to do anything. "Harold," she tells him, "you might try talking to him. Go talk to him. Reason with him. Try joking with him — make him laugh. Nobody ever died from having a sense of humor. Fighting shouldn't be the first choice in such situations. Do everything you can to talk it out. Sometimes, the best muscle in your body is the one between your ears. Polio didn't hurt that a bit. Use it."

She pauses, stops the massaging a moment, and looks at him. "However, there will come a day when, no matter how hard you try, reason doesn't work, and you have no choice but to fight. When that happens, you fight like hell, and you win."

The physical exercise has helped, and after some months, improvement is obvious. Grant has put up a swing set in the backyard, and Harold's favorite activity is hanging off the top bar, doing pull-ups, and hanging by his knees on that bar and the trapeze. Many days, he is off in the circus tent of his imagination. And he is happy.

One day, after working out at the bar, Margaret watching him through the window, Harold comes into the house, and Margaret begins to rub with the warm towels. Harold sits quietly until she has finished, whereupon she turns him around, looks him in the eye, and says with conviction: "Harold, I am so proud of you. "He looks back at her for a moment and asks somewhat bluntly:

"May I call you 'Mom'?"

Margaret hesitates, frozen briefly by the suddenness of it all, until finally, quietly: "There is nothing in the world I would like more." She takes the boy in her arms and hugs him close as a tear runs down her cheek.

Harry soon picks up on his big brother's words, and from that moment on, the boys have a "mother." Grant, quietly noting the change, says nothing to acknowledge it, although, through a smile, he thinks to himself, *I have a family.*

TULSA, OKLAHOMA
JUNE 1935

Grant, the new Chief of Detectives—the first in Tulsa's history—finishes his breakfast before leaving for work. Margaret sits with him. Harry hurries to finish so he can catch a ride with his dad to his job at De Van Nursery near downtown. The De Van family had purchased Margaret's flower shop and property from the estate's owners shortly after they passed, a few years after she and Grant were married. They branched out into a full-scale nursery, and Margaret decided to quit and concentrate on her new family.

Harry, who does a lot of the heavy lifting for De Van's, is, at thirteen, showing signs that he will be tall like his father and his Uncle Jim. Harold, at nineteen, appears to have peaked at five-eight and a half, but his body—regardless of the obvious indent to the muscle just below the shoulder of his left arm—is very muscular.

Shirt on or off, he has Hollywood leading-man good looks but doesn't know it.

Grant and Harry having left, Harold enters the kitchen and sits down with Margaret. He has recently graduated from Tulsa Central High School and is undecided about his next step. He wants to go to college but is concerned about money. Art Griffith, his wrestling coach at Central, says Coach Gallagher at A & M wants him and that he should go. He is not lazy, having managed two paper routes since age twelve, but he knows wrestling for Gallagher leaves little time for a job outside class and training.

"At least go over there and talk to him, son," Margaret says to Harold as he sits across from her.

"I barely have enough for the bus ticket, Mom," Harold says.

"I've got a little rainy-day bank I keep. I'll give you what you need," Margaret says.

Harold doesn't respond. His face says no.

"If you don't at least go and find out what's possible before you make up your mind, you'll regret it all your days." She reaches into her apron pocket, takes out a ten-dollar bill, and slides it across to him.

Harold looks at her. "I'll pack a satchel," he says as he picks up the bill. "Will you give me a lift to the bus station?"

Margaret nods.

The bus trip to Stillwater takes about two and a half hours. Upon arrival, Harold walks the few blocks from the bus station to the campus and, after asking for directions, soon finds himself in the athletics administration building. Everything seems quiet, Harold assumes, due to the fact that the spring semester has just ended.

The ground floor is dominated by dark woodwork, and each office door is matching drab, brightened only by a small plate announcing its occupant. He knocks on a door titled "Clerical."

A lady's voice responds, "Come in," and Harold opens it. It isn't until that moment that he fully comprehends the fact that he has come all this way without an appointment to talk to Coach Gallagher.

"I'm sorry to bother you," he says to the lady sitting behind the desk closest to the door.

"Yes. What is it, young man? How can I help you?" she asks.

"I was wondering how I can find Coach Gallagher?" Harold asks.

"Do you have an appointment?" the lady asks.

"No, ma'am," Harold says. "I was just hoping to talk to him."

"Well, school hasn't started yet. He might not be in his office."

The lady, sensing Harold's disappointment, adds, "But knowing Coach Gallagher, he's usually in his office at least part of everyday—school or no school—you might get lucky and catch him."

She pauses. "Down the hall, last door on the left. 115."

Harold thanks the lady and heads down the hall to 115. He hesitates before knocking. *What do I do if he's not there?* Harold thinks. *Go back to Tulsa? No, I'll wait here 'til I find him. I'm not going home 'til I see him.*

Harold finally knocks and waits. No answer. He knocks again and tries the door handle, realizing it is locked. He sets his satchel down on the hard tile floor beside the door and sits down next to it. He looks at his watch. It is almost noon. *I could go find something to eat and then come back*, he thinks, *but what if I miss him?* Concerned with what to do that morning, he had failed to take advantage of his mom's breakfast before he left, telling himself he wasn't hungry.

Having finally decided to go find food, Harold stands up just as an older but healthy, fit-looking man in casual clothes enters through the nearby door. Seeing Harold, he stops at the door to 115 and addresses the young man.

"What's up, son? What do you need?"

"I'm trying to find Coach Gallagher," Harold says.

"And why do you want to find Coach?" the man asks.

"I want to talk to him about school. Wrestling."

"You a wrestler?"

"Yes, sir," Harold says. "Just graduated from Tulsa Central. Light heavy, mostly."

"One of Art Griffith's boys. What's your name, son?"

"Harold Pilkington, sir."

The man immediately perks up when he hears the name. "Wait," he says and turns to unlock the office door. He sets his briefcase down inside, then turns back to Harold. "Give me your tote."

Harold does so, and the man sets it down near his own. He closes the office door and locks it. "You hungry?" he asks. "Cause I'm starving."

"Yes, sir, I could eat."

"We'll head over to the student union. The cafeteria there is good," the man says as he heads out the door, followed by Harold. "By the way," he adds as they walk, "I'm Ed Gallagher. But you can call me Coach."

Over sandwiches and unsweet tea ("Those colas and sweet teas just give you extra weight you have to work off in training," Coach says as they go through the food line), they talk about the wrestling program at A&M. Already legendary because of Gallagher's leadership, the program in Stillwater is one of, if not the best, collegiate wrestling programs in the country.

"Coach, my main worry is being able to pay for school. My folks can't help. I'll have to work."

"First of all, classes are important here," Gallagher says. "We expect our boys to take a full load each semester and make their grades. This is, after all, an educational institution. You come here to graduate. Prepare yourself for the future." He pauses a moment. "But along with that, we believe that athletic activity is important. The effort our boys put in to succeed at the highest level takes a lot of work. It takes long hours of training. It takes dedication. You must want it all."

"I believe I can do that, Coach," Harold says with conviction. "I did it in high school."

"I know, Harold. I've talked to Coach Griffith. What I'm telling you is that with classes and training, holding down even a part-time job is going to be very difficult. And this darn

Depression—there aren't that many jobs available. Next year, we've got the Olympic team to work toward. We want to be well represented in that. Trials are in the spring, so there's a lot to do." Harold looks down at his plate, and though he has just eaten, he feels an emptiness inside. Coach Gallagher looks at him.

"How about you go to Admissions today before you leave? Talk to them. Get a firm idea of what you're going to need expense-wise, and then decide."

Gallagher pauses and looks at Harold as the young man turns and gazes out the cafeteria window. He tries to imagine himself as a student—out there, walking by, books in hand, heading to the gym.

"Whatever you decide, Harold, please call me about your decision." The coach takes a small notepad out of his pocket, jots something down, tears off a page, and offers it to Harold. "Either way. Call me, OK? That's my number."

"Yes, sir, I promise. Either way," Harold says.

They both push their chairs back and start to rise when Gallagher motions for Harold to sit back down.

"One more thing, Harold. Art—Coach Griffith—told me that you may not be the best wrestler he ever coached, though you might be one of the best. But he did say that you may be the greatest athlete he ever saw. One of his young assistants told me he thought you were the Jim Thorpe of high school athletics in Oklahoma. I admire that you accomplished all that and would be honored to be your coach in the future."

With that, they rise and walk back to the office, where Harold retrieves his satchel, shakes the coach's hand, thanks him, and leaves.

Instead of going to the Admissions Office, he goes directly to the bus station and buys a ticket back to Tulsa. On the ride, he thinks of all the wrestling and gymnastics meets, football games, track meets, and various other athletic events he participated in as a high school student. Through all of that, his father had never come. Not once.

Grant Pilkington was not an outwardly religious man, Harold knew, but the one time he asked his father to come to school to see him wrestle, Grant had quoted the Bible as his way of saying no.

"When I was a child, I spoke as a child, I understood as a child, I thought as a child, but when I became a man, I put away childish things," Grant told him.

Long before the bus returned to Tulsa, Harold knew he wasn't going back to Stillwater.

A few days later, Grant takes the day off work and goes fishing with Tom and Lena. Grant, who loves to fish as much as they do, often accompanies them when they take a day to go upriver on the Arkansas for that very purpose. Fishing is not a sport, a "childish thing," Grant justifies, therefore not contradictory to Corinthians.

Instead, he concludes, *the Bible says that: 'fishing is about life itself.'*

Harold has borrowed Margaret's car to, as he puts it, "run some errands." Leaving the house, he heads toward downtown, pulls up near the corner of Sixth and Cincinnati, and parks. He has borrowed the car primarily so he can go to his former school and visit his old coach. He feels like he owes the man an explanation after the coach had highly recommended him to Coach Gallagher. It may be summer, but Harold knows he'll be there. He's always there — a dedicated man, Harold thought. He always told his boys, "If you want to be the best, if you want to win, you have to be dedicated. You have to work hard."

Tulsa Central High School looms large above Harold as he walks toward the athletic facilities and Coach's office. The facility is said to be the second-largest such school in the United States, with nearly 5,000 students, sophomores through seniors. It even includes an indoor pool and an indoor track—facilities Harold has come to know well in recent years. During those years, he excelled in wrestling but had also been a significant contributor on the track, gymnastics and tumbling, football, and swimming teams.

Coach's office door is open when Harold reaches it, and he immediately sees the man huddled at his desk, studying. Harold taps on the doorjamb to announce himself.

The coach jumps slightly at the sound, his deep concentration broken; he looks up and sees Harold.

"Harold, Harold! Come in, come in." He rises, reaches out to Harold, and they shake hands. Coach motions, and they both sit.

"I tried to catch up with you at graduation—to say congrats, wish you well, and all. But there were so many, so many. I didn't find you."

"I didn't stick around long, Coach. Had dinner with Mom and Dad, and that was about it." He pauses, looking briefly at the ceiling. "About A&M..."

"I know," Griffith interrupts him. "Gallagher called me. Said you called him right after you visited Stillwater."

"I'm sorry, Coach. All things considered, it just wasn't going to work out."

"He understood, son. He was disappointed, but he understood." Griffith leans back in his chair. "Jobs are scarce, I know. Our country got itself into a mess these days with this damn depression. They say western Oklahoma is a dust bowl."

A moment passes between them, eye to eye, as they share an unspoken, brief regret. Coach nods. Harold rises to go. "Well, I just wanted to come by and tell you thanks for everything."

"Take care of yourself, son," Coach says, and Harold turns and leaves.

Griffith sits, thinking of the exchange between him and Harold for only a moment before returning to his work. He always taught his boys not to dwell on a loss. "You get back on the mat and get back to work," he always told them.

Leaving Central, Harold decides to go see his Aunt Hannah, Grant, and Jim's older sister. She has raised two daughters, Mona and Jessie, and although he is not close to his aunt, he has always had a special fondness for Cousin Jessie. Older by four years, she has always shown an interest—compassion—for him. On those occasions that he and Harry had spent time at their home, she played with both boys, always with a smile and sincere interest.

She participated in girls' athletic teams in high school and, when visiting from Springfield, where she attended school, would often take in a match or a game in which Harold played.

"Harold. What a surprise," Hannah says as she opens her front door. "Come in."

Harold does so and, at his aunt's urging, sits at a table in the kitchen as she pours them a glass of iced tea.

"I understand you've graduated now, heading out into the world. What are your plans?"

Harold has always felt an unease in his aunt's house. On only two occasions through the years since his mother left has he seen her, both here. In the years before his parents' breakup, she and Hannah had a warm sister-in-law relationship—a friendship that seemed to survive the turbulent divorce. Whenever Virginia visited Tulsa, in the years since, she would always make a welcome visit to Hannah's home. Encountering Harold and Harry on those certain visits seemed natural to their mother, who hugged them as if it were just another day gathered around a warm family hearth. Harold, unsure of how he was expected to feel, would exit the room as soon as he could, retreating to the understanding arms of his cousin.

Before he can answer, Hannah begins an update. "Mona, you know, married a minister. They are going into missionary work. Live in Springfield now," Hannah says. "Mona says they may soon be assigned to the Philippines. Can you imagine?"

"I have enough trouble imagining Springfield, let alone trying to picture the Philippines," Harold says.

"Well, if you're going to do what they're fixing to do, Springfield's a good place to start. Heart of the 'Bible Belt,' you know."

"And Jessie?" Harold asks. "She left Springfield, I hear."

"She did. Lawrence quit his railroad job and bought an interest in a place up by the new lake. It's a restaurant, soda fountain, hotel—you name it, they do it all," Hannah says. "Had a partner at first but has since bought him out. Just the two of them now," she adds.

"The new lake?" Harold asks. "I don't know it, I guess."

"Up in central Missouri. They call it Lake of the Ozarks. Biggest in the country, they say. Their place is on the main highway not far from the dam."

"So, she's happy there? Likes it?"

"Seems to." She looks at Harold for a moment. He is suddenly quiet. "So, what about you, Harold? What are your plans now that you're a man of the world?"

"Not sure yet. I'm working on it."

Harold has barely moved through his home's front door when he hears the phone ring. Margaret picks it up.

"Hello. Yes, it is. Oh, nice to hear from you. No, we're fine. Everybody's fine. And you? Good, I hope." A pause. "Yes, I believe he is. I think I heard him come in just now. Hold a moment. I'll get him for you."

She lays the phone receiver down and steps to the door into the hallway. "Harold, telephone for you. It's your cousin Jessie."

"Harold?" A pause. "It's Jessie."

"You won't believe this, but I just came from visiting your mom," Harold says as he picks up the phone.

"I know, she called me," Jessie says. That seems rather quick, Harold thinks. She must have grabbed the phone before I pulled out of her driveway.

"Mom says you're not going to school. No more wrestling?"

"Can't afford to go to school just so I can wrestle," Harold says. "And there's not a lot of wrestling jobs available."

"Still like to joke, I see."

"Only with you, Jess. Only with you."

"What would you think about coming here and working for Lawrence and me?" Jessie asks after a brief pause.

"A job? With you, up there? What would I…? The only thing I've ever done is deliver papers," Harold says with reluctance. "What would I be doing?"

"Everything," Jessie says. "Just like us." She pauses. "Look, Harold, I'll be very honest with you. It won't pay much at first. But we're confident in the future here. And you'll have room and board. Right here at the Whitehouse."

"Sorta like the Roosevelts, huh?" Harold muses.

"Exactly," she says. "You have all the qualifications for this job: You're young, you're strong, and you're smart."

"And I've had polio."

"That's only good for the sympathy vote. Not worth much in a depression." She senses Harold's interest. "I know this is kind of sudden. Out of the blue. So, why don't you think it over for a few days? Then give me a call." She knows him well and understands he has to come to a decision on his own.

"I will do that. I'll call you and... thanks, Jess. I mean that."

"One more thing, Harold," Jessie says. "I think you'll fit right in."

"How's that?" he asks.

"Most of the folks here live on hillsides. One leg's shorter than the other."

"Very funny," Harold says and hangs up.

30

PART II
THE HILLBILLIES

LINN CREEK, MISSOURI
JULY 1923

Named, they say, for the Linn or linden trees prominent throughout the hills, Linn Creek is a tributary of the navigable Osage River. The town of Linn Creek, situated near its banks, is the busy county seat of Camden County in south-central Missouri.

A brief walk from the main street of the community is a draw that locals have dubbed "Possum Holler" because it is said to be home to a large population of possums.

Five-year-old Theora Robinson and her sister Phyllis, a year older, have never seen one of these infamous possums despite playing each day in the front and side yards of their home, a short walk up the holler from town. They have seen deer, squirrels, rabbits, and other assorted wildlife as they play, but never a possum. Phyllis says it's because they only come out at night. "And we're in bed asleep."

The girls' parents watch them play from the front porch of the house. It is a hot and typically humid midsummer day. Lena sits on the porch swing, quietly snapping fresh beans from their garden.

Her husband, Bert, stands nearby, smoking his pipe.

"What do you make of all this talk of a dam?" Lena asks him.

"Talk's all it is, seems like. We've been hearing these rumors on and off since 1912. Nothing ever happens."

"Must be some truth to it," Lena says. "Mrs. Boots said there were two men—in suits, mind you—walking around town a few days ago asking questions."

"I heard," Bert says. "Speculation is that if they build it, it'll be at a site about three miles upriver from Bagnell. That being the case, this whole valley will be flooded." He pauses a moment. "Those two company men, they're just trying to figure out how they're gonna deal with that."

"Maybe the time has come," Lena says.

"Maybe so," Bert says. "I've got a few more days of interior work to do on the Jones' house. I'd like to finish it and get paid before they flood it." Bert laughs. Lena makes a face and grunts.

"Then," Bert says, serious now, "we'll look into selling this place and moving on."

"Bagnell?" Lena asks.

"That's what I'm thinking," Bert says.

"Daddy! Help!" It is little Phyllis yelling as she hurries around the corner of the house. "There's a snake!"

Instinctively, Bert reaches inside the front screen door, grabs his shotgun, and hurries around the side of the house, Lena following with Phyllis. At the far edge of the sideyard, the ground begins to elevate as it moves up the hillside and is outlined with a large grouping of bare boulders. Bert sees it immediately. A large timber rattler is coiled on top of one of the boulders in a pre-strike pose. A few feet in front of it, standing frozen, is Theora.

"Sugar, don't move, alright? Not 'til I tell you," Bert says quietly. He slowly moves in the direction of the rattler until he is the same distance from it—though a few feet to the side—as Theora. He is attempting to keep the snake's attention directed at him. "Sugar, I want you to slowly back straight up until you get to your momma. You understand? OK?"

"Daddy, I'm scared."

"You'll be fine," he reassures her as he slowly lifts the shotgun's barrel, wiggling it slightly to keep the snake's attention. "Start backing up now. Slowly." She does so until she is safely at her mother's apron.

To Bert, there are times in life you can "mess around," take your time. But this is one of those "don't mess around" times, he thinks as he unloads both barrels of the shotgun into the snake, who obliges him by dying.

"Come on inside, girls," Lena says. "You can help me make dinner."

That night, as they lay in bed, Phyllis wonders briefly whether the possums are out and about before sleep takes her. Theora needs a little longer to fall asleep. She is thinking of the snake.

BAGNELL, MISSOURI
SPRING 1924

Having sold their Linn Creek home in the early fall of 1923, the Robinson family settled into a house just a few blocks from the bustling town and the river. Bert has taken a job managing the gravel plant located on the riverbank, his reputation in the construction trades preceding him. The plant is designed to dredge the river and bring up the gravel from the bottom—gravel necessary for roads and other construction work. The plant supplies some jobs to the local community but is not the primary economic factor.

The Bagnell "spur" of the Missouri Pacific Railroad was built for only one purpose—to bring out the thousands of locally cut and hewn railroad ties. The multiple small farms throughout the Osage Valley in this area of the northern Ozark foothills were populated by endless stands of old-growth oak forests. From those trees, farmers cut railroad ties to supplement their meager incomes.

Hauled to the riverbank, the ties were floated in raft-like formations to the railhead at Bagnell. So successful was this "cottage" industry that Bagnell was given the undisputed title of the "Railroad Tie Capital of the World." Engines turned around in the roundhouse, picked up the train of tie-loaded cars, and took them out. They held the rails that helped America maneuver through its "manifest destiny."

Phyllis is finishing her first year of school, while Theora waits each day for her return. It is their only time apart since the younger of the two was born. When Phyllis looks at her language book each night, Theora sits beside her so close you would think they were wearing the same dress. They have two older sisters. Dorothy, nineteen, is the oldest, and Frieda is three years younger. Both have their share of suitors, all older than they — part of their attractiveness.

There are two brothers as well. Clyde, the second oldest of the six children, plans to work part-time for his dad at the gravel plant and as an apprentice carpenter when he graduates from high school in May. George, the last born before the lengthy interim that came before the arrival of the two youngest, has two more years of high school before he plans to head out to the big city of Jefferson to "make his mark."

"Momma, I don't feel good," Theora says to her mother early one morning in late spring. Lena feels her forehead, detecting a mild fever.

"Where do you feel bad, Sugar?" Lena asks.

"All over, Momma. I feel hot, and my head hurts."

Lena lifts her daughter's nightgown, noting red rashes beginning to appear all over her midsection. "Could be the measles," she says to Bert as he enters the girls' room.

He looks her over and says, "That's the damnedest case of measles I ever saw. Aren't they usually just around the head and neck? She's got spots on her tongue. Call that new young doctor in Eldon. He might come out just to find new patients. I think we need a doctor to look at her."

"What new doctor?" Lena asks.

"You know. He's in there with ol' Doc Horner. Name sounds like part of a house or something."

"Part of a house? You must be thinking about Doctor Attic," Lena says.

"Yeah, him," Bert says. "Call him."

"Momma, is Sugar going to be alright?" Phyllis asks.

"Don't you worry, honey. She'll be just fine," Lena says as she hugs Phyllis reassuringly.

The young doctor named for part of a house comes ten miles from his office in Eldon.

"Uh-huh," he says, beginning his diagnosis. "Yes, uh-huh. Yes… yes… yes." He looks at Lena. "It's not measles," he says. "It's scarlet fever.

"Try to keep her as comfortable as possible. Use a cool, damp cloth to wipe her off. The biggest concern right now is keeping her temperature down. It's way too high. I'm going to leave you with these aspirin tablets. They're cut in half. Lot we don't know about aspirin, but the consensus is they'll help bring her fever down. I'll give her one now — a half. Check her temperature in a few hours. If it's not down a bit, give her another half. Then, every six hours as needed. I'll call you tomorrow to see how she's doing."

"Is she going to be alright, Doctor? I know this is serious." Lena looks directly at the doctor.

"Yes, it's serious. I won't lie to you. But it is very survivable. A major concern is that it doesn't lead to rheumatic fever. That can be very dangerous. We will keep an eye out for that." He pauses a moment and adds, "Your family will need to quarantine for a while. Just until the fever breaks. I'll put a quarantine sign in the front window as I leave."

Young Doctor Attic closes his bag, picks it up, and turns to go. At the door to the room, he stops and turns back to face Lena. "Mrs. Robinson, in all those years I spent in medical school in Columbia, I learned only one absolute — 'the good Lord looks after kids, cats, and drunks.'"

A week later, the temperature was back to normal, and the red rashes were gone; also, the quarantine sign was removed. The only aftereffect was the one day Theora complained of achiness in her joints, a symptom related to the doctor by phone. Concern in his voice obvious. Dr. Attic tells Lena to see how it is the following day, and if more severe, he will drive down to see the girl. But by the following day, her joints felt fine, and that was that.

"I'm glad you feel better, little sister," Phyllis says to Theora the day the aches go away.

"Me too," Theora says, smiling. "I felt bad."

"Just don't think about it, little 'sis,'" she says. "Think past it."

BAGNELL, MISSOURI
1927-1932

ALL THE TALK, all the rumors, all the crazy speculation finally becomes truth when, in August 1929, construction on a hydroelectric power plant begins on the Osage River at a site about three miles upriver from Bagnell. Already a bustling river port with its ferry, the railroad spur, and the tie industry, the town becomes a nucleus of sorts for everything, good or bad, that will become a part of the massive undertaking.

The Bagnell "boom," as it is called, includes hotels and boarding houses, banks, restaurants, clothing, and grocery stores, and nearly equal doses of churches and saloons—God be praised, and Volstead is damned. Settling in as well are a few ladies of questionable virtue, helping to dispense the booze, if not the communion wine. And almost as soon as the first spadesful of dirt are turned on the project, the Great Depression rears its ugly head.

As the only major construction project in the country at the time, people come from all over seeking employment. Not until Harry Truman brought home the Ft. Leonard Wood project and its resultant Army basic training center near Waynesville in 1940 would there be that many folks visiting the Ozark foothills of Missouri from out of state. Though, in neither case did such visitors ever consider themselves "tourists."

The sudden and overwhelming influx of engineers, foremen, laborers, and their families to the project and the community strains housing to the point that tents are constructed on wooden platforms in the surrounding fields to shelter them. The Robinson family, as do the others, adjusts. Bert and Lena do their best to shelter their two youngest still at home.

At their school, each of the girls has many new classmates, a result of this new depression-driven culture in which America finds itself.

Among the workers are two young men employed by Boston's Stone and Webster, the engineering and construction company that has been brought in by the original permit holders, Ralph Street and Walter Cravens. George Haage, though not much younger than her father, takes great interest in Dorothy. George works closely with Bert at the gravel plant and, in preparation for the beginning of primary construction on the dam, works to develop the concrete that will be used in the build. In the process, he designs a system to mix concrete and deliver it "alive" in large quantities to the pour site — the possible "birth" of the ready-mix concrete industry. He and Dorothy marry, and when Street and Cravens go bankrupt, the couple leaves for Kansas and other work.

Babe Lambert, a handsome man of French heritage, also comes to the project early from New England. He manages to woo the young and beautiful Frieda, and with the Street-Craven's failure, marries her, and the couple leaves to go back east.

Despite the loss of their primary permit holders, Union Electric takes control, and, not surprisingly considering the times, the dam is completed ahead of schedule, and the roadway is officially opened in late May 1931. The first Bagnell fire came just a month before, in April. Several businesses and a residence in town are destroyed. The second does similar damage later in early '32. But it is a smaller fire between the two that becomes embedded in memory.

One of the young Boots boys sees it first, walking the dirt road home from school just ahead of the Robinson girls. A large tent, a family's home, suddenly erupts in flames in a field a block ahead of them. The boy, seeing it, quickly turns around and runs back toward town, yelling: "Fire! Fire! There's a fire!"

Pedestrians in town hear the boy, and soon an alarm sounds, and the fire wagon and a number of volunteer firemen rush toward the scene. Having seen the fire, the girls start running toward home, passing the boy as he hurries by. They, too, are yelling, but for Lena.

"Momma! Momma, there's a fire! There's a fire!"

Lena, having heard them, quickly comes out of the house onto the front porch, sees the fire, and hurries to meet the girls at the gate to the yard. At that very moment, she sees a woman, engulfed in flame, run from the tent, screaming. The first volunteer to reach her struggles to get her to the ground to put out the fire, but the screaming abruptly ends.

"Girls, I want you to go inside now," Lena says as she ushers them onto the porch and into the house. They do so reluctantly, their curiosity giving way to the seeming horror of the scene.

Lena steps back onto the porch and notes Bert among the volunteers at the fire. He sees her looking and shakes his head. Lena walks down and through the gate into the road as Bert begins walking toward her.

"Bert?" she says as he reaches her.

"It's bad, Lena. A woman and her two kids - all gone. Dead." Bert shakes his head and looks down. "Awful, damn awful," he says finally.

"Momma?" Phyllis has slipped back onto the porch, Theora behind her, watching them. "Momma, what's that smell?" she asks. "It smells terrible, Momma," Theora says.

LAKE OZARK, MISSOURI
JUNE 1934

"So, how are you going to do that, Theora?" Marion Clayton asks. "Waitress and go to school too?"

"Well, Marion, I'll have a lot more free time now that I don't have all your papers to write," she says with a laugh.

Phyllis, sitting in the front passenger seat as Marion drives, laughs loudly. She loves it when her little sis gets "his goat." They are in Marion's stepfather's Studebaker, Theora, in the back seat. They have just pulled out of Bagnell Road, turning left onto Highway 54, and headed to the Dam. Marion's family had moved to Bagnell from southern Illinois in the twenties in anticipation of what was widely rumored to be major growth coming to the small river town. They are restaurant people and opened a diner near the old downtown, not far from the river. It prospers.

The three have recently graduated from the School of the Osage High School, though they have never spent one day in class there.

With the building of the Dam, growth in population, and the increased tax base, Bagnell High School has been replaced. A new building for all grades, first through twelve, has been built at a site about a mile southwest of the Dam in the town newly born there. Aptly named, the town is called Lake Ozark. The school building is completed just in time to accommodate the 1934 Baccalaureate and Graduation. The three, along with their other nine classmates, are honored to be the first.

Marion and Phyllis have been a "couple" for most of their high school years, and Marion, whose other primary interest is basketball, doesn't always find time for the joys of academic life.

He, therefore, often enlists Theora's help to write his papers, as in, "Theora, will you write my paper?" Phyllis won't do it, so Theora, feeling sorry for his predicament, does. The joke is that, prior to graduation, when Marion's name is called, Theora will automatically rise and walk to the podium. Fortunately, when the night comes, Marion manages to get there himself.

Theora reads a lot—always has. She read most of the "age-appropriate" books available to her growing up: *Little Women, Little Men, Penrod, Penrod and Sam*. She even read some Kipling, rooting, of course, for the mongoose. Fellow Missourian Twain's books about life in a booming river town remind her of the world around her, though her river is a "tad" smaller. Huckleberry's guilt about Jim contributes greatly to her instinctive attitude about justice for all. She has an innate desire for knowledge and more schooling, but this is the Depression, and money is, quite simply, hard to come by. She graduated from high school with Phyllis's class because she skipped a grade on the way to senior year—seventh, to be exact. Now, with the knowledge that she is allowed 12 years in public school, she has approached the superintendent with the idea of doing post-graduate study.

"There are a few classes I wanted to take but didn't find time for in the past two years," she tells him.

He agrees, including allowing her to come and go when she is not in class, thus allowing her to work at the same time.

Phyllis has started working as a waitress at the diner for Marion's mom and dad. Like Theora, Phyllis is also a reader, but her primary focus lately has been Marion—now work and Marion.

Theora approves of him, too.

"Why else would I write his stupid papers?" she tells her sister.

She likes the idea of waitressing and is on her way to a new restaurant just southwest of the Dam to see about a job.

Marion follows the highway up the hill, past the Pope house, and around the Route W intersection, a road that takes you out and across the north shore of the lake. At Highway 54's peak, before starting the downhill approach to the Dam's north end, you can see in the distance the vastness of the new reservoir. The road—the approach to the huge concrete structure—amounts to two lanes running through a "cut" in the hill: two vertical, sheer slices of rock that loom eerily above the vehicle. The road narrows as they move onto the Dam's roadway surface and remains so as they drive the half-mile length and are delivered into the town. A short distance later, Marion pulls head-first directly into a spot right near the front door of the Lakeside Casino, their destination.

"We'll just wait here while you talk to them," Marion says. "Maybe walk down by the lake a little way."

"Good luck, Sis," Phyllis says.

The restaurant, a large wooden structure painted deep forest green, appears smaller, nestled as it is against the gently sloping hillside. Theora walks to the door and enters. Before her is a large open room filled with tables and chairs of a similar green, though not as dark. To her left, running along most of the length of the room is a bar with stools. Coming from the bright sun of midday summer into the restaurant's dark interior, Theora doesn't immediately see the lady approaching her from behind the bar. "Hello, young lady," a welcoming voice says. "What can I do for you?"

As Theora's eyes adjust, she sees a tall, handsome lady of about thirty standing, smiling at her, awaiting an answer.

"Oh, hi. I'm looking for Mrs. Gordon," Theora says.

"I'm Mrs. Gordon. Bernie Gordon. What can I help you with?"

"I am interested in a waitressing job. I was told you might have a need for a waitress," Theora says, getting right to the point.

"Possibly," Mrs. Gordon says. "Who told you we had an opening?"

"Actually, no one, Mrs. Gordon. I just wanted to plant the idea in your head. In case you didn't."

Mrs. Gordon is amused.

"Come. Let's sit down here for a minute." She motions to a table nearby, and they sit. "Let's start with your name?"

"Theora Robinson. I'm from Bagnell."

"Bert Robinson, your dad? On the school board?"

"Yes, ma'am," Theora says. "I just graduated from the new school, and I want to work."

"Do you have any experience?" Bernie asks.

"No, ma'am, but I learn fast," Theora answers, trying to make her case.

That's okay, Bernie thinks. *I can spend more time training her and not waste time correcting bad habits.*

"Let me ask you, what's the first thing you would do when a group of new customers sits down at a table?"

"Well, I would say hello to them and welcome them to the Casino Restaurant," Theora answers.

"Uh, well, yes, of course," Bernie says. "That too. I was thinking that we should always arrive at the table with a glass of fresh ice water for each person. It's also a way of saying, 'Hello, we're glad you're here.' Always give them menus first thing as well," she adds.

"Now." She pauses briefly. "This is a full-service restaurant. Not a café. Not a diner. We serve three meals a day, which means your schedule could change weekly according to needs. Will that be a problem?" she asks.

"No, ma'am. I don't have a car, but I'll be able to get rides. It'll be fine." She stops momentarily, remembering. "There is one thing."

"Yes?" *Here we go*, Bernie thinks.

"I'm available anytime all summer, but I am taking some classes at the high school when school starts in the fall. Part-time," Theora says. "Will that be a problem?"

"We can work around it. Business slows down in fall anyway," Bernie says. "I'm confused, though. I thought you said you graduated?"

"I did. It's post-graduate work. A few courses," Theora answers.

"Oh," Bernie says, thinking to herself that nobody normal goes back to high school once they get out.

"May I ask you a question?" Theora ventures.

"Ask away," Bernie says.

"Is the food good here?"

Bernie chuckles. "Oh, darling. It's excellent."

"Great!" Theora says. "I'll take your word for it then and tell everybody I know."

"Can you start on Monday?" Bernie asks.

"I'm hired?" Theora queries to make sure.

Bernie nods.

"Yes, ma'am, I can be here Monday," Theora says.

"No more 'ma'am.' Just call me Bernie."

She is amused by the young lady, and only when the girl stands to leave does she take actual note of how diminutive she is. Theora, at sixteen, has seemingly topped out at 4'11" — five feet when she lies, which, as to her height, is frequent. And she's pert, Bernie thinks.

"You're a cute girl. Love the freckles. Customers will love 'em too, I'm thinking."

"Got the freckles from God, Bernie," Theora says as she shakes her new boss's hand. "And I refuse to give them back."

"Well, did you get it?" Phyllis asks when Theora returns to the car.

"I start Monday," she says as she settles into the backseat. "Need to confer with you, Marion, about your schedule. You'll be driving me."

Marion just grunts as he pulls out onto the highway. Instead of heading back toward the Dam, he turns south and drives further up into town.

Red Moore, Marion's stepdad, upon hearing where he is headed, asks the boy to take a look at a small building near midtown. Word is the space recently became vacant, thus available.

Business at their Bagnell restaurant had tempered greatly since the completion of the Dam in '31, and he and Carrie had been thinking about moving the diner into Lake Ozark.

Bagnell, now on the "road less traveled by," as the poet once said, was dying. Once the U.S. Highway 54 roadway across the Dam opened, the focus on the new reservoir and the massive concrete gravity structure holding it in place was immense. Although the Lake of the Ozarks, as it was dubbed, did not fill to full reservoir at 660 feet until 1933, folks from all over the Midwest came to see it. And those folks needed to eat.

Marion and the sisters get out and look at the building, peering through its locked door and windows. They like what they see, and Marion considers that if he and Phyllis were helping Red and his mom here, it would be easier to get Theora to her work, too.

"What are you kids up to there?" a voice from across the parking lot says. "Can I help you?"

Turning to look, they see a man in his late twenties or so standing in front of the building next door. He is of medium height, wears a small sliver of a mustache, and is looking at them.

"Hello, sir," Marion says back across the parking lot. "Just looking at the vacant store. My folks are interested in it."

"Well, then, come on over here. I know the owner. I'll get you the name and his telephone number," the man says as he turns to enter the Whitehouse.

The three follow him.

"They have ice cream here, Phyllis," Theora says as they enter. "Marion can buy us a cone."

They go to the fountain at the rear and sit on stools as the man approaches them from behind the counter. He hands Marion a piece of paper.

"Are you Mr. Fry?" Marion asks him. "You're the owner here? Of the Whitehouse?"

"I am. Lawrence Fry. I own the business, but we only lease the building. The DeGraffenreid family owns the building."

Theora, thinking of the ice cream, interrupts. "Can we get an ice cream cone, Mr. Fry?"

"Sure can. One minute."

He steps to the kitchen door, opens it, and says, "Jessie, got some fountain customers."

Momentarily, a tall, lean young woman in her mid-twenties comes from the kitchen to behind the fountain. She is smiling. "She'll take care of you," Mr. Fry says as he turns and heads back outside.

"Great! What'll you folks have?" Jessie asks.

Phyllis orders first. "I'll have a strawberry cone." She points at Marion. "He'll have chocolate. Theora?"

"Strawberry sounds good," she says. "A cone."

Jessie busies herself, making the cones. Theora watches her a moment, then asks, "Do you like working here, ma'am? How long have you worked for Mr. Fry?"

"My name's Jessie. You can call me that."

She hands the first cone to Phyllis, smiles, and laughs lightly.

"How long have I been working for Mr. Fry? Well, I would say that has been the case ever since I married him."

"Oh, you're Mrs. Fry," Theora says as Jessie hands her a cone.

"Jessie, please," Mrs. Fry says. "And you are?"

"I'm Theora Robinson. This is my sister Phyllis. Chocolate over there is Marion Clayton. We're all from Bagnell."

"Robinson? Sounds familiar. Your dad on the school board?"

"Yes, that's him," Theora says.

"I heard about the new school," Jessie says. "Haven't been by to see it, though. Heard it's nice."

"It is. We just graduated," Phyllis says.

Marion, having devoured his cone rather quickly, gets up to leave. "Come on. We gotta go. I gotta get back."

The sisters follow.

"Thank you, Jessie," they each say in turn. "Nice to meet you." She smiles and waves at them as they exit.

Marion's report to Red prompts his stepdad to investigate further, and it isn't long before the V. Red Moore Restaurant is a fixture in Lake Ozark.

LAKE OZARK, MISSOURI
JUNE 1935

"Hello. Welcome to the Lakeside Casino. My name's Theora. Water and menus. Take your time. I'll be back to take your order in a moment."

A veteran waitress, Theora, has just seated a couple for dinner. Her year of post-graduate work at the high school completed, she has begun to accept that this may be her future, though she harbors dreams of something else — something better — but knows not what. Sister Phyllis and her boyfriend, Marion, continue to help Red and Carrie at their diner, and there has been talk of marriage, but nothing definite yet.

"Are you folks ready to order?" she asks when she returns to their table.

"A question, Miss?" the man says as he looks at the menu.

"What is a 'chicken-fried steak'?"

Theora smiles at him. "You folks aren't from around here, are you?"

"We live in St. Louis," the lady says.

"Well, you're in for a treat. We take one of our finest cuts of meat and tenderize it 'til you can cut it with a fork. Then, it is rolled into the same batter that we use for our fried chicken and pan-fried, smothered with milk gravy made from the drippings, and served with mashed potatoes and green beans. You'll love it."

"All right, then. I'll try that and coffee — black," the man says decisively.

"Chicken and dumplings for me," the lady says. "Can't remember the last time I had that. And iced tea with lemon."

While the St. Louis couple eats, Theora takes a moment to speak to her boss. "Bernie, can I leave right at closing, at nine tonight?"

"What's up? You have a date?" Bernie asks.

"No. Nothing like that. Phyllis and Marion asked me to go with them to the Whitehouse. They've got a band from Jeff City tonight, and we can dance," Theora says. "It's in that side dining room. They serve set-ups if you're 21 and have your own bottle. We just have a Coke. Sometimes a sandwich."

"You go on, honey. Have fun. If Paul wasn't so tired from being in the kitchen all day, I think we'd join you," Bernie laughs. "Wishful thinking, huh?"

"Well, folks, I hope you enjoyed your meal," Theora says as she removes some dirty dishes from in front of them. The man's plate is licked clean.

"That chicken-fried steak was great," Mr. St. Louis says to her.

"I'll have to remember that one."

The dining room at the Whitehouse is somewhat crowded when the sisters and Marion arrive, but they manage to crowd around a table with one of their schoolmates from Bagnell, Lawrence Quinn, and others. The band is small but Whitehouse-affordable and is on break when the three arrive.

"Oh, hi, Mrs. Fry," Theora says as Jessie approaches their table to take their order.

"Well, hello," she says, recognizing them. "It's the Robinson girls." And, nodding to Marion: "And chocolate."

"It's Marion," Marion says.

"Cokes all around," Phyllis says.

"Mrs. Fry? Who are those people sitting over there?" Lawrence asks, indicating a table of three across the room. A middle-aged woman sits at a table with her teenage girl and young son. The girl is surveying the room while the boy appears bored. A fifth of bourbon sits on the table as the woman enjoys what appears to be a highball.

"Oh, that's Mrs. Barker and her son and daughter," Jessie says. "They're from Kansas City. They come down and stay at Mrs. Allen's Cottages over on the point. I believe her husband has passed, so she's available, Lawrence."

Everyone laughs except Lawrence.

"Thank you," Lawrence says as he gets up. "It's the daughter I'm interested in. Going to ask her to dance."

"Jessie!" An employee has come out of the kitchen looking for her and is standing at the door to the dining room. "There's a phone call for you."

Who could be calling so late? Jessie thinks as she hurries to the kitchen and picks up the phone. "Yes? This is Jessie Fry," she says into the phone.

"Jessie?" she hears from the other end.

"Harold? Is that you?"

"Sorry to call so late," he says apologetically. "I just now made up my mind. You still want me? Job still open?"

"Absolutely!" Jessie says. "When are you coming?"

"I'll be on the Monday bus," Harold says.

"Great! I can't wait," she says.

"Jessie?"

"Yes?"

"Do you have her address? In Springfield?" Harold asks.

Jessie hesitates a moment before answering. "Harold? Are you sure you want to do that?"

"Yes. I need to," he says.

Jessie gives him the address, and they hang up. Well, if he's truly smart, he won't tell Uncle Grant, she thinks.

On Monday morning, Harold, valise in hand, hugs Margaret and takes the 8:00 a.m. bus to Lake Ozark, with a stop in

Springfield. About three hours later, the bus arrives near the square in downtown Springfield, and after asking for directions, Harold decides to walk to his mother's house. He has known for a while about his half-sister, Virginia's daughter, with Taft but has never seen her. She would be eight now, he believes but is not sure. I would like to know her, he thinks. I always thought having a sister would be nice.

Harold arrives at the address and begins walking toward the front door. Just as it opens, a tall, middle-aged woman and a young girl appear. They meet midway down the walk.

"Yes, can I help you?" the woman asks.

"Mother. It's Harold."

She looks at him for a moment, surprised, not knowing how to respond. "Harold. I didn't recognize you. What... what are you doing here?" she says finally.

"I'm on my way to Jessie's," he says. "At the big lake. I just wanted to stop and say hi."

There is a pause, Virginia very much caught off her guard. Then finally: "This is your sister, Harold. Her name's Virginia, but we call her Ginny. Tell Harold hello, Ginny."

"Hello, Harold," the girl says, smiling.

Harold reaches his hand out to take hers, and she responds by taking his. "Hello, Ginny. I'm so happy to meet you," Harold says, smiling at the little girl.

"Me too," she says.

A lady approaches them, coming along the sidewalk, and stops at their walkway. "Well, good morning, Mrs. Taft," the lady says, greeting them.

"Good morning to you as well, Mrs. Ward," Virginia responds nervously.

"I see you have your beautiful little daughter with you today."

"Oh yes, we're on our way to her dance class," Virginia says. "And late, as usual."

"Well, good day to you then," Mrs. Ward says. She glances at Harold. "And to you, young man."

Harold nods to the lady as she turns to go.

"I should go too," Harold says. "I have a bus to catch."

"Ginny, please go wait by the car," Virginia says, motioning to the driveway running along the side of the house. The girl does as she is told.

"Bye, Harold," she says.

"Bye, Ginny," he says.

After the girl has left: "Harold, I would have introduced you to that lady, but no one here knows I have other children."

Harold doesn't respond; just looks at his mother.

"I must go now. Have a safe trip to Jessie's. Please tell her I said hello."

Harold doesn't watch them as they back out of the driveway and turn to go in the opposite direction. He simply turns away, walks back to the station, and boards the next bus to Jeff City, with a stop in Lake Ozark.

Two and a half hours later, the bus pulls into the driveway in front of the Whitehouse. Harold is the last passenger to get off, studying the building as he waits for the others.

When he steps off, he immediately walks, valise in hand, to the edge of the roadway as if studying the town in each direction. Looking northeast, he can barely see a portion of the dam and lake beyond. He is so immersed in his study that he almost bumps into a pedestrian walking along the roadway, heading southwest.

"Sorry, sir," Harold says. "I didn't mean to bump you."

The middle-aged man stops, looking Harold over from head to foot, and notices his scuffed older brown shoes. Dressed in a pair of dungaree-style work pants and a long-sleeved work shirt with the sleeves rolled above the elbows, Harold reminds the man of a leftover worker from the dam-building days.

"What boxcar did you just roll out of, son?" the man asks.

"I just got off the bus there," Harold replies.

"Where from?" the man asks.

"Oklahoma," Harold says.

"Oklahoma? I thought you 'Okies' when you left home, all headed west."

"I got on the wrong bus," Harold says.

The man laughs, shakes his head, and turns to leave.

"Sir?" The man turns back to face Harold. "Are you one of those Hillbillies I've heard so much about?"

"Dyed-in-the-wool, son," the man says. "Dyed-in-the-wool." The man begins walking back up the road as Harold turns his attention back to the large white building behind him.

PART III
THE TWAIN MEET

It is late August 1935, and in the few months Harold has been at the Whitehouse, he has settled in and learned his various tasks well. There are many of these tasks, and Lawrence and Jessie have come to rely on him like a manager. Lawrence, who has grown up in Springfield, the heart of the "Bible Belt," and was raised by a very religious mother, has never had an alcoholic drink in his life and has no plans to do so. However, always sensing an opportunity, he opens a liquor store in a small room just off the front entry because, as Lawrence always reminds anyone who inquires, "Liquor isn't for drinking; it's for selling." The entire back wall of the room is lined with shelves loaded with all the favorites, and as the folks in this area of the Ozark foothills are majority "Scots-Irish English" via Kentucky and Tennessee, straight bourbon and sour mash whiskey are the best sellers. Gin runs a pretty good second. There is just enough room behind a short counter for a clerk.

In Missouri, since repeal, the law says that unless you are twenty-one years old, you cannot possess, drink, buy, or sell alcoholic beverages. Harold, therefore, being under twenty-one, is not allowed to help with the liquor store. He does, though — door locked, after hours — do a little restocking and occasionally enjoys a late-night "highball" with his cousin Jessie, who, unlike her husband, does partake.

Missouri law also says that bars and restaurants cannot serve "liquor by the drink," although an individual can bring their own bottle in and purchase "set-ups" — usually a bucket of ice with glasses and a mix of choice, mostly Coke or 7-Up. An individual can get a license to sell beer and wine, though, and Lawrence has had that for some time now. But you can't do any of that on Sunday. The repeal of Prohibition has probably struck the greatest blow for "states' rights" since the Constitution was written — not only states' rights but county rights. Post-Volstead, there are counties, mostly in the South, that are "dry" right next to a county that is "wet." And right near the county line, on the "wet" side, is a bar or liquor store that is quite busy. In the dry county, gasoline sales are strong. It seems there is nothing state legislatures like to do more than fiddle with liquor laws. In Oklahoma, in contrast, Prohibition is not repealed, and 3.2 alcohol by weight beer is the only legal beverage. No fiddling there.

Lawrence, a very astute businessman, has created another profit center for the Whitehouse that will, over time, prove to be most worthwhile.

Harold, who has taken to enjoying coffee and an occasional cigarette, is doing so, sitting at the counter early one morning when Jessie comes out of the kitchen, cup in hand, and sits down beside him. She lights a cigarette.

"Harold, there's not much going on today. Why don't you take the morning off? Go do something. You haven't done anything but work since you arrived."

"I don't know what I'd do. I'm okay with the work, Jessie."

"Go look around. Take the car. You've never even been across the dam."

"I did once when I went to Eldon to buy some clothes," Harold says.

"Why don't you go to the casino down by the dam and have lunch?" Jessie says. "There's a cute little waitress there. You might want to take a look at her." Jessie smiles at Harold and pokes him lightly on the shoulder.

"I don't need another female to contend with right now, Jess. You're all I can handle," he says, laughing.

"Okay. What about this? Go to the UE dock down the hill behind us and go swimming. I'll bet you haven't been in the water since the last time you were in Central's pool."

Harold looks at Jessie for a moment, thinking. The idea appeals to him.

"That I'll do," he says. "That sounds good. I did bring my old practice trunks from Central."

Harold puts his cigarette out, finishes his cup of coffee, and gets up.

"I'll see you later, Cuz," he says.

Harold, wearing his swim trunks under his pants, T-shirt on, towel in hand, walks down the path a few hundred yards behind the Whitehouse to the lakeshore. The cove is not as large as most of the Lake of the Ozarks coves tend to be, and across its width, there is one cabin camp with eight or so units nestled on the shoreline. It has a dock with several fishing boats tied to it. A small house on a mid-sized parcel sits next to it. At the top of the hill near the far end of the cove, a few houses line up along a road he later learns is called Lake Road 1-A, as it has the honor of being the first roadway leading from the main highway just south of the dam. A road leading from it runs to the cabin camp and neighboring house. On the opposite point, a nearly perfectly round hill juts out into the main channel. Here, the Allen family has begun to build a cabin camp, with many of the units already in place around the hillside. A large house, complete with a screen porch on three sides, is nearing completion. It is a very pleasing sight, Harold thinks as he studies it in the distance.

"Fish or cut bait, stranger?"

Harold is brought from his reverie by an unusual request. He has been so engaged by his admiration of the point that he has not noticed the young man sitting at the end of the dock, holding a fishing pole.

"Neither," Harold says. "I was going swimming."

"Do me a favor and hold off till I finish fishing, and I'll share my catch with you."

"No need for that," Harold says. "I'll wait for you."

"Good. Thanks."

"What are you fishing for?" Harold asks.

"Crappie," Marion says. "Got a crappie bed right under here."

"What's a crappie bed?" Harold asks.

"After Christmas each year, we gather up a bunch of cedar trees—used Christmas trees—tie rocks to 'em, and sink 'em in a bed about ten to twelve feet down. Crappie spawns there. Fishing's best over a bed in the spring when they're spawning."

"So, how many have you caught so far today?" Harold asks.

"None. So far," Marion says.

"None? So, let me get this straight. I take your deal earlier. I get one-half of nothing. That's about right?"

"That's exactly right. You know your math, that's for sure," Marion says.

After a moment: "Go ahead and swim. It won't bother me."

"That's okay. I'm fine."

"You look familiar. Have I seen you up at the Whitehouse?" Marion asks.

"I work there, yes. For Jessie and Lawrence."

"The Frys. I've met them. Nice people."

"Jessie Fry is my cousin. Name's Harold. Harold Pilkington."

"Marion Clayton," Marion says in return.

"So, Marion, what's a crappie?" Harold asks.

"Oh...well. It's a small fish in the perch family, I believe," Marion says. "You have to scrape the scales off when you clean 'em, roll 'em in a batter, and fry 'em up. Great eating fish."

Marion pauses speaking while he adjusts the position of his line, moving it and the bobber to a different location.

"You fish?" Marion asks.

"A couple of times with my dad. Arkansas River. Runs through Tulsa. Didn't care much for the catfish, though. Too muddy tasting," Harold says. "Better than starving, though, Dad always said."

"Yeah, me too. Don't like the muddy taste," Marion agrees. "Except—except below the dam, in the Osage. Spoonbill. You ever eat spoonbill?"

"I don't know what that is," Harold responds.

"Spoonbill catfish. Monster fish. Only find 'em in the Osage below the dam. Big. Big ugly fish with a big ol' ugly snout that sticks out. Flat on the end. Ugly fish."

"Monster fish. Doesn't sound very tasty," Harold says, shaking his head at the thought.

"Well, they are, strange as it is," Marion says. "Lot of waste when you clean 'em, though. Have to cut away an outer layer of red meat to get to the white meat. But it's worth it. Doesn't taste a bit like a catfish."

"What do you use for bait? To catch them?" Harold asks.

"Nothing. You have to snag 'em with a big 'ole treble hook. Throw a line out and try to snag 'em. Lots of fun."

"If they're so good, why aren't you down there snagging them now?" Harold asks.

"They're protected," Marion says. "Only a short season in the spring and fall. Fall season will be coming up soon, though—in a few weeks."

"I'll have to try that, I guess," Harold says.

"And I need to go," Marion says as he reels in his line, snags the hook on the reel, and picks up his worm can. "Gonna be late for work."

"And where's that? Work, I mean," Harold asks as he strips off his t-shirt.

"Red Moore's," Marion says, pointing in the general direction up the hill. "Red's my stepfather. He and Mom own it."

"Well, see you, Marion," Harold says as he begins to strip down to his swim trunks. "Thanks for the fishing tips."

"It's better than giving you half my catch," Marion says. "Like they say: 'Give a man a fish, you feed him for a day. Teach him how to fish, and you feed him for a lifetime.'"

"Unless they're not biting," Harold says.

"Yeah." Marion turns to go but stops himself with a lingering question. "You mind if I ask? What's with your shoulder there?"

Harold glances down at his left shoulder and rubs it. "Oh, this. Gator bite. You should have seen it. Bloody mess."

"Sorry to hear that," Marion says, shaking his head. He looks at Harold. "Where'd you say you were from?"

"Oklahoma. Tulsa."

"Oh, yeah. You did say Tulsa, didn't you?" Marion says. "Well, nice to meet you, Harold," he adds as he turns to go.

"Likewise, Marion," Harold says as he turns and dives into the water off the end of the dock.

Marion heads up the hill, pondering — surprised to know there are alligators in Oklahoma. *I'll be damned,* he thinks to himself. *I didn't know that.* At that, he pauses in his trek uphill and turns to look back at the water, where Harold swims first freestyle, then backstroke, then butterfly, then freestyle again.

Damn. He didn't learn how to do all that by thrashing around in the creek, Marion marvels. *This guy's an athlete.*

"Gator bite," Harold, amused, mutters to himself as he swims.

That'll fix him for that tall tale about monster catfish in the Osage River.

Harold is standing in the doorway to the dining room, talking to a middle-aged workman — a technician — who has been running wiring for the new speaker system his company is installing. Lawrence and Jessie have talked about the possibilities of increasing revenue by promoting the Whitehouse as a place to come, listen to music, and dance to gather. It can't help but boost liquor and food sales, they conclude. Young people in the area are already tending to hang out on Saturday nights, meet their friends, talk, and dance. A few recent Saturday nights with a live band from Jefferson City have worked out well, but it is costly and not a solution for the other nights of the week. The new system will allow them to hook up a radio or a phonograph and play music for customers to listen to and dance. The system will include two speakers in the dining room, one in the main front room, and one outside above the front door. There is also a panel to turn the system off and on and a volume control. A microphone and stand complete the package.

"Just about done, Harold," the technician says. "A few minor adjustments, and I'll go over with you how it all works."

"Let me know," Harold says. "I'll be right here in the front."

The technician turns and goes back into the dining room as the front door opens, and a middle-aged man walks in. Harold recognizes him as the man he spoke to when he got off the bus on his first day here.

"Well, if it isn't the Okie who took the wrong bus," the man says with some surprise. "You still lost?"

"No, sir, Mr. Hillbilly. I got taken in by the Frys. They adopted me and put me to work." Harold intends to give as good as he can take, as the immortal "they" say.

"In that case, then," the man says, "you got cigars up there on that rack with all of them cigarettes you're selling?"

Harold turns back to look.

"Short, fat Roi-Tans if you got them?" the man adds.

Harold scans the shelves, finally finding the brand.

"This what you're looking for?" Harold asks as he turns around with a handful of the requested items.

"You got it," the man says. "I'll take whatever you got in your hand there."

Harold puts the cigars in a bag, takes the man's money, and gives him back the change.

"You got a name, son?" the man asks as he takes the bag from Harold.

"I'm Harold. Jessie Fry's cousin."

"Now that I knew," the man says.

Harold looks at him with some surprise.

"Small town," he says, explaining. "Nice to meet you, son. I'm Ward Atteberry. My brother Hoyle and I own the grocery store across the street."

Ward extends his hand, and Harold reaches out and shakes it.

"I normally sell these cigars, but my supplier left me short this week. He forgets that I'm my own best customer."

"Nice to meet you, Mr. Atteberry," Harold says, smiling now.

"I notice that you're putting a speaker out front there," Ward says. "Some advice: put the Cardinals game on the radio on that speaker out there. Folks will stop, get a soda or coffee, linger, and listen to a couple of innings. They always make time for the Cardinals. It's a religion."

Ward pauses a moment. "You do know who the Cardinals are, don't you?"

"Yes, even in Tulsa," Harold says. "Most everybody's a fan. Only team west of the Mississippi. And," he adds, almost as an afterthought, "they're winners."

"Yep. Diz is having another good year. And ol' Frisch still got some gas in his tank, still making a fair amount of starts." Ward knows his Cardinals. "Thirty-nine years old, still going strong. He may play forever."

Ward pauses. "Well, gotta go. Thanks, Harold. See you again."

Ward turns and goes out the front door, lighting a cigar as he leaves. Momentarily, the door opens, and he sticks his head back in.

"I'm serious about putting the game on the speaker," he says. "It'll bring business. "And he exits again.

The technician is at the door. "Ready whenever you are, Harold."

"Can you tell me what radio station we get here that broadcasts the Cardinals' games? I want to do that."

"Not a problem, I'll show you," he says.

Theora and her co-worker and friend, Jo Atteberry, are just finishing their assigned tasks at the casino after their breakfast-lunch shift. Jo wants to go to the Whitehouse in the evening to dance, and Theora wants to see the movie at the Eldon Theatre.

"I saw this cowboy type from Oklahoma in the store this week," Jo argues. "My sis says he's single. I want to see if he comes to the Whitehouse."

"Is he handsome?" Theora asks.

"Not particularly," Jo answers. "But cowboys aren't supposed to be handsome. They're supposed to be 'rugged.' He's rugged."

"But the movie, Jo. It's Gable. Gable. He's rugged and handsome."

"All right," Jo says, willing to compromise. "We'll go to the early show, then to the Whitehouse. Okay?"

"Okay. Pick me up at six-thirty? Gotta go. Marion and Phyll are waiting."

The movie is 1934's *It Happened One Night*, a pre-Code release that has taken its own sweet time getting to Eldon, and both girls enjoy it as if they were attending the premiere. Jo agrees with Theora about Gable.

"Rugged and handsome is good," Jo says on the way back to Lake Ozark after the show. "Especially that Gable fellow."

Theora, however, is intrigued by Claudette Colbert's cleverness in handling Gable.

"She outwitted him a few times," Theora says. "Knew how to outsmart him."

"They still ended up together in the end," Jo says.

"Yes. But she was in charge."

The Whitehouse seems busier than usual this Saturday night, as it is Labor Day weekend, and come Tuesday, summer will officially be over. Most out-of-towners will head home, and the locals will be left to their own devices — and vices. Whatever. It is Saturday night.

Jo and Theora find Marion and Phyllis sitting at a table down front near the dance floor and move quickly to join them. Jo immediately starts looking around the room for her cowboy. When she spots him, he is sitting across the room at a table with a young local dairy farmer named Ira Stith. Ira is a big man who appears to be quite strong, owing most likely to his occupation. Large milk cans aren't light. The two appear to be getting along, engaged in an animated conversation with two other young men at the table. Though no liquor bottle is evident, it would appear that they each may have imbibed a bit before they arrived. Seeing her cowboy, Jo alerts Theora.

"That's him there, sitting with Ira Stith. The tall fellow, you see him?"

"Dark hair. I see him," Theora says. "Why, he is kind of handsome, Jo. And certainly rugged, like you said."

Through most of Harold's shifts in these first two months at the Whitehouse, he has worked the front counter, pumped gas, and, in the evening, helped in the kitchen with prep — both food and setups. Most evenings, Lawrence watches the front and the liquor store while Jessie oversees the servers in the dining room. Only once has she asked Harold to come help her, and that was because she thought there was going to be a fight. But remembering what Margaret taught him, he managed to defuse the situation, cajoling the participants until they were best friends. So, along with everything else, Harold is now the resident bouncer as well.

Therefore, when the discussion at Ira and the cowboy's table starts to sound a bit combative to Jessie, she goes into the kitchen for Harold.

"There is some commotion at one of the tables, Harold," she tells him. "Not too serious yet, but I don't want it to get out of hand. It's halfway down on the left. Jack Wickham's sitting there with them. You met Jack."

"Oh, yeah, I've met Jack." And indeed, he had. Jack's car wouldn't start one recent night at closing, and Harold had driven him home. Good thing, because Jack was drunk and Harold wasn't. Harold was just irritated. Jack lived way out in the country at Bear Creek, and Harold got lost trying to get back to the Whitehouse. "Next time, Jack walks," Harold assured himself afterward.

Harold walks out of the kitchen and pauses in the doorway to the dining room, surveying its occupants. He notes where Jack is sitting and walks to his table. Jack looks up and sees him coming.

"Here comes Harold, boys," he says to the others. "No trouble now."

"Hey, Jack," Harold says when he reaches the table. "What are you boys up to? Having a good time, I hope."

"We are at that," Jack says.

"How's your old car running?"

"Rode with Robby here tonight," Jack says, indicating the fourth man at the table. "Rob Trapp from Brumley."

"Hey, Rob," Harold says, acknowledging Trapp. He looks at Ira. "You're Ira Stith, right? Been wanting to meet you. I've drunk my fair share of your milk since I've been here. Good stuff."

Harold extends his hand and shakes Ira's.

"I'm Harold Pilkington."

"You certainly are," the cowboy says.

Harold turns and looks at him. He seems very familiar, but Harold can't place him. *I hope he's not trouble*, Harold thinks. *I don't need that, and he doesn't look like a pushover.*

"The last time I saw you, Harold, you were lying on top of me on the football field at the 'Res.'"

"Damn," Harold says, finally realizing. "Jay Rice! What the hell are you doing here?"

"What the hell are you doing here?" Jay replies.

"I work here," Harold says. "I'm Jessie Fry's cousin."

"Not much future around Tulsa now, Harold," Jay says. "Came here to work. Got on at Union Electric as an apprentice lineman. Decent pay." He points to Ira. "Got to know Ira, been running some lines out his way."

"You ever milk a cow, Harold?" Ira asks.

Harold, amused, responds, "I can't say that I have."

"It takes a while, and the more cows you got, the more 'while' it takes," Ira explains. "But they got these automatic milking machines now, and if we get electric, we'll give 'em a try. Electric lights in the barn early mornin' before dawn are kinda nice, too. Jay, here's my best friend now."

"Harold here played sports for Central back in Tulsa," Jay says to the others. "He and his boys used to come out to the reservation and play us. Whupped our butts every time," he adds, laughing.

"Well, we had almost five thousand students in that school," Harold says. "School on the res, not that many." He pauses, takes Jay's hand, and looks at him.

"We're countrymen, you know, me and Jay. Our fathers were both born in Indian Territory. We share that."

"We have been talking here, Robby and me, about which one of these fellas would win if they were to arm wrestle," Jack inserts into the conversation. "Rob says Ira would, but I'm not so sure. What do you think, Harold?"

"Well, now, I don't know," Harold says. "I'm partial to Jay. He used to put a few of us on the ground, too. He's strong."

Harold looks closer at Ira for a moment.

"But you look pretty strong, too, Ira."

He evaluates the match-up for a moment.

"It's a draw. In a friendly match-up, which it would be. It's a draw."

Jo has been watching all the happenings at the cowboy's table and makes sure Theora is paying attention, too. And she is, but the cowboy is not the reason.

Jo turns to Theora and suddenly gets up.

"I'm going over there and rescuing that fellow before he gets into trouble," she says.

Jo crosses the room, grabs Jay's hand, and drags him toward the dance floor.

"Come on, cowboy. Let's dance!"

"But I'm not a cowboy, Miss. I'm an Indian. I'm Cherokee," Jay says, though he doesn't resist the girl's advances.

"The next best thing," Jo says. "And probably a better dancer."

Harold and the others laugh as Jay gets pulled away to the dance floor. "I gotta get back to work," Harold says. "Tell Jay for me if he's off tomorrow to come by and have some breakfast with me, will you boys?"

"Will do," Ira says, and Harold turns and walks back to the kitchen.

Theora has watched closely everything that has taken place in the last few moments, especially Harold, and enquires to anyone who will listen. "Who is that fellow talking to cowboy and Ira?"

Marion, who has also been watching, responds. "That's Harold Pinkerton, something like that."

"You know him?" Phyllis asks.

"Yeah, a new friend of mine," Marion says. "He's from Oklahoma. Jessie's cousin."

"What's a detective doing at the Whitehouse?" Theora asks.

"He's not a detective. That's his name—Pilkerton. Harold Pilkerton."

"He sure is handsome," Phyllis says, stating the obvious. Theora, though silent, agrees.

"Well, he's not perfect," Marion instructs. "I saw him with his shirt off. Got a big hunk of muscle missing from his left shoulder. Gator bite."

"Marion," Theora says, "there aren't any gators in Oklahoma."

He looks at her, thinking for a moment. "There aren't?" he finally says.

"No, Marion," Phyllis agrees.

"That son of a bitch," Marion mutters. "I'll get even with him."

That night, at home in Bagnell, as she lies in bed trying to sleep, Theora thinks about the new fellow from Oklahoma. "I couldn't tell for sure from a distance, but I think he has blue eyes. I like blue eyes."

Early the next morning, a Sunday, Harold sits on the bench just outside the front door. He is drinking coffee while he waits for the 7:30 bus from St. Louis. With the bus comes the Sunday papers from St. Louis—the *Post* and the *Globe-Democrat*. The paper from Kansas City, the *Star*, won't come until the 9:00 a.m. bus out of Sedalia. The Whitehouse is the only local place to buy the papers, and with the churchgoers and others out and about on a Sunday, the papers are normally sold out by noon. Harold likes to browse through the sports pages, check the Cardinals' standings and stats, and see if there is any talk about the Olympics next year — an event he has yet to put out of his mind. When finished, he carefully puts each paper back together and places them back on the stack to be sold.

The 9 a.m. bus having come, he has just finished the *Star* — nothing there — when an old, beat-up Ford pickup pulls into the driveway, and Jay Rice steps down out of the cab.

"I see you didn't get any of that Osage oil money," Harold says, motioning to the pickup.

"And neither did most of the Osage. Greedy white guys stole it."

"Well, as you can tell by my employment status, neither did I," Harold says.

"Where's that free breakfast I heard about last night?" Jay asks.

"Follow me, and we'll find it," Harold says as he gets up from the bench and leads Jay inside.

In the kitchen, Maggie, the cook, is finishing up after the spurt of customers from the 9:00 bus.

"This is Maggie," Harold says. "The only cook this place has seen since the Frys started the business in '32. This is my friend from Tulsa, Jay Rice. If we're nice, can we get a plate of breakfast, Maggie?"

"That depends. You like country-cured ham, biscuits, and gravy, Jay?" Maggie asks.

"If you fixed it, it's bound to be good," Jay says.

"Grab a plate, boys, and I'll serve you up some," Maggie says. "Get Jay a cup of coffee, Harold."

"Maggie, Jay is Cherokee. Off the reservation near Tulsa." He turns to Jay. "I should have said earlier, Jay. Maggie's married name is Custer, and she's got a chip on her shoulder."

"That's spelled Cherokee. Two E's on the end," Jay explains. "Not Sioux with one X on the end."

"I'll go easy on the poison then," Maggie assures, chuckling.

Plates and cups in hand, the two Oklahoma boys settle in at a small wooden table in the center of the kitchen and eat.

"Who was that girl you were dancing with last night?" Harold asks.

"You don't know?" Jay asks. "Daughter of a neighbor of yours. Atteberry. Owns the grocery. Her name's Jo."

"Yeah, yeah, I've met her dad. Smokes Roi-Tans."

"Yep. That's her uncle, Ward. Her dad's name is Hoyle," Jay says. "I only met her last night. She was with some friends. Two sisters and a fellow named Marion, I believe."

"Marion? I think I know… A fellow about five-eight, clean-shaven, decent looking?"

"Sounds about right," Jay says.

"I know him. Gave me a long-winded story about a monster catfish in the river below the dam."

"Well, you know, to the Osage and the Missouri, those waters are sacred," Jay says. "Cherokee, too. There could be a monster catfish living there to keep away the evil spirits."

"Whatever you say, Jay," Harold says, amused.

"One of the sisters, Phyllis, the tallest one, is Marion's girlfriend," Jay says, rerouting the subject.

"Sisters?" Harold asks.

"Last night," Jay says, "with Marion."

"Oh, yeah. Yeah."

"The short one," Jay says, "name's Theora. She's unattached, I think. I could get Jo to fix you up," Jay adds. "We could go out together."

"I don't know, Jay," Harold says, obviously hesitant. "Let me think about it."

"That's Bert and Lena Robinson's girls, Harold," Maggie chimes in. "Phyllis is a pretty one, but Theora is a cutie, Harold. She's a cutie. I'm telling you."

"Alright," Harold says to both. "Alright, I'll think about it."

On the following Tuesday, Harold takes a rare day off and walks down the street to Red Moore's restaurant. Everybody has told him that Red has the best chili in the county, and he decides to try it. "It's an old family recipe," they all say. "Very good." Harold likes chili; he really liked Mrs. Newton's during his time in Texas, but then again, bad chili is illegal in Texas. His dad's was terrible. It was Depression chili—colored water at best, though it did improve some when Margaret took over the kitchen. Of course, it's Marion's stepfather's restaurant. Great chili might be another tall tale.

Harold sees Marion, who is busily busing tables near the back of the room, almost as soon as he enters. The room is long, with a row of tables along one side and a counter running nearly the same on the other. Behind the counter, near the front, is a cash register, firmly in the control, appropriately, of Marion's mom, Carrie. At the back is the grill, manned for the moment by Red himself.

It is lunchtime, and the diner is very busy. Harold finds an empty stool and sits at the counter. Phyllis, busy with others down the counter, sees him, recognizing him from Saturday night at the Whitehouse. At her first opportunity, she approaches him with a glass of water and a menu. "What can I get you to drink, sir?"

"Hi, uh, do you…" Harold hesitates, wondering if this is Marion's girlfriend that Jay told him about. She sure is pretty, like Maggie said, he thinks.

"Sir? Your drink?"

"Do you have tea, iced tea? Unsweet?" Harold asks Phyllis.

"Unsweet is the only way we serve it. You want it sweet. Sugar's right there on the counter."

"I want to try your chili," Harold says, handing her back the menu. "I hear it's the best in the county."

"No, sir, it's the best in the state. You want crackers with it?"

"Saltines?"

"You got it," Phyllis says, nodding. "Bowl of the state's best. Up front," Phyllis yells toward the back grill.

Marion comes around behind the counter carrying a tray of dirty dishes and begins scraping the waste into a trash can below the double sink. He places the dishes into a sink full of hot water and begins washing them. When he looks up, he sees Harold sitting right in front of him, drinking his tea.

"I came to try the chili," Harold says to a surprised Marion.

"It's an old family recipe," Marion says.

"So, you take old family members, cut 'em up, and put 'em in the pot?" Harold says. "Who is it today? Great-great-grandpa?"

"Very funny," Marion says, drying the dishes he has just washed and stacking them on the back counter. "Actually, it's made with gator meat. We import it from Oklahoma."

"About that…" Harold starts to explain.

"Yeah, about that. There's no gators in Oklahoma."

"I didn't explain it very well. I'm sorry."

"Uh-huh," Marion murmurs.

"I was in high school," Harold explains. "I got a job working at the zoo. Got a nice zoo in Tulsa. I cleaned cages, helped feed the animals, stuff like that," he continues. "Well, there is a gator exhibit, and it's very popular because there are no gators in Oklahoma. One day, I was in there with the trainer, and he had just laid out some food for these two." Harold pauses, watching Marion slowly washing the dishes. "One was an aggressive eight-footer; the other was a six-footer. The eight-footer goes for it all just as the trainer turns his back, and the six-footer jumps up and grabs my left shoulder." Harold pauses again, then: "You should've seen it. Bloody mess."

"Here's your chili, sir," Phyllis says as she sets a bowl down in front of him. "Hope you like it. I'll get you some more tea."

"If it's as good as Marion says it is, I'll probably need another bowl," Harold says.

"Harold, this is my girlfriend, Phyllis," Marion says.

"Nice to meet you, Phyllis," he says as she pours him more tea. He tastes the chili and smiles big. "You're right. This may be the best chili I've ever had."

Marion follows Phyllis a short way, stops her, and says quietly, "It was the zoo, Phyllis. He worked at the zoo."

"The zoo? What are you talking about, Marion?"

"The gator bite," he says, pointing to his left shoulder.

"Oh, for God's sake, Marion."

It's a weekday afternoon in September, and Harold has been busy with gasoline customers. The Cardinal game is on the outside speaker, and a couple of locals have been sitting on the benches, listening. The Cards lead the Pirates 3-2 going into the seventh, and Frisch, player-manager, inserts himself into the lineup to pinch-hit for Paul Dean — Diz's brother, the one they call "Daffy." He's had a good six-inning start, giving up only two earned runs and striking out seven, but Frisch

76

plans to bring in a left-hander to close out the last three innings. Collins and Durocher are on first and second.

Lawrence Quinn, who is one of those sitting on the bench, got gas earlier, parked, and decided to listen to the game.

"Come on, Frankie," Lawrence says and takes a drink of his Coke. "Belt it outta there. You won't have to run as hard to try to score. He's getting older — don't want him to overdo it."

"He's got this, you think?" Harold asks. Lawrence and Harold have become casual friends in recent days and often talk over a day game.

"I hope so," Lawrence says. "We're holding on to second place, but there are only nine games left. Don't think we can get to first place."

Frisch looks at two strikes — one, a fastball down the middle, and another the announcer says should have been a ball.

"Frankie gave the ump a glance back after that one, and he didn't like it," the announcer says. "He better watch that — he could get tossed."

Harold, Lawrence, and the other man listening stop, waiting for the next pitch.

"Here's the windup, the pitch, and — oh my! The 'Flash' puts the wood on it. It's going outta here! It's going swimming! Goodbye, ballpark — hello, Mississippi!"

"Cards lead 6-2," Lawrence says. "I need to get to Eldon, or I'll be late to work."

"Our stats guy just informed me — that is the first home run Frisch has hit all year," the announcer says, "and it couldn't come at a better time."

"Spread the word, Lawrence. We've got a band coming Saturday night," Harold says.

"I'll do it. See you then."

Lawrence gets in his car and drives away toward the dam and Eldon.

Ward Atteberry walks up right then. "Did I hear that right? Frisch hit a home run?"

"You did. Cards lead 6-2," Harold tells him.

"See, I told you this would be good for business," Ward reminds him.

"Other than gas customers who pull in, get gas, and leave, I've sold one Coke and one coffee," Harold tells him.

"Well, son, at that rate, you'll be retired by the time you're thirty," Ward says.

At the casino on Saturday night, dinner customers are few, and all are gone by closing time at nine. Bernie says it's a pattern for September—summer's over, school's started, and many of the older travelers haven't gotten out and taken their fall drives yet. When the trees give up their bright colors in October, they'll come, she says.

Theora and Jo finish cleaning up and go into the ladies' room to change clothes. They plan to meet Phyllis, Marion, and Jay at Atteberry's and go together to the Whitehouse. Word is, the band, out of Jeff City, is new and good, and a big crowd is expected.

Bernie has even talked Paul into going for a while, a rare event. "One or two dances," she says, "and it'll be bedtime. But that's something."

Not surprisingly, parking in the area of the Whitehouse is limited, but Marion, who has picked up Jay at his rented place at Mrs. Knoch's Cottages on 1-A, planned ahead. He has marked off a spot in front of Red's restaurant with a wooden barrier and a sign that says, "No Parking." After he and Jay have picked up the girls and parked, he places the sign directly behind his car. The girls have told Bernie to have Paul park there behind Marion's car, placing the sign behind it. It works, and their walk to the Whitehouse is a matter of feet.

Maggie, the Frys' longtime cook, has opted to work only breakfast and lunch in the fall, leaving any dinner activity to a couple of younger cooks she has been training throughout the summer. Her husband has been having some health issues in recent days, and with the farm and all, she needs more time away. With Jessie and Harold's help, the kitchen manages to function fairly well without her in the evenings. The decision has been made to offer only sandwiches after seven p.m. on weekends. Maggie has made sure there are multiple platters of sliced "city ham" and turkey, lettuce, and tomatoes in the walk-in cooler, providing many choices as long as they involve cold ham or turkey with American cheese, lettuce, and tomato optional. Also piled high in the cooler are stacks of cases of Coke, 7-Up, and beer.

The place is already packed with people by the time Marion, Jay, and the girls arrive. The tables are all taken, and there are people standing along the walls. Many of the people they do not recognize, and it is assumed that some of the patrons have come from the surrounding towns — Eldon, Camdenton, and even Jeff City. Mrs. Barker, who traveled that morning from Kansas City with her seventeen-year-old daughter, Virginia, and young son, Harry, is camped at a table near the front. Lawrence Quinn, now a fixture with the Barkers when they are in town, sits with them. They came early to have dinner and for Mrs. Barker, a pair of highballs and a bottle of Kentucky's best prominent on the table. Lawrence has managed to secure two folding chairs, which he guards carefully.

Seeing Marion at the door, Lawrence gets up and goes to him. "Mrs. Barker and Harry are leaving in a minute, and I've got two extra chairs. Come on over."

Marion, Jay, and the girls follow him. Phyllis sits on Marion's lap, Jo on Jay's, and Theora on Lawrence's after asking Virginia if she minds. "No," she says. "It'll help hold him down."

Theora happens to notice Harold appear briefly in the dining room doorway just as Mrs. Barker asks her if she has a boyfriend.

"Not yet," she replies, smiling.

After securing a promise from Lawrence that he will have Virginia in by no later than eleven— "midnight maybe"— Mrs. Barker and Harry leave, making it slightly less crowded at the table.

In the lobby, Lawrence Fry has been kept busy in the liquor store, somewhat nervous about checking I.D.s and making sure he sells only to those over 21. When Bernie and Paul come in, having successfully navigated Marion's parking plan, Paul steps into the liquor store.

"You're Lawrence Fry, aren't you? I'm Paul Gordon. My wife, Bernie," he says, indicating her (she waves), "and I run the Lakeside Casino."

"Yes, nice to meet you, Paul," Lawrence says, shaking his hand. "Jessie and I had dinner at your place recently. Very good. Enjoyed it."

"The kids that work for us keep telling us we should come in some Saturday night and dance," Paul says, "but if I can get a pint of Ten High from you, I'll just have a drink and listen."

Lawrence laughs and complies, and Paul, bottle in hand, joins Bernie, who is peeking through the dining room door. Theora and the others have been trying to get sodas since first sitting down; the waitress, one of two, along with Jessie, tells them she is behind. They are all behind, the attendance much larger than anyone had expected. Jessie is circulating all over the room, busing tables, taking orders, and simply trying to move the process along, but she feels she is moving in reverse. Theora, seeing Bernie at the door, motions for her to come to their table. She grabs hold of Paul, and they work through the crowd.

"Bernie, I'm going to ask Jessie if I can help," she says. "They've got a problem; the waitress says everything's backed up. Holdup is in the kitchen, I bet."

"Might be. Paul, give me the bottle."

He does so, and Bernie takes a drink. "Go ask her, and I'll go with you."

Theora goes to find Jessie as the band, who have been on break, begins to play again. Good, Jessie thinks. Maybe dancing again will take their minds off the slow service.

"Jessie? Theora Robinson. Phyll and Marion, Bernie Gordon too. We want to help," Theora says when she catches up with Jessie. "Is the problem in the kitchen? We can help?"

Jessie is surprised but pleased. "Are you sure?"

"Of course."

"Meet me in the kitchen."

Theora goes back to the table and gets Bernie and Phyllis, and they head toward the kitchen. As soon as they enter, Phyllis immediately sees the pile of dirty dishes, announces she is going back for Marion and leaves. Theora immediately sees Harold busily making sandwiches.

"Harold, this is Theora," Jessie says. "She's going to help you."

"Stop just a moment, young man," Theora says to him. "Let me see your eyes."

He turns to her, obviously irritated. "Young man?" he says.

And then he sees her. *Damn,* he thinks. *She is cute. And that bosom.*

How does such a little girl — ? Damn.

"Your eyes?" Theora states. "They are blue."

"My eyes? I know what color my eyes are. Now, are you going to help or discuss anatomy?" As soon as the word is out of his mouth, he regrets it. *Anatomy,* he thinks. *Damn.*

"You don't have to be rude, young man," Theora says. Her eyes are fine, and she is amazed by how good he looks up close. *My goodness, he is handsome,* she thinks.

The kitchen door opens, and Marion and Phyllis enter. Phyllis points to the pile of dishes.

"Damnit," Marion says as he rolls up his sleeves.

"Jessie, Theora, and I can handle the food prep," Bernie says, "So Harold can be free to tell us what he needs."

"Great, thank you," Jessie says.

"One favor?" Bernie says. "Can you get some Cokes and a 7-Up with a glass of ice to our table where Paul is? He'll be so happy to have his highball."

"It's done," Jessie says as she loads a tray and leaves the kitchen. Harold explains the sandwiches offered to Bernie, who naturally takes charge.

"Theora, you do bread, mayo, and cheese," she says. "I got the ham, turkey, lettuce, tomato, and you," she says, turning to one of the two young cooks, "plate them, pile on the chips, and put them in a line. Harold will make sure we get the orders right; the waitresses get what they need."

With the assembly line in place, the group gets to work.

Phyllis, drying as fast as Marion can wash, turns to Harold.

"Got a stack of clean plates for you."

"Thanks," Harold says and takes the plates to the assembly line. A waitress comes in needing fresh ice buckets, and Harold retrieves them, fills them with ice, and sets them out for her while she loads a tray with the glasses and drinks she needs.

Turning back to Phyllis, he asks, "The little one there," indicating Theora, "she's your sister?"

"Yes," Phyllis says, then loud enough for Theora to hear, "She's adopted," to which Theora turns and gives her a dirty look.

"What about the pearl diver there?" Harold asks. "He adopted too?"

"Somewhat," Phyllis says. "He showed up one day sophomore year. Played good basketball. So, we kept him."

"You want half my catch, Zoo Boy? I'd be happy to share."

"Monster catfish?" Harold asks.

"Children, children. Enough."

She turns to Harold. "I should have introduced myself earlier," Bernie says. "I'm Berniece Gordon from the Casino. But everyone calls me Bernie."

Theora looks at her. "Berniece!" Theora says. "You never told me that."

The kitchen door opens, and Jessie leans in. "Harold, we may have trouble. Two guys are about to get into it."

"I'm coming," Harold says, heading toward the door.

"You need help, Harold?" Marion asks, drying his hands.

"No, I got this," he says firmly and leaves. Marion follows.

"Down front," Jessie says. "I think the guy on the left started it."

Jay, aware of what is happening, follows Harold. "I got your back, Harold, if you need it."

"I'm good, Jay. I got this," he says.

"Gentlemen, what's going on?" Harold asks as he steps between them, his back to the shorter one. The big one's got a couple of inches on him. The band, aware of the commotion, stops playing.

"This asswipe is messing with my girlfriend, and I'm going to wipe the floor with him," the big guy says.

"What about that, sir?" he says to the one behind him without turning.

"I didn't do a thing. I got my own date," the man says. "Right here," he says, pointing to the girl sitting behind him. "He's drunk and mad 'cause his girlfriend keeps dancing with everyone else."

"Why aren't you dancing with your boyfriend, ma'am?" Harold asks the big guy's date.

"He doesn't know how," she says.

"That true, mister?" Harold asks.

"Screw it. I'm going to kick his ass anyway," the big man says as he tries to push Harold aside.

Harold puts his hand out to stop him. "No, no, no. Why don't you and I take a walk outside and cool off?" Harold says as he reaches for the man's arm to lead him out.

The man suddenly swings his free hand toward Harold's jaw, but before it can connect, Harold blocks it. Immediately, Harold spins the man's arm around into a semi-half-nelson and applies pressure upward and in on his wrist. Placing his free hand near the man's other shoulder, he starts walking him out of the dining room. The man complains about the pain but does not resist as Harold moves him quickly toward the front door, the crowd parting as they go.

Law enforcement jurisdiction for the unincorporated town of Lake Ozark lies with the Miller County Sheriff's Office in Tuscumbia, and as usual, there is only one deputy on duty for the whole half of the county hosting the town. But tonight, he is conveniently located in the parking lot just outside the Whitehouse. It is the only place he can hear music and get a cup of fresh coffee, the rest of his beat being quiet.

He sees Harold as he comes out the front door with the man he is escorting and asks, of course, if he can be of help.

"You want to press charges, Harold?" Charley asks.

"No need to. He just needs to sleep it off somewhere safe," Harold says.

Charley cuffs the man and puts him in the backseat of his car.

"He can ride around with me for a while, and I'll get him a room in Tuscumbia when I check in at the end of my shift."

"Tell him he should take dance lessons when he gets out, Charley. Might keep him out of trouble."

Marion, who has followed Harold outside, sees the deputy, a friend, and approaches him, shaking his hand. "Hey, Charley, how's that application to conservation going? You heard anything yet?" Marion asks.

Charley has applied to the Missouri Department of Conservation to become an agent; Marion knows and is interested.

"I should know something next week," Charley says. "Looks good, I believe."

"Charles Fleetwood. Game Warden," Marion says loudly. "It has a nice ring to it."

Charley laughs. To Harold: "Need me around anymore tonight, Harold?"

"There won't be any more trouble tonight, Charley," Harold says. "We're good."

When they come back in, Jessie goes to tell the band to start playing again, and couples get up to dance. Jo, feeling the need to help, starts busing tables and carries a tray into the kitchen. Marion walks over to Jay.

"I've never seen anything like that, Jay," Marion says to him quietly. "It was so fast. One second, the guy's swinging. The next, he's out the door."

"Back home, the last couple of years, everybody knew not to take him on. Even me," Jay says. He pauses and looks at Marion. "He's the nicest man I ever met, Marion. Likes to joke around, have fun, stay calm when he's tested, and doesn't want trouble. Doesn't like to fight. But you don't want to mess with him. You can't beat him."

Phyllis sticks her head through the kitchen door, looking for Marion, and yells, "Marion! Dishes." He walks toward the kitchen, mumbling something profane.

With the extra help, the rest of the evening goes fairly smoothly, and most of the customers seem happy with their evening out. The band plays their last song at 11:30 in preparation for the midnight closing, and Harold switches the radio to a music station on the speakers. Many of the couples begin to make their way to the parking lot, among them Lawrence and Virginia—he, more worried about being late than his date.

At closing, Jessie invites everyone—her staff and the volunteers as well—to sit down in the dining room and relax. She has fixed highballs for Paul and Bernie and a very welcome one for herself. Harold, Marion, and Jay each enjoy a cold beer.

"Thanks to all of you for your help," she says. "Lawrence and I very much appreciate it. Seems we had created a monster and didn't see it coming. Hopefully, we'll be better prepared next time." "You know, Jessie, every time someone from out of town comes across that dam to visit and leaves happy," Bernie says, "we're all the winner for it. Chances are good, they'll come back."

Theora looks over at Harold, whom she has noticed, keeps glancing at her when he thinks she doesn't see him. A hit song, Glen Gray's *Blue Moon*, begins playing on the radio, and Theora gets up, goes to Harold, and takes his hand.

"Come on, 'Blue Eyes,' let's dance."

He doesn't hesitate and follows her to the floor, and they begin to dance.

"You work tomorrow?" she asks.

"Just 'til noon," he answers. "Until the Sunday morning buses are in and out."

"Pick me up at 1:00 then," she orders. "There's a matinee at 2:00 at the Eldon Theatre. I live in Bagnell, Robinson house. Look for Marion's car. He's always there."

Jessie, amused, watches the two. *He's done*, she thinks. *Doesn't know it, but he's finished.*

Later that night, after everyone is gone, Harold approaches his cousin and asks her, "Jessie, tell me. How can such a little girl like that, Theora, have such a large bosom?"

"They're called breasts, Harold. A gift from God. And yes, they're quite ample."

The next day, Harold arrives at the Robinson home promptly at 1:00. He finds the house easily; Marion's car is there. Bert and Lena are sitting on the porch, and Marion also, as Harold, steps up and introduces himself. Theora decides to wait before coming out, wanting to see how Harold manages his interrogators. Phyllis waits with her. Lena asks some usual questions: "Where are you from? What do your parents do?" etc.

"What do you do for a living, son?" Bert asks, finally entering the conversation.

"I'm a jerk," Harold says without breaking a smile.

Lena looks confused. Marion laughs lightly.

"Well, I'll be the judge of that," Bert says.

"Oh, no, sir," Harold says quickly. He glances at Lena. "I meant soda jerk. We have a soda fountain. I make ice cream sundaes, malts—you know, things like that."

"Uh-huh," Bert mumbles.

"And I also pump gasoline, help the cook, clean up, meet the buses, whatever. Shovel coal into the furnace."

"So, you're a jack, then," Lena says. "As well as a jerk."

"A what?" Bert says.

"A jack-of-all-trades," Lena says.

"Yes, ma'am," Harold says, smiling. "I think you've got it."

"And master of none," Bert mumbles to himself.

Theora and Phyllis come out of the house onto the porch.

"Come on, Marion, we've got to go," Phyllis says. She looks at Lena. "We're going on a picnic with Jo and her boyfriend, Momma. Out at the swinging bridges, by the creek. We'll be back by dinner."

"We're going to a movie, Momma," Theora says. "In Eldon. Be back by 5:00."

"Perhaps Harold will stay and have dinner with us also?" Lena says directly to him.

"Let's see how the movie goes first, Momma," Theora says.

"Yes, Mrs. Robinson. Let's see how the movie goes first," Harold says, smiling.

"Come on, blue eyes, let's go," Theora says. "We don't want to be late."

Once in the car, Harold asks Theora what the movie is, to which she replies, "I don't know. Does it matter?"

The movie went well—it was a comedy, and they laughed together. Afterward, Harold had dinner with the family, including Marion.

At work, Harold helped Lawrence and Jessie improve the system to make sure there would not be a repeat of the overwhelming previous Saturday night. A decision was made to have a band only one night a month. The young people were coming to the Whitehouse to listen to the music regardless of the source. They had begun to adopt the dining room there as a place to gather — to talk as well as listen. There was always a good crowd, particularly on a Friday night after a home basketball game. Area business remained strong through October, helped by a fall color that year that far exceeded expectations. Harold and Theora continued to date as their work schedules allowed.

One morning in mid-October, Marion comes into the White House to have coffee with Harold and announce the opening of snagging season. Harold will "finally get to see the monster catfish," he tells him. "We'll go down below the dam and watch until someone gets one," he says.

Harold, though skeptical, works around his schedule so he can go that night. Jay agrees to go as a witness.

At 7:00 that night, Marion, Harold, and Jay, with a few bottles of beer on board, drive across the dam, up the hill, and turn right onto the road into what locals call U.E. Village, or simply "camp." The view of the dam and lake from this vantage point is the best, unchallenged view of the two unique man-made landmarks together that exist, and Marion pulls off and parks so the three friends can take it in. From this point, at a parking spot behind a fenced-in substation, you can see down to the parking lot and the administrative offices and power plant facilities that provide the electricity to power up the lights of St. Louis. And with my help, Jay concludes, power to help Ira get his milk out to market faster. Rural electrification has become a big issue during the devastating Depression America is experiencing, and Bagnell Dam plays a small yet significant part in it.

Marion points out the line marking the area above which you cannot fish. This limit is intended for the protection of fishermen and sightseers alike. The line is for both bank fishermen and anyone fishing from a boat. At low water times, it may not be as dangerous, but at high water in the lake above, the open floodgates can increase the risk to everyone in the area. "Fishing is generally better above the line," Marion says, "but don't get caught. The fine is pretty hefty."

Back in the car, the boys drive on until they come to a large, one-level building nestled among some trees. There is an ample parking area on one side.

"They call that the clubhouse," Jay says. "I had some classes in there when I first started work at U.E. Got a couple of nice pool tables in there. We'd play during class breaks."

At the clubhouse, the narrow roadway makes a hard-right turn, runs down the hill, and settles onto a large, gravel-covered parking area. From here, you can walk to the riverbank, but you can't approach the dam and its offices due to a fence and a locked gate. There are several cars in the lot, this being the first night of snagging season. The boys, each carrying a beer, walk down near the bank and see several fishermen lined up, throwing their treble hooks out. Intrigued by the scene, they are unaware of someone approaching them from behind.

"All right, you three," a voice says. "Let's see some I.D.s."

All three freeze in place as Marion mumbles, "Damnit." When they finally turn, they are surprised to see newly minted conservation agent Charles Fleetwood, in full uniform, standing there smiling.

"Damnit, Charley," Marion says. "Don't do that!"

Charley laughs, then says, "Actually, guys, my supervisor is with me, about a hundred yards downriver, so you might want to finish the beers and trash the bottles before he gets back up here." They do so quickly and make a deposit in a nearby trash can.

"Too bad, Charley," Harold says. "We were going to offer you a beer."

"I would like nothing better right now, except the boss frowns on it," Charley says.

"Seeing many caught tonight, Charley?" Marion asks.

"A few. One-a-day limit now, so those caught are gone already."

A young boy of about twelve, fishing with his father a bit downstream, has just cast his line out into the slow current when there is a heavy jerk and drag on his line.

"Dad, I got one! I got one!"

The boy's father comes to him quickly, encouraging him. "Okay, Elmer. Just hold tight to the rod and start reeling. Lift, then reel as you come back down," the father says. "Lift and reel, Elmer. Good boy. That's it."

The guys and Charley walk quickly to where the boy and his father are fishing and approach just as the boy pulls his catch up to and slightly onto the gravel riverbank.

The guys look down at the catch.

"Hell, Marion, that's a paddlefish. Hell, Harold, that's no monster catfish," Jay says. "That's a paddlefish. We got those in the Arkansas River. You never seen one?"

"Nope. Never seen one," Harold says. "And actually, they're not that ugly."

"Not like those big old flatheads you see on the Arkansas," Jay says. "Now that's one ugly fish."

"I did see one of those once," Harold says. "Dad caught it and brought it home. Fried it up." He pauses, thinking back. "That was an ugly fish. I didn't eat that night."

All of a sudden, out of the unforeseen nowhere that is everywhere, Jay looks to the sky, stretches out his arms, palms up, and starts chanting: "Eey, yah wah, ho yah, yah, pu, pu ya-sah." "Is he okay, Dad?" Elmer asks. His father shrugs his shoulders.

"What are you doing, Jay?" Marion asks.

"I was praying to the Great Spirit," Jay says. "Thanking him for the abundance of food given up here by the sacred waters."

"These fish are older than the dinosaurs," Charley points out.

"So is the Great Spirit," Jay says.

"Was that Cherokee?" Marion asks.

"Yeah," he says. "Old Cherokee phrase meaning gobbledygook."

"Gobbledygook?" Harold questions, amused.

"It means I have no idea what I said."

"Kind of like when Catholics speak Latin?" Marion says.

"Yeah, kinda like that," Jay says.

"You boys may want to head out," Charley says to them. "I see my supervisor heading back up this way."

Taking his advice, the guys get back in the car and are only halfway up the hill when suddenly Jay bursts out laughing.

"Monster catfish!" He laughs some more. "Monster catfish. That's a good one."

One evening, a few days later, Harold leaves the Whitehouse and drives to the Casino at closing to pick up Theora. They don't have any specific plans, just that he will pick her up and drive her home. There is a mid-October chill in the air, and as they come out of the restaurant, Theora buttons up her coat and puts her arm in Harold's.

"Have you ever walked across the dam?" she asks him.

"No," he says. It's never crossed his mind.

"Let's do it," she says playfully. "It doesn't take long."

"All right. If you want to."

Harold buttons up his coat as well, and the couple begin walking toward the dam. The structure has been built to accommodate a two-lane roadway with a two-person-wide walkway running the length of it on the riverside. It is a clear night, and a full harvest moon is highly visible. Theora, the lover of literature and shoes, imagines herself as Cathy with her Heathcliff, walking arm in arm through the English countryside. No, no, she thinks. Harold is not Heathcliff; he's not a lost, lonely soul adrift in the moors. He's from Oklahoma.

"Were you busy tonight?" Harold asks. "It was pretty quiet at the Whitehouse."

"A few tables. Probably half of them were locals."

"Will Bernie close for the winter?"

"She did last year," Theora says. "She and Paul went to Tulsa; they both have family there. Stayed until March."

"I didn't know they were from Tulsa," Harold says. "Small world stuff, huh?"

"Do you plan on staying here, working for Jessie? Or will you go back there?"

"Staying. I have no other plans," Harold says. "The Fry's will remain open because of the daily buses. People have come to depend on us for their newspapers, magazines, and such. They'll keep me on."

"And the weekend dances, that too?" Theora asks.

"Oh, yeah. I think so. Folks seem to like it, not just the kids," Harold answers. "What will you do when Bernie and Paul close?"

"Well, last winter, I was still going to school. This year, not sure. Might be able to fill in at Red's part-time," Theora says.

They have reached the midpoint of the dam, and Theora stops and looks out over the river and the valley below. From her vantage point at the height of the dam, both seem so far away.

"I often think of going someplace," Theora says. "I'd like to travel. See New York. The Statue of Liberty. You?"

"Haven't thought about it much. Maybe drive to St. Louis one day, see the Mississippi." A beat. Amused, Harold continues, "I'd probably wait until ball season, though. Catch a Cardinal game, too."

Theora continues looking out over the valley below, the river running through it. Harold takes her shoulders, turns her gently toward him, and kisses her. When they part, she looks up at him, studying his features.

"If my mother knew I had kissed a man as handsome as you," Theora says, "she would 'tan my hide.' If you were ugly, though, not a problem."

"What's all this handsome stuff?" Harold protests. "I'm not handsome. I'm bow-legged, I'm kinda short, got cauliflower ears from wrestling, and I've got an indent in my left shoulder."

"My, you are a mess, aren't you," Theora agrees, shaking her head. "By the way, Marion told Phyll and me about your arm." She laughs. "Gator bite."

"Well, he fed me some tall tale about monster catfish in the Osage, so I gave him a tall tale back."

"What did happen?" Theora asks seriously.

"It's a long story. Goes back to my rodeo days. I'll tell you some other time."

"OK," she says, then glances at her watch. "We should go; I've got the breakfast shift in the morning."

And with that, the couple walk back to the car and drive toward Bagnell.

The second week in November, Jessie calls Bernie and asks her if she could stop by later in the day and visit.

"Of course," Bernie says. "We're closed. Just come around to the side and knock. I'll have the coffee pot on."

"Harold says you and Paul will go down to Tulsa soon?" Jessie asks Bernie after she arrives at the casino.

"The second week in December, probably. Stay until early March."

"You'll be in town on Thanksgiving, then?" Jessie asks.

"As far as I know now. No plans. What's on your mind, Jessie?" Bernie asks finally.

"We have to be open for bus customers in the morning—just rolls, coffee, that sort of thing—but otherwise, plan to close by noon, and I've been thinking." Jessie sips her coffee and leans in. "This community has been good to Lawrence and me, and we know there are lots of others like us—you and Paul. People new here with no family."

"I understand," Bernie says. "That's us, all right."

"I want to open up our dining room on Thanksgiving and invite anyone without a place to go to join us for a meal. We'll do a turkey and ham, gravy, stuffing, and potatoes." Jessie is very animated now, enthusiastic, and Bernie is paying close attention to every word. "We'll ask everyone to bring a dish, their own bottle, of course. Maybe Atteberry's would supply the rolls from their store. What do you think? Would people come?"

"I absolutely think they would, Jessie. I love the idea!" Bernie says. "I need to check with Paul first, but I'm sure we'll help out. I'll do another turkey here, a pan of stuffing and gravy. Bring some cans of cranberry sauce."

"It would be nice to have other locals come—those that normally would have their own family gatherings," Jessie says.

"Can we get them to join in, you think? Like the Robinsons?"

"I don't know," Bernie says. "What I do know is that if nobody comes, Lawrence and Paul will have a lot of leftovers to eat."

They both laugh. "I'll talk to Theora and see what she says."

"Okay. I'll talk to Marion. Maybe have Harold talk with him," Jessie says. "If he could get Red and Carrie to get involved, that would be nice. Even better if she brought along a couple of pies. That woman can certainly bake a pie."

"So, I've heard," Bernie says.

Jessie finishes her coffee and gets up from the table. "Bernie, think about it. This town we're living in didn't even exist until four years ago, and we're some of its first residents. We should celebrate that."

"Yes, we should. But, Jessie, we have to remember that to many of these local people, we are, and always will be, outsiders." Bernie gets up and pushes her chair back under the table. "We represent the folks that took their best valley land, covered their towns with water, moved their cemeteries. It will take a generation or two for that to be totally forgotten."

Jessie nods her head in understanding. "Well, we'll see what happens."

"I'll make some calls, Jessie. Let you know what I find out."

"I'll do the same," Jessie says as she goes out the door.

Not long before Harold had come from Tulsa to work for Lawrence and Jessie, the Frys had purchased and moved a small, one-bedroom cottage onto the Whitehouse property. There was space on the land just to the left of the main building, and the cottage was successfully hooked onto the septic system, with water and electricity easily accessed as well. The addition afforded the Frys some privacy from the fishbowl world that often surrounded the Whitehouse. For Harold, this meant some welcome privacy, too, as he was usually the only person housed on the second floor. If it was necessary to hire a waitress from out of town, room and board could be offered to help reduce the wages paid. This was rarely the case, though, and the few times it occurred, they didn't stay long. For transients during the Depression, a better life was always just a boxcar away.

Maggie did keep a room upstairs in case of an emergency, weather being the primary reason. The road going to her small farm crossed two creeks, and the low concrete-slab bridges could flood easily in hard, constant rains. Snow was not so much a problem, as she proudly said, "I could track with the best of them." She kept a change of clothes in the room and some personal items but rarely ever stayed. She always wanted to get to her farm and see about Fred, her husband of forty-some years. He had been injured some years before—a nagging back issue that wouldn't go away—and his ability to help on the farm was limited. Maggie worried about him, of course, because she loved him.

Jessie told Harold one day, not long after he first started dating Theora, that if he wanted to know what love is, all he had to do was take a drive out to Maggie's place and watch her and Fred. She had once, she told him, ridden out with Maggie to pick up something she had forgotten, and Fred was telling her all he had gotten done around the farm. They were not heavy tasks—his health kept him from that—but they were important to him. They were things she would not have to do after working all day. Maggie made sure she thanked him for "getting so much done; it's a huge help" and then kissed him. It wasn't praise he wanted, Maggie told Jessie that day—it was respect. Respect from the one he had made the life bargain with in front of a preacher those many years ago.

"In their small living room, I noticed," Jessie told him, "two rocking chairs sitting side by side in front of a wood stove—darn near in the middle of the room." She continued, "If you ever want to know if you're in love, try to imagine yourself forty, fifty years in the future. If you can picture that person sitting in a rocking chair next to you and you're both smiling, there's a good chance you're in love." She paused and smiled. "Or senile."

Jessie, with Harold's help, had spoken with Red and Carrie, and they had agreed to participate. Marion's brother Ross and his wife, Gladys, were back in Illinois, where Ross was apprenticing as an electrician with an old friend of the boys' dad and wouldn't be coming home. Their older sister,

Ruth, and her husband, Art Hanson, as well as their adopted sister, Nelia, and her husband, Paul Wolfe, all lived in the Chicago area. There was concern about the predicted bad weather, and therefore, they did not want to make the long drive. So, encouraged by Marion, they would be there, pies in hand — "mostly pumpkin, maybe a pecan or two."

And the Atteberrys — both families — had agreed to help and attend, providing dinner rolls, green beans, and corn (canned, of course). That meant Jay was all in for the feast because, as he said,

"Every Thanksgiving gathering should have a token Indian."

Bernie made a special trip down to Bagnell and, with Theora and Phyllis's help, spoke with the Robinsons. The sisters were very favorable to the event, as Marion and Harold were committed — Harold by work, Marion by Mom.

"Momma," Theora said, "we can take some of your fresh-churned butter. Everybody will love that."

"And how about we make a couple of cakes, Momma? I'll help," Phyllis said. "Nobody can resist your cake!"

Lena was considering. She knew that her son George was committed to going to his new wife's family upstate. She had a daughter and wanted her to be near her aging parents. Dorothy was busy having babies in Kansas — four at last count — and wouldn't be home. Frieda had been back to Bagnell only once since she left and was not expected. Son Clyde and his wife, Pebble, would normally be at home.

"Well, Bert, what do you think?" Lena asked her husband. "Will Clyde and Pebble go with us?"

"Clyde is like me, Lena. He doesn't care where he eats as long as he gets fed well."

"That settles it then," Theora announced. "Bernie, we'll be there."

That same day, Jessie got a call from Mrs. Cunningham, the new barber's wife. Her name was Dolly. "Named for the First Lady," she said. "Your young fella there told my husband that we can come for Thanksgiving, and I wanted to make sure that was okay. George can get confused sometimes."

"Of course," Jessie said. "We want the gathering to bring people together — newcomers like you and me and those who were here before."

"I bake. Can I bring cookies?" Dolly asked. "George has a sweet tooth, and I make him cookies all the time."

"That is a wonderful idea. Please do," Jessie said.

"I'll make a bunch up while he's working and hide them from him. What time, Mrs. Fry?"

"People will begin gathering about 2:00, and we'll eat about 4:00," Jessie said. "And Dolly, call me Jessie."

An open invitation is circulated to the offices at the power plant. Turner White, the plant superintendent, and Mrs. White talk to Bernie about their regrets. Their family connections are in St. Louis, and they need to go there for a few days. Mrs. White, who serves on the local school board, has shown sincere interest in the community and is respected for that.

Local employees at Union Electric, for the most part, are very active in the area, in their churches, and the school, and a few families from the "UE Village" respond positively to the invitation. Among them is a young engineer named Bruce James and his wife, Helen. Mr. James has worked at Bagnell Dam since 1931 and has recently gotten to know Harold. He is always the first one each Sunday morning to meet the 7:30 bus from St. Louis to get the newspapers. Union Electric, being a St. Louis-based company, values keeping up with news and events from the city, which is worthwhile to an energetic young employee. Harold has come to admire the young engineer for that.

If everyone who has committed comes, it will be a success, Jessie and Bernie agree. But two days before Thanksgiving, Paul suddenly decides there may be a shortage of food and puts a large roast in the oven. "There may be some folks there who don't care for turkey or ham; we might want to have a few slices of beef just in case," he concludes. "I'll make some brown gravy to go with it."

It has been confirmed that a rather large pan of sweet potatoes with marshmallows is coming to the gathering, and Jessie is making mashed potatoes. However, Paul is concerned about having enough mashed potatoes, so he peels a large bag of spuds and makes more, a container of which Bernie describes to Jessie over the phone as being "bigger than my pillow."

Thanksgiving Day is sunny and warmish for late November, and Harold takes care of the few passengers on the buses that morning. Maggie had made pans of sweet rolls the day before to serve passengers, and that, along with coffee and soft drinks, is all that is offered. There is, however, a young mother traveling with two small children who expresses concern about food farther down the road. She is on her way to Ft. Sill in southwestern Oklahoma to join her husband stationed there, and Jessie quietly makes three ham sandwiches and wraps them up for her to take along for her family.

Paul and Bernie arrive at noon, their car loaded with pans of food, including the mashed potato "pillow." Harold and Lawrence, the day before, have arranged a row of tables near the front of the room where the food will be placed, and people can be served cafeteria-style. The remainder of the tables are arranged so they can seat eight each to facilitate the mingling of folks, a desired result of the gathering.

The Robinson girls and Marion arrive soon after, as they have volunteered to help set up, and Jo, with Jay in tow, walks across the street to help as well.

Lawrence's youngest brother, Don, who has recently turned sixteen, has been given permission by his mother to drive them from Springfield to Lake Ozark, adding to Lawrence's anxiety. He is very fond of the boy, whom he calls Donnie, and dotes on him — perhaps as an unconscious way of making up for the loss of their father at his young age. His middle brother, Harvey, and his wife, Vivian, have settled in nearby Eldon but have committed the day to her family and will not be attending. Donnie and Mrs. Fry plan to drive there later that afternoon to visit for a few days. When his mother and brother arrive on time and in one piece, Lawrence relaxes and puts the boy to work helping Harold with whatever needs to be done.

More food arrives with Red and Carrie, and Mrs. Cunningham's cookies have to be hidden until later because George is on the scent. Bert and Lena, butter and cakes in hand, arrive, and Lawrence immediately tests the fresh-churned butter, spreading it on a piece of bread, eating it, and announcing loudly, "That is not butter; that is a sin!"

Others, food in hand, begin arriving at the suggested time of 2:00 p.m. Among them are Coach Henderson and his wife, Helen, as well as the new Superintendent of Schools, Leland Mills, and his date, Lenah Becker, the first-grade teacher. Bud Henderson is the new School of the Osage's first basketball coach and also serves as principal. Helen teaches English, Speech, and Drama, even though Coach jokes that the cheerleaders cheering and a close ballgame should be enough of the latter. He coached Marion in his senior year and has just completed his second season with Lawrence Quinn in his last.

As for Lawrence, he is present as well. It seems Mrs. Barker — Clara, that is — has come down from Kansas City with Virginia and Harry to join in the festivities, having begun to feel more at home here than there. Virginia, being "smitten" by Lawrence, has a lot to do with that. Clara has carted along a few groceries from a Kansas City market to offer up and has her usual bourbon bottle in hand.

Donnie has happily jumped right into helping Harold, and the two have become friends. Donnie notices that whenever this girl named Theora, whom Harold has introduced him to, is around, Harold is very attentive. He is also "smitten" with the "older woman," who responds to him by telling him he is "such a sweet boy." And then there is the issue of the other "older woman"—the wife of a young engineer at Bagnell Dam. She has become "smitten" with Harold, and anytime she can get close to him, highball in hand, she does—whether with a question, a need for a helping hand, or a wink. Theora watches this amusing dance from a middle distance as Harold does his best to dodge the married woman's advances. Her husband, equally enamored with highballs, is seemingly oblivious to the dance.

All this smiting—if that's what you call plural "smitten(s)"—could lead to sore cheeks, but it doesn't. The only somewhat "tense" moment of the entire day occurs when Jay Rice fields a question from another guest.

"What's it like to live on a reservation in Oklahoma, fella? You like it?" the man asks.

"Well," Jay begins, sensing a hint of prejudice in the man's tone, "if we are to believe our ancestors—and we are—then it's not nearly as nice as it was before that SOB Andy Jackson made us take the great walk from the Carolinas."

Jay exchanges a glance with Harold, who nods and doesn't say another word. The man smiles slightly, excuses himself, and moves to talk with another group.

Marion, somewhat aware of Harold's background as an athlete, introduces him to Coach Henderson, who inquires about what sports he was involved in. Harold doesn't elaborate, saying only,

"My primary interest was in wrestling."

"You know, Harold," Coach says, "every athlete I ever played with or coached, whether in high school or college, who also wrestled told me it was the most demanding of all the sports. Would you agree with that?"

"Yes, with the possible exception of long-distance running," Harold says. "I can't say for sure, though, because I never ran the distances. But as to individual sports — yes, wrestling."

"How did you train? What did your coaches teach you?"

"Well, Art… Coach Griffith stressed that we needed to develop all of our muscles for strength, but not at the expense of looseness and agility. Being loose, agile, and quick was more important than what he called 'brute strength.'"

"Probably true for most sports," Coach adds.

"He also taught us to keep moving and make the other guy move with you. Constant motion — to do that, you have to be in good condition. And leverage," Harold says, almost as an afterthought. "Leverage. Understanding leverage is one of the most important things he taught me. If you understand that and do it better than the other guy, you'll win every time. But to your original question — conditioning, just like any other sport, is of utmost importance. In wrestling, as you know, Coach, there are no free throws or huddles in which to catch your breath. You have to be in great condition to outlast the other guy."

"I teach a class in physical science each semester," Coach says. "What would you say to coming over to school one day and talking to my class about these things, like leverage? Hearing you apply these things to something as basic as self-defense is a way for them to learn."

"I'm not a teacher, Coach, but I'll come if you want me to," Harold says.

"Great," Coach says. "I'll call you."

Later in the day, as things begin to wind down, Marion, Jay, and Harold, along with the Robinson girls and Jo, are sitting together eating. They have been busy serving and are among the last to eat. They appear to be in a good mood and happy with the way the day is going.

Theora suddenly remembers something and turns to Harold, smiling. "Harold, you were going to tell me about the shoulder — your rodeo days."

Everyone looks toward Harold. Marion mumbles, "What, now?" and Jay chuckles — he knows there's a tall tale coming.

"Shoulder? Rodeo days? What happened to the zookeeper?" Marion asks with a "gotcha" look on his face.

"That was just a tall tale because you fed me that BS about monster catfish, Marion," Harold says in his own defense.

"That wasn't a tall tale," Marion says. "I showed it to you!"

"It wasn't really that much of a monster, Marion," Jay says in Harold's defense.

Marion grunts.

"Well, Harold, tell us the real story then," Theora urges.

"Yes," Phyllis urges, "tell us the real story."

"Look, it's kind of embarrassing, actually," Harold says hesitantly. "I was a city boy, but one day, I hitched a ride out to this ranch. Decided that I wanted to be a cowboy because I was from Oklahoma. Told the guy there, and he says I gotta ride a bull first before I can qualify for training."

"It's true," Jay says. "Those dumb cowboys out there believe that unless you can sit atop a bull for eight seconds, you'll never make it as a cowboy. That's why they're all bow-legged. It isn't just from riding their big horses—it's mostly from straddling the bulls. We Indians only ride our small, fast ponies."

"Shut up, Jay, and let Harold finish," Jo says.

"Thank you, Jo," Harold says. "So, they get this big, old, mean bull into the chute. All the cowboys gather, sitting on the fence of the corral where they're gonna let this bull—with me on it—loose." He pauses to let the suspense build.

"Indians will never get on a bull," Jay interrupts again. "It's stupid. You ever see a bow-legged Indian?"

They all turn to look at him, though no one answers. He's the only Indian they've ever seen.

"So, I climb up the side of the chute and slowly get on the back of this huge mountain of an animal. A fellow hands me a rope handle—reins, I guess you'd call it—and says, 'Hang on to this.' Then he takes off his hat, plants it on my head, and says, 'This may help,' before opening the chute."

Harold takes a deep breath and lets it out slowly. "That damn bull flies out of that chute like a house afire. Goes straight to a fence post on the left side and slides me across it. It takes a big hunk out of my shoulder, and I'm on the ground."

A pause. Harold reaches up and rubs his shoulder. "You should've seen it. Bloody mess." Then he stops, and everybody looks at him—except Jay, who is looking at the others for a reaction.

"I found out later that bull's name was Big Cactus because riding him felt like straddling a large cactus."

"Well, did it?" Phyllis asks.

"Did it what?" Harold asks.

"Feel like straddling a large cactus?"

"I don't know—wasn't on it long enough."

All things considered, the day was a success — at least in the opinion of Bernie and Jessie. A varied assortment of people came, and there was ample food, even a few leftovers. And no arguments or fights to dampen the spirits — unless you consider the brief disagreement over what was taking place in Germany.

Someone commented that Charles Lindbergh was favorable toward the Hitler regime, whereupon someone asked Brooksie Bowlin her thoughts on the matter. Brooksie, attending with her fiancé, Ray Behrens, was one of the fabled first twelve graduates of the School of the Osage and a friend of the Robinson girls. She had worked for Union Electric in their offices on Camp Road above the dam in recent years.

Lindbergh, an original American hero, had visited the project, and Brooksie had been assigned to show him around. Brooksie noted, "Lindy was a nice man — tall, handsome, a gentleman. The loss of his child may have affected his view of things," she suggested.

Another at the table, with firsthand knowledge of Lindbergh's visit to the lake, was blunter: "But he was not of exceptional intelligence."

"I think those Krauts are gonna be a problem in the future, just like they were in '14," someone else said. "That Churchill fellow — all the Limeys think he's crazy — but he says the same thing."

Someone else asked if America should still attend the 1936 Olympics in Berlin.

"Yes. Dropping out — not going — that's like saying we're afraid. We gotta go and show them what we can do."

Harold, reflecting later on the overheard conversation, remembered only two things from it: "Berlin" and "Olympics."

Later that evening, as they finish cleaning up, Theora finds herself alone with Jessie in the dining room. They have just moved a table and sit for a moment to rest.

"Jessie, what actually happened to Harold's left shoulder?" Theora asks.

Jessie looks at her for a moment. "Are you in love with him, Theora? I wonder if you might be."

Theora gives her the only answer she has at this point. "I don't know, Jessie. I don't know."

"He had polio when he was a child," Jessie says quietly. "It ate up a part of the muscle in his left shoulder."

"Oh," Theora says. "Oh, my gosh."

With Fry's blessing, Harold goes home for a few days at Christmas. The bus trip takes longer than usual due to a four-hour layover in Springfield because of heavy snow. Removal from Route 66 takes longer than expected. In addition to the snow — or perhaps because of it — there is also a major vehicle accident to clear. Harold considers calling his mother or even walking to the house but quickly decides against it. If she wanted to see me, she could have come to the Lake at any time, he thinks.

Harry, at fourteen, though slender, is already taller than Harold and is happy to see his big brother. Margaret has begun to get exasperated with the younger boy and is also happy to see Harold. *Finally, a Pilkington who will behave,* she thinks. Mainly, she wants Harold to talk to him because Harry admires his older brother. She thinks Harold can talk some sense into him about skipping school and making poor decisions on friendships — all the self-imposed obstacles to his intelligent development. She is also happy to see Harold because she loves him, and he loves her.

Perhaps the time has come to divert briefly from the narrative to address the proverbial "elephant in the room." Harold, Harry, and Harrison (that's Harold's middle name, for God's sake) are all the same or derivatives of each other. Throw in Henry and Harvey — also derivatives — and shake your head and ask why.

(Just for the record, there is no proof that Virginia Shannon or Grant Pilkington had anything to do with naming Harvey, Lawrence Fry's middle brother. Mrs. Fry is responsible. Or Harry Barker? Clara is. Or Henry V, whom Bill Shakespeare refers to as "Harry the King" — and who knows what else.)

Back to the question: Why are two male siblings of the same parentage, born six years apart, pretty much named the same? Nobody has any earthly idea. Perhaps the English royals will explain it someday; they've had their share of Henrys and derivatives through the centuries.

Perhaps Edward will when he becomes king in January.

"You start high school next year," Harold begins a conversation one day. He is taking his brother to have lunch — a chance to spend time together and talk. "How about sports? Are you going to play sports?"

"I don't know," he says.

"You have no interest in it?"

"Maybe. Maybe not," Harry says.

"Harry, Mom is concerned about you. Says you've been skipping school. Got suspended. What's going on with you?"

"You got a girlfriend, Harold?" Harry attempts to change the subject. "Up there, in Missouri?"

"Uh… well, I— There's a girl there I've been dating. Only the one, so yes, I guess."

"She died, you know."

Harold looks at Harry, not understanding. "Mrs. Newton. Down in Texas."

"I didn't know," Harold says, reflecting. "Dad didn't tell me."

A pause. "She was a nice lady."

"Yes." Then Harry, very direct: "You went to see her, didn't you?"

"What?"

"Mother. In Springfield. You saw her."

"What makes you think that?" Harold asks, surprised at the subject.

"You always told me that if you ever got to Springfield, you'd go see her."

The boys stare at one another for a few moments.

"Yes, I saw her."

"And? What happened?" Harry asks, anxious to know.

"She had no interest in talking to me."

"Bitch!"

Other patrons in the diner react to the sound, staring at the boys.

The owner, standing behind the counter, looks at them. "Boys, we'll have none of that talk in here, you understand? One more outburst, and I'll have to ask you to leave."

"Yes, sir. Sorry, sir," Harold apologizes, then to his brother:

"Harry, you don't talk like that about your mother."

"That's what Dad calls her," Harry says.

"You're not Dad," Harold says.

Harry sits back in the booth, food half-finished, indicating he is.

"I saw our little sister," Harold says. "Her name's Virginia."

"Half-sister," Harry says pointedly.

"Whatever," Harold says with some exasperation as he picks up the check and gets up from the booth. "C'mon, let's go."

Harry follows.

In the car, before he pulls out into traffic, Harold turns to Harry. "I want you to promise me you'll do what Mom tells you. No skipping school, okay? Do your homework."

"Yeah, yeah, okay," Harry says without conviction.

"Dammit, Harry, she's hard on you because she cares. She does it because she loves you."

Before Harold goes back to Missouri, he does two things. First, he tells Harry that if he starts to hear better reports from their mom, he can come to the lake and visit. Harry reacts positively to the offer and promises his brother he will do better.

He also calls Coach Griffith to ask about the trials for the Olympic wrestling team.

"They're scheduled for the first week in April. Des Moines," Coach tells him. "These are just preliminary trials. Sixteen will be on the team and make the trip. Final trials are to be held on the boat going over. It's possible to make the trip and still not wrestle. You thinking about coming to the trials?"

"You think I have a chance, Coach?" Harold asks.

"You get in shape. Make weight. You got as good a chance as any to make the team. You thinking light-heavy?"

"I can make that and keep it, I believe," Harold says. "You taking some Central boys?"

"Yeah, a couple. I'm not that hopeful, but it will be a good experience for them. The Iowa boys — we have to contend with them most. They've got some good ones. They'll give Gallagher's kids a good run."

"Will you send me the details when you get them?" Harold asks.

"Even better. I'll call you."

Harold takes the bus back to Lake Ozark on December 29. He has promised Jessie and Lawrence he will be back in time to help set up for New Year's Eve. They've booked a band and expect a good crowd for the party. Theora is at the

Whitehouse waiting for him when his bus arrives, signaling the possibility that she might have missed him.

"I was at Red's, waiting for Marion and Phyllis to get off work, and just happened to walk up here. Jessie told me you were due," she said, offering a perfectly normal explanation for her presence.

Harold didn't say so, but he believed she was there because she missed him. At least, he hoped so.

The New Year's party at the Whitehouse is a success, with a large, well-behaved crowd, and though Harold is working, he finds time to dance with Theora several times. At the end of the evening, when he finally gets to bed, he is unable to stretch his legs out. After struggling with the covers a bit, he gets up, pulls them all the way back, and discovers someone has short-sheeted the bed. There is a note, and he picks it up and reads: *This bed has been made up for a bow-legged cowboy."*

Up until the time he finally falls asleep, he mumbles to himself, "That damn Marion. That damn Marion." He vows to get even.

In January, Harold gets permission from Coach Henderson to work out in the school gym when there are no classes. This gets him out of the bad weather of winter, though he does run outside when there is no snow or ice. The longer straight stretches are best to build stamina, he thinks, and his favorite place to run is the dirt road to Bagnell. With the Robinsons' permission, he parks the car in front of their house early some mornings and heads out, running the road all the way to Highway 54 and back — a round trip of about two and a half miles.

He is always invited in for coffee after, and he always accepts. The coffee is very welcome after the long run, and he usually has a biscuit but avoids the butter and jam — Lena's best. Shamefully, while he eats the biscuit, he often finds himself staring at the dish of her fresh-churned butter.

"Harold," Lena asks him one morning, "where do they do this Olympics?"

"In Germany," he answers. "In Berlin, in August."

"Oh my gosh," she says, realizing, "Isn't that where that Hitler fellow is?"

"Yes, ma'am, but he's not entered in any of the events."

"Lots of folks think he's going to be trouble in the future," Bert says. "I heard Harry talking about him on the radio, and I trust Harry's judgment."

"Harry?" Harold asks.

"Truman," Bert says. "Senator Truman."

"Of course," Harold says.

One morning in early February, as Harold is leaving the Robinson house, Phyllis steps out onto the porch with him. No one else is around, so he speaks to her quietly. "Phyllis, is everything all right with you and Marion?"

"It better be," she says. "Do you know something I don't?"

"It's probably nothing. I shouldn't say."

"What? C'mon, tell me. What do you know?"

"I don't want you to be hurt," Harold says, holding back.

"Harold, tell me," Phyllis says to him with her "or else" look.

"While I was running, Marion passed me in his car, heading toward 54," Harold begins.

"And, so?"

"There was this girl in the car with him," Harold says, not holding back. "She looked like that cute blonde from Eldon that comes into the Whitehouse a lot. Dishwater blonde."

"I'll kill him," Phyllis mumbles.

"You know the one—short, everybody wants to dance with her?"

"I'll kill her too."

"I have to go," he says, stepping off the porch. "I'm sure there is an explanation, Phyllis." She is still mumbling to herself as Harold drives away.

Harold continues his routine, training when not working, and in between, tries to spend as much time as possible with Theora, who tells him Marion is looking for him. Harold knows he would be better off if he had a "sparring" partner to train with, but so far, the only one worthy is Marion. However, it is a different kind of sparring.

"I wonder what he wants?" he says to Theora.

"I don't know," she says, "but he got into serious trouble with Phyllis. She thought he was cheating on her. Turns out it was just a couple of new mops he bought for the restaurant. Someone told her they thought it was a girl with him in the car. The way they were propped up in the front seat, it must have looked like someone sitting there." She looks at Harold knowingly. "You wouldn't know anything about that, would you?"

"No. Sounds like an honest mistake, though," Harold says.

A few weeks later, in early February, the two couples take advantage of a warmish late winter day and go to the newly built Lake of the Ozarks State Park for a picnic. The park, a CCC project, is one of many from Roosevelt's alphabet soup of public works designed to provide employment opportunities during the Depression. What they see for the first time impresses them: a swimming beach, campsites, and picnic tables with nearby playgrounds for children. It's midweek, and there are only a few patrons in the park, so the foursome easily finds a covered picnic table with a clear view of the lake.

Phyllis has made the sandwiches for the day—chicken salad with lettuce on Lena's homemade bread. The girls have also packed a jar of homemade pickles, and Theora has brought tea in a large jug with ice. Marion and Harold's only job is to bring beer if they want it. And they do. Harold has brought a six-pack of GB, a St. Louis beer, and Marion has brought a six of PBR, a Milwaukee product.

"Why GB?" Marion asks Harold.

"It's a Missouri beer, and it's cheaper than Budweiser, that's why."

"Yeah, but Pabst is cheaper than GB," Marion counters.

"We'll try both then," Harold says. "Think how much money we're saving."

At a point in the otherwise pleasant conversation, Phyllis assumes a serious look, turns to her sister, and says, "Theora, Marion, and I are going to talk to Mom and Dad tomorrow and tell them we're getting married."

Everyone looks at her. Marion grunts.

Theora, acknowledging the worst-kept secret in the world, asks, "When is this happy event going to happen?"

I said, "Tomorrow.'"

"No, I mean the wedding, Phyllis."

"Oh. Well, next Tuesday," Phyllis says. "We have an appointment with the Christian minister in Eldon at 2:00 p.m. Can you get off and go with us? I want you to be there. My witness."

"Can I? ... Well, let's see... There is that shoe sale I wanted to go to. I hate to miss that. You know how much I love shoe sales."

"Theora! I'm serious."

"Of course, I'll be there!"

Phyllis looks at Marion. "Go ahead, Marion."

He looks at Harold. "Harold, I was wondering if you would stand up with me?"

Harold, surprised, looks at him. "Are you sure, Marion? I mean, you have…"

"Our friend from school, Garland Payne—he graduated with us—will come and drive us there. We made a deal in high school that whichever one of us got married first, the other would drive him to the wedding to make sure he got there. Garland insists on honoring his promise." Marion pauses. "But I need a best man. Yeah. I'm sure, Harold."

Harold glances at Theora, who smiles at him broadly, and then looks back at Marion. "I would be honored to stand up with you, Marion."

He glances around the table at the others, who all have a "well, that's settled" look on their faces, and reaches out to shake Marion's hand.

"He just wants you there, Harold, so he can keep an eye on you," Phyllis says, and they all laugh.

Late the next afternoon, Marion's car pulls into the drive just in front of the Robinson yard, and Theora jumps out of the backseat, enters the gate, and crosses onto the porch. Marion and Phyllis remain in the front seat of the car, talking. Bert, who is on the front porch sitting in the swing, acknowledges his youngest. "How was work, Sugar?" he asks.

"Good, Daddy. I made good tips. Momma inside?"

"Yeah, unless she escaped through the back door and I didn't see her. Phyllis and Marion getting out?" he asks.

"I think they're discussing the weather," Theora says, smiling.

"The weather? Not a cloud in the sky, and the sun's shining."

"Marion thinks there's a storm coming," she says as she enters the front door.

Bert is busy fiddling with his pipe—loading tobacco, patting it firmly, and lighting it—as Phyllis exits Marion's car and comes onto the porch. Marion is not far behind. Bert notes their presence.

"Phyll. Marion."

"Going inside to see Momma, Daddy," Phyllis says. "Marion wants to talk to you."

Bert perks up. Now what, he wonders. Marion remains awkwardly on the porch as Phyllis goes inside. Bert stares at him until finally…

"Mr. Robinson?" Marion says firmly.

"Yes?" Bert says.

"Mr. Robinson?" Marion says again. He hesitates.

"For God's sake, son. Sit down and spit it out," Bert says, motioning to a chair near the front door. Marion sits.

"Mr. Robinson." He pauses a moment, then 'spits it out.' "I'm asking for your daughter's hand in marriage!"

Bert, unaffected by Marion's sudden boldness, just stares at him.

"Mr. Robinson?" Marion tries again. Then, finally…

"My daughter's hand. You want to marry my daughter's hand? What the hell am I supposed to do with the rest of her?"

"Dammit, Bert! You know what I mean." Marion is on the offensive now and intends to state his case. "We've been together since the tenth grade, and we intend to get married."

"You're both eighteen. I can't stop you," Bert says. "Go ask her mother. Lena's the one you gotta convince."

"Dammit, Bert," Marion mumbles as he stands up and goes inside the house.

Phyllis has just finished telling her mother about her plans.

"What's your hurry, honey?" Lena argues. "You're young yet. Enjoy it."

"I have to marry him, Momma. He can't keep his hands off me."

Theora laughs, eliciting a "that's enough out of you" look from her mother.

"Well, then… that settles it," Lena says.

"Settles what, Mrs. Robinson?" Marion says as he comes into the kitchen, where the ladies have been talking.

"That you can call me Lena now that you're going to be my son-in-law."

"It was a unanimous vote, Marion," Theora tells him. "We all abstained."

The following Tuesday at noon, Garland Payne, with Marion on board, picks up Harold, who is carrying a paper sack, and they head toward Bagnell. As soon as he gets in the car, Harold starts the checklist.

"Got the rings?"

"Yeah, I got the rings," Marion answers.

"Got the license?"

"That, too," Marion says.

"Bottle of bourbon?"

"Bourbon?" Marion questions.

"Phyllis may want a couple of stiff shots after she realizes what she's done," Harold explains. "And you may want a highball, too."

"I know a place near Eldon," Marion says. "We'll pick up a bottle on the way."

"Not necessary," Harold says as he picks up the paper sack.

"Wedding present."

"Phyllis will be thankful," Marion says.

"What else?" Harold asks, looking for a prompt.

"Got my shotgun in the trunk," Garland says. "Double barrel."

"Double barrel," Harold acknowledges.

"One for Marion if he tries to run. The other for the 'best man' who lets him get away."

"Pick up the girls, that's next," Marion says.

They are quiet for a few moments. Though they are young, they are not unaware of the seriousness of the events of the day. Marion has known about the inevitability of this day for a very long time, and now it is here. He's ready.

"Theora tells me you were raised by a stepmother, Harold."

"I was. Mother left me and my little brother when I was nine. It was fine. Dad remarried. Mom—my stepmother—is a wonderful lady." Harold pauses a moment and laughs a bit. "She's got her hands full now, trying to raise up my little brother. He finishes eighth grade this spring if he doesn't skip too many days. He's already as tall as me. Mom has her hands full."

"My mother was married at fifteen," Marion says. "Can you believe it? Not long after, she got pregnant. Gave birth to twins who died. Not sure she knew at the time where they came from."

"Your dad?" Harold asks.

"He was older—thirty, I think," Marion says. "Mine foreman in southern Illinois. Made a good salary and paid his bills, but he drank. Mom had three babies—sister Ruth, brother Ross, and me. And she raised a niece, Nelia. She was my dad's sister's girl, my cousin. Parents died when she was young. Nelia had an older brother, Roy, who died in the war, and Nelia used the government benefits she got from his death to put both her and Ruth through nursing school."

Marion glances back at Harold, who listens intently. "Dad was a good man, though, I believe, but eventually, he and Mom parted ways. Mom married Red, and we came here."

"I met your brother. Electrician, right?" Harold asks. "Where is your sister now?"

"He is — brother Ross. I think he and his wife are going to settle down and stay here," Marion explains. "Sister Ruth and Nelia, too — nurses, both married and live in Chicago."

"I've got a half-sister, I found out recently," Harold says. "My mother had a baby with the fellow from Springfield she ran off with. Always thought it would be nice to have a sister. Now I got one but can't have a relationship with her."

"You don't see your real mother at all?" Marion asks.

"Don't think she has any interest at all in Harry or me," Harold says.

When they arrive at the Robinson house, there is no one on the porch, not unusual for this time of year. The two young men get out, walk to the front door, and knock. Theora answers the door and lets them in.

"It's Frank and Jessie," Theora jests. "Or is it Wyatt and Doc? Garland not coming in?"

Harold gives her a quick kiss. "Says he can best watch the escape routes from there."

Marion grunts.

"Everyone is in the kitchen," Theora says. "Come on."

"You boys need to eat something before you go," Lena demands as they enter the kitchen.

"I'd have maybe a piece of your homemade bread with some of your butter," Harold says.

Marion looks at him. "How can you eat?"

"I'm not getting married."

"You a little nervous, are you, Marion?" Bert says. "Today's the easiest you'll ever have."

"Says a man who hasn't lifted a finger in the kitchen except to eat in thirty-some years," Lena says.

"See what I mean, Marion?" Bert says.

Harold finishes his bread and turns to Marion. "We need to go, don't you think?"

"Yes, we need to go," Phyllis says. "Unless you've changed your mind."

Marion just grunts.

"You take good care of my daughter, Marion Clayton," Lena says pointedly.

"I promise," Marion says directly to her.

Bert and Lena follow the foursome out onto the porch and, after some hugs, watch them as they leave.

The wedding goes without a hitch. "I dos" are said, papers signed, and the preacher paid. Marion left his car in the church parking lot earlier, and with his job completed, Garland leaves the foursome to figure out the next step.

Before they leave the church parking lot, Harold opens the bourbon bottle and passes it around. Phyllis and Theora agree that they prefer it with 7-UP, which prompts Marion to question his best man's competence.

"You forgot the highball mix?" Marion accuses.

"It wasn't on my checklist," he answers in his defense.

After an early dinner at a nice restaurant in downtown Jefferson City, Marion drops Harold and Theora off at the Whitehouse, where Harold has access to Jessie's car. Marion and Phyllis go to Mrs. Knoch's place on Lake Road 1-A, where they have rented a small cottage. It will be their new home for a while.

When Harold drives Theora home later that evening, she seems sad.

"I don't ever remember one night sleeping in this house that Phyllis was not also here," Theora says.

Lena is lying in bed awake when Theora comes in, and after she has settled into her bed, she hears her mother's voice.

"Everything go okay, Sugar?"

"Yes, Momma, it went fine," Theora answers.

"Well, so be it, then," Lena says.

"Momma, Marion Clayton has been a part of this family since Phyllis first saw him playing basketball and pronounced him 'kinda cute.'"

"Would you both shut up and go to sleep?" Bert says loudly.

The weather, for the most part, remains mild, allowing Harold to continue his outdoor conditioning. In mid-March, Coach Griffith calls. "Trials are set for April 4th," Coach tells him. "You need to be there on the 3rd. I put your name in, so they're expecting you."

On the evening of March 30th, Harold is not feeling well and, with Jessie's blessing, excuses himself from work and goes to bed early. Sometime in the middle of the night, Harold awakens feeling terrible and barely makes it to the bathroom, where he erupts from both ends. When he is not downstairs early the next morning, as is usual for him, Jessie calls up the stairs. When there is no answer, she ascends the stairs to check on him. One look is all it takes, and she immediately goes downstairs to call Dr. Attic.

"Yeah. Uh-huh. Mmmm… he's sick," Dr. Attic diagnoses after looking him over. "Got an elevated temperature, diarrhea, general malaise," he tells Jessie. "There's some kind of influenza going around this spring—a 'flu bug,' as they say. Not much we can do; it has to run its course." He begins to pack his black bag. "Chicken soup, water, plenty of liquids. Give him an occasional aspirin as needed until the temperature goes down. And bed rest. Best you can do for now."

"Jessie," Harold says to her after the doctor leaves, his voice weak, "the trials?"

"It's only the thirty-first, Harold," she says. "Let's see how you're doing tomorrow." She smiles. "Right now, I'm going to the kitchen to see if Maggie has that chicken soup done."

Theora is in the kitchen with Lena that morning when Lena mentions that Harold's car is not in the driveway outside their house. "That's not like him. He never misses a day now," she says.

"Maybe he's working early today, Momma," Theora says.

"Maybe he is," Lena says.

"I'm sure that's it."

After her shift that day, Theora goes to the Whitehouse to ask about Harold, and Jessie tells her. "He would have to leave here some time on the second to get to Des Moines in time," Jessie explains. "But he's a very sick boy right now."

Theora goes to Red's after speaking to Jessie and tells Marion and Phyllis. The next day, April first, Harold is not better—not eating well, obviously depressed. No one at the Whitehouse is making the usual Fool's Day jokes; the inappropriateness is well understood. Late in the afternoon, Marion shows up at the Whitehouse and informs Jessie that he has a bag packed, a full gas tank, and believes he can get Harold to Des Moines in "seven, maybe eight hours tops. Pack a bag for him, Jessie, so he'll be ready to go the minute he's up to it."

"Alright, Marion, I'll tell him," Jessie says. "I'll pack a bag, but he's still very sick."

"Even if we don't leave until tomorrow evening, I can still get him there before dawn on the third," Marion says. "If he's up to it and can get to the car and stretch out in the back seat, we'll get there."

"I'll go up and tell him now," Jessie says. "You go home and get a good night's sleep, and we'll hope he's better tomorrow."

"One thing, Jessie. If you tell him I said 'stretch out,' assure him it was not an April Fool's joke."

Jessie looks at him quizzically. "He'll understand."

The next day, Harold is a little better but still moves slowly down the hall to the bathroom. He knows he must make a decision and considers taking a shower but can't muster the energy at that moment. Marion is in the house by noon, having called Jessie first thing for an update. Maggie feeds him, he offers her a job, and she tells him she can't improve his chili, so he takes back the offer. Theora comes into the Whitehouse late in the afternoon and sits at the counter with Marion, drinking coffee and talking to Jessie. Around five, Jessie goes upstairs to see about Harold. She sits on the edge of the bed. He speaks to her very slowly, very quietly, very directly.

"If I let Marion take me, I would barely be able to contest a match. My body will not respond the way I would need it to in order to prevail. And if I can't win, I have no right to be there." He pauses in an effort to refresh his strength. "And if I am still sick, contagious, they won't want me anywhere near that building. It is not fair to the other guys."

"Are you sure, Harold?"

"Yes. Would you call Coach Griffith at the hotel in Des Moines for me?" Harold asks. "The hotel name and phone number are on that piece of paper on the table."

She goes to the table, picks up the paper, and turns to leave.

"What do you want me to tell him?"

"Just tell him I'm sorry and thank him for me," Harold says.

Marion and Theora look up at Jessie as she comes down the stairs. She looks at them and shakes her head. "No," then goes into the kitchen and picks up the phone. It takes a moment for the hotel desk to find Griffith, who mutters profanity on the phone and then apologizes for it to Jessie.

"Tell him I'm so sorry it didn't work out," Coach says. "I was hoping he'd help us put that SOB Hitler in his place."

"Don't worry, Coach. Others will step up, I'm sure." "Thanks for calling, Jessie," he says and hangs up.

Theora and Marion have overheard the conversation through the kitchen door. Marion is sad; he truly wants to help.

Theora gets up from her stool and says to him, "I'm going upstairs to see Harold."

"Theora, he may still be contagious. Maybe you shouldn't."

"I don't care," she says as she walks up the stairs to the second floor. She easily finds Harold's room. She hesitates briefly before she steps in, and when she does, she sees him just lying there, staring at the ceiling.

"Harold," she says.

He looks toward the door and sees her. "Theora, you shouldn't be here. You might get sick."

"Jessie told me," she says.

A single tear begins a slow movement down his cheek, and Harold quickly turns his head away as he wipes the cheek clean. He doesn't want her to see him weak. He doesn't want anyone to ever see him weak. But she has seen it. The tear is shed. It can't be put back. And she takes it up and places it in her heart to live forever.

"I love you, Harold," she says. "Very, very much."

She turns and walks out of the room and knows for certain, for the first time, that she is in love with Harold Pilkington.

The first day Harold starts to feel "normal" again, he washes his workout clothes in the bathroom sink and hangs them up to dry. Later, when they are dry, he folds them neatly and puts them away in the back of a drawer — symbolically putting away his childhood.

The next day, he tells Jessie that he is going for a walk around the lakeshore and wanders down the path to the dock below the Whitehouse, where he first meets Marion. From there, he walks—meanders at best—around toward the back of the cove, stopping occasionally to look for a good rock to skip. Halfway around the other side, in the direction of Allen's Point, he finds the perfect skipping rock. *This is multiple skips, at least*, he thinks.

As he reaches down to pick it up, he inadvertently kicks over a larger rock sitting in the shallow water, revealing a large crayfish that has been hiding under it. The crayfish moves back and forth in the shallow water briefly, then momentarily glides gently and quickly into the deeper water and disappears.

"Watch your back, little fellow," Harold says to the departing crayfish. "There is an ugly, mean, hungry catfish out there just waiting for you."

He looks up and out at the water, rears his arm back, aims, and sends the skipping rock out and on its way into skipping legend.

"One," he counts, then quickly, "two, three, four, five, six, and… barely, yes, seven," and— "plop"—it's gone.

He continues walking until he reaches the end of Allen's Point, where he sits down on a large boulder on the shore and looks out at the water and the dam in the distance.

The walk has all been about Theora, Harold knows. It is all he has contemplated on his journey. *She said she loved me. How does she know that? Do I love her? I don't know, and how do you know? Jessie's rocking chair test? I'm not ready to imagine myself that old, let alone her. And what is there about being seventy-something that makes you want to smile about it? I know that I like her and care about her more than any other girl I have known. I miss her when she's not around. But is that love?*

Finally, the issue "unsettled," Harold walks the distance back around to the dock, up the hill to the Whitehouse, and back to work.

At lunch the next day, Harold walks to Red's and orders chili.

"You've got to be a whole lot better now if you want chili," Phyllis says.

"I waited a day or two to make sure," Harold says.

"A bowl of the state's finest, upfront. For Harold," Phyllis yells.

Marion, busing tables at the back of the room, looks up, picks up his tray, and comes around to where Harold is sitting at the counter.

"Chili? You sure?" Marion asks.

"Phyllis wouldn't let me have it unless I promised not to tell stories about you," Harold says.

Phyllis, who has come back to bring him a glass of iced tea, rolls her eyes.

Harold pauses and stirs some sugar into his tea. "I came here mainly to thank you for having my back. Jessie told me what you did."

"I'll do anything to get out of work," Marion says.

When he has finished eating and gets up to leave, Harold seeks out Marion and reaches out to shake his hand. "Thanks again for what you did. I won't forget it. Anything I can ever do for you, let me know."

Marion laughs. "That's what I'm afraid of."

Harold laughs with him.

With the dream of Olympic glory behind him, Harold puts all his effort into his work and pursuing Theora. Since the day she came to his room when he was sick, she has not uttered the words "I love you" again. Perhaps, Harold thinks, because he has not reciprocated—something he chooses not to do until he is sure.

They talked about his family—what he felt when his mother left, his father's reaction, his stepmother's love.

"I want what Phyllis and Marion have. And I want it for a lifetime," he says one night when they are talking seriously about the future. "My children will have their parents."

Theora has always held out a dream that she would leave this place, travel, and see things she has read about in books. She wants adventure in life, and she wants it now while she is young. She remembers her mother's words to Phyllis—the three Y's, she calls it: "You're young yet"—and embraces them. So, love Harold or not, is she ready for permanence? For the moment, she is unable to answer the question and refuses to hurt Harold the way he has been hurt before.

Within two months of the marriage, Phyllis learns she is pregnant. This fact further emboldens Theora to do something she has wanted to do since she graduated—go to New York and visit her sister, Frieda. *I'll work extra shifts and save more of my money, go in the fall when business slows down before it gets cold,* she tells herself.

That's a good plan. I'll write Frieda and tell her—or ask her, she concludes.

At first, she tells nobody of her plan, not even Phyllis, until she realizes she needs Harold's help. When she tells him, he is surprised—and, if he is to be honest, a little hurt— though he tries not to show it.

"But why?" he says when she has finished telling him her plan.

"Why?" she responds, surprised at his response. "Because I want to see my sister. I want to see the Statue of Liberty. That's why."

"New York's just another big, sprawling city with too many people," Harold says.

"Like Berlin?" Theora counters. It is the first time since he was sick—since *that day*—that she has mentioned his lost dream. She regrets saying it as soon as it comes out.

"I didn't want to go to Berlin, Theora," he says. "I wanted to represent my country at the Olympics."

"I'm sorry," she says.

"So, what do you want me to do?" Harold asks.

"Would you drive me to Jeff City, to the train station? I want to research the train schedules."

"I'll drive you to St. Louis when the time comes," Harold says. "That money might be the difference in you eating for a few days."

Theora writes to her sister, Frieda, who, by return mail, tells her, "That's a great idea! I can't wait to see you." This exchange occurs before she tells her parents, who, when she does, express concerns—the least of which is money.

"How will you pay for the trip, Sugar?" Bert, the practical man, asks. "We can't help you much, if any."

"I don't expect you to, Daddy. I've been saving for a long time now—from my pay and tips." She pauses a moment. "I looked into the ticket costs. And Harold offered to drive me to St. Louis to save the cost of the train from Jeff City."

"So, Harold knows about you going?" Lena asks.

"Yes, why?"

"She just wondered, Sugar," Bert says. "I think she likes the boy."

"Oh, Bert, hush!"

In late August, Harold notes, on the sports pages of the St. Louis Post-Dispatch, the results of several events in the Berlin Olympics. An Oklahoma boy from A & M, Frank Lewis, wins gold in freestyle welterweight, and another A & M boy, Ross Flood, wins silver in freestyle bantamweight. Americans pick up two other silver medals—one for an Indiana boy, another from Massachusetts. Ed Gallagher is listed as an honorary coach. Harold experiences only a brief moment of regret for what might have been—regret more for the results of the team's efforts than for himself. "I thought we might do better," he mutters to himself.

The first week in October, three days before Theora leaves, she and Harold drive into Eldon to Reid's Department Store, where she buys a pair of shoes she wants to go with a new dress she purchased, especially for the trip. Afterward, they have a sandwich and soda at the drugstore lunch counter.

"What are the chances you'll like it so well in New York that you decide to stay and never come back?" Harold asks Theora, only half-jokingly.

"What are the chances you'll go back to Tulsa while I'm gone and never come back to Missouri?" Theora answers.

That subject, minus any answers, is, for the moment, put to rest and never discussed again before she leaves.

With Jay on board for the company on the return trip, Harold and Theora leave for the St. Louis train station early on a Sunday morning to make an 11:00 a.m. departure. While Jay waits in the station cafeteria, Harold walks with Theora to her train. She is apprehensive and forces a smile because that's what you do when you leave your boyfriend on the train platform. Or so it is in the movies.

"Are you okay?" Harold asks.

"I'm a little nervous, I guess," Theora says.

"Where's that natural self-confidence that you usually show?"

"As soon as I settle into my seat, it'll come back to me."

When the conductor gives the "all aboard" call, they kiss.

"I best go," Theora says.

"Yes, you should," Harold says. "I'll see you soon when you get back."

Theora boards and settles into a seat next to a window, from where she can see Harold, and waves to him as the train departs. He watches until the train is out of sight, locates Jay, and together, they leave for Lake Ozark. She'll be gone for two weeks.

Theora dwells briefly on the image of Harold alone on the platform as the train leaves the station. *He looked sad,* she thinks, *and I will miss him, but I don't know how much.* Her gaze fixates on the scenes outside her window as the train moves toward the Mississippi River and across it into Illinois. *So wide,* she thinks. *It is so wide; the Osage seems so small now.* She has brought along a book from the Eldon Library that will be due before she returns, but the small fine will be minor compared to the cost of buying the book. It is a bestseller recently released, called *Little House on the Prairie,* and though she is anxious to read it, she is more interested in the potential sights outside her window. She is heading east while Laura Wilder heads west, and right now, "east" is her focus.

As her train heads out, Theora settles in and eats a ham sandwich that her mother has sent, washed down by a Coke from the train vendor. The terrain in Illinois and then Indiana rolls by, and it is hard to know one from the other. She sees very few signs of the variety of colors nature will give up as fall comes on and is, so far, disappointed in the scenes outside her window. The larger cities have been few since St. Louis — until the train comes to Indianapolis. Here, for the first time on her trip, she sees the lingering signs of the "Great Depression." Along the tracks coming into town are the "Hoovervilles" she has only read about. She sees the downtrodden and lost faces of the men lined up at the soup kitchens and wonders why Roosevelt's alphabet soup is not being served. *Perhaps it is,* she thinks, *but it is not enough.*

An older gentleman across the aisle from her watches her reaction to the scenes of poverty and ventures into a conversation.

"Excuse me, Miss," he says.

Theora, surprised, turns at the sound of his voice. It is the first time she has spoken to a fellow passenger since she left St. Louis. "Yes, sir?" she says in response.

"All that farmland coming across Illinois and Indiana — you see?"

"Sir?"

"It can feed a lot of families when it is farmed by farmers," he says. "But nowadays, it's farmed by bankers. And they don't know diddly-squat about getting a good crop out of the ground."

"Diddly-squat?"

"Diddly-squat," he repeats.

The stop in Indianapolis is longer than those thus far in the trip.

A major stop usually means a changeover in passengers, and this city is a crossroads. The older gentleman from across the aisle gets up, gathers his belongings, and starts to go.

"Have a nice day, Miss," he says to Theora as he turns to leave.

"Sir, I hope you don't mind my asking — what do you do?" Theora is being bold; *that's how you learn,* she thinks.

"I was a small-town banker, but I work in accounting for the WPA now," he says. "Have a nice day."

Darkness is coming as the train leaves the city behind; the days are getting shorter, and the train is moving eastward. Theora decides she will have dinner in the dining car, being a "woman of the world" now. She leaves a reserved card on her seat and goes there. The waiter gives her a menu as soon as she sits, and the first thing she sees is "French fries." *That's what I want,* she thinks. *If they have ketchup — and surely, they do.*

The waiter says "yes" to the ketchup and asks, "What else would you like?"

"Oh, I don't know. I have a small appetite," Theora says.

"May I make a suggestion?" the waiter asks.

"Oh, of course, please," Theora says.

"How about a sandwich cut in half—eat half now, wrap the other in napkins to take with you?"

"Why, that's a wonderful idea. Thank you. Let's do the ham with Swiss, lettuce, and mayonnaise."

"May I make a suggestion, Miss?" the waiter says.

"Oh, of course, please," Theora says again.

"The mayonnaise," the waiter says. "As you are taking half with you and will not be eating it for a while, I would be concerned about non-refrigerated mayonnaise. It can go bad and could make you sick."

"Of course," Theora says. "You are so right. I'm not a big mustard fan, but I suppose that will have to do."

"May I suggest honey mustard, Miss?" the waiter says. "It's something new; the harshness of the mustard is softened by the sweetness of the honey. Pairs well with ham."

"Well, I'll try that then. And tea."

And she does, and she likes it, and she fills up on fries with ketchup and half a sandwich. She has neatly wrapped in paper napkins and a half sandwich for later or tomorrow.

Before she pays and leaves the table, her waiter brings her a paper cup filled with tea.

"For you to have with your sandwich later," he says. "No extra charge."

"Thank you so much," Theora says. "You have been so helpful and kind."

And when she pays, she leaves nearly a 20% tip—more than ever in her life. That man is trying to make a living, she thinks and deserves to be paid well for his service. If not for people tipping me fairly for good service, I wouldn't be able to make this trip.

Back in her seat, the dark outside her window leaves her with little to think about, so she retrieves the book from her bag and attempts to read. Struggling with concentration, she finds herself glancing about her car indiscreetly, noticing new faces she had not seen before, among them a young man of about thirty years. Dapper and well-dressed, he sees her make eye contact, assumes it is meant as an invitation, and gets up.

Uh-oh, Theora thinks. Harold warned me. Don't make eye contact. Always project confidence, like you know what you're doing. It is innocence that bad people prey on. Harold offered her a long list of precautions before she left, compliments of his police officer father. This was just one.

Not that Theora thinks the man coming down the aisle toward her is "bad people"; she is just not in the mood for small talk from a suitor. Quickly, she takes an orange out of her bag and holds it up. An orange? Lena, again, for her breakfast.

"I couldn't help but notice you sitting here all alone," the man says as he stops by her row. "Perhaps I could join you for some, uh… conversation."

Theora leans in the man's direction, puts her finger to her lips in a sign of quiet, and begins to whisper just loud enough so only he can hear. "I must warn you, sir. I would not want you to get sick." She looks him directly in his eyes and, with the most serious of serious looks, says, "I have scurvy." She holds up the orange. "My medicine. I will take it first thing in the morning. It helps, but until then, I am highly contagious."

"Scurvy?" the man mutters as he steps back a little. Theora nods.

"You have scurvy. I'm so sorry, Miss. I hope you get better soon. I won't bother you anymore." He turns to leave, thinking, *Scurvy? … That sounds awful, whatever it is. I hope I didn't get too close.* When he gets back to his seat, he doesn't stop, instead moving farther away to the very front of the car.

I'm sure glad I read all those adventure books when I was young. Theora prides herself. *Especially the ones about pirates and scurvy and citrus.* And grog, she thinks, concluding her assessment of her cleverness. *I'll order grog in a restaurant when I get to the ocean.*

The rest of the evening and into the night, she dozes for a while and studies the exterior view for a while, until just past Columbus, she decides to sleep. The conductor told her they would reach Pittsburgh an hour before dawn, and she wanted to see it. It is the place of the industrialists' glory, a town that helped make the "Gilded Age" of America's Victorian period. It is near the disaster of the Johnstown Flood. So much history. And the Whiskey Rebellion? *I need to read up on that one,* she thinks. *All I remember is that it had something to do with taxes. It's always about taxes.*

Theora puts her window-side arm through the straps of her purse, folds her arms, and settles back in her seat, head against the window. And she sleeps. Imperfectly, but she sleeps.

At 5:00 a.m., she is awakened by the conductor's voice announcing, "Next stop, Pittsburgh, Pennsylvania." He repeats it, and Theora, in her groggy state, is irritated that he says "Pennsylvania." *Everybody knows that* she thinks until she remembers that there is more than one. There is one in Kansas—a Pittsburgh, Kansas, she knows—because her oldest sister, Dorothy, lives there.

Now fully awake, she realizes she is hungry and contemplates going to the dining car, but it is too early. Remembering the sandwich, she takes it out and, justifying it for breakfast because it contains ham, begins eating it. *And it is good,* she thinks as she washes it down with the remainder of her now warm tea.

They enter Pittsburgh, still in darkness, and all she is able to recognize is the river she saw as they crossed into downtown. The landscape is crowded with tall smokestacks, many of which are idle, she concludes, because of the Depression. The stop is at least thirty minutes, and there is a significant changeover in passengers, more boarding than departing, and by the time the train moves again, her car is nearly full. It is the first time it has been full since it left St. Louis.

It is just beginning to get lighter as the train pulls out of town and moves into the daylight. Continuing east, she begins to see the hilly landscape, which she finds refreshing as it reminds her of home and Bagnell. But more than anything, it is the color splashed across the landscape that holds her attention as she realizes that she is now farther north and east than home. Fall is alive here, and she loves it. It keeps her attention out her window almost exclusively all the way across Pennsylvania.

Theora's train does not pass through Philadelphia, a fact that disappoints her, but rather makes a straight path toward New York, a fact that doesn't. She is now on the last major leg of her journey and, from this point on, is more interested in Pennsylvania Station than Pennsylvania.

Harold concentrates on his work and puts in extra hours to keep his mind off Theora's absence. Although he never speaks of it, everyone around him knows it—he misses her very much. Marion knows, and one early morning, convinces Harold to join him at the dock to fish for crappie. They are biting well over the "bed," and in the local vernacular, the two men catch "a mess of 'em." Harold agrees to come to the Claytons' apartment that night, where Marion fries some up, and they feast on the fish, although Phyllis complains of the frying fish smell lingering in their cramped living space.

Phyllis's pregnancy is going well, although Lena worries anyway. Bert tells her it gives her something to do as if fall canning is nothing to do.

"I don't know what it is with these Robinson girls. They just keep having babies," Lena complains to Bert when they hear from Dorothy that she is pregnant again.

"Why are you surprised? You had six," Bert reminds her. "Besides, what else is there to do in Kansas?"

Lena is not wrong about this Robinson population growth. Dorothy is up to three, she calculates, with one on the way. Frieda has two, and now Phyllis. And Theora… Theora is in New York! "Good God," she mutters to herself, *"and they wonder why a mother worries."*

Theora has called them once — a quick call from Frieda's home to tell her parents she has arrived and is safe, but that's all since she left. Oh, and they are going to the ocean tomorrow, the beach. She will write. Bye.

When Frieda first brings Theora to her home, Theora is amazed that the city is left behind, and there are farms, empty lots, and little towns.

"We live on Long Island, Theora," Frieda instructs, "not in the city."

In a shop at the beach, Theora buys postcards to send home — pictures of the beach, the Statue of Liberty, the Empire State Building, and the Radio City Rockettes — but she will not send them until she has witnessed these things firsthand. They have lunch at a small diner at the beach, and Theora asks the waiter if she can have a "grog" to drink.

"First of all, you have to be 21, and you're obviously not," the waiter explains. "Secondly, we don't have any. Finally, the only place that currently serves that beverage is the English Navy — and only on board their ships."

"I'll have iced tea," Theora says.

"Tell me about your young man," Frieda asks during lunch at the beach on the first day. "Momma made me think you came here to decide how you feel about him."

"He's nice, very handsome," she says. "I know he likes me."

"But do you like him? Do you love him?"

"I think I do," Theora says. She pauses and looks away. "I don't know. I always thought I would leave Bagnell, go to unusual places, see things, see the world."

"Well, Sugar, I did. And I ended up in a small town on Long Island surrounded by vegetable farms. Going to the city to see the sights with you the next few days will be one of the few times I've been in the city since we came here."

"You don't go to the city?" Theora is surprised. "You're so close."

"Babe goes on occasion because of his work, but I have no reason to."

Theora looks out the restaurant window and across the ocean. *It has to end somewhere,* she thinks. There are exotic destinations at its end.

"Sometimes, Theora, it's not where you go. It's who you go with. Not what you do, but who you do it with." Frieda pauses, studying her sister for a moment. "As for this young fella, Harold, the only issue is: do you love him? And is he worthy of your love?"

Frieda arranges for a neighbor to watch her two children, Donald and Phyllis (named for her sister, of course), both preschool age, and she and Theora embark by train on their adventure into the city. When she arrived, the entire family had come to pick her up in their car, and she saw little of the city on their way home. But today, they take the ferry out to what is probably the best-known and most-visited site in America—the Statue of Liberty. Theora is excited. She walks around its entirety, stands, and studies it from every available perspective, finally returning to the front and looking at it for the longest time.

And then, it suddenly occurs to her. *I'm underwhelmed. It's smaller than I imagined it.* In the movies and in the history texts, every image of *the* Statue she has ever seen made her assume it was like the Great Pyramid or the Great Wall—a colossus meant to inspire awe. She doesn't share her thoughts with her sister, though, saying simply when asked her opinion, "It's unbelievable!"

The Empire State Building, however, does impress her. Upon completion, it is the tallest building in the world, and standing on the sidewalk below, Theora leans her head back and tries to see the top.

"Come on, Theora, you'll strain your neck," Frieda cautions, amused. "There is an observation deck at the top."

They take the elevator up and, from there, see the city through the available telescopes. Theora is amazed at how the tall buildings seem to emerge into the air right at the water's edge and cover the entire island, creating the infamous "canyons" she has read about. Only Central Park, it seems, offers some relief from the vertical climb of the city.

"I hope they never build tall buildings, even four and five stories, along the shore of *our lake* at home," Theora says to Frieda as they emerge from this true colossus. "It would ruin the beautiful scenery forever."

"I wouldn't worry, Theora. That will not happen."

Theora looks back at the tallest building in the world. "I bet there are more people working in that place than there are in all of Miller County."

On another day, Frieda and Theora spend time in the city wandering around Rockefeller Center, an emerging complex of buildings in Manhattan still under construction. Of those that are finished, there is the Radio City Music Hall and its already famous Rockettes, and the two ladies take in a show. Theora is proud to learn that the group originated in St. Louis some years before as the Missouri Rockettes, and she briefly entertains the idea of joining the group—until Frieda reminds her that her legs are too short.

"And I'd have to take dancing lessons," she admits.

In the evening, she sits down at a table in her room and writes postcards to send home. The one to Harold has a picture of the Rockettes, and she is certain he will appreciate the gesture. On the back is a message ending simply with "Miss you, Theora." Others she sends to Marion and Phyllis, her mom and dad, and Bernie and crew at the Casino. This is her only correspondence to anyone during her entire trip.

On her last day at her sister's home, the entire family takes a driving tour around Long Island. During a stop at a quaint restaurant on the bay shore, she walks by herself down steps toward the water and onto a large dock filled with a variety of boats—skiffs, trawlers, and large sailboats. She pauses, looking out across the water, and for a moment, she is Nick Carraway—not on his initial encounter with the East, but at the disillusioned end before returning to his Midwest.

Theora stands "in awe" at the thought and is haunted by it. Today, she finds herself, as did Nick, seeing the "inessential houses melt away fresh" for the "Dutch sailors' eyes." *My God, it must have been beautiful.* Theora has come to realize *I live every day next to miles of awesome, untouched beauty.*

Standing below the dam, riverside, looking up at the monument of concrete and steel, one is reminded that this massive structure holds back 650 billion gallons of water. This water "seeks its own level," flowing along the original riverbed and into the valleys and hollows and other low places, creating beautiful "arms" and coves that curve along and through the surrounding hills. And it does so for 1,376 shoreline miles.

One ancient world compromised to create another.

So much untouched beauty. So long, Possum Holler—hello, Lake Ozark. I miss it, Theora realizes, *and I want to go home.*

At the Lake, business is good throughout the month of October, and Theora arrives home just as the fall color hits its peak, reaffirming her conclusion that she lives surrounded by beauty—Harold included.

As Harold has turned twenty-one in late summer, he is now able to take more responsibility for running the liquor store, and Lawrence and Jessie make plans to go to Springfield for Thanksgiving. Lawrence's mother has requested they do so, and brother Harvey and his wife, Vivian, will be there as well. Bernie and Paul have closed the Casino for the winter and leave for Tulsa before the holiday, thus preventing a repeat of the prior year's community-wide gathering.

On Thanksgiving morning, Harold and a waitress take care of the few bus passengers coming through, and he loads the newspapers into the new racks that now sit just outside the front door. You can get a newspaper without paying, but, not surprisingly, each day, the nickels in the coin slot equal the newspapers gone. Harold closes the Whitehouse at noon and drives to Bagnell, where he has been invited to the family gathering. It will be the first time since he met Theora that he has been a part of any such event, and he is a bit nervous.

Theora's trip is now old news. All talk is about Phyllis' imminence. Due in mid-December, she looks like she has already had turkey—all of it, whole. The baby's anxious, Phyllis is anxious, and Marion is, well… Marion.

When Harold arrives, he finds himself in the driveway in front of the house with the Robinson brothers, George and Clyde, along with Dorothy's husband, George. They are all, in the vernacular, "out at the cars." This means only one thing, Harold learns—they're having a drink, a *snort.*

Bert would be there too, but Lena is keeping him very *busy,* they explain, laughing.

Introductions were made, and they offered Harold a drink.

"Thanks, fellas, but I best go pay my respects to the lady of the house first," Harold says, begging off. "Don't want to get off on the wrong foot with the boss today."

Further introductions are in order when Harold enters the house, and Theora does the honors.

"This is Pebble, Clyde's wife, and Elenor, George's. Now come into the kitchen and meet the Haages."

On their way to the kitchen, they share a quick kiss — further indication that things appear to be fine between them since Theora's return, perhaps even a bit better.

"Hello, Mrs. Robinson. Happy Thanksgiving," Harold says as they enter the kitchen.

"Harold, you best call me Lena or *Mom* today, or no-body'll know who you're talking about," Lena says as she goes about her business.

"This is my sister Dorothy from Kansas," Theora continues. "You met her husband outside, I believe. And this is her brood — George (we call him Sonny), the oldest; Barbara; and Phillip."

Harold nods and smiles at them all. He is a bit over-whelmed; introducing his family only takes long enough to say the word "Harry."

Phillip walks over to his mother and gently pats her midsection. "And this," he announces, "is my little brother Charley."

Sonny laughs. "Phillip wants the same thing I have — a little brother to pick on." Everyone laughs but Phillip.

The day is a pleasant one for Harold, a relief from the routine at work and a reminder of things that matter — family foremost. Bert's prayer before the meal is the longest grace Harold has ever heard, and he and Theora exchange a glance during it.

Later in the evening, as the festivities wind down, Harold thanks everyone and says goodnight. "Some things need to be done at the Whitehouse before the day's end."

When he leaves, Theora follows him out and sits with him in the car. It is dark outside, and the porch light is on. A half-hour goes by, and Theora is still not back, which is bugging Marion.

"Bert, when I was dating Phyllis," Marion says, "and we'd come home and sit in the car out front, we wouldn't be there five minutes before you'd start blinking that damn porch light to tell her to get in the house. I called it a BC, named what you did after you.

I'd tell Phyllis, 'Bert's doing a BC again.' So," Marion comes to his point, "Why no BC for Harold?"

"Lena likes him—believes he can be trusted," Bert says.

"Meaning you didn't trust me?"

"Well, look here, you did get Phyllis pregnant!" Bert says.

"After we were married!" Marion contests.

"Well, just barely," Bert says.

In the car, Harold notes the porch light blinking and asks, "Is that the famous BC I've heard so much about?"

"No," Theora says. "That's a Marion."

As Phyllis's mid-December due date approaches, she agrees to have the baby at home in Bagnell, with Dr. Attic and a midwife delivering. And so, one midmorning, when Phyllis's water breaks while she is standing in the kitchen of their small apartment, she alerts Marion, who calmly picks up a pre-packed bag and walks her gently to the car. While she waits, he goes back in, quickly calls the Robinson house, and informs Bert, who answers, "Baby's coming. We're on the way."

Marion and Bert await the baby on the porch, even though it is a somewhat cold December day. Bert fiddles with his pipe, lighting and relighting it, while Marion smokes several cigarettes. Lena is in the room with the midwife and doctor while Theora waits just outside the door should another hand be needed.

At approximately 4:15 that afternoon, Theora hears a baby crying, but it is a little while before Lena cracks the door to the bedroom and speaks to her.

"Tell Marion he has a baby girl. Vital signs are excellent. Phyllis is fine," she says. "And then tell him to come in. The doctor wants to speak to him."

Theora senses something is not right just from the worry on her mother's face but puts on a wide smile when she relays the message to the new father.

When he enters the room, the doctor tells him to sit down on the edge of the bed next to Phyllis so the three of them can talk for a moment. Phyllis is cuddling the baby, who is wrapped in a light blanket.

"What's wrong, Doc? Something wrong?" Marion asks.

"The baby is healthy — heart, lungs, pulse, all her vitals are excellent," the doctor assures them. "It's her hands."

"Her hands?" Marion asks. "What about her hands?"

"There are bands of skin that have wrapped around her fingers and stunted them. Three, on one hand, are severely stunted. Two on the other, a little."

"Marion, we have a beautiful baby," Phyllis says to him. She wants to be strong, to assure him that things will be all right. Tears come from her eyes, and Marion looks at her and knows now, more than at any other time before, why he loves her.

"What is our beautiful baby's name?" Marion asks.

"I wish to call her Ruth," Phyllis says.

Marion looks down at the baby. "Then, hello, little Ruthie. I'm your daddy." He turns to Dr. Attic. "So, what next, Doc?"

"Let's look together at her hands while I tell you what I recommend," the doctor says, and Phyllis unwraps the baby's arms and hands.

"Damnit," Marion murmurs when he first sees Ruthie's hands.

"I need to make some calls," the doctor begins. "I believe that the recommendation will be for surgery."

"Surgery?" Marion protests. "She's a baby."

"At some point, the bands will have to be removed, Marion. Not right away. The surgeons will want her to be older, stronger."

The doctor pauses and rises from the bedside chair he has been occupying. "You treat her just like any other baby. Feed her, diaper her, and love her. I'll research the matter and call you."

The doctor turns to Lena and the midwife. "Ladies, would you like to see me out?"

The three exit the room. Theora goes to sit with her mother in the parlor while the midwife goes into the kitchen.

Dr. Attic comes out on the porch, where Bert is sitting alone in the swing. "Where's your medicinal bourbon, Bert?"

Bert leans forward, reaches behind him, and takes out a half-full pint bottle and a small glass. He pours three fingers into the glass and hands it to the doctor.

"Normally, I would not recommend two folks drinking out of the same glass," the doctor instructs Bert. "That's how you can spread sickness. But when the glass contains medicinal bourbon, any disease you catch while drinking it is cured at the same time." With that said, the good doctor empties the glass in one swallow, bids Bert goodbye, and leaves.

Phyllis has, with Marion's approval, named their baby Ruth after his older sister, and when Marion calls his mother to tell her about the baby, he asks her to call sister Ruth and tell her. "And, Mom, will you ask her if she and Art can come home at Christmas? I want her to see the baby. Nelia, too, maybe?"

Not only do both ladies work at the Children's Hospital in Chicago, but Nelia is also chief of nursing. Marion and Phyllis obviously want their opinion on the options available to help their baby.

Later that evening, Theora calls Harold to tell him. "I don't know what to do, Harold, to help my sister."

"Just be there for her. And Marion, too," Harold says. "I don't know what else you can do. Tell Marion whatever he needs, I'm here for him. I'll try to get away and come by there tomorrow."

"Harold, when I was in New York, did you really miss me?" Theora asks, leading him.

"Yes. The picture of those dancers helped me through it, though."

"Good for you." She pauses. "Harold?"

"Yes?"

"I know a way you can help baby Ruthie."

"How?"

"By loving her Aunt Theora."

"I already do," Harold says. "Goodnight." And he hangs up.

He just said he loved me, Theora realizes. He's never said that before. "Well, I'll be," she murmurs to herself.

When Dr. Attic calls Phyllis and Marion two days later to check on the baby, he informs them that the baby's condition, though rare, is not unknown and that there is a doctor at the University Medical Center in Columbia who has experience with her "issues." "I've informed them, and they are expecting your call," he tells them.

Later that day, sister Ruth calls Marion and, in the conversation, asks him if he can get a camera and take pictures of the baby's hands, sending the film in for processing now. "Art and I plan to be at Mom's around the twenty-third, but we need to return on the twenty-seventh," Ruth tells Marion. "Sometimes getting film processed and returned takes a while, so the sooner you get pictures, the better. And, Marion, take lots of pictures, every angle." Having the pictures to take back, Ruth explains, will give her and Nelia visuals to discuss Ruthie's situation with their doctors. "The doctors and surgeons here have seen just about everything; they have vast experience."

"Should we go ahead and call the Columbia doctor or wait until Ruth comes home, Marion?" Phyllis asks.

"I say we go ahead and call. It might take time to get an appointment," he decides.

Marion, through Harold, locates a camera from Jessie. It's a Kodak, "basic, nothing fancy," Jessie tells them, "but it should do what you want." Marion and Phyllis take the pictures, tears streaming down while the baby cries in some pain.

"Damnit, damnit," Marion mutters.

Marion calls Columbia and makes an appointment for early January. Upon coming to Bagnell for Christmas and seeing the baby, Ruth better understands the concerns. "We have seen similar cases like this," she tells Marion and Phyllis. "No two cases are exactly alike, but the issues are similar. I want to take the pictures back and talk with Nelia and the doctors, and I will call you. In the meantime, go ahead with the Columbia appointment. Can't hurt to have another opinion."

Harold does go home for Christmas, but only for a few days, and, learning that Harry has been doing better, promises him he can visit Lake Ozark when summer comes. For the first time, Harold tells Margaret about Theora. Grant is at work, and Harry is out with friends one morning, and over coffee, Harold feels the need to talk with his mom.

"Do you think you're in love with her?" Margaret asks.

"I think I am, but I don't know for sure. I miss her when she's not around; I miss her now."

"And how does she feel, do you think?" Margaret asks.

"She told me she loves me," Harold says. "But she's only eighteen, Mom. Does she really know what she wants at that age?"

"It depends on the person." Margaret pauses, reaches across the table, and takes Harold's hand. "It's always been about that."

"Well, in some ways, she reminds me of you. Very strong-willed."

Margaret laughs. "That settles it then. Marry her."

"Did I mention she's also a smart aleck?"

In December, the new King of England becomes the ex-King without explaining the Henry and derivatives issue, and the world remains in darkness. His younger brother, Albert, is crowned King George. Go figure.

More importantly, while Harold is away, though it is only for a short time, Theora misses him more than she has ever felt his absence at any time in the past. "I am truly in love with him," she realizes, "and there's no going back for me now."

New Year's Eve at the Whitehouse is fairly tame except for a brief exchange between a fellow from Jeff City and Jay. The fellow is very drunk and, upon learning that Jay is of the Cherokee persuasion, tries to recreate Wounded Knee. Jay obliges him by recreating Little Big Horn instead, followed by Harold escorting the gentleman from the building. Theora and Harold find time to dance during the evening, and Harold offers a compliment.

"Watching those Rockette dancers has made you better, I think."

"Harold, if I did all of what those girls did in that show, you'd be escorting me out of the building."

"Or upstairs to my room," he says, raising his eyebrows as he speaks.

"Hey, remember, my mother lives just down the road," she warns him.

Midnight comes, and 1936 becomes history, while at the same moment, 1937 emerges as a period of time that has to be lived. Humanity's job is to not take time for granted, and mostly, they do their job well. After all, although time is infinite, lives are not. And for Marion and Phyllis, there is no desire to waste time; they want to help baby Ruthie, and they want answers now.

Their appointment in Columbia goes as expected, and the doctors essentially tell them that surgery to remove the bands is the first step. "There is, however, no way to change the fact of the unformed and stunted fingers." They basically offer no second "step." One nurse proffers when the doctor is not present, this supportive advice: "A blind man develops all his other senses far stronger than most people. A deaf man sees everything." And she smiles.

"So," Marion concludes from that advice, "my daughter won't be able to hold a glass of juice, but she'll smell it better than anyone else."

"No, Marion, she will develop the fingers she has left better than anyone else, and she will do things just as well as anyone else," Phyllis tells him pointedly. "We will make sure of that."

Though it is the remedy proposed, surgery must wait until the baby is a bit older and stronger. When they call Ruth to tell her the results of the appointment, she relates that her doctors believe that "on the basis of the pictures and not having seen the baby, surgery is the first step," but they believe more can be done to help. There may be a second step. But all in all, surgery must wait.

Marion and Phyllis decide that Chicago is the best answer for baby Ruthie, as her aunts will be right there, and the couple begins to make plans for what is to come.

Phyllis' work schedule is limited with the new baby, but with Lena's help, she is able to get some time in. To make up for it, Marion works extra hours and even helps Harold at the Whitehouse on the busiest nights. The two men have become somewhat synonymous around town now; it is no longer Harold or Marion or Marion or Harold. It's Marion and Harold, Harold and Marion. No one knows why it happened that way—it just did. Someone referred to it as evolution in its crudest form. Neither Harold nor Marion understood the statement, so they just ignored it.

On their anniversary in mid-February, Marion and Phyllis invite Harold and Theora to go to dinner with them at a restaurant on the square in Camdenton. It's not expensive—they didn't want that. It's out of town—they wanted that. Ever since the baby was born, things have been busy and stressful, and they simply wanted a view of different walls, a change of scenery. While the girls are in the restroom, Marion asks a pointed question of Harold: "When are you and Theora getting married?"

"I was waiting for you to grant your permission," Harold says, avoiding an answer with the delicacy of an average politician. "I assumed you put it off to avoid being related to me."

"Well, it wouldn't be 'blood' relation. That's the good news."

"Tell you the truth, Marion, I think I'm a little afraid," Harold shares. "The situation with my dad and mom sticks in my craw. I want kids someday, but I want to make sure they don't grow up in a broken home."

"My parents divorced too, Harold," Marion says. "I have no way of knowing, but my plan is Phyllis and I are going the distance."

"I know, Marion, I know."

"You ask Theora to marry you, and she says yes—no hesitation—she'll still be there when you die," Marion says. "The Robinson girls make a commitment. It's gospel."

When the girls return to the table, Phyllis asks them what they were talking about.

"The Cardinals season," Marion says. "They're due to report to spring training soon. Harold's unsure about them, but I think they look like a good team."

Theora reaches over and places her hand on top of Harold's, and smiles at him.

Damn, that's it, Harold realizes.

Even though it is late when he returns to the Whitehouse, Harold calls his mother. "Mom, I'm in love with her, sure of it now."

"Well, then, ask her to marry you before she gets away."

Two days later, Harold and Theora go for a drive out State Road HH. It is known locally as Horseshoe Bend, a large peninsula that forms an indent into the main channel of the lake, thus the bend of a horseshoe. A couple of miles out, they pull off onto a level spot at the top of a bluff that offers an excellent view of the wide main channel. The pair exit the car and sit on a smooth boulder facing the water.

"They call this 'Lovers' Leap,'" Theora says. "There's another one where we turned off the highway."

"I know the story. There's a couple of Lovers' Leaps in northeast Oklahoma, too," Harold says. "They're everywhere."

"Well, anyway, I'm not jumping off the cliff with you, Harold," Theora says firmly.

Harold picks up a small rock and throws it out over the edge of the bluff. "When my father took Harry and me to live in Texas, left us there with Mrs. Newton, I felt abandoned," Harold shares. "First, my mother, then Dad. I didn't understand what was going on. It still bothers me." Harold turns to look at Theora. "I don't understand how someone can say they love you and then leave."

"Is this about my going to New York?" Theora asks.

"No," Harold says emphatically. "You came back."

"I said I would."

"Do you want children when you marry, Theora?"

"Very much so. I thought you knew that."

"I want their mother and me to always be there for them," Harold says.

"I want the same, Harold," Theora says, a bit irritated. "I always have."

Harold picks up another rock and throws it out toward the water. "I love you, Theora. Will you marry me?"

"I love you too, Harold. Yes."

Harold looks at her. "Now what?" he asks.

"Well, I guess we could shake on it," Theora says matter-of-factly.

"Are you trying to be funny?"

"No, actually, I wasn't," she says.

The growth in Lake Ozark has brought about the need for a post office. When the U.S. Postal Service announces a decision to fill that need, Lawrence Fry decides to apply for the civil service job of postmaster. Harold has told Jessie and Lawrence privately that he and Theora are planning to get married, and soon after, the three of them sit down together to talk.

"Harold, we bought some land up on 1-A," Lawrence says.

"Jessie and I are going to build a house there."

"That sounds great," Harold says, truly happy for them. "Jessie deserves it."

"Amen," Jessie says. "Obviously, we hope you are planning to stay with us — I mean, now that you're getting married and all."

"I don't have any other plans if that's what you mean," Harold reassures them.

"We won't be as easily available to the business as we have been," Lawrence says. "Even more responsibility will fall on you." "It will come with a substantial raise, though, as it should," Jessie assures him, looking to Lawrence for consensus.

"Yes, of course," Lawrence says. "Helpful, we hope, now that you are getting married."

Harold nods his head agreeably. "What about your little house here?" he asks. "Would Theora and I be able to move in there?"

"Well, not right away," Jessie says. "It will take a few months for the house to be ready."

"You know I took the exam for postmaster," Lawrence interjects. "I have some contacts in Jeff. They tell me it looks good. Part of the deal is our making that building available as the temporary post office."

"We may have to move back into the Whitehouse for a while," Jessie says. "Until the house is ready."

"We'll manage," Harold says.

A short time later, Lawrence Fry is appointed the first postmaster of Lake Ozark, Missouri.

Wherever people find a need for distilled spirits — bourbon and such — an equal need for redemption is generally posed. Therefore, folks in Lake Ozark make an effort to provide for those needs as well. The Baptists have already successfully managed the needs of their parishioners in the form of the Bagnell Baptist Church, long the spiritual home of Bert and Lena Robinson. Father Larkin, a Catholic priest, is sent from Jefferson City to round up the available flock in and around Lake Ozark for Sunday Mass. There is, however, a small group of Protestants, mostly younger people, who favor the Christian Church and, with the help of a young minister from Eldon, have services on Sunday mornings in an empty storefront just up the street from the Whitehouse. Among them are the Claytons, the Frys, the Gordons, the Jameses, Theora, and, on days she can rescue him from work, Harold Pilkington.

Harold has grown up with little organized religion in his life, although a belief in God and a savior has always been innately understood. However, with Theora's gentle nudging, he will adapt and do as he is told. And so, on Easter Sunday, 1937, he attends the service with Theora. It is held at 12:30 p.m. due to the reverend's commitments to his Eldon church, thus allowing Harold to leave work. During the service, everyone prays for little Ruthie — together and quietly — each in their own way.

A few days after Easter, and after Harold's talk with the Frys, Harold, and Theora have dinner with Marion and Phyllis at their apartment.

"We're getting married," Theora tells them.

"Pardon me if I don't act surprised," Phyllis says. "But congratulations. When?"

"We're thinking June," Theora says. "But we want to know if you have scheduled your trip to Chicago yet."

Phyllis looks over at Marion, who looks down at his drink. "They want to begin in July — surgery, then go from there," she says. "I'll leave with Ruth the first week in July."

"Then it will be June," Theora says. "We're not doing it without you being there."

"You good with that, Marion?" Harold asks him. "You stand up with me?"

"Yes—and do a better job than you. I'll remember the mix."

Later, after dinner, Harold and Marion step out onto the porch to have a cigarette, and Harold asks Marion if he is surprised that he finally asked Theora to marry him.

"Harold, everybody in this town knew the minute she saw you that she was going to marry you. We were surprised that you held out as long as you did."

The second week in June, Harold picks up Marion and Phyllis at their apartment and heads to Bagnell to pick up Theora. Both men are wearing suits, and Phyllis is equally dressed up. As they pull into the driveway, Marion says, "Here we go again," and Phyllis laughs; Harold just looks at him. Once inside the house, they join Bert and Lena in the kitchen as they wait for Theora.

"You nervous, Harold?" Bert asks.

"No, no. I'm fine."

"You boys hungry?" Lena asks. "You should eat."

"I'd have a piece of that cake on the table there," Marion says. "I'm not the one getting married today."

"Not for me, I'm fine," Harold says.

"Harold," Bert begins, "everything will be fine as long as you do what you're told. It's worked for Marion. Should work for you, too."

Lena gives him a look. "And you, Bert—what's worked for you? You never do what you're told."

Bert ignores her and steps to the bedroom door. "Theora, you about ready? The boys are waiting on you."

Theora finally comes out wearing her nicest dress and a new pair of shoes purchased just for the occasion, and the wedding party departs for Eldon. As they leave, Bert, standing on the porch with Lena, notes tears coming to her eyes as she watches the car go up the road toward the highway. He walks over to her, puts his arm around her, and pulls her close.

"She's my baby, Bert. My last one."

"He's a good boy, Lena. She'll be fine."

"No, Bert, he's a good man," she corrects.

At the church, the reverend, though he has known Theora for a while, questions her age.

"Are you sure, Theora? You don't look eighteen," he asks.

"If you don't believe me, call my home and ask."

"All right. We don't want to get in trouble here." He picks up the phone and dials. Bert answers.

"Mr. Robinson, this is Reverend Cartwright in Eldon. Your daughter is here with a fella wanting to get married. I wasn't sure she was old enough. Is she eighteen, or, if not, do you give your permission for her to marry?"

"What does she look like, Reverend?" Bert asks.

"She's short, pretty, has freckles."

"Hold on. Lena, do we have a daughter—short, pretty, freckles?"

"What? Give me the phone." She takes the phone from him. "This is Lena."

"Reverend Cartwright in Eldon. Your daughter is here to be married. I'm just calling to confirm she's old enough."

"She's eighteen, Pastor—almost nineteen," Lena says. "And she has our blessing."

"Very well. Thank you, Mrs. Robinson. Goodbye." He hangs up, performs the ceremony, papers are signed, the preacher paid, and goodbyes and thank-yous said.

As they are leaving, the reverend asks Theora, "Your dad's a Baptist, isn't he?"

"Yes, he is," Theora answers.

"I thought so."

In the car, before they leave the sanctuary of the church parking lot, Marion retrieves a metal cooler containing bottles of iced 7-Up and a paper bag holding a fifth of bourbon. "Drink off the top of the 7-Up, pour in about a jigger full of bourbon, put your thumb on the top, and turn the bottle upside down three or four times. Instant highball."

The foursome toasts the newlyweds and drives to Jeff City for a nice early dinner. After the return from the city, they go by Red and Carrie's to pick up Ruthie and drop the threesome off at their apartment. When they arrive back at the Whitehouse, which is now closed for the night, Theora asks Harold if he is going to carry her across the threshold, as is customary.

"Which one?" Harold asks. "The front door to the building or the door to our room?"

"Both," she says.

"Both?"

"Everybody keeps telling me how strong you are. Prove it."

And he does.

Arrangements are finalized for Phyllis' Chicago trip. She is to take the train from St. Louis and will be staying with Nelia Wolff's in-laws, her husband Paul's parents. They live closest to the hospital — walking distance, in fact — making it the most convenient for Phyllis. She will have to wean Ruthie on the trip, as there will be prolonged separations during their stay in the city. Harold offers to drive Marion and family to St. Louis to give him company on the return trip, but he begs off. "I think I'd like the time alone," he says. But Lena insists on going with him, and he agrees. During the first week in July, early one morning, Marion, Phyllis, Ruthie, and Lena get into the car and head to St. Louis. Harold and Theora join Bert at the house in Bagnell to see them off. Ruthie gets more good-bye kisses than Phyllis, and there is concern she may have a permanent lip mark on her forehead.

At departure time in St. Louis, everyone tries to be brave, but when Lena starts to cry, Phyllis can't hold back. Marion hugs her close and says, "You're one hell of a woman, Phyllis. You can do this."

"I'm scared, Marion," Phyllis says through her tears. "I don't want them to hurt our baby."

"Ruth and Nelia will be right there with you every day."

Marion helps Phyllis and the baby get settled on the train, and when the conductor motions for him to leave, he does. Phyllis watches Marion and her mother through the window as the train pulls out, holding Ruthie up so they can see her. And then they can't. It is mostly quiet in the car on the way back to Bagnell, both occupants needing time alone with their thoughts.

The trip to Chicago takes approximately eight hours but feels like eighty to Phyllis, as it makes numerous stops along the way. Her efforts to wean the baby are somewhat successful, but as Phyllis already knows, Miss Ruthie has a mind of her own. *Reminds me of her father*, Phyllis thinks.

Nelia meets Phyllis and the baby at the station and drives them to her in-laws' home. On the way, she passes by the hospital to show Phyllis where she will be going the next morning. It is a short, easily walked distance, which Phyllis finds quite pleasing. The Wolffs, Phyllis is happy to note, are a gracious retired couple in their sixties and quickly make her feel at ease.

The next morning, she arrives at the hospital before eight, checks in, and shortly after, a nurse comes out, asks a few questions, and takes the baby. An hour later, Marion's sister Ruth comes out to the waiting room, hugs Phyllis hello, and sits down to talk to her.

"The doctors, of course, are seeing the baby for the first time, so the majority of the day will be spent making decisions about the preferred treatment," Ruth explains. "It's good because decisions are made by a group of doctors—you're getting multiple opinions at the same time."

"Will I be able to take her with me at the end of each day?" Phyllis asks.

"No, honey. I know it won't be easy, but you can't. Babies' immune systems are not well-developed, and therefore, the ward is in permanent quarantine. We have to limit access for the sake of all the children."

Phyllis experiences a brief moment of panic, fearing she won't see her baby. "You mean I won't see her before I leave today?"

"No, you will, Phyll," Ruth reassures her. "Later today, a nurse will come and get you and take you back where you can prep—wash up, put on a mask—and a doctor will meet with you and the baby to explain the course of treatment. I suspect they may do surgery as early as tomorrow."

"I just sit here until then?"

"Unfortunately. I need to get back to work now, but if I can, I'll sneak out and meet you. We could have some lunch in the cafeteria. I'll try." Ruth gets up to go.

"Ruth, how do you kiss your baby when you have a mask on?"

Ruth looks around to see if anyone's watching, reaches up and pulls her mask down, kisses the air, replaces it, smiles, and, with a wink, leaves.

She and Ruth do have lunch together and talk about everything but the hospital. At four in the afternoon, a nurse ushers her back, preps her, and hands Ruthie to her to hold. A doctor comes into the room and goes over the medical team's recommendations. Phyllis listens, but none of what he says registers. All she can think about is that she will soon have to leave here without her baby.

Momentarily, the doctor leaves, and the nurse comes to her.

"Mrs. Clayton, it's time for you to leave now. I'll have to take the baby."

"Give me a minute, please," Phyllis says to her, and the nurse nods, turns away, and busies herself with notations in Ruthie's file. Phyllis quickly pulls her mask down, leans in, and kisses her baby, holding her for a long while. Finally, she gives Ruthie a last hug and hands her to the nurse. Ruthie immediately starts crying.

"Don't worry, she'll be fine," the nurse says. "She'll settle down. You must go now." Phyllis turns and walks out of the room, out of the hospital, and cries all the way back to the Wolff home — and does so on her walk home every day thereafter.

The surgery was successful, she is told — the bands of skin removed so that the fingers, or what remains of them, are unrestrained. And afterward, there is post-operative recovery, during which she is unable to see the baby. Ruthie, in fact, is restrained, a necessary measure to keep her from touching her hands. Everything after is called rehabilitation, and Phyllis continues to struggle to understand it.

In Lake Ozark, Marion tries to adjust to existence without his wife and baby — difficult for a man who has been attached at the hip to the same woman since he was fifteen years old. He works all the possible hours at the restaurant. It helps keep his mind off missing his family, but he also needs the money to help pay for Ruthie's medical bills. Harold hires him to help out at the Whitehouse on Friday and Saturday nights, and to all who have known him since his basketball days, he becomes the brunt of all the bad "bouncer" jokes. "You gonna bounce me outta here, Marion?" they say as they imitate bouncing a ball. "Don't you double-dribble me" is a favorite. Reacting appropriately, Marion requests a double-barrel shotgun to help him do the job and is immediately turned down by Harold. "Not in the budget," he says.

Theora, too, misses her sister, adding to the normal issues attributed to starting married life, and she often sits with Marion just talking, letting him "let go." She continues to work for Bernie and Paul at the Casino Restaurant, refusing to leave them without another experienced waitress — especially during the busy season. And, too, that is probably best for the marriage, considering that the "boss thing" was settled at the altar.

Phyllis writes home every day — to Marion, to Bert and Lena — her way of talking to someone close to her, getting things "off her chest." There are occasional phone calls, but the service is expensive, and they are short. She works part-time, doing so to help pay the bills but also because most days, she is unable to see Ruthie and doesn't understand why.

Phyllis sees sister Ruth most days at the hospital, and occasionally, they have lunch together there. Nelia sees less often — her administrative duties keep her constantly busy at work. When she does, it is usually at the elder Wolffs' home after work hours. Both experienced nurses assure her that what the medical staff is doing is what's best for Ruthie. "I'm watching out for her, Phyllis," Ruth says to her sister-in-law. "I won't let anything happen to my namesake." Phyllis' answer to her is always the same: "But a child needs its mother."

Finally, one morning, after several weeks, she makes up her mind and tells Ruth at lunch that she is going to check the baby out and go home.

"But Phyllis, the doctors have not completed their work yet," Ruth cautions her, though she is only mildly persuasive. "Are you sure that's best for the baby?"

"What's best for the baby is she needs her mother, Ruth. Me," Phyllis says. "I'm going to take her home and let her live a normal life. If she needs to pick up something, she'll figure it out—she'll adapt just like every child ever born. That's what she'll do. And every night, her mother and father will be there to kiss her goodnight and tell her how much she's loved."

Ruth studies Phyllis for a few moments. "Your mind's made up?"

"My mind's made up," Phyllis echoes.

"I'll alert the doctors and the office and have her ready for dismissal the day after tomorrow," Ruth says. "Is that enough time for Marion to arrange to be in St. Louis?"

"Yes, I'll call him tonight."

They both stand up and carry their trays to the counter. At the door to the cafeteria, they pause, and Phyllis takes Ruth's hand.

"You don't necessarily think I'm wrong, do you?" Phyllis asks.

Ruth hugs her. "I, too, just want what's best for the baby."

Two days later, Phyllis and Ruthie board the train to St. Louis to go home.

October is in full color when Phyllis returns to Lake Ozark, and because of it, business is good. She settles in, returns to work part-time, and tries to put Chicago in her past. But often, when she hugs Ruthie, she tears up. "It will take time," Marion tells her.

Harold and Theora attend Thanksgiving dinner at the Robinsons in Bagnell, but the Haages do not make the drive this year. Phillip's "little brother to pick on," Charley, has been born, and Dorothy is expecting again, which was not un-expected. This year, Harold joins Marion, Clyde, and George out at the cars for a celebratory drink. They enjoy the day with a plan to drive to Tulsa on Friday, returning on Sunday. Lawrence and Jessie, with Marion's help, cover for Harold while they are gone. It will be Theora's first introduction to her in-laws, and she is nervous but won't admit it.

By car, Harold expects the trip to be about six or seven hours, and they leave just before dawn the next morning, heading southwest on Highway 54 to Highway 5 South at Camdenton. At Lebanon, they pull onto U.S. Highway 66 and enjoy an improved stretch of road all the way to Tulsa. At Claremore, they stop for lunch at Will's Diner — named, no doubt, for native son Will Rogers, who died in 1935 and is buried here. A movie fan, Theora is well aware of who he was and insists they take time to visit his grave, Harold reluctantly agreeing. In doing so, their arrival in Tulsa is delayed until late afternoon, and Margaret worries.

"They'll get here when they get here, Margaret. Quit worrying," Grant tells her.

They do, and Harry is immediately smitten by his sister-in-law, asking his brother when they are alone if there are any more like her back where he lives.

"No, they're fresh out, Harry," he tells him. "I got the last one."

It is obvious from the beginning that both Grant and Margaret like Theora, too. She easily jumps right in to help Margaret without being asked — something "down-home folks" appreciate — and describes herself as just a "hillbilly girl" from Missouri, even though she sounds more like a girl who has read a few books.

Saturday morning, Grant announces to Theora that he's going to take her to meet a real-life bank robber.

"A what?" she asks.

"You'll see," he says.

At noon, the five of them load into his big Buick and head east on Admiral Place, Route 66.

"Old Willis Newton has a bar and grill, and we'll have lunch there," Grant tells them. "I told him Harold and his wife were coming in, and he said he'd like to see you."

"Willis and his three brothers were the most successful bank robbers in American history," Harold tells her. "They gave it up after a daylight train robbery in Illinois in '24 that got fouled up.

"They all did some time — Willis, four years, I believe."

"Four it was," Grant says. "He's a model citizen now." Grant chuckles at the thought.

"It was his mom that Harry and I lived with in Texas that time," Harold tells her as she glances at Grant, who has turned his head to look out the side window.

The restaurant, Newton's, is about two miles east of the city limits. Willis joins Grant's family group at their table and has lunch with them. Harold tells him he was sorry to hear about his mother's passing and how much he remembers her — especially her cooking.

"He's right. She could really cook a lot of different things," Harry adds. "We ate good there, that's for sure."

"I'm glad to know you boys got to eat decent at some point growing up," Margaret says, smirking.

"No, no, Mom," they both chime in. "You're a great cook. Love your cooking."

"She did great with what they call Tex-Mex now," Harold tells her. "An Americanized version of Mexican food. It's a Texas thing."

"Any of her recipes on the menu here?" Theora asks.

"No, none exist that I know of," Willis says. "It was all in her head. She couldn't read or write."

"May I ask a very personal question of the two of you?" Theora ventures. "Please stop me if I'm out of line."

"Go ahead, young lady. We've got tough hides," Willis says.

She points to him and then Grant. "You're a bank robber, and he's a police officer. How is it that you've been friends so long?"

"Retired bank robber," Willis corrects, smiling.

"Willis, and off and on, his brothers have lived in Tulsa for many years," Grant tells her. "In all that time, they never broke the law here—or, for that matter, to my knowledge, in Oklahoma. We have never received a warrant of any kind from out of state asking us to pick them up and hold them. You can't arrest someone if they don't break the law. You can't arrest them for a rumor."

Willis laughs. "And there were plenty of rumors, I'll tell you. If we had done every job we've been accused of through the years, we would have been dead from exhaustion a long time ago."

"Early on, we somehow came to a mutual understanding—an unspoken respect," Grant says. "It's hard to explain."

"If you want to go straight, then spend a little time in a federal prison in Leavenworth, Kansas," Willis says. "A lot of those Chicago mobsters in there, and they are not pleasant people."

Later that day, Harold, Grant, and Harry sit around a fire pit in the backyard, the older men enjoying some distilled spirits—compliments of Kentucky. A lot of their talk revolves around how Harry is doing in school, and Harry keeps trying to change the subject. Inside, Margaret shares a quiet conversation with Theora about the man she has married. Theora has questions, and Margaret is willing to answer as she can.

"Yes, he was sickly when Grant and I married, and no, it wasn't me that made him better—it was sports." Margaret shows Theora Harold's yearbook with all the sports pictures. Underneath each senior's picture is a saying or caption considered applicable to them, and the one under Harold's picture states: *The glory of young men is in their strength.*

"Of character, you think?" Theora asks.

"That, too," Margaret answers.

Sunday morning, Tom, Lena, and Ruth come to Margaret and Grant's home for breakfast and to meet the newest member of the family. They have a nice visit, and all seem to approve of Theora. Tom mentioned that Harry had already called him on Saturday to announce that "she's a winner." Everyone notes that Harry and Theora blush simultaneously at his statement.

After the meal and a visit, Harold and Theora excuse themselves to pack, load the car, and say their goodbyes. Theora speaks quietly to Margaret before they leave. "Thank you for helping me to know my husband better." His mom hugs her tight, and they leave to drive home.

On the drive, Theora tells Harold about Margaret showing her the yearbook. "Marion was right," she says. "He said he believed you were a very good athlete at almost everything you did."

"Theora, I excelled at wrestling. People who know wrestling know we were good nationally. But most fans just know—just care about—the team sports. The average fan doesn't come to track, swimming, or gymnastics meets. They want to see a basketball or football game." Harold laughs at the memory.

"What's so funny?" Theora questions.

"At the same time I was at Central, Tulsa University had this fullback." Harold glances at Theora. "That's an important player on the football team."

"Okay, understood."

"He was, and maybe for a long time, the greatest athlete in TU history." Harold pauses and glances toward Theora. "His name was Ish. Ish Pilkington. I not only wasn't the best athlete in Tulsa—I wasn't even the best athlete in Tulsa named Pilkington." Harold laughs again at the thought.

Theora is quiet for a moment, and without looking at Harold, she says, "Ish… 'Call me Ishmael.'"

"What's that?" Harold asks.

"It's the opening line from *Moby Dick*. A story about a big whale."

"Yeah, I've heard about that book," Harold says. "Never read it, but you should recommend it to Marion. He likes monster fish stories."

In December, business is slow for the places that remain open—Red's and the Whitehouse among them. Customers are mostly locals out and about running errands, but occasionally, a few out-of-towners will pass through. "We want to see the lake and surrounding hills in winter," they explain.

It snows a lot, and Harold and Theora make no plans to return to Tulsa at Christmas. This being their first Christmas together, Theora wants to share it with her family—something Harold truly understands. The social event of the season, though—in the Robinson family, anyway—is Ruthie's first birthday party in mid-December.

Grandma Lena makes the cake because Lena makes the best cake in the county. Her secret is her fresh churned butter, but her special icing is an old family recipe that only old family members know. She tells Phyllis and Theora that when they become old family members, she will pass the secret along.

At the party, Phyllis shows everyone how the baby is attempting to grasp small objects and is often successful. She has been working with her and explains that she believes Ruthie will instinctively adapt and learn. "She doesn't know something is missing," Phyllis says. "She will get whatever she gets done with what she's got. That's simply it."

The other thing family members remark about is how cheerful and good-natured the baby seems to be, considering all she has been through.

Later, at home after the party, Theora remarks about the baby smiling all the time.

"She's very much loved," Harold says, "and she knows it."

Theora smiles at her husband.

"Phyllis is right, you know, about how she will adapt," Harold says. "Mom taught me that even though I was missing muscle in my left arm, there was still plenty left to develop."

"She's going to be alright, isn't she?" Theora states, more than questions.

"Yep, she is," Harold says.

PART IV
AND WELCOME OTHERS

The house on 1-A that the Frys are building is completed in early 1938, and they move out of the Whitehouse, allowing privacy for the Pilkingtons that they have not enjoyed before. The little cottage at the front remains the post office, with no plans for that to change anytime soon, and Lawrence and Jessie commute the short distance each day to work.

Business has just begun to pick up as the spring season gets underway when a tragedy occurs. Red Moore's restaurant catches fire in the early morning hours of a Sunday and is a complete loss. Volunteer firemen from Bagnell come to the aid, and a truck is dispatched from Eldon, but the fire has taken all it can by the time they arrive. Business and building are a complete loss. Red and Carrie Moore weigh their options and decide that, after 22 years in the restaurant business, beginning in southern Illinois, they are done. And overnight, Phyllis and Marion are out of a job.

Harold uses Marion as much as he can at the Whitehouse, but he needs more, and when Mr. Jones, "Jonesy," at the locker plant, offers him a job delivering ice, he jumps at it. With the coming of electricity to Lake Ozark, Jonesy has built a freezer facility in which he can produce ice to sell to numerous emerging customers. In addition, he rents space to individuals to freeze and store their foodstuff—say, a hunter's harvested and dressed deer in season—until they need it. He also has developed a good business with local restaurants, supplying frozen meat products to them on an as-needed basis. Each day, when Marion mounts up in Jonesy's old truck to make ice deliveries, he says a brief prayer—which works—because each day, he returns home safely.

Bernie hires Phyllis at the Casino, happy to have an experienced waitress instead of training a new girl, and she and Theora, as expected, make a good team. The Moores, though worn out with the restaurant business, are not ready to retire and thus acquire a vacant lot halfway between the Casino and the Whitehouse and build a building there. At the front is a retail space, and at the back are ample living quarters, prompting them to sell their home in Bagnell and move into the new building. And the V. Red Moore Gift Shop is born.

As to inventory for the new shop, souvenirs are the most logical. Postcards, pennants, and other items featuring the obvious—dam and lake foremost—are often requested by visitors and others just passing through. Also, there is a growing demand for items made from the local cedar. With little previous interest from "outsiders," craftsmen have for some time made various objects from the beautiful red and amber hues hidden under the tree's bark. The aroma released from the wood is considered so pleasing that small pieces of it are placed in drawers, and closets in newly built lake cabins "must" be cedar-lined. Small souvenir items include keepsake boxes, ashtray holders, and salt and pepper shaker sets.

In mid-April 1938, a young man in his mid to late twenties stops by the Whitehouse and asks to see the proprietor. Harold, standing behind the front counter, asks why.

"I'm a woodworker, a craftsman," the man says. "I make small pieces—keepsake boxes, trays, that sort of thing—but also larger items: chests, small tables. I make them out of cedar mostly, some walnut."

"You want us to purchase these items for resale?" Harold asks.

"Not necessarily," the man says. "If you don't mind stepping outside with me, I'll show you what I have in mind."

"Lead the way. I'm willing to hear you out."

"During the warmer season, when the weather permits, I'd like to set up a table right here and sell my products." The man indicates a spot under cover between the post office and the front door. "I'd pay you, of course."

"Can I see what it is you're selling?" Harold asks. "You have some products with you?"

"In my truck right here." The man leads Harold to the back of an old pickup and pulls a canvas cover from a large piece positioned there. "I make these cedar chests. They're clear-finished on the outside, as you can see, but inside" — he opens the chest, and it is completely unfinished aromatic red cedar — "the chests I make are 100% local cedar, the prettiest cedar in the world."

"Well, I can't speak for the rest of the world, but the chest impresses me," Harold says. "By the way, my name's Harold Pilkington. I'm the manager here."

The man reaches out to shake Harold's hand. "I'm sorry, I should have said earlier. Lon Stanton. Nice to meet you, Harold."

"What else you got, Lon?"

Lon opens a large canvas bag sitting next to the trunk, reaches in, and brings out a cedar tray holding an inexpensive clear-glass ashtray. "This is a cheap way to dress up a simple ashtray. Women love it." He reaches in again and pulls out a small cedar box with a hinged lid and an unfinished interior. "I make this jewelry box — that's what I call it — in two sizes: five-inch and eight-inch."

"So, what would you pay me? For the space?" Harold asks Lon.

"Days I sell nothing, I pay nothing. Otherwise, 10% on all sales of property. I have a $200 day, you have a $20 day."

"Sounds fair," Harold says. "But I would need to clear it with the owners first. Can you come by again early next week?"

"Of course," Lon says. "I'll see you next Monday."

"Before you go, I have a first anniversary coming up in June, and I was wondering..." Harold decides that Theora would love the chest — a place to store her memories. "What would it cost me to have you make me one of those cedar chests? Just like that, for my wife."

Lon begins to calculate. "Well, normally I would sell that chest for $55, but for you, $50 — less your commission of $5, which should be yours personally because you're the buyer — $45, half in advance."

"You've got a sale. Can you have it ready by early June?"

"Or before, if you want," Lon assures him.

"Wait here. I'll get your down payment." Harold goes into the Whitehouse and shortly comes back out and gives Lon $25. "I owe you $20 on delivery."

"Thanks, Harold. I'll see you Monday." Lon and Harold shake hands, and Lon gets into his truck and leaves.

Harold watches as Lon drives away south. *Well, I just gave a stranger $25,* he thinks. *I'm gonna look pretty stupid if he doesn't come back.*

The next Sunday morning, Harold is standing behind the counter doing paperwork when a large, long black vehicle — a limousine — pulls up to the gas pumps in front of the Whitehouse. Seeing it, Harold goes to the kitchen door and calls to Theora.

"Got a gas customer, Theora. Can you watch the front?"

"Coming." Theora, who is dressed nicely to attend church later in the morning, comes out of the kitchen carrying a cup of coffee.

Harold comes out of the main door just as three young men in their thirties get out of the car and head to the door.

"Can we get a cup of coffee inside?" the rugged one asks.

"Yes, sir. There's a lady at the counter. Go right in."

"Fill it up," the driver says. "You got a bathroom inside?"

"Yes. When you get to the back counter, go to the right. It's down the stairs."

Inside, the three men approach the counter and sit down on the stools there.

"Can we get some coffee, ma'am?" the rugged one says.

"You sure can," Theora says as she goes about pouring three cups of coffee. "Sugar is here. Would you like cream?"

"I would, please," the most handsome one says. He looks at Theora. "You seem very dressed up to be waitressing this morning."

"I'm going to church later," Theora says.

"Quit flirting, Ty," the third man says.

"I'm not flirting, Hank. I'm simply making conversation."

"Not to be rude, but may I ask you a question?" Theora ventures.

"Which one of us?" the rugged one asks.

"All of you." The rugged one nods his head. "That's a very fancy car you're in out there. You look familiar. Who are you?"

"We're actors," the one called Hank says. "Making a movie here in Missouri."

"Been shooting out at a place called Lovers' Leap," Ty says.

"Which one?" Theora asks. "There are several."

"Oh, uh, it was right out the highway, just off the road there," Ty says.

"It's about Jesse James," Hank says.

"What's it called?" Theora asks.

"Jesse James," Hank says. "I'm Hank Fonda, miss, and this is Ty Power."

"Oh my gosh! I thought you were... I know you both. And you, sir..." She is looking at the rugged one, unsure.

"Just call me Randy, miss. My job's riding around with these two matinee idols, keeping 'em out of trouble." Harold comes back in and stands by the cash register at the opposite end of the counter, waiting for the driver. Randy nods in his direction. "That your husband, miss?" he asks.

"Yes, he is. His name is Harold," Theora says, smiling.

"He is quite a handsome man, but a pretty girl like you—I would expect nothing less," Randy says, then turns to his two companions. "Zanuck ever gets a look at him, you boys are going to be out of a job."

The driver comes up the stairs and walks to the register. "Gentlemen, I suggest you use the bathroom if you need to," he says, addressing his three companions. "I don't want to stop again until we get to Springfield."

"Checked your oil; it's good," Harold says. "That'll be $2.19."

The driver hands him a five-dollar bill and asks for a receipt. Harold writes out a receipt and gives the man his change. "Thank you," Harold says. The man nods and goes out.

The three men quickly finish their coffee and stand up to go.

"What do we owe you, ma'am?" Randy asks.

"Oh? Uh, nothing," Theora says. "Coffee is on the house." Each man reaches into his pocket, takes out a dollar, and leaves it on the counter.

"A tip then, ma'am," Randy says, then nods at Harold. "Sir." And the three men turn to go.

"I'll be damned," Harold mutters as it suddenly dawns on him. "I'll be..."

"Do you know who that was, Harold?" Theora says excitedly.

"Of course I do, Theora. I'd know that voice anywhere. That was Randolph Scott. He does Westerns. Zane Grey stories."

"Randolph Scott?" Theora can't quite place him.

"Hawkeye, *Last of the Mohicans*! Last year. You wanted me to go see it."

"Hawkeye? That Randolph Scott! *The Last of the Mohicans*. I loved that story."

"I thought it was sad," Harold says.

Harold has cleared the Lon Stanton deal with the Frys, and on Monday, when Lon stops by, he and Harold shake to confirm it.

"Until summer comes, I will probably just do weekends," Lon says. "Most of my customers are going to be visitors, I think."

"Some locals, they see the chest," Harold says, "or that small side table — they'll be buyers, I bet."

"Well, I'll try a day or two, then."

"You might catch some during the mornings with the bus passengers, too," Harold says. "The small things, anyway."

"That settles it, then," Lon decides. "Mornings and weekends.

The rest of the time, I'll build my inventory. When's the first bus?" "7:30 a.m. Out of St. Louis, heading to Springfield."

"I'll see you then." Lon departs.

He came back, Harold thinks, congratulating himself. *I'm still a good judge of character.*

Lon does well with sales at his position in front of the Whitehouse during the spring, and both he and Harold and the Frys are happy with the arrangement. On June 12, Lon informs Harold that his cedar chest for Theora is in the truck, and together, they unload it and carry it into the dining room, where Harold hides it, covered, in a corner. Early on June 14, his anniversary, Harold slides the chest out to the middle of the room, places a large bow and anniversary card on it, and goes to find Theora in the kitchen.

"Theora, grab your coffee and come with me. I want to show you something."

"Aren't you going to give me a big hug and kiss first and say, 'Good morning, honey'?"

"Can you just come here, please?" he says again. "I need your help."

Theora follows Harold into the room and quickly sees the chest sporting the big bow. She walks slowly over to it, sees the card, and picks it up. It reads:

"Dearest Theora – As we make memories together through the years, I thought you might want someplace to store the best ones. Love and Happy Anniversary, Harold."

"Harold, I...."

"Go ahead and open it up," Harold says. She does, and from her reaction, he knows she loves it and is certain at that moment that the end result of the day will be a lot better than jumping off Lovers' Leap.

"I know what the first keepsake I will put away in it will be," Theora says, anxious to share her idea. "The shoes I wore when we were married."

"The shoes you... what if you need to wear them again?"

"I'll know where to find them, then."

"Of course you will," Harold says, accepting the logic.

"Oh, honey, I love it. How about the hug and kiss now?"

They embrace and kiss, and Harold contemplates the age-old question that has haunted men since Adam: "Will I ever understand women?"

In late June, Harry's long-awaited trip to visit his brother happens. Harry will be seventeen before he starts his senior year at Central, and the following summer, he will be, as he puts it, "long gone." He has a girlfriend, Maxine, back in Tulsa, and she has "slowed him down a bit," in Margaret's words, but there's "still a lot of piss and vinegar left," also Margaret's words.

"I thought about stopping in Springfield," Harry confides to Harold when they are alone that first night. "Dad said if I did, not to come back, so I didn't. He would know, too, wouldn't he?"

"Yeah, he would. It's the cop thing."

"Harold, I'd like to go back to Texas. Maybe when I get out of school. I liked it there."

"You were only four or five years old, Harry," Harold says. "How could you remember it?"

"I just do," Harry says.

"Why don't you enroll at TU?" Harold asks. "Get a degree."

"Been thinking about the service," Harry says. "Might join up."

"The service?"

"Actually, the Coast Guard," Harry says. "I like the idea of working on the boats without going way out to sea. I talked to some guys. They said they get more shore leave than you ever would in the Navy. The married guys like it that way."

"That's probably true," Harold agrees. "A lot of their water deployments are standard shifts—eight to twelve hours, I imagine."

"I talked to a recruiter there in Tulsa," Harry relates. "He told me that firefighting was a major part of what they do—putting out fires on other ships or onshore fires."

"Sounds like good training for civilian life after you get out."

"Yeah, he showed me what Tulsa firefighters start at," Harry says. "Pretty damn good."

"How about you concentrate on finishing high school first," Harold reminds him. "Right now, we need to get to bed."

The next morning, Jessie comes into the Whitehouse early, having ridden with Lawrence when he came to open the post office. Harold is inside at the back counter when she comes in, and he pours her a cup of coffee.

"That's exactly what I needed," she says. "Got a call last night from Mona. She and her husband are driving up from Springfield to visit. Be here about noon but need to head back about five, she said. Wants to see you and meet Theora. I told her Harry was here also, and she would like to see him as well."

"That's great, Jessie. Theora is off today. She can help Maggie, and we'll set up a nice lunch in the dining room."

"That won't work, Harold. The three of you will have to come up to the house. About two o'clock. Give us time to have a quiet lunch."

"Alright, sure," Harold says. "That will work. We'll be there."

"It's the liquor store, Harold," Jessie explains. "Doesn't stop Mona, but her husband won't go anywhere there is liquor. He won't come in the Whitehouse."

"Better hide your bourbon bottle, Jess," Harold says, amused.

"Already safely tucked away in the basement," she says. "No matter how much he wants a drink, he won't find it."

"A soul saved," Harold says triumphantly.

"When you come, bring Lawrence with you, please," Jessie says. "I've got the car, and I need to go to the grocery store."

Later, when Harold tells Theora the plans for the day, she says she is excited to meet Mona and the reverend but has a question. "How are you supposed to save souls if you don't go where the lost ones are?" Harold understands the logic behind the question but offers no answer.

"Jessie thinks Mona is coming to tell her that she and her husband are being sent to the Philippines finally, and she wants to say goodbye," Harold says. "It's been talked about for a few years. The church must have made a decision."

"What denomination are they?" Theora asks.

"I don't really know," Harold says. "Not Baptist, but some other Protestant branch."

"The Philippines, I don't understand," Theora says. "Why send missionaries to a country that is already heavily Christian? The Spanish influence has been there for many years. They're all Catholic."

"Maybe they're going to save the people from Catholicism?" Harold says with a chuckle.

"Save them from the evils of communion wine?" Theora says, laughing shamelessly along with Harold.

Jessie has a nice lunch with her sister and her husband, and the reverend remains somewhat quiet as the two young women talk of their shared past. When Mona finally tells Jessie that the main reason she is there is to tell her goodbye for a while, Jessie does not hesitate to relate her concern.

"Why the Philippines?" Jessie questions. "They have been mostly Christian for many years, haven't they? American and Spanish influence?"

"We are being sent to take over an existing mission and school near Manila," Mona explains. "It's our largest facility there." She glances at her husband. "It is a great honor, great promotion. I'm very proud of my husband."

Jessie looks at the reverend. "Yes, of course, absolutely. Congratulations!"

The conversation when Harold, Theora, and Harry arrive is mostly congenial. Mona, like Jessie, is a naturally decent, good person, and Theora takes to her as she has Jessie. Showing concern, she mentions the recent newspaper reports of Japanese atrocities in Nanking, China. "Japan is so close to the Philippines; aren't you concerned?"

"The Philippines are Ameri…" Mona begins.

"They are sovereign now," the reverend interjects. "MacArthur is there with American forces at their request, but armies aren't the solution—they are the problem."

"Yes, perhaps," Theora decides to drop the subject.

Harry, unconcerned about the brief awkward mood prevalent in the room, jumps right out of the "frying pan." "Mona, do you see Mother in Springfield? I know you are friends."

"Harry, leave it alone," Harold cautions.

Mona smiles at both of them. "It's alright, Harold," she says. "Yes, Harry, I have. Not recently, but I have."

"And?" Harry asks.

"She is fine. Your sister is twelve or thirteen now. Sweet girl, you'd like her."

"Mother? Does she ask about us?" Harry presses.

"Harry. Let it go."

"She does, Harry," Mona says. "I'm unable to tell her much because I don't see you boys often enough, but she does."

"Why doesn't she come see for herself?" Harry says.

"You'd have to ask Uncle Grant," Mona says.

When the time comes for Mona and her husband to leave, the goodbyes are bittersweet. As their car pulls out of the driveway, Harry notices tears coming from Jessie's eyes and steps over, puts his arm around her, and hugs her.

One day, not long after Harry goes back to Tulsa, Theora and Phyllis make a shopping trip to Eldon, and while browsing the book and magazine rack at the drugstore, Theora finds a pamphlet: *Learn to Play Bridge: A Beginner's Guide,* by Harold S. Vanderbilt, 15 cents.

"Phyllis, we're going to learn to play bridge," she announces excitedly to her sister and anyone else in the store as she pays for the book. "Everything we need to know is right here."

Two days later, Phyllis and Marion come to the Whitehouse, and the two couples settle down at a table in the dining room to learn to play the game. Theora begins reading from the book as they lay out four practice hands—men against women—and count up high-card points.

"Okay, I'm the dealer, so I bid first," Theora says. "I have fourteen points—two Aces, one King, and three Jacks. Enough points to open, and a five-card suit in hearts with Ace, King, Jack, seven, five. I would open 'one heart.'"

"Wouldn't you bid five hearts 'cause you got five?" Marion asks.

"No, you see, the bid is for how many 'tricks' you believe you can take more than the basic six."

"Then you should bid seven, right?" Harold says.

"No," Theora says. "There are thirteen tricks in all. The bidding is about making a contract with your partner about how many tricks over six you believe you can make." She looks at Harold's hand on her left, and he has fifteen high-card points, a void in hearts, with a strong five-card spade suit. "Moving on, I believe Harold would bid one spade. Phyllis doesn't have much—three points, only two hearts—and she would pass. Now, Marion has eight points, including a bunch of my hearts, and four spades to support Harold. He would bid two spades."

"What then?" Harold asks.

"We keep going until there are three straight passes. I would, therefore, pass, not having any support from my partner. Harold would bid three spades. Phyllis, then Marion, then I would pass, and Harold would try to take nine tricks.

We play our hands, and Marion's is laid on the table for Harold to play 'cause Marion is the 'dummy.'"

"Marion is the dummy," Harold repeats. "That is the first thing I've understood all night."

"Wait a minute," Marion interjects. "Why am I the dummy? Phyllis's hand is worse than mine."

"Hey, Marion, look at it this way," Harold explains. "It's not like poker where you have to say 'deal me out' while you go get a fresh drink. This gives you an excuse, a chance to do that. We should call the dummy the bartender instead."

"OK then. I'm the bartender. What'll you have, Harold?"

"Bourbon and Seven, emphasis on the bourbon."

"For the love of God," Phyllis says.

Shortly after re-designating the "dummy" as "bartender," Theora gives up and tells Phyllis that they should find two other females to learn the game with, then come back and teach their guys.

"Amen," Phyllis says; then, to Marion: "Hey dummy, fix me a highball."

The last Sunday of summer, on the Labor Day weekend, the 7:30 a.m. bus from St. Louis is ten minutes late, and a handful of locals are hanging out waiting for their Sunday newspapers. Longtime driver Sam White steps down from the bus, followed by another man in a driver's uniform. Both men are carrying stacks of newspapers.

"Sorry we're late, Harold," Sam says, handing him the stack. "Breaking in a new driver today."

"No problem, just put them down on the bench there for now," Harold says.

"Harold, meet Anthony Bertone," Sam says. "He'll be driving the St. Louis to Oklahoma City route on Sundays now."

"Call me Tony, Harold," he says, extending his hand.

"Hey, Tony," Harold says, shaking Tony's hand. "You're changing routes, Sam? You can't be retiring. You're too young."

"No, I'm taking a job with Busch," Sam says. "Delivering Bud in the St. Louis area. Still on the road, but home every night."

"So, Tony, you a St. Louis boy?" Harold asks.

"Yes sir, Italian boy from The Hill. Born and bred."

"The Hill?" Harold asks.

"You don't know The Hill? Italian neighborhood not far from downtown. Great restaurants, great food. You gotta try it sometime."

"Sounds good. Will do if I can ever get away to St. Louis."

"Oh, I should tell you, too," Tony says. "We won't ever be late again. Gotta live up to my nickname."

"What's that?"

"On-Time Tony," he says. "Got it when driving city buses." Sam and Harold laugh.

"You're like that fellow Mussolini, then," Sam says. "They say he made the trains in Italy run on time."

"Yeah, but he's cozying up to that SOB Hitler," Tony says. "Can't be good for Italy."

"Unfortunately, you're probably right," Harold says. "Well, grab yourself some breakfast. Drivers' meals are on the house." Sam and Tony go inside while Harold places some newspapers in the outdoor racks and carries the remainder inside.

There are several locals sitting at the tables in front of the soda fountain having coffee and four or five at the counter having breakfast. "The news in this paper is just as bad as it was yesterday," one of the groups says to the room.

"You must be reading the sports section," another says. "Damn, Cards are still 16–17 games outta first."

"No, I'm talking about these damn Germans," the first man says.

"It's not the Germans," a lady at the counter suggests. "It's the Nazis!"

"Well, they're still Germans," another lady says. "You don't hear about any French or English Nazis, do you?"

"Hell, the French and the English are too busy quaking in their boots," a third man says. "There's going to be a war in Europe again, and the French could stop it right now if they would give them damn Germans an ultimatum. Quit building weapons and your army, or we'll stop you before it goes any further."

"He's right. Stop the move into Austria," the first man says. "The Versailles Treaty says they can."

"The chances of that happening are about as good as the Cards finishing first," the second man says as he closes up the sports section. "The Frogs ain't got the balls."

"Agree to that," the first woman says.

"We better get going, Tony, before we get caught in the crossfire," Sam says, chuckling, as he gets up from the counter. To the room: "Bus to Oklahoma City, loading up, leaving in five! See you around, Harold. Thanks for everything."

"Take care, Sam. Don't be a stranger," Harold says. "And we'll see you next week, Tony? 7:30?"

"On the dot," Tony says as he exits, smiling.

After his probationary period, new conservation agent Charles Fleetwood has been assigned to cover the Bagnell Dam area, along with the surrounding countryside and state park. Soon after his posting, he and his wife Jean rent a small housekeeping cottage from Hale's Fishing Camp located on a side road just off 1A. The proprietor, Clark Hale, maintains a number of fishing boats and guides groups on trips up the lake. He knows where all the crappie beds are because he put most of them there. Charley and Jean can usually be found on weekend nights at the Whitehouse, partying with all their friends. Clark, on the other hand, usually stops by on quiet winter mornings and engages Harold in a gin rummy game, penny a point.

On one slow autumn night, before the snagging season, Harold and Marion go fishing below the dam, having heard that channel cats are biting well there and seem to be abundant. Of all the catfish, these are the best tasting — river or lake, they believe — and the chance to put some on their dinner table is tempting.

After about an hour of casting their lines with no success, Marion gets restless and tells Harold he's going above the line.

"Marion, don't do it. Charley might be around."

"Even if he sees me, he won't write me a ticket," Marion says. "Besides, with deer season getting ready to start, he'll be out in the woods looking for early starters."

"All right, but keep an eye out and be careful. I'm going to go downstream a little way and try my luck there." That said, Harold moves fifty yards or so downstream while Marion moves ten feet or so above the line.

Agent Fleetwood happens to be on duty this night but not out in the woods preparing for pre-season poachers. His supervisor, his boss, has come down from Jeff City, and together, they have spent the day on the water checking fishing licenses and catch limits, including an encounter with a group led by Clark, anchored over a bed in Pumphouse Cove. But no tickets are written. Clark has gone out legal as always, even though he might have had a heads-up from Charley. That evening, before he heads back to Jeff, the supervisor decides they will do a check of activity below the dam. On the Camp Road above the dam, they pull into and park behind the substation. They get out of the car, and here, binoculars in hand, the supervisor begins surveying the riverbank leading up to the dam. After a few moments, the supervisor sees Marion, still above the line, and hands the binoculars to Charley.

"I believe I see someone fishing above the line down there," the super says to Charley.

Charley takes the binoculars, looks down toward the line area, and immediately recognizes Marion. "I don't see anyone, Super. You sure these things are working all right?"

"Of course, they're working all right," the Super says. "You need to get your eyes checked." He looks through the binoculars again. "There sure is somebody down there way above the line. Come on, get in the car. We're going down there."

Charley, upset because he may have to write Marion a ticket, drives as slow as he can to get below the dam until his supervisor yells at him. "Good God, Fleetwood, can't you go any faster?" Charley speeds up a bit, and they pull into the parking area below the dam and quickly make their way toward the perpetrator, Marion.

"Sir, you, sir," the agent yells at Marion. "Pull in your line there. You're breaking the law."

Marion looks up and sees the agent and Charley and mumbles to himself, "Shit, it's Charley. I'm screwed." Harold, hearing the commotion, sees what is happening and works his way back toward the dam and Marion. He is carrying his stringer with two nice-sized channel cats attached.

"Let's see your driver's license and your fishing license, sir," the agent demands. Marion complies as he glances at Charley. "Go get your stringer and bring it here too." Marion goes and retrieves his stringer with three very nice channel cats attached.

Charley acknowledges Marion by touching the brim of his hat. "Mr. Clayton. Did you not see the sign posted behind you there, sir?"

"The sign?" Marion says. He looks behind him and reads the sign. "Well, by gosh, I did not see it. I apologize."

"Nevertheless, I am going to have to write you a ticket for fishing above the line," the agent says. "Ignorance is no excuse."

Harold, having just arrived at the group, tries to help. "Why? Ignorance has always worked for him before. This is my mentally handicapped brother-in-law. He can't help what he does sometimes."

"You his fishing companion?" the agent asks.

Harold nods, "Yes."

"We will have to confiscate your catch, both of you, as illegal contraband," the agent says. "Agent Fleetwood will return your stringers in a few days."

"What do you do with the fish, may I ask?" Harold says to the agent.

"They will be donated to the homeless shelter in Jefferson City," he says.

"Homeless shelter? Jefferson City? There's no such thing," Marion contends. "Everybody there is either employed by the State, is a priest or a German Catholic farmer."

"Or all of the above," Harold adds. "There's no unemployed people in Jefferson City."

"Don't argue with me, Mr. Clayton. Here's your ticket. Have a good day," the agent says. "Let's go, Fleetwood." The two agents place the fish in their trunk, get in, and drive away.

Two days later, Marion and Phyllis and Harold and Theora are invited to the Fleetwoods' cottage for dinner. Jean is in the kitchen cooking when they arrive, and Charley fixes them all a highball. Marion wanders into the kitchen, highball in hand, and notices Jean is frying fish.

"Harold, come here," Marion says. Harold, also highball in hand, does as requested. "Do those fish look familiar to you?" Marion asks.

"Yeah, they're from the homeless shelter in Jeff City."

Weekend nights at the Whitehouse continue to be very busy that fall and Theora gives Bernie notice that she would be leaving the Casino employ when they closed for the year in November. She and Harold had talked about it and agreed it was best. With the blessing of the Frys, she is given a small salary and becomes an employee of the Whitehouse. Bernie understood, and the two remain close friends.

Though the talk around the tables most nights is of popular music — Bing Crosby, the Dorsey brothers, Benny Goodman, and the newest country anthem, Roy Acuff's "Wabash Cannonball" — conversation finds its way to talk of war. The older people present prefer not to speak of it, though they quietly fear it's coming. The younger generation, too, fear it, though they tend to embrace its romanticism. Nazi Germany's takeover of Austria earlier in the year has not gone unnoticed. And although the newspapers are filled each day with news of Japan's atrocities in Manchuria and China, the focus for most remains on Europe.

In September, British Prime Minister Neville Chamberlain returned from Germany with the Munich Agreement and declared to the English people there would be "peace for our time." In response, Winston Churchill, totally opposed to the appeasement policy, called the Munich Agreement "a total and unmitigated defeat." The great majority of Americans are isolationists and want nothing to do with a war in Europe. President Roosevelt reads the room well and complies with popular opinion. In the fall of 1938, the ancestors of the majority of Americans were Western European, with a decent fraction from Eastern Europe, but the prevailing thought was that not again in this century would Americans fight on that continent. And Japan is only vaguely on their minds.

To most inhabitants of Lake Ozark and the surrounding area, the primary conflicts of immediate interest that fall were those the Osage High Indians basketball team engaged in. Conference games were usually held on Tuesday and Friday nights, and if at home or at nearby Eldon or Camdenton, there was considerable activity at the Whitehouse afterward. The soda fountain was popular, and many an ice cream soda or malt was consumed with two straws.

Donnie Fry, now a student at Southwest Missouri State University in Springfield, would drive to Lake Ozark on occasional weekends and help at the Whitehouse. Harold and Theora became quite fond of him and welcomed his help, as did Jessie.

Jessie and Lawrence hosted the Fry family Thanksgiving that fall at their new house on 1A, and Harold and Theora stopped in to say hello before going to Bagnell for the Robinson gathering. Donnie brought his mother from Springfield, and Harvey and Vivian came from Eldon, the latter now frequent visitors to the Whitehouse and friends of the Pilkingtons and Claytons.

At Christmas, Harold and Theora were back at the Robinsons' in Bagnell for the family dinner, with plans that Grant and Margaret would drive up to visit from Tulsa on the 26th. They had agreed to do so without Harry, as he was committed to work at the De Van Nursery through the holidays. Though the Christmas tree-selling season, a large part of their business, was over, there remained a lot of heavy lifting that needed to be done before the first of the year. Grant had obtained a promise from his youngest son that he would stay out of trouble, suggesting that Harry spend the time when he is off work with his girlfriend. "Less chance you'll get in trouble than when you hang out with your buddies," Grant told him.

The trip for Harold's mom and dad is a rare event. Neither had been more than an hour out of Tulsa in many years — Grant, not since his trip to Texas to retrieve his sons in '24;

Margaret, never. They make a few stops along the way out of curiosity — Margaret's.

From Joplin to Lebanon, where they get off Route 66 onto Highway 5, places selling oak and walnut bowls, boxes, odds, and ends catch her attention, and she insists Grant stop. At the final stop in Lebanon, she buys two walnut bowls, one for Theora and one for herself. Turning onto Highway 54 at Camdenton, their first view of the Lake is when they travel across the Glaize Arm on the Grand Glaize Bridge, referred to as "the upside-down bridge." It is impossible to see what makes it famous as you are crossing it, and if you do see it, you are on your way to the water yelling, "Help." It is best to buy a postcard later.

"Well, Uncle Grant, what do you think of the Whitehouse?" Jessie asks him on his first morning over coffee in the dining room.

"Damn near perfect, I'd say, Jess."

"Oh?"

"Well, you've got everything you need," Grant explains. "A bed, a bath, a liquor store, ice cream, and a big ole' room to dance in."

"A room to dance in?" Margaret interrupts, surprised. "When did you ever dance?"

"Dad, you forgot to mention fishing, just down the hill," Harold reminds him. "Marion's coming over with an extra rod in a bit, and we'll go down and try our luck."

"Fishing. That does it, son. I think you're living in heaven," Grant says.

"Oh, Margaret, I've got to show you what Harold bought me for our first anniversary," Theora says. "Don't let me forget when we go back upstairs."

"That reminds me," Margaret says as she reaches down and picks up a sack sitting on the floor by her chair and hands it to Theora. "This is for you."

"Oh, my. Margaret, what…"

"Take it out, Theora. I hope you like it." Theora does and immediately understands the craftsmanship in the beautiful walnut bowl she is holding. She understands it even more after having gotten to know Lon Stanton. He has helped her to understand and appreciate the blessing of Missouri's woodlands, with their old-growth oak walnut and cedar.

"I liked it so much I bought one for myself," Margaret says.

"I love it," Theora says. "Missouri Black Walnut. It's a beautiful wood. And a beautiful bowl. Thank you."

"Thanks, Mom, it's beautiful," Harold says.

"Margaret, grab your coffee cup and come upstairs with me," Theora says, getting up, still holding the bowl. "I can't wait to show you." Margaret does so, and the two women start up the stairs.

"Excuse me, too, gentlemen," Jessie says, getting up. "I need to speak to Maggie in the kitchen. Leave you two alone to catch up."

"You know, son," Grant begins after the women have left. "I'll have thirty years in at the Department next year. Thinking about retiring then."

"What'll you do? You've always been a cop."

"You remember that place we went to eat in Tulsa?" Grant asks.

"Willis Newton's?"

"That's it," Grant says. "Willis' place. He's been talking about selling and going back to Texas."

"What do you know about running a bar and grill, Dad?"

"What did you know about running this place before you got here?"

"I had Lawrence and Jessie to teach me," Harold says.

"Willis said he would stay on for a while till we get up to speed," Grant says.

"And Mom, what does she think about this?"

"You're gone. Harry's about raised. I think she likes the idea of something new to do. A challenge."

"And Newton?" Harold asks. "He'll wait on you?"

"We've discussed it. I'll officially retire in June, sell the house, and do the deal."

"Sell the house?"

"You don't remember," Grant says. "There are living quarters attached to the back of the place. It amounts to a small house. Plenty of room for when you come to visit."

"Well, if it's what you both want. As long as Mom's happy."

Upstairs, Theora ushers Margaret into a spare room housing some of Harold and Theora's things, including the cedar chest, and shows it to Margaret.

"It is so well-made, Theora," Margaret, amazed, says. "The varied colors in the wood are beautiful. Is this local wood?"

"Yes, the local cedar. Like you won't find anywhere else. And look inside." Theora opens the chest, and the pleasing aroma is still quite evident. "Unfinished. So, the natural smell remains."

"May I ask what the shoes are for?" Margaret queries.

"Well, Harold intended the chest as a place to store our memories, uh... mementos," Theora says. Margaret looks at her quizzically. "These are the shoes I wore when we got married."

"What if you want to wear them again?" Margaret asks.

"Then, I'll know where to find them," Theora explains. Margaret nods. "And I am going to place this special bowl you gave us here as well. And when I want to use it..."

"...You'll know where to find it," Margaret says.

Theora settles onto the floor next to the trunk, facing Margaret, who is sitting on the edge of the bed.

"Margaret," Theora starts quietly. "What happened between Grant and Virginia when the boys were little? Or do I have a right to ask?"

Margaret thinks for a moment, choosing her words carefully.

"I believe you have that right as someone who may be living with the consequences of it. And you are, aren't you?"

"The feeling of abandonment stays with Harold after all these years, I sense," Theora answers. "Make no mistake, Margaret. To Harold, you're his mom. Not only does he love you very much, he respects you very much. And he knows you love his dad."

"The only answer I can give you is what Grant has shared with me, and it is not much," Margaret says. "He believes that she was seeing Taft before he met me, but he didn't know it, didn't suspect it. They were having problems, money a part of it. Harold's polio added to the stress on the marriage. She found out he would stop by the shop and visit with me sometimes and accused him of having an affair with me." Margaret pauses a moment and looks directly at Theora. "But I can guarantee you that wasn't true."

"Relationships end, I understand that," Theora says. "It happens. But a mother and her children? You can't divorce that."

"Virginia is the only one who can explain that to you, Theora," Margaret says.

"Yes, I suppose."

"I will say this," Margaret offers. "I think she just couldn't be bothered with it. It was too damn much trouble for her."

Marion has come and met Grant and Harold, and the three men head down to the UE dock just below the

Whitehouse to fish the crappie bed. It's December, there's a nip in the air, and even though it's only 9:30 a.m., Harold has a "nip" in his coat pocket in the form of a pint of Jim Beam.

"You remember the worms, Marion?" Harold asks.

"Yeah, right here," he says. "You got the seasoning?"

"Right here," Harold says and takes out the bottle, opens it, takes a drink, and passes it to his dad. "Won't hurt you to drink after me and Marion, Dad. It's medicinal bourbon. Doc Attic says it kills germs while you're drinking it." Grant takes a strong drink and passes the bottle to Marion, who takes a drink and sprinkles a drop or two on the worm he has just put on his hook. He hands the bottle back to Harold, who also "seasons" his worm, and then hands the bottle to his dad, who takes a stiff drink.

"You boys aren't going to make a fool out of this old man with that silly 'season the worm' business," Grant says, and he puts a worm on his hook and lets his line down about eight feet. Within five minutes, Marion and Harold each have two very nice-sized crappies, and Grant hasn't had a nibble. When Marion hooks his third fish, Grant surrenders:

"Give me that damn bourbon bottle," he says, takes a drink, then dribbles some on the fresh worm on his hook.

By noon, the threesome has two full stringers of fish and plans a fish fry for the next evening at the Whitehouse. And they are out of "seasoning."

Grant and Margaret drive back to Tulsa on the 30th to avoid New Year's Eve Day traffic. They feel their trip was successful, including a visit with the Robinsons. Bert and Grant, both hard-working men with limited education, find common ground in common sense. Margaret and Lena share an innate understanding of motherhood. And there are no shopping stops on the return, which pleases Grant.

New Year's Eve, 1938, at the Whitehouse is very popular, partly attributable to the new band hired to play the event.

The Doerhoff Family Orchestra from Jefferson City is very attuned to the "big band" music that is popular and plays it well. Just before the beginning of the school year in September, the School of the Osage had purchased a new piano for the music department, and Jessie had purchased the old upright from them and had it moved to the Whitehouse dining room. Its first major use is for this particular evening.

Marion and Phyllis work alongside Harold, Theora, Jessie, Lawrence, and other staff to help make the evening a success. Two-year-old Ruthie plays in the kitchen, which she likes. The big news of the night is that Jay and Jo have slipped off to Oklahoma and gotten married, returning in time for New Year's. A toast to the couple is offered by the band during the night. Lawrence Quinn is with the Barkers, who are there, as has become customary in recent years. Even though young Harry and his mom stay till midnight, Harry finds a young lady to dance with. And at midnight, a year passes into history while a new one "rears its ugly head."

Unlike any other year in history, 1939 opens the entire world to a long ride on the road to what seems like hell for many. Germany invades Poland; Britain and France declare war on Germany. Mussolini in Italy joined his friend Adolph in the Fascist cause, and Japan, a member of what has come to be known as the "axis," continued to terrorize the Pacific Rim countries. For many decades to come, the world will be deeply affected by the events that are set in motion in the year we are now entering. Millions upon millions of people will die in Europe, the Soviet Union, China, Japan, and other parts of the world. And America again will give up many of its best and brightest to stop an insanity not of its making. If that's not a definition of hell, then it cannot be defined.

Though many in the local area may be nursing a hangover on this New Year's Day, 1939, not so for Harold and Theora. They are up early to take care of bus customers, having let all the staff off for the day.

Regardless of the day, the buses still run, and people still travel. And it's Sunday, and if Tony is on duty, the 7:30 bus from St. Louis will be on time, and the papers will be published, and Tony will have them.

Harold gets up early, comes down at six, turns on the coffeemaker, and walks over to the dining room while he waits for the coffee to brew. We left ourselves a pretty big mess to clean up. Still, he thinks as he looks in. They had decided to leave the work till the next day when they would be rested and made it to bed by 1:30 in the morning. Harold makes a note to reward himself with a nap later after the buses have come and gone and they have closed again. He heads back into the kitchen, pours a cup of coffee, walks to the front door, unlocks it, and steps out. A frost is evident everywhere he looks, but as the sun comes out, as predicted, it will be gone before Tony is back on the road. The parking area in front has little trash on it, as is often the case after a Saturday night—a testament to the nature of the customers who frequent the Whitehouse. Hearing Theora calling him, Harold reenters the building and goes to the kitchen.

"Just the sweet rolls, coffee, and juice, right?" Theora asks. "Is that what we decided to offer this morning?"

"Yes, that's it," Harold answers. "I'll turn on the oven to preheat."

Theora goes into the walk-in and retrieves a large tray of sweet rolls that Maggie has prepared in advance with attached baking instructions. She makes another trip and brings out the container of frosting that Maggie has also prepared.

"Cinnamon rolls, they do look good," Theora says as she places the baking tray in the oven, noting the time. "I woke up hungry this morning. Did you ever take time to eat last night?"

"Marion and I sat down in the kitchen about nine and shared a sandwich with Ruthie," Harold answers. "Did you?"

"No. I don't think Phyllis did either. When Phyllis took a breather, she was usually checking on Ruth."

"Little Ruthie did well; coloring her book seemed to keep her busy," Harold says, smiling. "Every time I'd come in the kitchen, she'd look up and giggle." Harold pauses, walks over to the back door, and looks out toward the lake. "Ever since I came here, Theora, I've saved a little money from every paycheck," he says.

"I know," Theora says. "I've saved some also."

"I understood from the beginning, I believe, that I was never going to be able to accomplish anything unless I could run my own business," Harold says. "Not just this business, but a business. When Jessie asked me to come here, she didn't offer me a job — she was offering me a future. It has never once occurred to me to go back to Tulsa."

"Have I told you lately that I'm glad you came?" Theora says as she walks over to him and touches his back. Harold turns around to face her. "And that you stayed." He kisses her.

"If this business can sustain a few grosses like we saw last night, we could do very well," Harold says. "What would you say to us talking to Lawrence and Jessie about buying the business?"

"You think they want out?" Theora asks.

"I've heard Jessie talk about wanting to have a baby, and Lawrence is so dedicated to his job, the Whitehouse is his afterthought. Lawrence is up by five and in the post office every morning before six, and Jessie wants to be home in the evenings to fix dinner and share it with him. I've heard her say so."

"Why don't you sit down with them and discuss it if you think there is interest?" Theora says.

"Why don't we do it together?" Harold says.

"Alright, together," Theora says. She glances at the clock. "I think the rolls are done."

Before Harold and Theora have an opportunity to speak with the Frys, sadness comes to the Whitehouse family. Fred Custer, Maggie's husband of nearly 47 years, dies quietly in his sleep. Maggie, of course, needs time off to take care of the necessities of his passing—funeral arrangements most prominent. The couple's grown son, an insurance salesman from Wichita, is of little help. He spends most of his time trying to convince his mother that she needs to sell the farm and move to town.

"Jessie, I don't want to move, and I want to continue to work," she tells her friend one day before the funeral when her son is not around. "But I may have to sell some of it. It'll be too much to manage without Fred's help."

"Maggie, don't worry about your job—it'll be there when you're ready to come back," Jessie tells her.

On the day of the funeral, friends and family gather at the farmhouse after the services, and as is the custom on such days, positive remembrances of the deceased are shared. The favorite is from one of Fred's old friends from youth, who recalled people constantly asking him if he was related to the General. "Old Fred would tell 'em, 'Yeah, he's a distant cousin of some kind, so's they tell me.' Well, one time this fella asks him who 'the hell is this Custa' fella you'se talkin' 'bout?' Old Fred looks at him and says: 'The dumb son-a-bitch went un got his self killed!'" Everybody within earshot laughs, including Jay Rice, until he sees Maggie looking at him, faking a frown his way. Jay hugs her before he leaves. Within a week, Maggie is back at work.

Harold and Theora finally get together one evening in mid-March with Lawrence and Jessie, and Harold opens the discussion with a simple, straightforward question. "Would you have any interest in selling the business to Theora and me?"

Jessie smiles broadly and looks at Lawrence, who nods at her. She looks at the Pilkingtons and says simply, "Yes."

"We've been thinking about the same thing recently," Lawrence says. "We had planned to discuss it with you."

"We're very happy you are interested," Jessie says.

"Harold, I think we can work out a contract with a very minimum down payment," Lawrence says. "I'm sure you don't have much money saved. And we'll set it up so payments can be based on your sales rather than a set figure. We'll carry the paper; you won't need to apply for a loan. Oh, and I talked with DeGraffenreid. The lease is transferable, and they'd be fine to work with you."

"We appreciate that," Harold says. "Do you have a sales price in mind?"

"I need to take some time to look at the books and do some figures, Harold, but I promise you it will be fair," Lawrence says.

"I appreciate that, Lawrence. And I appreciate all you have done for me since I've been here."

"There's something else, Harold," Jessie says. "You know how dedicated Lawrence has been to his responsibility as Postmaster. How it has limited his time to help with the Whitehouse. There's another issue, also."

"Is there a problem, Jessie?" Theora asks.

"No, no. We've been talking about starting a family," Jessie says, smiling.

"I know the Whitehouse is probably not the best place to raise a family," Theora says.

"You want to have a baby?" Harold says. "Good for you, Jess." He hugs her as soon as his wife has finished doing the same.

"So, you see, your timing could not be more perfect," Jessie says. "I may be even less available than before."

"I'll get the figures together in a few days, and we'll sit down and talk," Lawrence says.

"Great, thanks," Harold says.

As early spring comes in, and with it the little crocuses that seem to appear out of nowhere, a few day-trippers appear around Lake Ozark: sightseeing, browsing, anything that will cure "cabin fever." With them, Lon Stanton returns to his spot in front of the Whitehouse, hoping to pick up a little business to help make up for the slow winter. That first day back, he and Harold talked over a cup of coffee.

"Back in November, I bought a small piece of ground out alongside the highway and have been building a small building out there," Lon tells him. "It's been slow going — weather and all — but I hope to have it finished by mid-April."

"So, what are your plans?" Harold asks him.

"I'm setting it up so I've got space at the back for my shop — saws and all — where I can work," Lon explains. "But I'm making an area up front to display my things for sale, a retail space. That way, I can keep working when I don't have any customers."

"Makes perfect sense to me," Harold says. "When do you hope to be ready out there?"

"I think Easter weekend would probably be my last here if that's still alright?"

"Of course it is," Harold assures him. "We'll miss you. I know you've been good for our business."

"I hope I have; you've been good for mine. I appreciate everything you've done, Harold."

"When the time comes, and you want to do any whole-saling, I'll put up a table in the front inside with a few items for sale," Harold offers. "Small items, and if you have a brochure or business card, we'll put them on the table."

"I appreciate that," Lon says, finishing his coffee and shaking Harold's hand. "Right now, I better get back to it so I can pay for it all."

Maggie decides, going into spring, that now is when she needs to sell—if ever. Anyone buying would want to get a crop in the acreage, and plowing and planting can't wait. So, when a neighbor approaches her with an offer, she negotiates to sell 70 acres, keeping the house and barn and the five acres they sit on. Then, she makes arrangements for a farm sale at the property to sell her tractor, implements, tools, and other items of interest she no longer needs.

On the day of the sale, Harold and Marion go out to the farm to help her do the heavy lifting if needed, even though she has hired a local auctioneer with experience to conduct the sale. Halfway through, Harold is standing near the back of the crowd, and an older man standing next to him turns and introduces himself.

"You're Harold, aren't you? Harold Pilkington?" the man asks.

"Yessir, I am," Harold says, offering his hand to shake.

"I'm Morgan Crowder, one of Maggie and Fred's neighbors," he introduces himself and shakes Harold's hand. "Maggie always speaks high of you and your boss, Jessie."

"Nice to meet you, Mr. Crowder," Harold says. "I'll pass your kind thoughts along to Jessie."

"You know, Harold, there's only one thing sadder in a rural community than a funeral," Mr. Crowder ventures. "And make no mistake about it—this is still a rural community. We got our Dam, and we got our Lake, but at heart, we're still a rural community."

"Yessir, I think so," Harold agrees.

"One thing sadder," Crowder repeats. "A farm sale like this. Maggie will look out that front window for a long time to come, imagining Fred out there on his tractor. And when she walks into the barn after dark, she won't see that tractor stored there anymore. Won't see the tools that his hands took up to task with every day. When you have a farm sale, it's not about property — it's about a culture, one man's way of life."

"Our hope is that Maggie will do alright, sir," Harold says. "We'll certainly do our best to help her."

"I know you will, Harold." Crowder pauses. "You know what they say about a house — that it's not a home?"

"Yessir."

"Well," Crowder adds as he turns to leave, "a farm's not a farm without a farmer, either."

Easter Sunday, April 9th, there were several out-of-towners around the Lake Ozark area — a large number the entire weekend. Many were in occupancy at the cabin camp-style family resorts that were becoming more prevalent each year. A lot of the visitors were there to fish, particularly as the crappie were expected to be spawning. Clark Hale and other local guides would take the men and boys (mostly) out fishing while the women and girls browsed around town.

Theora did manage to get away from her work long enough to attend church services, still being held just up the street in the same empty storefront — but for the last time. The parishioners had been given notice a month before that the space had been leased to a permanent occupant. The congregation, which calls itself the Lake Ozark Christian Church, had appealed to the Frys to hold services in the dining room at the Whitehouse. As members of the Church, Lawrence and Jessie accommodated, and it was agreed that a service would be held at 11:30 a.m. after the last morning bus had come and gone. Their first service there would be the following week.

That same Sunday, the 9th, NBC radio broadcasts a concert by Marian Anderson on a stage constructed on the Lincoln Memorial. The event is arranged by Eleanor Roosevelt after the DAR turns down a request to allow the concert at Constitution Hall. It is reported that more than 75,000 people are in attendance. Subsequently, the First Lady resigns from the DAR.

Lon Stanton had one of his best weekends ever over the holiday, including taking deposits on three cedar chest orders and one for a walnut table. Of course, he sold a considerable number of smaller items. When you let a visitor get a whiff of the local cedar and tell them how much better their drawers will smell if they put a little piece of it in the drawers that hold them, they buy. Lon had taken to putting the cedar shavings — sawdust from the manufacturing process — into muslin bags, which a local woman had sewn up neatly for him to be sold as pet beds or a small one as a sachet for a drawer. Theora tells him that his "genius knows no bounds" — a phrase she read somewhere. When he loads up at the end of the day, he thanks Harold for the support and promises to stop in some mornings and have coffee with him.

The last week in April, on a Thursday, Theora is standing behind the counter at the soda fountain when a young girl of about eighteen — attractive, neatly dressed — enters and walks up to her.

"Are you Mrs. Fry?" she asks quietly.

"No, she's not here," Theora answers her. "May I help you with something? I'm Theora Pilkington. My husband, Harold, is the manager."

"I'm here to see about employment," the girl says. "I was hoping you might be hiring."

"Yes, we might. Let me get my husband, and we'll sit down and talk. Wait here, please." Theora goes into the kitchen, where Harold is stacking warm beer into the walk-in cooler.

"Harold, there's a young lady out front asking about employment. I think you should talk to her."

"Alright, good. I'll be right out," he says.

"We'll be in the dining room."

When Harold comes out of the kitchen, he grabs a quick 7-Up at the fountain and enters the dining room.

"Would you like something to drink, miss?" he asks the young girl before he sits down at the table with her and Theora.

"No, thank you, sir. I'm fine," she says.

"I'm Harold Pilkington. I manage the business here. You're interested in employment, I understand."

"Yes, sir. My name is Pauline Vaughn. I would like to work here."

"Do you have any experience, Miss Vaughn?" Theora asks.

"Not job experience, ma'am," Pauline explains. "I live on a farm and help my mother with my younger brothers and sisters. Help with cooking and cleaning—that sort of thing. When I'm not in school."

"I grew up in the city," Harold says. "One brother. My only job before I came here was delivering papers. You may have more experience than me."

"How many brothers and sisters do you have?" Theora asks.

Pauline smiles and laughs lightly. "I lost count. Momma, too, I think. Anyway, a whole bunch."

"You mentioned school?" Harold asks.

"I finish the Friday before Memorial Day. I can work weekends only until then. Afterward, every day, you need me." Pauline pauses. "Mr. Pilkington, I was told that you may be able to offer room and board with the job. Is that possible? I don't have a car."

"Yes, it is," he says.

"Harold and I live here," Theora says. "There are eight rooms on the second floor. We have two of them. One is reserved for Maggie, our cook, and one we use for storage. You would have your choice of one of the remaining four. There is, however, only one bathroom."

"That's better than at home," Pauline says.

"I'm sure you understand that with room and board, your salary would be a little less than otherwise," Harold explains. "There would be tips later, though," Theora says.

"We would start you in the kitchen with our cook," Harold says. "She's a farm girl too. You'll learn a lot from her."

"Mrs. Custer?" Pauline asks.

"Yes, you know her?" Theora answers with a question.

"Our farm is not far from hers. It was very sad about her husband passing."

"Yes, it was," Theora says. "But she's a strong lady."

"You willing to start the day after tomorrow?" Harold asks. "This Saturday?"

"Yes, sir!" Pauline says with a smile.

On the Friday evening before the Memorial Day weekend, Pauline Vaughn moves into a room on the second floor and becomes a part of the Whitehouse family.

Harold and Theora sit down with the Frys on June 1st and sign the papers transferring ownership of the Whitehouse business to them, following which they immediately go back to work. Jessie promises to be available to help whenever they need it. Theora has just turned 21 years old, and Harold is just short of his 24th birthday. And they just bought a business. To celebrate, the couple have a highball together that evening and begin to make plans for the future.

A few days later, Harold calls Grant and Margaret to tell them the good news, and he asks his dad about his retirement plans. The subject had not come up again anytime they had talked since the Christmas visit.

"I've decided to hold off into next year," Grant tells him. "Got a case that I've been working on for a long time now and would like to see it through."

"What about Willis?" Harold asks. "He still wants to sell?"

"I think he'll wait on me," Grant says. "Says he's in no hurry."

Since April 16, the parishioners of the First Christian Church of Lake Ozark have held services on Sundays in the dining room at the Whitehouse with hopes of having their own building one day. With that in mind, a committee is formed to look into the feasibility of that hope. Lawrence is made chairman of the committee because of his financial and business expertise, and Phyllis is selected secretary.

The space the church group formerly occupied opens with its new tenant, Overfelt's Grocery. A young man named Sam Overfelt and his wife and young son, Sammy, move to town and open their business, a competitor of Atterbury's Market, almost directly across the street. The town is, of course, "all abuzz" about the new place, concerned that the town can't support two grocery stores. Talk calms down some after Bernie Gordon speaks out, saying: "For several years, the Whitehouse Café, the Casino Restaurant, and Red Moore's all sold food, and all made a living. People eat a lot more meals at home than they do in restaurants. Two grocery stores should do just fine."

To add to this "boom" in business activity, a man named Frank Frudegar, along with his wife and teenage son, buys the small house next to Hale's cabin camp and begins building cottages to rent on the attached parcel. At the lakefront, he puts in a dock and adds a few fishing boats. Frank and Clark Hale get along fine, and there proves to be enough business to go around — which, considering the lake holds 650 billion gallons of water, means enough fish to go around also.

Harry, having graduated from Central High School at the end of May, continues working at the nursery, saving as much of his paycheck as possible. Toward the end of the summer, he and a friend buy an old but mechanically sound automobile and plan a trip to Texas. He is intent on going back to see the area he has mostly pleasant memories of — the place he and his brother were boarded during the breakup of his mother and father's marriage. The Newton place near San Antonio is still ranched by Jess and Joe, who will remember him and his brother and their stay with the family. They know that brothers Willis and Doc still keep in touch with the boys' dad in Tulsa. In fact, they are aware of the talk between Willis and Grant about the sale of the bar and grill.

Harry, a tall, strong young man at six feet, three inches, can certainly take care of himself in a fight but is not of the sort to go looking for trouble. His companion, Sonny, however, at 5'9", is the tough, scrappy sort who tends to lead with his mouth instead of his left or right. All goes well for several weeks until one night in San Antonio.

In Texas, though most counties are wet, it is illegal to drink if under the age of 21. Also, in most counties, if an 18-year-old wants to drink, he'll find a place to do it. One night, while hanging out with some of the hands from the Newton ranch, the boys are drinking in a bar on the edge of town. Harry, who is large, can hold quite a few beers, whereas Sonny, who can't, tries to keep pace with him. Consequently, Sonny's mouth springs a leak while he is conversing with a very large, muscular cowboy over the age-old question of who the better football team is — Oklahoma or Texas. It isn't long before Sonny is forced to continue the discussion from the floor, and Harry is obliged to defend his friend. His defense includes beating the fellow who attacked Sonny until he falls limp to the floor, whereupon several of the man's friends decide to come after Harry. One of Newton's hands grabs Harry and quickly escorts him out a back door.

"Come on, kid," the cowhand says. "I'm taking you to the bus station. You're headed back to Oklahoma."

"But I can't leave Sonny," Harry protests.

"Deputies arrive. They'll haul him in for disturbing the peace. Maybe a fine, couple of days in jail."

"But he didn't do anything," Harry protests. "I'm going back for him."

The cowhand stops him. "Listen to me, you dumb Okie. The way you beat that guy, his buddies will claim you tried to kill him. They might charge you with attempted murder. They ain't gonna come to Oklahoma looking for you, so I'm putting you on the first bus to the Oklahoma border."

"You sure he'll be alright?"

"Yes, he's got your car," the cowhand says. "When he gets out, he can drive home." The cowhand gets Harry on the midnight bus heading north, and with a couple of changes, he's back in Tulsa by noon the next day. Hoping that his dad is at work, he calls and asks Margaret to pick him up. All he tells her — and later, Grant — is that he decided to come home, but his friend wasn't ready.

As Harry's luck "wouldn't have it," Joe Newton calls Willis in Tulsa and tells him what happened and to check and see if the boy is alright. Willis, concerned, calls Grant.

"Willis Newton called me today," Grant says that evening at home in Harry and Margaret's presence. He looks at Harry. "Your buddy, Sonny, got a fine and three days in jail. Should be out tomorrow and on his way home."

"Did he say anything else?" Harry says an obviously worried look on his face.

"The fella you beat up is in serious condition but is expected to live. They're charging you with attempted murder."

"Dad, he was beating Sonny! Sonny didn't swing first. That guy started it!"

"And resisting arrest," Grant adds. "Look. Here's how this works."

Harry, incredulous, looks at his dad. "Are you going to turn me in?"

"No, of course not. You were defending your friend," Grant says. "They'll have somebody do a drawing of how the witnesses say you look, print up a poster, and circulate it — wait till you come back. Which you're not going to do."

"No, I'm not going back," Harry says adamantly.

"There's a thing called statute of limitations — usually seven years — but I'd wait longer if I were you."

"Yes, sir," Harry says.

"There's another thing — may help," Grant says. "They know your last name is Pilkington, and your dad is a Tulsa detective. They won't want to make me mad over a trumped-up charge."

"I appreciate it, Dad," Harry says.

"Well, appreciate this," Grant says, intending to end the discussion. "You need to find better friends before one of them gets you into real trouble. You understand?"

"I understand, sir."

Shortly after Sonny returns to Tulsa, Harry sells him his half of the car. That same day, Harry goes to the Tulsa Fire Department Administrative Offices downtown to get information on entering their Training Academy. In the evening, he discusses it with his dad, who is very favorable to the idea.

"You'll make a whole lot of better friends there," Grant tells him.

In July, Lawrence Fry's committee investigating possible new homes for the Lake Ozark Christian Church gives a report to church members at a meeting immediately after a Sunday service.

"There is a parcel of land available right on the highway just across from the school road that the owner is willing to sell," Lawrence tells the members present. "It's at the corner of 54 and Lake Road 1B."

"That's a good location, very convenient, nice piece of ground," are some of the positive comments heard coming from the gathering. Only one comment, though, truly reflected the bottom-line issue: "Can we afford it?"

"The owner wants $800 for the parcel," Lawrence tells them. "We give him 25% down — $200 — he'll carry the rest for one year.

Gotta pay the remaining $600 by the end of one year, or we lose it." Lawrence asks Phyllis, who is acting as church treasurer as well as committee secretary, to report on church finances.

"We average about $55 a week and pay the minister $15 a week, which is our only expense considering we have free meeting space — the cost of which has doubled since Harold and Theora have taken over the building's lease. It is now double zero."

"The reverend is our only current cost, netting us about $40 per week," Lawrence says. "Phyllis, what is our bank balance?"

"With today's contributions, and after the reverend was paid, we will be at about $317.50."

"Our committee has voted to approve the purchase and present it to the entire congregation for a vote right after next Sunday's service," Lawrence reports. "I would hope that all of you, regardless of how you feel, would encourage all to attend next week and vote. The committee believes this is a very doable purchase." With that, the gathering adjourned, some stating intentions to drive by the parcel on their way home.

The Sunday following a vote is taken, and the purchase is overwhelmingly approved and is expected to be paid off by year-end. A request for plans and costs of a building will be given to local contractors per committee specs in January in hopes the congregation will be able to build their first real home.

On September 1st, Germany and the Soviet Union invaded Poland, marking the beginning of World War II. On September 3rd, Britain and France declare war on Germany. Prime Minister Neville Chamberlain appointed Winston Churchill as First Lord of the Admiralty — his first time in the government since June 1929. President Roosevelt stated that every effort would be made to keep the United States neutral, and on September 5th officially declared the country's neutrality.

In mid-September, Harold takes a drive out the highway to visit with Lon Stanton at his new place. The building is humble, but a large sign announces "Cedar-Craft Novelties." Lon is working in the back when Harold enters, so he steps back to the shop. As soon as he does, he hears the sound of two more cars pulling into the parking lot. They say activity breeds activity in business, and that appears to be the case at the moment, Harold thinks. Lon, who is busy on one of his saws, doesn't hear him.

"Lon, you got business! Hey!" Lon looks up, acknowledges Harold, and turns off the saw.

"Hey, Harold. Come on in."

"I think a couple of cars pulled in behind me — you may have some real customers out front," Harold says.

"Good, it's been kind of slow today." The two men walk to the front of the shop, where two elderly couples browse the items on display there.

"If I can help you, let me know," Lon says to the customers, who all respond, "Just looking, thank you."

"How's this working out for you?" Harold asks.

"It's not bad. Allows me to continue working when I'm not out here selling something." Lon pauses. "The key for me is to be able to produce in quantity and sell wholesale in large quantities — to places like yours or all over. The only way I'll ever be able to make a good living out of this."

"I think you'll get that done someday," Harold says.

"Come here a moment." Lon walks to the front of the building and looks out across the roadway; Harold follows him. "Directly across the road there, down the hill. There's a parcel — several acres, not much for farming, all woods. I'm looking to buy it. Cheap."

"You have to build a road in then?" Harold asks.

"Yeah, about a half-mile to get to some level ground," Lon says. "There's a little creek that runs through it there. Great spot to build my factory."

"You'll get it done too, won't you?"

"Yeah," Lon says. "I'll get it done."

Harold shakes Lon's hand. "I best be going before Theora fires me."

"Just think, Harold. Someday, our kids will be sledding in the snow down that hill. Safe, away from the highway."

Harold laughs. "We have to have some kids first." Lon chuckles with him.

Now that the busy summer has passed at the Whitehouse, Pauline is a seasoned veteran and can fill in for Maggie in the kitchen when needed. She knows the soda fountain well, but because of her age — though she can serve set-ups — she can't serve beer. Therefore, except for Sundays, Harold or Theora, Marion or Phyllis, and sometimes Jessie need to be in-house when the business is open. Pauline has begun attending church services with the others in the dining room on Sundays while Harold takes care of any customers that may appear during that hour. Although Marion has offered, Harold is happy to cover during the service, saying Marion needs time with the Lord more than he does.

In August, showing signs of maturity, and much to the relief of Grant and Margaret, Harry applies for and is accepted into the Firefighter's Academy in Tulsa. Not unlike many young men of his generation, he knows there is the possibility of war in the future, regardless of the President's public statements. His plan is to finish training, work through his probationary period with the Department, and, should war become a reality, take a leave and join the Coast Guard. He shares his plan with Maxine Stewart, his longtime girlfriend, whose only question is: "Where do I fit in this plan?"

"After I finish basic training in the Coast Guard, we'll get married, and you'll go with me to my assignment," Harry assures her. "Duty stations are all stateside, so we'll find a place to live in my homeport."

"I like the plan better if you don't go in the Coast Guard," Maxine tells him.

"But it could be an adventure, a chance to see a different part of the country," Harry assures her.

"Like going to Texas?" Maxine says.

"No, you know what I mean. You'll be with me."

"Well, we'll see what comes," Maxine says.

"If there is no Coast Guard, then we'll settle in here," Harry assures her. "The Fire Department can be a good career."

In the fall, Marion continues his work hauling ice for Jonesy and fills in at the Whitehouse when needed. Phyllis occasionally helps Red and Carrie at the gift shop and also fills in at the Whitehouse when needed. Jessie has yet to become pregnant, and there is unspoken disappointment. There have been hopes of the prospect of a new playmate for Ruthie, who, by the way, is doing quite well, thank you. Always smiling, she never seems to get frustrated when taking on a new task and experiencing a setback. She just tries it again.

Sometimes at night, when her mother is putting her to bed, and she is saying her prayers, she asks God for a sister and, after saying "amen," looks at her mother.

"Will God give me a sister, Momma? I want a sister very much."

"I don't know, sweetheart," Phyllis says. "It is up to God, and only He knows what the future holds for us. Your momma and daddy would like that too—a sister for you."

"I will pray for it, okay?"

"Yes, continue to pray, but right now, you need to get to sleep."

"Goodnight, Mommy," Ruthie says.

Phyllis listens at the door for a few moments when she leaves Ruthie's room and hears her say another prayer for her sister, then silence as if she is waiting for an answer. She and Marion have discussed having another child on occasion since Phyllis returned from Chicago, but the discussion is always tabled. Phyllis swears she will never go through an experience like that again; will not watch another child in pain and separated from its mother. Marion understands and shares her fears but wishes it could be different.

Then, in early November, Jessie tells Harold and Theora that she is pregnant and that it is okay to tell others, so it is not long before Marion, Phyllis, and others know. There is much delight in the good news for Lawrence and Jessie, while at the same time, there is unspoken apprehension within the Lake Ozark family. Ever since Ruthie's birth, there has been a tendency to show subdued excitement in such matters.

"We leave it to God, now," a local said as if it had been left to someone else before.

Theora and Harold host the Robinson family at the Whitehouse on Thanksgiving, and the Haages come from Kansas to see everyone. George and Dorothy Haage's count is now at five, Margaret being the youngest. Robinson brothers Clyde and George and their wives are there also. Only Frieda is missing, but she calls during the afternoon and talks to almost everybody. All are excited about her latest child, also named Margaret. The call ends when Babe reminds her about how expensive a long-distance call is. Bert finds that humorous; Lena doesn't.

After dinner, which is preceded by one of the longest prayers ever offered prior to a meal, the men settle in over coffee while the ladies clean up the dishes. Talk drifts toward politics and potential war. The Robinson family has, for several years, considered themselves New Deal Democrats—supporters of Roosevelt's efforts to bring America out of the Depression. They are equally favorable to Harry Truman, senator from Missouri, because of his straight-talking ways. George Robinson and brother Clyde are acorns from Bert's tree, and Phyllis and Theora appear to toe the Democratic line as well. Marion leans toward the Republican point of view, probably as a reflection of his southern Illinois roots. Harold remains nonverbal on many of the political issues of the day, choosing to listen for the most part.

"In eastern Kansas, most people don't want anything to do with a war in Europe again," George Haage offers. "Their politics are probably going to lean in his direction as long as Roosevelt keeps us out of it." He pauses and looks at Bert. "Bert and I are too old for it, but not the rest of you. I have sons, too young now, but war is always in your mind if you have sons."

"Well, the Brits are in it now, and their guy Churchill told them years ago that it was going to happen," George Robinson says. "And they didn't listen to him."

"Harry Truman believes it's coming, and we'd better get ready," Clyde says. "And I believe Harry's right."

"Knowing the way Roosevelt operates, he's probably getting ready for it behind the country's back right now," Marion says. "Well, better than getting caught with your pants down," Clyde says.

"Don't worry, Marion," George Robinson says with a laugh. "Miller is predominantly a Republican county. You're safe here."

"I feel safer already," Marion says as he gets up. "But I'm going to have a shot to go with my coffee, just in case."

"Good idea, Marion," Harold says. "Bring that bottle over here to the table."

"Where do you stand on all this, Harold?" George Haage asks.

"Well, I have a wife and a business to think about, and I don't want a war. But if, or when, it happens, we'll do what we have to do, I guess. That's all I know."

Business is brisk on the Saturday night of Thanksgiving weekend, and the big news is the wedding ring on Virginia Barker's finger. She and Lawrence had gotten married the weekend before in Kansas City and were home sharing the news with the Quinn family and friends. A toast is offered from the bandstand during a break, followed by a big round of applause. The couple plan to reside in Kansas City, where Lawrence has taken a job, but everybody expects that sooner or later, they'll be back at the Lake.

In mid-December, Hollywood premieres *Gone with the Wind*, a film based on a popular book that came out in 1936. The premiere is held in Atlanta — a town that is burned to the ground in the movie. Fortunately, for those attending the premiere, the town has been rebuilt. The film, lasting nearly four hours, is mostly about a war that lasted four years. Some say it never ended.

Late afternoon on New Year's Eve, Lon Stanton stops in at the Whitehouse. He has come to have an early dinner and visit with Harold. Hearing the door chime, Pauline comes out of the kitchen.

"May I help you?" she asks in her quiet, polite way.

Lon, who is preoccupied looking around the room for Harold, reacts to her voice. "Is… Oh, uh, hi," is all Lon gets out, taking note of the pretty young lady who is standing there behind the counter. He walks over and sits down. "Yes, thank you, miss. I'm going to have some dinner."

"Let me get you a menu, sir," Pauline says.

"Do you still have that roast beef dinner with the potatoes and gravy?"

"Yes, we do."

"I'll have that and a beer," Lon says decisively. "Is Harold around?"

"Yes, sir, he is," Pauline says, setting a glass of water down in front of Lon. "I'll get him for you. He has to serve your beer." Pauline places silverware on the counter for Lon and goes into the kitchen. Lon watches her go.

Momentarily, Harold comes out of the kitchen and greets Lon. "Hey, stranger, been a while. What kind of beer do you want?"

"How about a GB," Lon says. "Griesedieck Brothers. Two things the Germans are good at. Making war and making beer."

"You staying busy?" Harold asks as he sets the beer down on the counter.

"Not selling much, just building inventory right now. I did go ahead and make a deal on that land, but it's going to be a while before I can do anything with it."

"Well, one step at a time, right?"

"That's about right," Lon says, taking a sip of his beer.

Pauline comes out of the kitchen with the dinner plate and another with two rolls. "I'll bring butter for your rolls, sir." She goes back to the kitchen.

"New girl, Harold?" Lon asks.

"New in June," Harold says. "But you'd know that if you stopped in more often."

Pauline reappears with butter for Lon. "Anything else I can get for you right now, sir?"

"No, miss. This is fine, thank you."

"Well, I'll leave you two gentlemen to visit then," Pauline says and goes back into the kitchen.

"New from where Harold?" Lon asks.

"Farm girl from up near Eldon," Harold says, smiling. "Her name's Pauline Vaughn."

"She's a good waitress, Harold. And the food's good. I'll try to come in more often."

Harold laughs. "I'm sure you will," he says.

New Year's Eve 1939 at the Whitehouse is not unlike those of the recent past. Always there is talk of the music; what's new, what's old but good. Glenn Miller's band is becoming more and more popular and is always much requested by the band playing for the night. There is one difference, though, as war seems to be a floating topic among the group, more so than in any previous year.

About an hour before closing, a near tragedy is averted and robs the staff of any semblance of cheerfulness they may have had regarding the coming new year. The cook on duty, work caught up, momentarily leaves the kitchen to go to the bathroom. Theora has come from the dining room, a tray of dirty dishes in hand when she suddenly pauses at the door to the kitchen. Harold, who is close behind her, sees her hesitate.

"I smell smoke, Harold," Theora says as she reaches for the door with her free hand.

Harold suddenly realizes what is happening and yells at her, "Don't open that door!" Theora stops and backs up.

"Theora, back away from the door and get away from it. Move to one side. Don't let anyone near it." Harold quickly goes to the fountain, grabs it, and wets down a bar towel. Moving back to the kitchen door, he wraps the towel loosely around his right hand and slowly touches the door at different spots with his left hand. Convinced that the heat is minimal, he slowly opens the door a bit, releasing some smoke. As there appear to be no flare-ups, he slowly opens the door and moves into the kitchen, holding the wet towel to his face, covering his nose and mouth. He quickly locates the source of the fire in a trash can that holds only paper items. He throws the wet towel on top of it, draws a large pan of water from the nearby faucet, and drenches the fire. The fire is soon out. It was only smoldering, but if unattended, it could easily have become fully enveloped and a serious danger to the wooden two-story structure that is the Whitehouse.

Harold sits at the kitchen table, relieved. "It's ok now, Theora. The fire's out."

Theora slowly enters the kitchen, sees the trash can where the fire had been, and sits down at the table with Harold.

"Some son-of-a-bitch must have put out a cigarette on a plate and left a crumbled-up paper napkin on top of it," Harold says, attempting to understand what has happened. "And we accidentally scraped it out in the paper bin." He looks over at Theora, who has quietly started to cry. "Theora, what's the matter? Are you okay?"

"Fire scares me," she says. "I hate it so."

Phyllis comes into the kitchen and sees Theora crying and Harold sitting with her. "Theora, what... Harold, what's the matter?"

"There was a fire in the paper waste, and I think it scared Theora," Harold tells her.

Phyllis seems to understand and walks over to stand behind her sister, placing her hands on Theora's shoulders. "Just put it out of your mind, Theora," she says. "Just think past it."

On New Year's Day, Harold calls home to wish Grant and Margaret a Happy New Year and tells them about the fire scare the night before. Margaret tells him that Harry, who has completed Fire Academy training and graduated just before Christmas, would have been helpful, which makes Harold laugh at the thought. Harry has been assigned to a nearby station to work during his probationary period, Margaret says, and Harold should be proud. He begins his work there the next day, January 2nd.

"I am proud, Mom. Let me talk to him," Harold says. "I want to congratulate him."

"Well, he and Maxine partied last night, and he's still in bed," she says. "And he hasn't been there that long."

"Well, I'll catch him another time then," Harold says. "How about you and Dad? Did you go out dancing last night?"

"Don't speak sacrilege now, son," she says, and Harold laughs. "He did take me out to dinner, though. Had a nice steak dinner at a fancy place. Back home and in bed by ten."

"Well, okay then, great. Gotta go. Love you, Mom."

"Love you too, son," she says. "Love to Theora too," she says just before hanging up.

One morning in mid-January, Marion and Harold are sitting in the dining room having coffee before Marion starts his job at the ice house.

"You heard anything about Union Electric doing some hiring down at the power plant, Harold?" Marion asks him.

"No, not a thing," Harold answers. "You talk to Jay? Maybe he knows something."

"Called him last night. He said there are rumors floating around that they're thinking about security. But nothing definite."

"Security?" Harold questions. "They afraid of sabotage, you think?"

"Don't know," Marion says. "But they keep in close touch with the government because of their importance as part of the electrical grid. All I know is they know more than we do."

"Everything I hear is that the military is rebuilding and has been since Roosevelt came into office in '33. New ships, new weapons. A slow buildup. That's what I read in the papers."

"I do think he's serious about keeping us out of the war in Europe," Marion says.

"Yes, but it appears he's doing it while quietly making sure we have what we need in case that changes," Harold says.

"Well, if UE is hiring security guards, I'm going to look into it and maybe apply," Marion says. "UE pays well."

"That's what I hear," Harold says.

Not long after their early morning talk, Marion applies for and is hired as a security guard at the dam and power plant facility. It will provide a steady schedule and paycheck that has been missing since Red's restaurant burned. He will have some overnight shifts, not unwelcome, as he realizes the importance of the job. He's especially excited about the prospect of keeping people from fishing "above the line." It is an issue close to his heart, as Harold is quick to remind him.

Lon has managed to stop by the Whitehouse a few times since New Year's Eve Day, once for dinner and on two occasions for early coffee. Each time, he is waited on by Pauline and visits with Harold. Then, on one occasion in mid-April, Harold is not in, and Lon visits with Pauline.

"Would you like to go out sometime?" Lon asks in a very straightforward manner. "Maybe a movie or something?"

Pauline is not surprised. She has come to realize that Lon may be interested in more than the Whitehouse's food. "You don't seem like the movie type of guy," Pauline says in response. "More the 'or something' kind of guy."

"Do you like to eat?" Lon asks.

"Well, yes," Pauline answers as if he has asked an inane question.

"How about you make us lunch one day when you're off, and we'll go to the state park and picnic?" Lon says. "I'll pay for the lunch."

"I'm off next Tuesday," Pauline says.

"Pick you up at noon?"

"Yes. What would you like to eat? For the picnic, I mean?"

"Surprise me," Lon says.

Grant calls Harold in April to tell him that he will officially retire on June 1 and that he and Willis have agreed to terms on the purchase of the Bar and Grill. He and Margaret will wait to close on the sale before putting their house on the market, Grant tells Harold. However, they plan to put out the word that it may be available soon.

"Will there be a party, retirement ceremony, anything like that?" Harold asks his dad.

"Just something brief at city hall, probably," Grant says. "Maybe some of the guys will gather at a local bar near downtown after the ceremony. Nothing big."

"Maybe Theora and I can make it to Tulsa for that, Dad," Harold says. "Can't promise, but we'll try."

"You don't need to do that, son. It's just another day."

"Thirty-one years, Dad," Harold says. "It's not just another day. You've been a cop since before I was born. I'm curious to see what you look like when you're not one."

"Alright, Margaret will call and let you know the plans."

Lon arrives to pick up Pauline on the preplanned Tuesday. She is carrying a large basket and a plastic checkered tablecloth.

"That's a big basket," Lon remarks as they get in his truck. "What did you make?"

"It's a surprise. Maggie helped me, so it should be good."

"Maggie's a good cook," Lon says. "I know that."

"The tablecloth was her idea. She found it stuffed away in the back of the storage room."

The drive to the state park isn't long: a few miles out to a left turn onto Highway 42, then a few short miles to the park turnoff. The day is sunny and warmish for a mid-April day, with no showers in sight. The redbuds have been flowering for several days now, and the dogwoods are coming in right behind them. Though the majority of the Missouri woods are mostly leafless at this time of year, it helps to make the two flowering trees, with their mixed blossoms of white and purplish-rose, dominate the forest. To a native Missourian, there is no more beautiful sight than this.

The couple finds a nice table near the edge of a heavily wooded area but still in sight of the lake. Though mid-week, the mild, sunny weather has brought out a number of folks who have also come to enjoy the rustic park. Pauline spreads the tablecloth out and begins to unburden the basket. First, the two ham and cheese sandwiches with mayonnaise, lettuce, and tomato. Then, the potato salad.

"Maggie made the potato salad," Pauline says as she sets out two heavy paper plates, real silverware, paper napkins, and a serving spoon for the potato salad. Then, she takes out a canning jar filled with medium-sized dill pickles. "These my momma and I pickled and canned just last fall." She lays out an extra fork to use for the pickles. Finally, she reaches into the basket and takes out a sizable container of iced lemonade and two paper cups. "The lemonade I made. And the sandwiches."

This is a great spread, Lon thinks to himself. "That looks great, Pauline. Can we eat? You're making me hungry."

"Sure can," she says. "Hand me your plate, and I'll serve your sandwich and some potato salad. Do you want a pickle?"

"I want it all," Lon says. "I love homemade pickles; sweet, dill, it doesn't matter."

The couple settles in and makes small talk while they eat.

"When the alphabet boys…that's what I call them, 'cause I can't remember whether it was WPA or CCC or whatever…CCC, I think," Lon tells Pauline. "When they first started building out here, clearing land, I would come out and ask them what kind of wood they were going to burn, and if there was any good walnut or red cedar or anything I thought I could use, I would ask them if I could have it."

"And were you able to make use of it?" Pauline asks.

"Yes. They usually would give it to me. A couple of foremen, I would have to slip a few bucks to, but most would just say, 'Yes, take what you need.'"

"So, you work mostly with walnut and cedar?" Pauline asks.

"Cedar mostly," Lon says. "If I find walnut already down or soon to come down due to age, I'll use it or save it. But I hate to cut a walnut tree."

"We have a couple on our farm," Pauline shares. "My brothers and sister and I would shell the nuts, pick out the meat, and save it. We would eat a bit along the way, but we wanted the nuts to last through the winter. At Christmas, when momma made cookies, they almost all had black walnuts in them. They taste better than any nut."

"And it took forever to get the stain off your hands," Lon says, laughing.

"It's the price we had to pay," Pauline says, laughing with him.

"You see that big white oak over there?" Lon asks, pointing to a large tree not far away. "The big one right behind that picnic table?"

"I see it," Pauline says.

"Some people like to use that wood for furniture," Lon says. "Good hardwood. You can take that shell from the walnut and rub it on a fresh-cut white oak board. It acts just like a stain. Like you were putting on a stain. Let it dry. Maybe another coat. Have to make sure you get it even, though."

"Your sandwich, okay?" Pauline asks.

"It's great! I just got to talking so much that I was forgetting to eat. I'll do less talking and more eating. I'd even take another pickle if that's okay."

"Sure, here, I'll get it for you," Pauline says. "I like hearing you talk about the trees, the wood. You obviously love it. The woodwork."

"I respect it," Lon says. "God gave us a wonderful renewable resource when he gave us trees. We need to honor that by replanting twice what we cut and use. And I'll never cut a redbud or dogwood."

"Without them, a day like today wouldn't be nearly as special."

"You know something else?" Lon says. "That's good potato salad. You should get Maggie's recipe."

"Why?" Pauline asks quizzically. "You think I'll need it?"

"You never know," Lon says, smiling.

One weekday night in early May, with Phyllis and Jessie covering, Harold and Theora go to the Eldon Theater to see the movie *Jesse James*. Released in late January 1939, it has become the third highest-grossing film of that year. It has taken its time getting to the small-town theaters because the majority of its prints are still in demand in the major cities. During the showing, Theora, among others, reacts out loud during the scene of the cowboy and horse falling off Lovers' Leap.

"That's it, Harold! That's Lovers' Leap," she says.

"I know, Theora. I see it. Sssh. Quiet."

"Don't you remember?" Theora asks. "It's where you proposed."

"No, not that Lovers' Leap," Harold corrects. "It was the other one, farther out on HH."

"You're right. I was just testing you."

Harold turns to look at Theora. "Women," he mutters to himself.

"Regardless, we'll tell everybody that it was the one in the picture," Theora says.

"Great. You want to shake on it?"

"Enough," she says. "Shut up and watch the movie."

"Randolph Scott is sure good in the movie, don't you think?" Harold says in a statement, not a question.

On May 10th, in London, Chamberlain resigned, and Winston Churchill became Prime Minister of the United Kingdom. On May 13th, he tells the House of Commons in a speech that "I have nothing to offer you but blood, toil, tears, and sweat." The consensus is that the Roosevelt administration is quietly relieved.

The women of the United States are soon pleased, as well. On May 15th, nylon stockings are sold in the country for the first time. It is reported that millions of pairs are sold on the first day. Later, during the War, along with chocolate bars,

G.I.s on a pass in Paris will find that a pair of stockings is invaluable.

British and French troops fighting on the mainland of Europe suffer defeats and are soon stranded with their backs to the sea at Dunkirk, France. They are potentially doomed until, beginning on May 26th, a flotilla of navy ships supported by civilian boats of all sizes begins to evacuate the soldiers. The process continues until June 4th, when the last of them are brought over. A total of more than 300,000 troops are rescued, essentially the difference between Britain having an army or not.

That same day in June, Churchill tells the House of Commons: "We shall not flag or fail. We shall fight on the beaches…on the landing grounds…in the fields, and in the streets…We shall never surrender."

With the Memorial Day weekend holiday over on Monday, the 27th of May, Harold and Theora make plans to drive to Tulsa on the 30th. Grant's retirement is planned for noon on Friday the 31st, his last day. They plan to stay and drive back on Sunday.

Again, Phyllis, Jessie, and Lawrence, with help from Marion in time away from his new job, cover for the Pilkingtons. Everyone seems to understand how important it is for Harold to be there and tries to do what they can so he can attend.

The ceremony at City Hall is brief, with a representative of the mayor in attendance, but not the mayor. The Chief of Police makes a brief speech, and a few of Grant's fellow department veterans tell stories. Grant smiles a lot and laughs some, but Harold thinks he just wants to get it over with. Margaret doesn't think that; she knows it. Harry has managed to arrange his schedule to be in attendance as well, and having both his sons there, along with Theora and Maxine, means more to Grant than anything.

After promising to meet some of his now former crew for drinks later at a local bar, Grant and his family leave and go to lunch at a nice downtown restaurant. During lunch, Harry comments that the ceremony seemed somewhat "blunt," considering Grant was the first chief of detectives in department history.

"To the city fathers, I represent the 'old guard' in the department ranks," Grant tells his family. "I remind them of the city's guilt. The sooner they can retire my generation— in the fire department, too, Harry—the sooner the '21 riot is lost in the past." "All these years, that still with you, Dad?" Harold asks.

"No place for it to go," Grant says. "Some things can't be left behind." He pauses and looks around the table at his family. "After lunch, we'll take the girls home, and then I want to take you boys for a drive."

Lunch completed and the ladies delivered home, Grant drives back downtown and pulls into a shanty-like old house near what was once the prosperous Greenwood area. Grant gets out of the car, telling his boys, "Come with me. There's someone I want you to meet." The three, led by Grant, walk across a roughly kept front yard and around the side of the house into the back yard. Situated at the very back is a large brick oven. Light smoke emerges from a chimney on top, and a tall stack of firewood sits beside it. On top, a wooden sign says, "Johnny's Smoked Meats." At the back of the house is a porch with an elderly black man sitting in a swing, moving slightly back and forth. Grant speaks to him.

"Mr. Boyd, you can't get any cooking done sitting on your backside."

"All I do, Mr. Grant, is light the fire. God takes care of the rest." Boyd rises from the swing, and as he does, Grant's sons react nonverbally, suddenly stopping where they are.

"These your sons, Mr. Grant? I don't believe they've ever seen a one-eared man before."

"You are their first, sir," Grant says as he reaches out and shakes Boyd's hand. "Try not to scare them."

"Your brisket's done, Mr. Grant. The ribs need about thirty more minutes. You can't rush God's work, so why don't you all grab a seat?"

They all settle in on the porch, and it's obvious to everyone that the boys can't take their eyes off Mr. Boyd's head.

"The short one there is my oldest, Harold," Grant says. "Lives in Missouri. The tall one is Harry. He just started with the Tulsa Fire Department. Boys, say hello to the best cook in Oklahoma, Johnny Boyd." Harold and Harry give a nod to Johnny.

"Word got around that you were retiring today, Grant," Johnny says. "Lot of bad guys happier now, I bet."

"Not any happier than the boys downtown. They were glad to put me to pasture."

Johnny turns to speak to the boys. "Your dad has a reputation for speaking his mind."

"The first morning after the riot, dawn, when I and the other officers first came back on the street," Grant begins, "We were told to arrest every black, no matter if they weren't doing anything. Some were still holding spots in what was left of some building or other and shooting at the white boys, setting fire to everything. But most were just protecting what little was left of their lives."

"They weren't arresting any white boys, that's for sure," Johnny Boyd says. "I had a very successful restaurant in the community. Everybody in Greenwood would eat there at some point. Then, that night, these three white boys came along and set my place on fire. I tried to stop them, and they grabbed me. One of them says to the other two, 'Hold 'em, I'm gonna cut his ear off.' And that's what they did."

"Why didn't they kill you, Mr. Boyd?" Harry asks.

"They can't humiliate a dead man, son," he answers. "Alive, they could drive by me anytime and brag to others what they done."

"The first person I saw when I entered Greenwood that morning was Mr. Boyd," Grant says. "He was leaning against the burnt-out wall of his building, in shock, I believe. The side of his head was bleeding. He kept repeating, 'They cut my ear, they cut my ear,' but I didn't know what he meant until I got the bleeding stopped and saw it."

"This other sergeant came by and saw us and told Sergeant Grant to put me in handcuffs, arrest me, and move on. Your dad yelled back at him, 'This man doesn't need arrested. He needs a doctor, and get the hell out of my face.'"

"I moved him around to the alley side of the building and told him to tell any other cop who came by that I said to leave him be. Then, I went to find the three guys. When I did and put them under arrest, my precinct commander came by and ordered me to release them. That we weren't arresting whites, only blacks. We had an argument, and I ended up looking for a doctor among the blacks they'd rounded up. When I found one, I took the cuffs off him and took him back to help Johnny."

"Later on, days later, after things cooled down a little, your dad had me point them boys out to him. He wanted to make sure he knew exactly who did this."

"I couldn't arrest them then, but I knew that sooner or later, they would break the law again," Grant says. "Men like that. They can't not do it."

"Did they, Dad?" Harold asks. "Did you catch up to them?"

"A year or so later, two of them robbed a local grocery and shot a clerk. He lived and testified against them, and we put them away in the state pen."

"And the other one, Dad?" Harry asks. "Get him, too?"

"He got in a fight in a bar one night," Grant says. "Shot the other fellow, and we put him away for manslaughter."

"He didn't serve out his sentence, though," Johnny says, smiling slightly.

"He was the one that actually cut Mr. Boyd's ear off," Grant says, smiling with him. "There was some Osage and Cherokee in that penitentiary, and they knew what he had done. One night, they got him down and scalped him. Must have cut pretty deep 'cause he bled out before help could get to him."

"You know, those Indians are minorities, too," Johnny says. "They're from the civilized tribes. Most didn't like what happened that night in '21."

"Boys, there was a time back before this country became a state. Back in Indian Territory, back in Oklahoma Territory, when the black man and the Indian and the white man got along fine. And then, along came oil and land grabbing and statehood."

Mr. Johnny Boyd finishes for Grant: "And greed and envy. Some men just can't live without another to be superior to." He gets up from the swing, goes to the smoker, opens it, looks in, and takes his long-handled fork to turn two slabs of ribs. "Those ribs are ready. I'll get them wrapped up to go for you. Get the brisket, too."

"Don't forget some of your sauce, Mr. Boyd," Grant says.

"All ready to go." Johnny looks at Harry. "Son, grab that can there, the one with the paper and rubber band around it. Don't spill it. That's got your sauce." To Grant: "How many of you for dinner? Six, you said?"

"Six it is, Mr. Boyd," Grant says.

"I'm sending along some baked beans with you, Mr. Grant. That other can there, Mr. Harold, that's got the beans.

Just grab that paper bag and put your two cans in that to carry." Johnny wraps the two rib slabs in brown paper and then newspaper. He mumbles something about finding a good use for the Tribune and puts the ribs and the pre-wrapped brisket in another paper bag. "Here you are, all set to go."

Grant pays Mr. Boyd, adding a little extra. His sons shake his hand, saying they are proud to have met him, and the three Pilkingtons, food in hand, walk back around to the front of the house and leave.

The three men don't drive far, Grant telling them he promised they would stop in at a local bar at five and have a beer with some of his now former officers. They are mostly quiet on the short drive to the bar, a favorite hangout of cops, and its closeness to the station house, making it probable cause. Inside, a small group of officers has already gathered, and there are introductions all around. Most know that Grant has a son, the tall one, who is a fireman.

"Grant, we're not gonna give your fireman son a rough time," one officer says. "He's too big to mess with."

"It's the short one you gotta worry about," Grant says.

Harold laughs. "I don't mess with the tall one," he says.

A man taps Grant on the shoulder from behind. He turns around and immediately recognizes an old friend.

"Murphy, you son-of-a-bitch! How in the hell are you?"

"Well, word got around they were throwing you to the curb, and I wanted to be here to cheer," Murphy says. "Here, got you boys a beer." Murphy hands each of them a bottle and taps them lightly. "To a long, peaceful retirement," he toasts.

"You boys remember Ryan Murphy, my old boss?"

"Nice to see you, Captain Murphy," Harold says, shaking his hand.

"Good to see you, sir," Harry says.

"Murph retired three years ago," Grant says. "I haven't seen him since. Where you have been hiding, you old Irishman?"

"Trying to stay busy. Fish a lot. Me and my son go different places around the state when he can get off work."

"I figured you would have gotten hitched again by now, the way you liked the girls," Grant jokes.

"They didn't like me then, don't like me any better now," Murphy says, laughing. "You know, boys, your dad worked under me for eighteen years before I retired, and not once did he do what I told him. He always had a better way. Stubborn SOB."

"That's not true. I always did what I was told."

"The only time he ever did what he was told was when Margaret told him what to do," Murphy says. "He was afraid of her."

"Reminds me," Grant interrupts. "Told your mom I'd have us and the meat home by six. Picked up some good smoked meat from ole Johnny Boyd."

"You still go by there, Grant?" Murphy asks.

"Now and again. You?"

"Not since that day."

"Let me run to the bathroom, and we'll get going, boys," Grant says and then leaves.

After he has left the room, Harry looks directly at Murphy and asks him: "Did you know our mother, Virginia..."

"Harry, leave it alone," Harold interrupts.

"It's alright, Harold," Murphy says. "I knew her, but not well."

"What happened between them, do you know?" Harry asks.

"Not really. If I had to guess, probably be the same thing that happened to my marriage. Never home and never any money. Sooner or later, they find something better."

"When your wife left," Harry asks, "did she take your son with her?"

Murphy pauses. He knows where this is going. "Yes," he says quietly.

"Here comes Dad, Harry," Harold says.

"Let's get going, boys." Harold reaches out to shake Murphy's hand. "Thanks for the beer. Call me, and let's go fishing. Okay?"

After saying goodbye to a handful of other officers, the three Pilkingtons leave the bar and walk back to the car. Harold sits in front with Grant, and Harry sits in the back seat. Grant reflects for a few moments before starting the engine.

"Ole Murph says he fishes with his boy a lot," Grant says finally. "He's lying. When his wife left him, she turned that boy against him. He never saw him again. He tried to connect with him a few years ago. The boy wouldn't have anything to do with him."

He has given Harry an opening he has wanted for a long time. "Is that what happened with us, Dad? Did you turn us against our mother so we wouldn't ever see her again?"

"No, dammit! She turned you against her when she left."

"Dad, maybe it's time we talked about it," Harold says calmly. "Harry... and I... I think we have a right to know what happened."

Harry leans forward in his seat. "We're grown men now, Dad. We need to know."

Grant half-turns in his seat to face both Harold and Harry. "All I can tell you is what I know. What I've told you before."

"You once told me that if you came to Missouri and she was in my house, you would leave," Harold says. "Is that not turning me against her?"

"I didn't say she should leave. I didn't say you couldn't see her. I, me… I do not want to be in the same building with her. You said it. You're grown men. You can do what the hell you want."

"What happened back then, Dad?" Harry asks. "Were you having an affair with Mom at the time?"

Grant is incredulous. "First of all, that is none of your business! I was a married man. Margaret had too much respect for herself. And you two. You will respect her also."

"I'm sorry, Dad," Harry says. Grant calms down a bit and looks at both of his sons.

"Alright. You boys heard what me and Mr. Boyd were saying today. I was making a salary of about $106 a month. We worked shifts, but you couldn't just stop in the middle of a case and go home, so there were a lot of extra hours. We had a son who had polio, and we didn't know what to do. Hell! Nobody else did. And then you came along, Harry. A woman like your mother wanted more. Tulsa then was prospering. Even the blacks in Greenwood before the riot were doing very well. Oil money was everywhere. Even your uncle Jim left the force and got in with it. Virginia looks around and sees all this, and she wants it, too. And I can't give it to her. Greed and envy almost destroyed Tulsa; it did destroy Greenwood. And it took Virginia with it."

"But not us," Harry says.

"I never told that woman she couldn't have her sons. I never told her I would fight her for you. I only told her that she would not keep me from you. And that I meant. She was there at the divorce hearing. Not once did she ask for custody or shared custody."

"Maybe she just didn't love us," Harry says.

"That is a question I can't answer, son. You'll have to ask her."

"I went to see her, Dad," Harold shares. "On my first bus trip to Missouri." Grant looks at him but says nothing. "Only spoke with her briefly in her front yard. A neighbor comes by, and she doesn't introduce me. Tells me after the neighbor leaves that no one knows she has other children. That did it for me. I left."

"He met our sister, though," Harry says. "Her name's Virginia."

"Maybe someday that Virginia can explain it to you, boys."

"What about Texas, Dad?" Harold asks gently. "Why that?"

Grant is quiet a moment, pondering the question; then, finally, he says, "That was a mistake. Texas was a mistake. I should have kept you with me. I'm sorry."

The three men are quiet for a time. Grant and Harold both stare out the front. Harry, who had been leaning forward into the conversation, settles back into his seat.

"Let's go home, Dad," Harold says.

"Yes, let's go home," Harry adds.

That night at dinner, all enjoying the smoked meat from Johnny Boyd, there is an unspoken awareness from the three men that they all finally belong at the same table.

The Lake Ozark family grows when, in late June, Jessie Fry gives birth to a healthy baby boy. He is named Lawrence Marion Fry, Jr., after his father, but from day one, he is called Larry. Jessie's mother, Hannah, makes a rare venture away from Tulsa. She comes to visit and help with the baby for a few days but soon returns to Tulsa after promising a return visit. Lawrence's mother comes a few days later to help as well and stays longer, visiting Harvey and Vivian, as well. At about the same time, the Jameses welcome a son, Bruce, into the local family. The boy is their second child, as their daughter Judy was born just about one year after Ruthie. To differentiate the boy, who is not a "junior," from his dad, they are referred to from early on as "Big Bruce" and "Little Bruce."

The business remains good throughout the summer in Lake Ozark, and Lon and Pauline continue to date. Theora and Harold both realize it is just a matter of time before they will be needing a new waitress. Ruthie continues to grow and learn new things and manages to improve her dexterity with her hands. Phyllis, aware that in a few short years, she will start first grade, work with her on such things as holding and using a pencil and coloring with crayons. Commenting on her new playmate, baby Larry, she is happy, though not overly excited: "He's the wrong kind, Momma," she tells Phyllis, who answers her, saying, "He'll just have to do for now." Eventually, Ruthie agrees, "He'll do for now."

In late August, Marion and his brother Ross get word that their father has died. He had been living near Columbia, where Marion had visited him once or twice, on one trip taking Ruthie along so he could meet his granddaughter. The brothers make plans to go to Columbia and have him transported to southern Illinois for burial.

"Marion, do you need me to go with you and Ross to help?" Harold asks him right after they make plans.

"I appreciate it, Harold, but it is something Ross and I need to do," Marion tells him. "Phyllis and Gladys aren't going."

"Can I ask you a question?"

"Of course," Marion says.

"Did either one of your parents ever try to turn you against the other?"

"No, not really," Marion says. "There was such a difference in their ages; I think they just naturally drifted apart." He thinks back for a moment. "I know Mom got irritated with him – he made good money and paid the bills, but he liked to drink. Mom had three kids, and he would be in a bar. But she rarely said anything negative about him in front of us."

"I just wondered," Harold says.

"And you?" Marion asks.

"All in all, I suppose not," Harold says.

On the trip, Ross tells Marion that his wife Gladys is pregnant but not to say anything because they haven't told Carrie yet. "Hard to understand the world," Marion says, "lose someone you love before you can have someone new to love." Ross is quiet but looks at his brother and nods his head.

On September 3, the so-called Anglo-American Lend-Lease agreement is signed by President Roosevelt. It will prove to be imperative to England's survival.

The first peacetime draft in U.S. history becomes a reality on September 16 when President Roosevelt signs the Selective Service and Training Act. It requires all males 21 to 36 to register with the Selective Service System. To many, there is no longer any doubt: America is going to war.

As do others affected by the draft, Harold and Marion register, while Theora and Phyllis gain another reason to worry. Paul Gordon and Lawrence Fry register also, as required, though they are approaching the cut-off age, and their wives worry less about that.

"Marion thinks there is a chance he would be deferred from the draft because of his security job," Harold tells Theora one day soon after the draft announcement. "Jay, too. Union Electric will request it from the government. They are essential to national security."

"They don't consider the sale of liquor essential to national security?" Theora asks, not totally with a humorous intent.

"Only for Congress, not the military," Harold answers, also not totally with a humorous intent.

"What will we do if you get drafted, Harold? I'm scared."

"It won't do to worry about it, Theora," Harold says, trying to assure her. "We'll deal with it if, or when, it comes."

"They will probably take the younger boys first unless we go to war, don't you think?" Theora asks, attempting to reassure herself.

"I suppose so," Harold says, wanting to drop the subject.

There is a rumor that a site in Iowa selected for a new U.S. Army training base may be rejected, and the base instead relocated to Missouri. The proposed site is near St. Robert, just off Route 66, about a 45-minute drive from Lake Ozark. Speculation around the Lake area is that such a facility should be beneficial to local businesses. It will also bring civilian jobs to help build the infrastructure necessary for the facility.

Young Larry is growing nicely, and every chance Ruthie can get to be around him, she asks to hold him. The more she holds him, the more she loves him, and finally, one day announces to her mother that "he'll more than do for now, Momma."

Bernie and Paul do not leave for the winter, instead opting to remain open on weekends, lunch and dinner only, throughout November and December. Phyllis and Jo work some shifts for them, and business is good enough to justify the decision. One morning in late October, Bernie ventures to the Whitehouse to have coffee with Harold and Theora.

"Theora, remember that year we all gathered here for Thanksgiving dinner?" Bernie asks.

"I do," she says, surprised at the question, "Five years ago, 1935."

"Lot of fun, but a lot of work," Harold adds.

"I've been thinking we should do it again," Bernie says, "but this time at the Casino."

"Are you sure? That's a big undertaking, Bernie," Theora cautions. "We'd help, of course."

"Harold, you know there's a chance that some of the locals might not be here this time next year, the draft and all," Bernie says. "It may be the last chance for a while."

"Hell, Theora, we might as well. Not going to Tulsa."

"Have you said anything to Phyllis, Bernie?" Theora asks.

"Yesterday, at work. She said, whatever the rest of us want to do. Can't be sure of Marion, though, until he knows his schedule. And Jo said she'll talk to the Atteberrys."

"They get involved, I'll approach Sam Overfelt to come in, too," Harold says.

"She's kept busy with Larry these days, but I bet Jessie, Lawrence too, will help," Theora says. "As much as she can, anyway."

"Well," Bernie concludes, "let's see what we can find out and talk again in a few days."

"I best clear this with Momma first, though," Theora realizes. "I don't know if Dorothy and her brood are coming this year."

"Hell, Theora, the more, the merrier," Harold says.

"One more thing, Theora… Harold, I'd rather keep this private for now, but…"

"Yes. Bernie, is something wrong?" Theora asks.

"I'm going to have a baby."

"Oh, my God, Bernie! You're… a baby. Wonderful. Congratulations!"

"Congratulations, Bernie," Harold says, laughing. "Tell Paul I said, 'Way to go.'"

One Sunday evening in mid-November, with plans moving along for the gathering at the casino for Thanksgiving, Harold and Theora invite Harvey and Vivian to dinner at the Whitehouse. They are joined by Marion and Phyllis, Lawrence and Jessie, and the Gordons. Vivian uses the occasion to tell the others that she, too, is pregnant. Word of Bernie's and Gladys Clayton's good news is no longer a secret. Theora reacts.

"My God, look what you have started, Jessie," she says, laughing. "The population of Lake Ozark will almost double in 1940-41."

"Theora, we live in Eldon," Harvey says.

"Well, yes, but you're Lake Ozark family." Everyone laughs as Theora starts counting on her fingers.

"We do plan on being at the Casino on Thanksgiving, especially with Mother Fry and Donnie here," Vivian says.

A few days later, Pauline asks to speak with both Harold and Theora in private. "I'm going to get married, so I will be leaving the job at the Whitehouse in late January," she tells them. "I wanted you to know so you can have time to plan."

"We appreciate that very much," Theora says. "I must say, we're not surprised. Congratulations."

"Anyone we know?" Harold asks, tongue-in-cheek. Pauline smiles.

"I am taking off Thanksgiving morning if it's okay, and I won't be able to help with the Casino," Pauline says. "Lon hasn't met my family yet, and I'm taking him home with me that day."

"It's not a problem; we'll manage fine," Harold says. "But what happens if your family votes against Lon? You're not worried about that?"

"Harold, that's not funny," Theora says. "I'm going to tell Lon what you said."

"I'll marry him anyway."

"That-a-girl!" Harold says.

"Did you know that Maggie is going with us to the Casino on Thanksgiving?" Theora asks. "And not just to help."

"She told me. I think she's tired of the drive to Wichita every year. Can't understand why her son and daughter-in-law can't come here and bring her granddaughter one year."

"Her daughter-in-law's family is all there," Theora says. "If we ever have children, I want them to know Harold's family."

"I want that too," Pauline says.

Thanksgiving morning early, Jay Rice meets H.H. Ranney at school. Mr. Ranney is the industrial arts teacher at the high school and also serves as the scoutmaster for Boy Scout Troop 21, which is sponsored by the school. He is a veteran of World War I and a respected teacher. Meeting them, there is 12-year-old Sammy Overfelt, a member of the troop and son of a local grocer. With the support of Union Electric, the troop has held a food drive to gather groceries for some of the needy families throughout the area, and the three are loading up Jay's truck to do deliveries. Earlier in the week, the boys in the troop sorted the donations into equal sacks of mostly canned and packaged goods. Just before heading out, the three add a donated fresh turkey from the school cafeteria walk-in refrigerator and a bag of fresh dinner rolls to each sack.

All are planning to be at the Casino gathering later in the day, so they hope to have their deliveries done by noon. Jay has volunteered on behalf of UE because, as a lineman, he knows the backroads around the area as well as anyone. There is another unspoken reason for his help as well. As a native of northeast Oklahoma, Indian Territory, he understands rural poverty firsthand.

After the first few stops, where they have been welcomed heartily, Jay tells the others they should stop and say hello to George and Opel Robinson and if time allows, his brother Fred and wife Ethyl. Each couple and family live on a small farm in the Bear Creek area and are brothers to Bert of

Bagnell. "George will be good for a free cup of coffee and a piece of fresh pie from Opel," Jay tells his companions.

When they arrive at George's, Jay knocks on the door, and when George opens it, he yells at Opel: "It's the Okie, Opel."

"Harold?"

"No, the ugly one," he yells again.

"Well, let him in any way," she yells back.

After introductions, and once the coffee and pie are served, George tells Jay not to stop by his brother Fred's house. "He'll just get talking too much and be late. He and Ethyl are picking us up, and we're all going to the gathering. We want to get there before Bert eats all the good stuff."

George gives them the names of a few families in the area he knows that could use some help, and the three leave the Robinson farm and continue their very welcome stops. At Jack Wickham's farm, they stop briefly to say hello.

"All's good here," Jack tells them, "unless you're delivering whiskey."

"I'm out of that," Jay says. "We only do that on the Fourth of July," Jay tells him.

"I'll look forward to that then," Jack says.

Before they go, Jack mentions a young couple that lives "just up the next hill a mile or so. They don't have anything. Just four walls, a roof, and a dirt floor. Might want to stop there. Go past the Beards, then up the hill, the first house you come to."

Jay leaves the Wickhams and, after a brief "hello" stop at the Beards, he drives on up the hill, and as he sees the house, he immediately recognizes it. There is only a small space to park as Jay pulls the truck off the gravel roadway. The yard, or what appears to be so, is overgrown with weeds. There is a small wood pile stacked against the outside front wall.

"I know this place. We ran lines up here," Jay says. "Young couple. I don't think the fella works, even when he can. Pretty damn sad." Jay turns to Mr. Ranny. "How about you two stay here and let me take care of this stop? I think Sammy has learned enough 'life lessons' for one day."

Jay gets out and goes to the door, which is already open, and knocks on the jamb. A young woman in a soiled dress comes to the door. She and Jay exchange a few words, and he hands her the sack of groceries. The two in the truck hear an inaudible yelling sound from inside the house and see Jay, smiling, yell something back. The young woman thanks Jay, and he leaves and returns to the truck.

"Well, gentlemen, we're out of groceries," Jay says. "Time to head back to town."

"Sammy, I think you have done more than enough today to finish earning that Citizenship Merit Badge," Mr. Ranny says. Sammy looks at him and smiles.

That same morning, Harold is up meeting the buses while Theora and Maggie take care of the few passengers passing through. All the newspapers that morning have the same story on the front page: confirmation that a new Army base will be built at the St. Robert site. According to reports, construction bids have been let, and land clearing and preparation will begin by December first. The as-yet-unnamed base is intended not only for basic military training of recruits and draftees but will also be the site of military engineer training. As a businessman who stands to see additional activity from the base, Harold's reaction is positive, though he knows that it could also mean the government is preparing for a possible war — a war that no one wants.

Dinner at the Casino is scheduled for 4:00 p.m., with folks starting to arrive at 2:00 p.m. Marion has had to work the 4:00 a.m. to noon shift, and after going home to clean up, he is there helping Phyllis by 2. Enough locals had joked about Marion making a big pot of chili to serve at the feast that he considered it. The memory of that old family recipe has faded slowly since Red's closed. His work schedule allowed him little time to do it, but it helped fuel a desire to someday get back into the restaurant business — a dream shared by Phyllis.

Paul has avoided making another "mashed potato pillow" but has managed to prepare a large quantity of sweet potatoes with marshmallows on top. In addition to a turkey and a ham, he has also managed to cook a beef roast because there are a few folks who only eat beef. Truth be told, he's mostly talking about himself, who is still the biggest fan of his own chicken fried steak recipe.

Maggie, whose stuffing is thought to be the best, makes a pair of large pans filled with it to prove that opinion correct. Her freshly made dinner rolls are a supplement to the fresh dinner rolls donated by Atteberry's and Overfelt's groceries. Many others provide dishes of green beans, squash, and other vegetables to round out the meal. Opel and Ethyl Robinson add plates of fried chicken to the menu as an added touch. Dolly Cunningham again comes through with a variety of baked goods, primarily cookies. That and Carrie Moore's pies and Lena Robinson's cakes ensure there will be dessert at the end of the day.

Conversation throughout the afternoon centers around the subject of the new Army base and the potential of war.

"Would they be building it if they didn't think we were headed that way?" one man asks.

"It's just precautionary," another offers. "Roosevelt doesn't want to be caught with his pants down."

"Roosevelt thinks it's inevitable," the first man says. "I think he wants to get in it now, sooner, to get it over with. But he knows he can't; the public would crucify him."

"Well, he doesn't have to worry about getting elected again for four years," a third man says. It was true. Roosevelt had been reelected at the beginning of the current month—the first U.S. President to ever be elected to a third term.

"Well," a lady sitting nearby injects into the conversation, "if he gets us into this war, he'll have to hide out in our Whitehouse up the street instead of the one in D.C. He may not be safe there."

A local young man, Leroy Black, who has done apprentice work as a heavy equipment operator, mentions the potential jobs at the site of the base. "I'm going over to St. Robert on Monday morning. I've been told there is a company there with a contract that's hiring already. Government money, jobs should pay well enough to make it worth driving there every day."

"One thing to keep in mind about government jobs, son," Lawrence Fry offers. "The taxpayers are the employers. More pay, more taxes. I know because I got one of those government jobs." Everyone laughs—not because Lawrence is seemingly poking fun at himself, but because he is respected as a businessman who understands financial matters better than any other resident of the community. It remains to be seen if Larry will inherit the good qualities of his mother and father, but for now, Ruthie approves of him and is constantly checking on him and wanting to hold him. The youngest, Clayton, will soon be four and often reminds her mother that "I'm a big girl now."

Late afternoon, Mr. Ranny has an opportunity to speak with Jay in private and asks him about that last stop they made that morning. "We could hear that man yelling from the truck but couldn't make out what he was saying. What was that about?"

"I could see there were a couple of babies in a makeshift bed in the back of the room when I handed the sack to the lady. One of them was crying. Her husband - he's sitting over on the side in a chair. When I looked over at him and smiled, he yelled, 'What the hell you lookin' at? Get the hell out of here!'"

"A real nice guy sounds like," Ranny says.

"That made me mad. I shouldn't have let it, but it did. So, I yelled back at him. I told him that if I ever heard of him hurting his family in any way, I'd come back and shove this sack of food up his rear end. And him to never doubt that I could do it. He shut up and looked away. The lady quietly said, 'Thank you, sir, but please go.'

So, I smiled and left."

"You think it will make any difference?" Mr. Ranny asks.

"No, think not. He's a no-good, lazy son-of-a-bitch. He isn't gonna change."

The gathering proved to be very successful, with only one complaint. Bert's brothers, George and Fred, objected to the length of the grace he was asked to say before the meal.

"I thought that prayer Bert said was mighty long, George, didn't you?" Fred says.

"Long?" George replies. "The Old Testament was shorter!"

"It takes a lot of words when I'm in the presence of a pair of sinners like you two," Bert offers in his defense. The issue remains unresolved at the end of the day as no one wishes to take sides in even a friendly family feud.

Leftovers are few, and clean-up does not take long with the ample help available. Marion and Harold, Paul, and a few others settle in for a quiet highball at the end just before heading home.

"You think we'll all ever be able to get together again like this in the future?" Paul ponders. "Possible war and all."

"Change is the only thing certain," Marion says. "None of us knows where we'll be this time next year."

"Well, yeah," Charlie Fleetwood says. "Look at you, Marion, one day you're fishing above the line, the next you're chasing people away from it."

They all laugh, and after it settles, Harold ventures to speak to the issue. "I am going to hold out hope that we all will still be here next year, swapping the same old stories and still laughing at 'em just like they're new."

Theora and Phyllis hear the exchange through the open kitchen door, and tears come to Theora's eyes. Phyllis notices her apparent sudden sadness. "Theora, what's wrong?" she asks.

"I'm worried about Harold being drafted."

"Don't let yourself worry about that, Theora," Phyllis says. "Just put it out of your mind; just think past it."

In Tulsa, on December 1st, Grant and Margaret close the deal with the Newton boys and move into the living quarters behind the bar. Harry, with help from a few off-duty firemen friends, helps them move. Trying to be romantic, Grant places a big red Christmas ribbon on the door and says, "Merry Christmas, Margaret." She, in turn, presents him with a beagle puppy for a pet. He immediately falls in love and names him "Brownie." Harry moves into a small house with two other young single firemen, and the Pilkingtons put their house up for sale.

For most of the period since his retirement, Grant has spent time at the bar and grill learning the ropes, with Margaret accompanying him on many days. They both take to the business. Margaret especially enjoying visiting with customers, something she hasn't done since her days at the flower shop. He enjoys cooking, though the Newtons have convinced him to keep the menu simple: burgers, hot dogs, fries, and other sandwiches. With help from Doc, he finally understands what makes good chili good — something only a Texan could teach him. On the day of closing, a new sign goes up that reads "Grant's Place," which he explains to everyone cost less than calling it "Margaret's Place" because the sign painter got paid by the letter.

The couple has chosen to keep the same schedule as the Newtons, closing on Sundays and Mondays, leaving some leisure time necessary for fishing. One quiet weekday night, just two weeks into their new proprietorship, Grant and Margaret are both standing behind the bar when a young man comes in, walks quickly up to the bar directly in front of them, and pulls a pistol out of his jacket pocket.

"Keep your hands up," he says, his focus primarily on Grant, who notices the man's nervousness.

"Just take it easy, son," Grant says calmly. "Just tell me what you want, and no one needs to get hurt."

"Give me all the money in your register, and hurry. Now."

"Okay, I'm going to do it now and get your money," Grant, still calm, tells him. "Just take it easy." Grant turns to the register behind him, the robber watching him intently. Aware of the empty beer bottle sitting on the bar near her right hand, Margaret makes an impulsive decision, grabs it, and slams it down hard on the man's gun hand. He immediately drops the pistol and starts yelling, "My hand's broke! My hand's broken!" Grant reacts quickly, jumping over the bar faster than a high school hurdler, and takes the man down.

"Margaret!?!" Grant yells. "Don't EVER do that again! You could have gotten us killed. Jeez!"

"I wasn't going to let him take our money," Margaret says, seemingly calm.

"Jeez! Margaret."

Grant's Place, located on East Admiral Place, also known as Route 66, two miles outside Tulsa city limits, is not under the jurisdiction of the TPD. Grant, therefore, calls the county sheriff's department, and a deputy soon arrives and takes the man into custody. The robber, still complaining about his broken hand, finds out it hurts even more when surrounded by handcuffs. He keeps looking at Margaret, telling the deputy to "keep that crazy woman away from me." The deputy knows Grant from his days in law enforcement, having been an officer at TPD before leaving and joining the sheriff's department, so he feels comfortable joking with Grant.

"So, let me make sure I have this correct now for my report," the deputy says. "Captain Pilkington was cowering in the back by the register while this strong, brave woman subdues the bad guy."

"Stupid woman," Grant corrects. "Tell her it was the wrong thing to do, deputy."

"It was the wrong thing to do, ma'am. Could've gotten you both killed. Money's not worth your lives."

"He would not have gotten much," Grant says. "I was taught a long time ago to occasionally clear excess cash from the register during the day. I used to teach that to new clerks on my beat in the early days. Try to keep it down to basic change."

"I'd better get this guy to lock up and get his hand attended to," the deputy says, then hesitates, recalling something. "Captain Pilkington? Didn't you work with or under Ryan Murphy, Captain Murphy, for a long time at TPD?"

"I did, a long time. Had a beer with him the day I retired. Why?"

"He killed himself a few weeks ago," the deputy says.

"Murph's dead? What…what happened? He seemed fine when I saw him in June."

"We got a call. A couple of kids found his boat loosely tied to the bank up on the Arkansas River. One shot to his head, his pistol lying in the boat beside him. No note, but the coroner ruled it a suicide."

"He had been divorced for a long time," Grant says. "Estranged from his son. I think maybe his job was all he had, and then he didn't have that."

"There was fishing gear and several empty beer bottles in the boat," the deputy says.

"It wasn't enough," Grant says.

New Year's Eve 1940 is busier than the Whitehouse has seen in several years. Among the crowd are a handful of Army uniforms, mostly officer or higher NCO ranks. They are, they say, part of the advance party from the Army engineers sent in to oversee the construction of the new base. They say they expect to have a sizable "permanent party" in place by early Spring. Their presence does not temper the celebration by the mostly local crowd; they enhance it, though they are a reminder of changing times. Nearly every young male in the crowd under 36 carries in his wallet this night a selective service card. None of them knows where that card may take them in the future, so they choose to make the best of this night.

Sensing a future need, the bus company has added a daily bus from what will be the main gate of the new base to Lake Ozark, leaving early in the morning and returning early in the evening. On Friday and Saturday nights, a late bus returns to the base at 11:00 p.m., arriving in time for the midnight bed check.

Harold and Theora have anticipated the increased business and hired Jay Rice and Jack Wickham to help keep the peace, with Jay also looking after Jack. Marion is working the overnight shift at the Dam, but Phyllis, Jo, and Jessie are in-house to help out as well. Larry is safely tucked in a playpen in the kitchen under the watchful eye of Vivian Fry and, of course, Ruthie. Lawrence sits behind the counter in the liquor store and is kept company by his brother Harvey.

"Have you talked to him, Lawrence?" Harvey asks.

"Haven't spoken to him since Christmas Day," Lawrence answers.

"He's just got a year and a half to go."

"You think he's serious about quitting?"

"Yes. After this semester," Harvey says. "With only his senior year to go. I know Mom wants you to talk to him."

"I'll talk to him, but if he's concerned about the draft, I don't think they're taking full-time students yet."

"He thinks that if he joins now, the Army Air Corps, he'll have some rank if, or when, the war comes."

"I can understand that," Lawrence says, then laughs. "And riding beats walking anytime."

"Well, anyway, try to talk to him, Lawrence," Harvey says.

"I'm surprised he's not here tonight," Lawrence says.

"Had a date with a special girl tonight, Mom said."

"Another reason not to enlist," Lawrence says.

Lawrence and Harvey look up at the sound of the front door opening just as their brother Don walks in. He is accompanied by a pretty blonde wearing a trendy winter coat. She appears to be cold, the night temperature, though dry outside, having reached below freezing.

"It must be super busy in here; we had to park halfway to the Dam and walk," Donnie says when he sees his brothers. "Can we go into the kitchen and warm up?"

"Of course, after you introduce us to your friend, who, if she's intelligent, will never date you again," Lawrence says. "Does mom know you came to Lake Ozark?"

"First of all, this is Suzy Wilson, who, if your band is any good tonight, will date me again. Suzy, my brothers Lawrence and Harvey."

"Hi, nice to meet you," Suzy says with a shiver. The brothers smile and say hello to Suzy, who unbuttons her coat, revealing a very shapely figure.

"Secondly, Mom knows because we're staying at your house tonight, Lawrence," Don says. "And thirdly, she's 21 and has a legal ID to prove it, so where is your private stock, brother Harv?"

"Vivian and Jessie are both in the kitchen; check with them," Harvey says. "After you get settled, Lawrence wants to talk to you."

Lawrence looks at Harvey. "We both want to talk with you."

"Oh, well, that should be interesting," Don says as he directs his date toward the kitchen. "Come, Suze. Cocktails in the kitchen; it's very romantic."

On their way to the kitchen, the young couple stopped and peeked into the dining room. All the tables are filled, and there are a number of people standing along the walls. Don and his date pause, listening for a few moments.

"The band sounds good," Suzy says approvingly. "I wonder who you have to know to get a table?"

"Let's head to the kitchen and see if we can find out," Don says. "Follow me." The two move toward and enter the kitchen just as Harold comes out.

Harold, not necessarily surprised, takes a quick look at Don, then his date, then back to Don. "Grab an apron and get to work, kid," Harold says, then moves quickly toward the dining room.

"Nice to see you, too, Harold," Don says to his back, then enters the kitchen. He immediately sees Jessie. "Mom, call you?" he says to her.

"She did. Asked that you call her when you get here. You must be Suzy." She takes the young girl's hand. "I'm Jessie, his sister-in-law." Indicating the others, "His other sister-in-law, Vivian. This is Ruthie, who is currently taking care of my son Larry, Don's nephew." Jessie pauses and turns to indicate Maggie. "And this is Maggie; she runs the place."

"Come over here by the stove and warm up, young lady," Maggie says.

"Where's your private stock, Jessie?" Don asks. "I want to fix Suzy and me a drink."

"Over behind that stack of dishes, and fix me one, too," Jessie says.

"None for me," Vivian, who is sitting at the table, says. "I'm pregnant, sworn off. Suzy, sit down with me. This is probably the only available table in the building." She does so just as Phyllis comes through the door carrying a large tray of dishes that she takes to the sink, whereupon Ruthie goes to her, wanting to be picked up. As she does, she sees Don making drinks.

"Make that one more, Mr. Fry, or we're hiring a new bartender," Phyllis says, then turns to Suzy. "Surely, you're not unfortunate enough to be with him?"

"That's me, Suzy Unfortunate. Hello to you."

"I'm Phyllis. Related to the family by marriage. My sister's." "Where's Marion?" Don asks.

"He's protecting Bagnell Dam from the Nazis tonight," Phyllis says. "Don't worry, though, he's doing an excellent job. None have been sighted so far."

"And Theora?" Don says.

"She's out in the dining room flirting with soldiers," Phyllis says. "That woman has no shame." Theora comes through the door just as her sister speaks.

"Who has no shame?" She sees Don. "Oh, hi, Donnie. You making drinks? Make me one, too."

"See what I mean," Phyllis says. "No shame."

Don comes to the table with three drinks and gives one to Suzy, one to Jessie, and one to Phyllis. He goes back to the counter, fixes two more highballs, and hands one to Theora. With the fifth drink in hand, he proposes a toast: "Here's to all the pretty girls gathered here in this spacious kitchen tonight, including the one I brought with me."

"Oh, hi, I'm Theora," she says, smiling toward Suzy for the first time.

"She's the one who promised me she would wait till I grew up, but fickle as she is, married that gruff fella you met briefly when we came in. Jilted me."

"I don't blame you, ma'am," Suzy says. "He's very handsome. I wouldn't have waited either."

"Speaking of waiting, Mrs. Pilkington," Don asks, "any way we can get a pair of seats in the dining room?"

"Maybe. Mrs. Barker didn't come from K.C. this year. I think young Harry had a party, and she didn't want to be away overnight," Theora says. "So, Lawrence and Virginia have the family table back in the corner by themselves. I have a couple of fold-up chairs you can take in and sit at their table. I'll talk to them when I go back out."

Harold, who is wearing a half-apron, comes through the kitchen door and looks around. "There is more partying going on in here than out there. Pauline and Jo need help."

"Doesn't Harold look nice in his bartender's uniform, Suzy?" Theora says. "I'm a sucker for a man in uniform." To Harold: "Honey, this is Suzy, Donnie's date."

"Ignore everyone in here, Suzy," Harold says. "They're all crazy… uh, except Ruthie and Larry." Maggie loudly clears her throat. "And Maggie."

"Suzy, are you a student at SMS, also?" Vivian asks the girl.

"Not directly. I'm in training to be an RN, a nurse, and the program is administered through the University in cooperation with St. John's Hospital," she explains. "We have classes at school, but the majority of the instruction is at the hospital."

"The demand for nurses is high right now from what I read in the paper," Vivian says. "You've picked the right profession."

"Even more so if the war comes," Suzy says.

The customers in the dining room are, somewhat unexpectedly for a New Year's Eve, congenial. Only a handful appear overly intoxicated but not belligerent; a few couples leaving early, evidently needing more than dance and drink to help them celebrate. Later in the evening, after 1940 is safely ushered into the past and 1941 is born, Lawrence and Harvey corner Don in the dining room to try and discuss his future plans. Suzy has asked to help with clean-up as needed, and her assistance is welcome.

"Are you thinking about leaving school early before you graduate?" Lawrence asks.

"I am. Army Air Corps," Don answers.

"If the war comes, the draft will get you sooner or later," Harvey says. "What is your hurry?"

"I'm interested in pilot training at the Air Corps. If I join now, I can pick where I serve, and if the war comes, I'll be ready."

"What about your eyes?" Lawrence asks. "I thought pilots had to be 20/20."

"If they don't accept me for pilot training, I'll opt to be a navigator," Don explains. "They're officer-ranked, too."

"Don, listen to me," Lawrence argues, "you only have a year left to graduate. Finish school first and then enlist."

"Big Brother, school will still be there when I get out," Don says.

"Will Suzy?" Harvey asks. Don doesn't immediately respond to his brother. "She's the first girl you ever brought home. Has to mean something."

"The Whitehouse?" Don asks.

"It's where your family is," Lawrence says.

"We have an understanding. She knows I have to do this."

"No one is making you," Harvey says.

"The semester ends two weeks after we get back from holiday break, then finals." Don pauses and looks at his brothers, hoping for understanding and acceptance. "Then I have to report."

"Well, hell, then," Harvey says. "It's already done." Don nods his head, and Harvey gets up and leaves the room.

In late January, Don reports for Basic Military Training at the newly named Ft. Leonard Wood, the facility still under construction near St. Robert, Missouri. It is located approximately 45 minutes from both Springfield and Lake Ozark. Don takes a "ribbing" from everyone about his training assignment, some paraphrasing the old WWI song lyric, "How are you gonna keep 'em down on the farm after they've seen Missoureee?" He gets the best of it, though, when he announces that after the first two months of basic training, he heads to flight school at a new base in Florida. "It's warm in Florida," he reminds everyone as they struggle to dig out of a late January snowstorm.

About that same time, Lon Stanton marries Pauline Vaughn, and she begins working with him in his wood manufacturing business, which has prospered. Like all the young couples in the area, there is uncertainty hanging over their lives. Talk of war is dominant in conversations, though many still believe that Roosevelt will be able to keep America out of it. This in spite of his declaration during a late-year Fireside Chat that this country will be the "arsenal of democracy."

Over time, a group of locals began gathering early every morning at the Whitehouse over coffee and the newspapers. "How do you manage to continue to provide supplies to one side in the European war without upsetting the other side?" one asks. "Sooner or later, Hitler's going to get mad."

"Let him," another says. "We'll kick his butt."

"He's already mad," Sam Overfelt says. "Those U-boats of his are already out there off the East Coast."

"Sam's right," Ward Atterbury says. "Our Coast Guard's already in this war. Trying to protect our civilian shipping."

"This is a historic moment," Clark Hale interjects. "Two grocers agreeing on something."

"Well, we agree on this," Sam says. "The price of coffee and newspapers at the Whitehouse is too high."

"Harold told me he charges extra for the entertainment," Frank Frudegar says, laughing. "Isn't that right, Harold?"

"Yeah, these jokers entertain themselves and pay me for a place to do it."

"Hey, Frank, isn't there a fish out there somewhere needing to be caught?" Ward says. "Take Clark with you; he knows where it is."

"Actually, Harold, we come here to watch you do Theora's bidding," Clark says. "That's our entertainment." Everyone laughs except Harold.

In Tulsa that same morning, as if he had been part of the conversation at the Whitehouse, Harry sits down with Grant and Margaret to tell them his plans to enlist.

"I've decided to go ahead and enlist in the Coast Guard," he tells his parents. "I've talked to the Department about putting in for a leave of absence. My job will be there when I get out; just have to take a refresher course."

"That's it, then?" Grant asks.

"All but signing and picking a date."

"Dammit, son! You could get killed," Margaret says.

"Mom, I go into burning buildings almost every day. That's a lot more dangerous than riding around in a boat off the coast of Connecticut."

"What I read says the Nazis got submarines just off our coast now," Grant says. "Tracking our ships."

"Then I want to be there to help blow them out of the water," Harry says.

"Have you told Maxine?" Margaret asks.

"She knows," Harry says. "Our plan is for me to get through training. When I get a home-port assignment, I'll take leave, come home, and get married. She'll go with me."

"Well, son, if that's what you gotta do, we can't stop you," Grant says.

"No, I guess we can't," Margaret says.

By mid-February, Harry is on a bus headed to Connecticut and Coast Guard basic training. He tells Maxine he'll be back, and she tells him she'll be waiting.

It was On-Time Tony that first got the locals thinking about it. One Sunday in March, during his early morning stop at the Whitehouse, he tells Harold and a few locals sitting at or near the back counter about his conversation with the Chinaman.

"He was from Los Angeles heading to New York," Tony relates over coffee. "Rode with me all the way from Oak City to St. Louis, sitting in the front seat. American-born Chinese, third generation, he says. Speaks better English than me."

"That's not saying much, Tony," one of the locals throws in.

"Better looking, too, I'll bet," another says.

"Hush up, boys, let him finish," Harold says. "He doesn't have much time."

"He tells me that you rarely hear anyone mention Germans, Nazis; it's the Japs," Tony says. "West Coast folks think our problem is going to be Japan. The Japs are in China, Manchuria, and Burma, just waiting to get a chance at the Philippines. This fella, Harry Chang was his name, sees them as pure imperialists. He thinks they have eyes on America. Need our oil."

"They have several aircraft carriers, from what I've read," one of Tony's passengers says. "You don't use those to protect your own land. You use them to get your guns closer to somebody else's land."

"Harry Chang said the same thing," Tony adds.

"Did this Chang fella say anything about Hawaii?" the passenger asks.

"Yeah, he did," Tony says. "They're coming for it. Just a matter of time."

"Damn," the passenger says. "I got a brother stationed there with the Navy."

"One more thing, then I got to get back on the road," Tony says. "The reason he left the West Coast and was heading to New York: he said there is growing prejudice toward anyone Asian out there. Chinese, Japanese, Korean. 'To many of the Caucasian folks,' he said, 'we all look alike. We're all Japs now.' He was headed to live with family in New York because they told him it wasn't like that there."

Tony gets up to leave as one of the locals, who has been listening intently, says quietly, "Hell, we could end up with a war at both our front and back door at the same time."

Approaching their fourth anniversary in June 1941, the subject of children comes up, as it has on many occasions in the past. Having delayed efforts to conceive, the Pilkingtons concentrate instead on efforts to succeed with the business. They have also been reluctant to bring a child into the "world" of the Whitehouse. It is a place where people party, dance, and often drink too much and fight; at the same time, it is their home, as it would be for their child. It is not likely to get any better—only worse with the possibility of heavy traffic provided by the new Fort. What is good for business, Theora thinks, is not the best for my child.

But there is that other Whitehouse—the one where people gather over coffee, discuss the news, see their friends, and it is not always over a drink. It is a place where church services are held each Sunday. It has become an extension of the life of this small community, and in Theora's mind, "not a bad place to raise a child."

Therefore, on this day, the discussion is finally over. The couple is sitting at the table in the kitchen, having their morning coffee. Maggie is there at the stove cooking. "I'm pregnant, Harold," Theora says nonchalantly. Maggie perks up, though Harold has not registered what she has said.

"I'm going to the restroom," Maggie says and quietly slips out of the kitchen.

"I saw Dr. Attic yesterday," Theora says. "He confirmed it."

Harold looks up from his newspaper. "What? Dr. Attic? Are you sick?"

"I'm pregnant. We're going to have a baby."

"A baby? What! Why didn't you tell me?"

"I just did."

"A baby," Harold says again. "That's wonderful! When's she due?"

"The baby, sex undetermined, is due in mid-January."

Maggie comes back into the kitchen and goes to the stove.

"Hey, Maggie, guess what," Harold says. "We're going to have a baby."

"Yes, I heard that. Congratulations!"

"You heard? Damn. Word sure gets around fast in this town."

Two weeks after Theora's baby announcement, she answers the phone at the Whitehouse, and a male voice at the other end says: "Is this Jessie Fry? Jessie?"

"I'm sorry, no, she's not here. This is Theora. Can I help you?"

"I was trying to reach Harold Pilkington, and this is the only number I had. Does he still live there?"

"Yes, he does," Theora says. "I'm his wife."

"Oh, I didn't know he had gotten married. Congratulations."

"Thank you," Theora says. "I can get him for you. May I tell him who's calling?"

"Tell him it's Art Griffith. Coach Griffith."

"Coach Griffith, yes, I've heard so much about you," Theora says excitedly. "Hold on, please. I'll get him."

"Coach, what a surprise," Harold says when he picks up the phone.

"It's been a while, I know, Harold," Griffith says. "You still there by the Bagnell Dam?"

"Still here, running a business called the Whitehouse about a mile from the south end."

"Don't know whether you would have heard or not, but Gallagher retired at A&M, and they gave me the job. I start this year."

"I hadn't heard, but I can't imagine them giving it to anybody else," Harold says.

"I'm going to a coaching clinic meeting at Columbia, Missouri University next week and saw by the map that you are on the way. I wondered if I could stop and say hello?"

"Absolutely, Coach," Harold says, surprised but excited about the idea. "Can you stay the night? We have plenty of room."

"Yeah, I could leave a day earlier and do that," Coach says. "Be great to catch up."

"I'll look forward to it. We'll be here."

"Alright then, Harold. I'll see you next Thursday."

"Great, sir, see you then."

In addition to speculation about what Coach Griffith may have on his mind, Harold and Theora spend time each day speculating on baby names. Theora favors the name John: "The best of the biblical names," which is fine if the baby is a boy. However, Harold is most fond of the name Sharon, whereupon Theora asks the obvious question: "Why?"

"I knew this girl in school, and her name was Sharon, and I always thought it was a beautiful name," Harold tells her.

"You want to name our son after an old girlfriend!?" Theora, incredulous, asks him. (Incredulous is very common with young couples; as in "You what!?" or "I don't believe it!!!" Older couples, not so much; a simple "Yeah, whatever" will usually do.)

"Not our son!" Harold, adamant, explains. "Our daughter." (The same theory applies here: Young couples, 'adamant;' older couples, 'yeah, whatever.') "And she was not an old girlfriend, just a classmate."

"Well, John, it will be then," Theora says.

"We'll nickname her Sharon," Harold mutters to himself as he exits the room.

As to the subject of babies, they have been arriving on a persistent schedule throughout 1941. As promised, there is a little girl named Linda now at Ross and Gladys Clayton's home, a Kay at the Paul Gordon's, and a Jane at Harvey and Vivian Fry's. Not a Sharon among them, Harold notes. "There is hope," he thinks.

Although he is only vaguely aware at this time, Larry is happy about all the new playmates. Ruthie, not so much: "Still not the right ones," she tells her mother.

Art Griffith arrives at the Whitehouse the next Thursday afternoon just as the Cardinal broadcast is coming to a close. He finds it humorous that it is being played on a speaker outside the building and notes the three or four patrons gathered there. They appear to be grumbling as the "Cards" have lost.

Entering the building and seeing Harold at the back counter, he says as a greeting: "Your customers out front aren't happy. You need to do something about that."

"You agree to manage the Cardinals next year. They might perk up," Harold says, seeing his old coach.

"You think that'll do it?"

"Can't hurt." Harold comes out from behind the counter, and he and Griffith shake hands.

"You look good, Harold," Coach says. "Still at your old fighting weight?"

"Yeah," Harold laughs. "Plus, a little. It may get worse. Theora's got a roast in the oven for our dinner tonight."

"Sounds good," Griffith says. "I'm anxious to meet your wife. I want to meet the woman who could 'pin' you."

"Come into the kitchen with me, and I'll introduce you."

Maggie is busy mashing potatoes when the two men enter the kitchen, Theora stirring gravy at the stove. She looks up when they enter and is surprised to see the Coach.

"Oh, Harold, you should have warned me," Theora says as she walks over to shake hands with Griffith. "Welcome, sir. We are so happy to have you here. Harold has talked very highly of you."

"I teach all the boys to lie," Griffith says. "It's part of their character development."

"Coach, this is Maggie Custer," Harold says. "She runs the place. We'd be lost without her."

"Hello, and please, folks, just call me Art."

"I'm going to ask a question now I never thought I'd be asking my coach," Harold says. "Can I fix you a highball before dinner?"

"Only if you join me."

"Not me, Coach," Maggie says. "There is an old saying that the only two professions in which everyone in them drinks is sign painters and cooks. I'm the exception to that rule." Everyone laughs heartily. "Harold, get your drinks. You all go sit in the dining room and relax. I'll bring the food out when it's ready."

"I set a plate for you too, Maggie," Theora says.

"No, you all go ahead. I'm gonna eat in here and let you all visit."

Drinks mixed, the three exit the kitchen, go into the dining room and sit down.

"You said on the phone that you're going to a coaching clinic?" Harold asks.

"Yes. In Columbia. They asked me to speak on making the transition from high school coaching to the collegiate level. My speech will be short: I have no idea."

"A lot of the team will be the same, won't it?" Harold asks. "Central always sent a lot of athletes to A&M."

"Oh, yeah. Three or four wrestlers there now," Griffith explains. "A couple of last year's team going to Stillwater with me, too."

"What about the Olympics, Coach?" Theora asks. "Will they ever do that again?"

"Doubtful for now, with the war in Europe and all. Many people think it is going to be impossible for the U.S. to stay out of it."

"My younger brother just joined the Coast Guard," Harold says. "The Army just built a large new training facility an hour from here. It'll be good for business. But a constant reminder."

"What's your status, Harold?" Griffith asks.

"I've registered, carrying a card. Haven't been called yet."

"We're expecting a baby, Coach," Theora says. "So, I certainly don't want him called."

"Well, congratulations! Harold Pilkington, a father. I still remember this little freshman, a bit of a runt. Comes to me to wrestle; not a doubt that he belongs. He'll make a good father, Theora."

Maggie comes from the kitchen with a serving platter of roast beef and a bowl of potatoes. Theora gets up and follows her back into the kitchen, and momentarily, the two return with gravy, green beans, rolls, and butter. They eat heartily, laugh heartily, telling stories; it's a good reunion, Harold thinks. When they are finished, Theora carries the dishes to the kitchen, leaving the two men alone. Harold starts to light a cigarette. "Do you mind?" he asks first.

"No, go ahead," Coach says. "You're a grown man. I don't need to tell you it's bad for you. You already know that."

"I think it comes with my job," Harold says. "Sometimes it can be stressful."

"Did you know that Jesse Owens smoked a pack of cigarettes a day?" Griffith says. "I know, I saw him in Berlin. They say he had many other things on his mind, not just running."

"Maybe the best overall American athlete since Thorpe," Harold says.

"Maybe in the world." Griffith pauses, sipping at the coffee he has been drinking with dinner. "Harold, five years since high school. I think you could still compete. And win. Would you consider coming back and going to school? I'm sure I could get a good job for Theora."

Harold surprised at the sudden direction the conversation has taken, looks at his old coach with a bit of shock. "Are you sure? Coach, I'm six years older. I haven't trained since the months before the '36 trials."

"I'm sure. Theora's probably kept you in shape doing her bidding." They both laugh. "It would be a chance to get a degree, Harold, if that is important to you."

"Right now, I need more hours in a day than a degree." It is Harold's attempt to be humorous, though neither man laughs. "Look, Coach, it's so sudden. I'm honored…and humbled." He pauses and looks back toward the dining room door.

"Let me talk to Theora tonight, and I'll give you an answer in the morning."

"Fair enough, Harold," Griffith says.

The following morning, early, Griffith sits at the counter drinking coffee and talking with Theora.

"After your meeting in Columbia, are you coming back through this way, Coach?" Theora asks.

"No, when I leave Columbia Sunday, I'll drive into St. Louis. There's a prospect there I want to talk to. See if I can get him to come to A&M. Then when I leave, I'll head straight down Route 66 back to Tulsa."

"Harold told me about your conversation last night."

"How do you feel about it, Theora? I know this is your home."

"I told Harold that it's his decision," Theora shares. "I told him that whatever he decides, I will be right there with him."

"And?"

"I think you'll know the answer before I do."

Harold, who has been out in front-loading newspaper racks and talking with bus drivers, comes in and joins Coach Griffith and his wife at the counter. "Hand me a cup of coffee, please, honey. I'm going to take Coach back to the dining room so we can talk privately." The two men, coffee in hand, go into the dining room as three passengers sit down at the counter.

"I can see this place does keep you and Theora busy," Griffith says as they sit down.

"We only recently purchased the business from the Frys, but there's growth potential here now we hadn't expected when we did," Harold says. "The new Army base at St. Robert will bring trainees, but permanent staff as well. Some, mostly the officers, may have spouses and families with them. People want to see this lake. And the dam. People eat and buy fuel and souvenirs. A person has to wonder. Had I gone to school and gotten a degree, would I have been in a better position than I am today?"

"Which begs the question," Griffith states, understanding.

"Yes, sir. Will I be better off with a degree four years from now than I would be staying on the path I'm on?"

"You would make a good coach, I believe. You'd need a degree for that."

"I love sports, Coach," Harold says. "I always have. Sports gave me more back than I ever gave to it. And I think you'd agree that I gave it my best. I always left it all on the mat, on the field."

"You gave it all back, that and more."

"Coaching is not for me," Harold says. "It takes a special person, a Gallagher or a Griffith. I'm not that person." Harold pauses; the two men exchange glances. "Do you want more coffee, Coach?"

"No, thanks, I'm fine."

"I'm married. I'm going to be a father," Harold says. "I have to think of that first. And this dam war that's hanging over everyone's head."

"Yes," Griffith says. "If I'm to be truthful, I have to say I'm convinced we'll be in this war within the year. And then I'll have to compete with the military to help my boys grow up a little before they go to it."

"I'm turning down your offer, Coach," Harold says, verbalizing the obvious. "But I want you to know how much I appreciate your remembering me and honoring me this way. It means more than you'll ever know."

Griffith gets up from his chair. Harold does the same, and the two men shake hands. "I best get on the road to Columbia. Need to be there by noon."

"Did you get your bag from upstairs?" Harold asks.

"Brought it down this morning, and it's already in the car. I want to go say goodbye to Theora before I head out."

"Alright," Harold says. The two men go back to the front, final goodbyes are said, and Griffith gets in his car and leaves. Harold doesn't say anything to Theora, but the look he gives her tells her all there is to know. I don't need to start packing, she thinks.

No one can say for sure when it started, but in mid-1941, there appeared to be a gradual, unspoken change in the way people approached their lives, mostly their leisure lives. Over time, an urgency began to emerge that wasn't evident before. Harold and Theora first began to be aware of it on the Friday and Saturday nights at the Whitehouse. It seemed the young people, particularly, danced the fast tunes faster, the slow ones closer, and drank more in between. They partied harder because they weren't worried about tomorrow. Or because they were. The war was there, and they felt the cold breeze of it on their necks.

Roosevelt's brilliant lend-lease policy was his way of trying to help protect democracy while appeasing the largely isolationist American public. "I won't sell you anything you need; you can't afford it anyway, but I'll loan it to you. Pay me back when you can." The Germans invaded Russia in June, and America was to include them in lend-lease as well. Born of necessity, lend-lease may be the perfect definition of "balance of payments deficit," as America began manufacturing ships, tanks, and other mechanized weaponry, ammunition at a cost that might never be returned. And, people sensed that may eventually include lives that will never be returned. For the time being, though, Americans were going back to work making things.

All of this led to expeditious growth at Ft. Leonard Wood, a fact increasingly evident at Lake Ozark, particularly on weekends. Though the Gordons' lease of the Lakeside Casino Restaurant continued, Union Electric, the owner of the building, brought in a small orchestra to play on the screen porch during the warmer months. This seemingly created a "supper club" atmosphere that many of the visitors had become accustomed to in the cities of their origin.

Regardless of this, business at the Whitehouse boomed, made obvious by the number of Army uniforms in evidence each week. Along with the uniforms came an increase in the local single girls squeezing their way in each Friday and Saturday night. Romances, though expectedly short, were numerous, ending for the most part with a promise to return when "this is over." An emerging urgency began to be a part of it all.

One Saturday night in late September, with a dance band in-house to play for the crowd, the dining room is packed, the crowd spilling out into the front counter and tables there. Lawrence is working at the liquor store, and Jessie and Phyllis are helping out. Ruthie, nearly five now, is looking after Larry in the kitchen. Maggie is there with a new assistant, Jane, who has been working out quite well since her hiring in mid-summer. Two somewhat new waitresses are continuing their on-the-job training in the dining room under Theora's guidance. Marion, who is off tonight from his job at UE, is helping Harold to keep order with the assistance of Jack Wickham.

Mid-evening, a young soldier carrying a half-empty bottle of beer wanders through the crowd in the dining room. He appears to be intoxicated as he weaves among the crowd, looking for a place to sit. As soon as he finds one and sits, other patrons arrive from the dance floor to reclaim their chairs. This goes on for a period until Theora tells him he needs to dance or find a place and stand against the wall.

"I don't know how to dance, ma'am," the soldier tells her. "I just listen."

"Well, listen from the wall then, soldier. Please, you're in the way," Theora tells him, then gives Harold a "heads up" about the fellow.

The soldier makes his way to the wall and squeezes between two couples when, momentarily, the two males of the foursome tell him to move on, which he does. Unfortunately, in an effort to accommodate them, he bumps into a table, spilling his beer and knocking over the table's contents. This, as it were, irritates a very large man with sergeant's stripes on his sleeve who is sitting at the table.

"What the hell!" the sergeant says. "You clumsy asshole, watch what you're doing!" He grabs the soldier by the collar to get his attention, simultaneously getting Theora's attention, who simultaneously gets Harold's attention, who hurries toward the altercation, arriving just before the sergeant draws his arm back to hit the smaller man. Whew!

"Sergeant," Harold tells him, grabbing his arm to stop the forward motion. "What's the problem here, sir?"

"This clumsy idiot bumped into our table. Knocked over the mix and ice. Spilled everything." Theora has arrived by this time and has started cleaning up.

"We'll take care of that, sir, on the house. The lady here will take care of you." Harold turns to the young soldier. "And you, young man, what about this?"

"The Sarge is right, sir," the soldier says. "It was an accident. I'm kinda clumsy when my feet are involved, I guess. I didn't mean to bump 'em."

"Alright, soldier, wait here just a minute, and then you and I will take a walk," Harold says and then turns back to the sergeant. "Now, Sarge, you and your friends sit back down and enjoy the rest of your evening." Harold looks pointedly at the big sergeant. "And keep in mind that this is a private business, and if there is any policing to be done here, I'm the one who will do it. Understood?"

The big sergeant, somehow sensing he may be out of his "league," sits down. "Understood," he says quietly.

"Follow me," Harold says to the soldier, who falls in line, if not in step with him. The two go into the kitchen, where Harold, followed by the soldier, sits down at the table. "I see on your uniform there your name is Walker. What's your first name, soldier?"

Walker points to his shoulder and says, "Corporal. Corporal Walker, sir." Harold gives him a look he quickly deciphers, and he says, "Oh, sorry, sir. It's Hiram." There is a pause as he glances up at Maggie and Jane. "But my friends call me Mississippi." Hiram smiles when he says it, followed by, "You know why?"

"You're from Mississippi," Harold says flatly, but smiling. Hiram smiles broadly. "I think you may have had too much to drink," Harold tells him.

"Oh, no sir, one beer," Hiram says. "Half of it. I spilled the other half. That ain't drinkin'. Some of my daddy's 'shine,' now that's drinkin'."

"Well, anyway, let's get you a cup of coffee," Harold says, nodding to Maggie. "You like coffee, don't you?"

"Yessir, I do." Maggie hands him a mug of coffee. "Thank you, ma'am."

"Follow me, Corporal," Harold says as he gets up and heads to the door. Hiram gets up to follow him, and as he does, Ruthie, who has been watching the entire exchange intently, waves and says, "Bye-bye, 'Missipipi.'" Hiram turns and smiles at her as he follows Harold out the door.

Harold leads Hiram outside to the bench directly to the right of the front door. "Why don't you sit here, drink your coffee, and wait for the 11:00 p.m. bus back to the Fort? You can hear the music from here."

"Yes, sir, Mr....?"

"Harold."

"Yes, sir, Mr. Harold."

Harold goes back inside, where Marion is waiting for him. "The boy okay, Harold?" Marion asks.

"He's fine," Harold says. "I'm just worried he might get tangled up with some hothead and get hurt. The boy's name is Hiram Walker. Does that ring a bell with you?"

Marion thinks for a moment, then points into the liquor store to a point on the shelf just above Lawrence's head. "Canadian Club," Marion says. Right beside it is a bottle labeled "Hiram Walker's."

"He did say his daddy made 'shine," but he's no Canadian," Harold says. "He's from Mississippi."

"Small world," Marion says.

Only thirty minutes passed, and, having consumed his coffee, Hiram got a bit antsy and considered if he could sneak in long enough to refill his cup. When the band begins covering Tommy Dorsey's 1940 hit I'll Never Smile Again, Hiram decides to try it. "Slow song," he thinks, "they'll all be swooning and won't see me." Peeking in the front door, he sees Marion at the dining room door. Deciding against that entrance, he walks to the north end of the building to a side door that enters near the bathrooms and stairwell. Finding it unlocked, he sneaks through the door and, crouching, makes his way behind the soda fountain counter and stops at the kitchen door. He peeks in. Ruthie looks up at him just then and smiles. Hiram puts his finger to his lips in a 'shush' motion, and Ruthie begins giggling. Hearing her, Janie, who is about the same age as Hiram and the only other person in the room, turns to see him and smiles also.

"Excuse me, but could I have some more of that good coffee there?" Hiram asks. Janie nods, goes to the pot, and fills his cup.

"Thank you, ma'am… miss?"

"Janie," the girl says. "That's Ruthie and little Larry, there in the playpen."

Ruthie giggles. "Hi, Missipipi."

"Hi, Ruthie," Hiram says.

"Mississippi, you can go out this back door, down the stairs, and back around to the front, and Harold won't catch you," Janie offers.

Hiram looks at the door and decides that it makes sense. "Thanks, Miss Janie," he says and goes out the door.

"Bye, Missipipi," Ruthie says.

When the 11:00 p.m. bus back to Leonard Wood arrives at 10:45, Hiram contemplates getting on it but doesn't. "I have an overnight pass," he thinks. "It's gloomy at the Fort. I'll stay here on the bench." Watching, he notices that a number of military personnel get on the bus, and he realizes that this should provide for some empty seats in the dining room now.

When the bus departs, he is not on it. Instead, he is headed to the door situated at the south roadside end of the building. It, too, is unlocked and provides him with a short hallway to pause in while he peeks around the corner. Noting that Theora's back is to him and Harold is not in the room, he sneaks along the front wall and finds an empty seat at a table with a young couple.

"May I sit with you?" Hiram asks the couple.

"Sure, go ahead, Corporal," the young man says. Hiram sits down. The band is on their last break of the night and will play a final short set before ending at midnight. During the break, the music is switched to the radio, and the Andrews Sisters are doing Boogie Woogie Bugle Boy. The dance floor is crowded and almost frantic as couples burn off some of the alcohol. That Janie is kinda cute, Hiram thinks. If I could dance, I'd ask her to dance. The next number coming across the airwaves is Hoagy Carmichael's *Stardust*, and Hiram really perks up. He turns to the young couple.

"They tried to teach me poetry in school, but I didn't much take to it; the Tree one wasn't bad, but this here is poetry. This song."

The young couple looks at Hiram as he settles back in his chair, closes his eyes, and listens to the music.

Sometimes I wonder why I spend the lonely night
Dreaming of a song,
The melody haunts my reverie…

I'd like to dance with Janie to this one, slow, Hiram thinks. If I could dance. The music ends, and Hiram slowly opens his eyes to see Harold standing over him.

"Uh, hello, Mr. Harold, I ran out of coffee."

"Corporal, did you miss the bus to the Fort?" Harold asks him.

"Well, I didn't exactly miss it, you see. I got an overnight pass, and I didn't want to go back, so I kinda didn't get on it." Hiram smiles.

"Come on," Harold says. Hiram gets up and follows Harold into the kitchen. Ruthie looks up as they enter and starts giggling.

"Look, Janie, it's Missipipi!"

"Hi, Mississippi," Janie says. "More coffee?" Hiram holds up his empty cup and nods. The joy is infectious as Larry begins giggling and dancing in his crib.

"Sit down with me, soldier," Harold says. Hiram sits as Janie pours him coffee.

"Do you have a way back to camp?"

"I hadn't thought about it 'cause I didn't want to go back 'til tomorrow."

"Where are you going to sleep?"

"I hadn't thought about it," Hiram says. "Your bench out front?"

"Sorry, no," Harold says. "Take your coffee and go sit out there for now. I'm going to check around and see if I can find you a ride back." Harold and Hiram leave the kitchen, and Hiram heads out front while Harold walks into the dining room. He approaches a few tables with the enlisted military and arranges for a ride for him at closing, then goes out front to tell Hiram.

"Got you a ride with Staff Sergeant Bowker and his wife," Harold says. "I told them you would be waiting right here for them at closing. So, don't go anywhere. Stay right here."

"Yes, sir, Mr. Harold. Right here." Harold hasn't been gone fifteen minutes when Hiram suddenly needs to go to the bathroom, the copious amounts of coffee taking a toll. Momentarily forgetting his ride, Hiram walks to the south end entrance by the restrooms and goes in to use the facilities.

While he is doing so, the staff sergeant and his wife come out, and not finding the corporal, walk to their car and leave. In the meantime, Harold walks out front and, not seeing the soldier, is relieved to know he is headed back to camp.

An hour later, Harold is doing his final check to make sure all the doors are secure for the night and is at the front when he notices Hiram stretched out on the outside bench.

"For the love of God," Harold mutters as he goes out and shakes the corporal awake. "Did you miss your ride?" Harold asks, exasperated.

"Oh, hi, Mr. Harold," Hiram says, sitting up. "I had to go to the bathroom, all that coffee, you know. I guess I missed 'em."

"Come with me," Harold says. Hiram follows Harold into the Whitehouse as he locks the front door, and the pair walk to the dining room.

"Stay here. Don't move. I'll be right back." Hiram did as he was told while Harold went upstairs, momentarily returning with a blanket and pillow.

"Now, you pick a spot on the floor over there and go to sleep. Don't be getting up and wandering around. You might scare someone. There's other people in the building." He pauses, takes a deep breath, and exhales. "Understood?"

"Understood," Hiram says as he watches Harold turn to go.

"Mr. Harold, would you call me Mississippi? All my friends do." Harold turns and smiles at Hiram.

"Goodnight, Mississippi. Sleep well."

"Goodnight, Mr. Harold."

The Christian Church parishioners in Lake Ozark are still meeting each week in the dining room of the Whitehouse despite having paid off the parcel of land they bought to build on. There is concern among some that they may begin construction and run out of funds necessary to complete the building as they have designed it. The plans that have been drawn up are somewhat ambitious. As drawn, they include the sanctuary with a baptismal font and a nave large enough for a congregation numbering more than two hundred souls—or bodies, souls to come later. At the rear would be a large dining room with a small kitchen, the space to be used for church potluck suppers, wedding receptions, and funeral gatherings. Down an adjacent hall would be the reverend's office, a cloakroom, two small classrooms for a future Sunday School, and restrooms. Near the front door would be a small bell tower with a bell.

There was a faction of the church flock who wanted to jump right in and start in hopes the money would come in as they made progress. Another faction wanted to wait until the treasury had built up sufficiently before breaking ground. The compromise faction suggested building only the sanctuary, with font and nave. This, they said, would provide the meeting space necessary for services and be the cornerstone for future development. The compromise appeared to have the most support, but the issue was tabled for now out of concern for the unknown future relative to war. The one thing everyone did agree on was that the growing number of visitors attending weekly services, compliments of Ft. Wood, would help the treasury grow faster, with a significant increase in the weekly collection already having been noted.

Harold, up early to let Beatrice, the morning waitress, in, bypassed waking Mississippi until the early bus had come and gone. He had simply closed the dining room door after checking to make sure he was still there. He was awakened about nine by Theora, who, having been told by her husband the night before that they had a houseguest, brought him a towel and soap.

"My name is Theora. I am the wife of the man who mistreated you so much last night. I am here to apologize for him.

Offer you a towel and soap so you may freshen up in the bathroom." There is a hint of sarcasm in her tone, and Hiram does sense it. "After that, please come to the kitchen, where I will fix you some breakfast."

"He wasn't mean, ma'am," Hiram says. "Mr. Harold was very nice. He let me sleep here."

"He'll be happy to know you slept well here because he may end up here himself some night."

"Are you expecting a child, ma'am?" Hiram asks.

"How did you know that?"

"I notice you have a bit of a baby bump, but I could sense it, too," Hiram says. "Congratulations."

"You're not a dumb Southern hillbilly, are you?" Theora says, chuckling.

"We don't really have many hills in Mississippi, ma'am," Hiram says.

Theora laughs. "Come on. Get up and go clean up, and I'll see you in the kitchen."

Theora leaves, and Hiram gets up, folds the blanket, lays the pillow on top, and goes to the bathroom. When he finishes and comes into the kitchen, he sees Maggie and says, "Hi" and "Where is Janie?"

"Janie is off today; she worked late last night," Maggie says. "You know where the cups are. Get yourself a cup of coffee."

"You did, too, work late."

"Well, I went upstairs and went to bed after the food sales shut down at ten. Everybody else, including Janie, worked till one a.m."

Hiram walks over to the stove to see what Maggie is making. "Sausage gravy?" he asks. He watches for a moment as Maggie reaches into the oven and takes out a fresh tray of biscuits. "Want me to stir?"

"If you know what you're doing," Maggie says.

"Sure do," Hiram says. "Momma taught me." He stirs a bit. "Do you think we need to put in some more thickening, Miss Maggie?"

"Do you think so?" she says. Hiram nods. "Maybe a might, just don't lessen the flavor. A couple of spoonsful of flour. A dash or two of pepper with it."

"Yes, ma'am."

"You know how to cook, do you?" Maggie asks him as she watches him work on the gravy.

"Yes, ma'am. Momma taught me. She told me," he says, pausing to put his hands on his hips, imitating his mother, "'Hiram, if you can hunt it or collect it or harvest it and cook it, you can survive it.'" He laughs. He turns back to the stove to stir the gravy. "My Daddy would add to that whenever Momma was out of earshot, 'and distill it.'" He chuckles, remembering.

"I had to make more this morning for the 10:30 bus coming in," Maggie explains. "Seems lately passenger numbers have picked up. You sit down now, and I'll fix you some breakfast. How do you like your eggs?"

"I can fix it, Miss Maggie."

She studies him for a moment. "Okay. Grab that pan there; there's eggs in that bowl." He does so and begins to fry two eggs, and when they are about done, Maggie hands him a plate with a biscuit. "Gravy?" she asks.

"Yes, ma'am, please," he says. She dishes gravy onto his biscuit, placing another biscuit on the plate for a "pusher."

Theora comes into the kitchen just as Hiram finishes frying his eggs. "Well, found a new helper, Maggie?"

"Oh, hi, Miss Theora," Hiram says, smiling. "Can I fix you some breakfast?"

"No, thank you," Theora says. "I ate already. Twice." She watches as Hiram dishes up his eggs and sits down. "Are you a cook in the Army, Hiram?"

"No, ma'am. Engineer."

Theora lets his answer register a moment. "God help us," she mutters as she goes out of the kitchen, passing Marion going in.

"Well, I'll be," Marion says when he sees Hiram. "It's Corporal Hiram Walker, United States Army. Good morning, soldier."

"Yessir, Mr. …?"

"Marion."

"You work today, too, Mr. Marion?" Hiram asks. "Weren't you here late?"

"Wife made me come in and help set up for church," Marion says as he pours himself a cup of coffee. He sits down at the table with Hiram. "We hold church services in the dining room because we don't have a church house yet. You're welcome to come."

"I'll help you set up if you want," Hiram says. "I've got to wash my dishes first." Hiram cleans his plate quickly and starts to get up.

"Relax, soldier, we have plenty of time." Hiram sits back down. "What do you do in the Army?"

"I'm an engineer," Hiram says, obviously proud.

"Now, how did that come about?" Marion asks. "A nice Mississippi boy like you?" He started to say "with three left feet," but he didn't, choosing not to be critical.

"My daddy made a lot of money making 'shine' and selling it starting when he was young, and he used it to buy earth-moving equipment. He started teaching me when I was young. I can run it all and could by the time I was sixteen."

"So, why the Army?" Marion asks.

"Well, you see, Mr. Marion, my dad never gave up on the 'shine. He had regulars that just wouldn't drink any other's spirits." He pauses.

"Uh-huh. Call me Marion. And, uh…?"

"One day, I was delivering an order for him," Hiram tells, talking slowly. "Had done it a bunch of times, but this one day, this sheriff's deputy." He looks at Marion. "I don't think he liked this fella I was taking it to. That day, he stopped me and arrested me, and the judge gave me a choice, jail or the Army." He pauses again, thinking back. "I think he wanted to make a sample of me."

"Example, you mean?" Marion corrects him.

"That, too," Hiram says. "I was eighteen, so I chose the Army, and it didn't take the Army very long to find out I couldn't march, so they asked me what I could do, and I told them. They put me in the engineers. We build things."

"What are you building now?" Marion asks.

"Nothing much. Civilians mostly—built airstrips and barracks. We're training recruits, getting more of 'em each week." Hiram pauses, gathering the "pride" in his voice. "That's what I do—teach 'em to run the machines. Did you know, Mr. Marion, we get city boys who've never even driven a car before?"

Harold comes into the kitchen and speaks to Maggie.

"Ten-thirty bus just came in. Just a handful of customers. Theora's got the counter." He sees Marion with Hiram. "You ready, Marion?"

"Yeah," Marion says, getting up. "Hiram's going to help us."

Hiram gets up, carrying his dishes, and heads to the sink. "I just need to wash these dishes first."

"Don't you worry about that, Hiram," Maggie tells him. "Just put them by the sink there and go help Harold and Marion."

"You sure, Miss Maggie?"

"Shoo, get out of here," she says, motioning him out.

Phyllis and Ruthie are with Theora up front when the three men come out of the kitchen. When Ruthie sees Hiram, her eyes light up like it's Christmas. "Missipipi!" she yells and runs, putting her arms around his legs. He immediately leans over and gives her a hug.

"Miss Ruthie!" Hiram says, exchanging greetings. "You look so pretty this morning, all dressed up."

"I'm going to church," she says.

"Well, I've got to help your dad set up for it now."

"I'll come and help," Ruthie says.

The phone rings, and Theora goes to pick it up. "Theora?" a female voice on the other end says. "It's Millicent. Herman is sick—very sick. Woke up this morning and spoke with Doctor Attic; he's meeting me at his office. We won't be at the service. I'm so sorry." It is all very hurried. Theora hardly has a chance to acknowledge the call before it abruptly ends.

"Herman is sick," Theora tells Phyllis. "Millie won't be here. No piano player. No music." Theora goes to clean up as the last of the customers at the counter get up to return to the bus.

"The service will be shorter," Phyllis says. "That'll make Harold and Marion happy." She goes into the dining room to the open storage room where the men have been taking out folding chairs. "I don't know whether we need the books or not," she says to no one in particular as she looks at the box of hymnals. "I suppose we need them for the readings and responses," she decides and takes an armful.

"You talking to yourself, Phyllis?" Marion says.

"Millie won't be here. Herman is sick," she says as she places a book on every other chair. "No piano. No music."

Hiram, who has been listening while he places chairs, looks up just as Theora enters the room. "Miss Theora, I can play the piano." Everybody looks at him but doesn't speak. "I can play," he says again. "Church music. Momma taught me."

"Wait a minute," Theora says. "You can cook, you're an engineer, and you play the piano. Anything you can't do?"

"I can't dance," Hiram says.

"Let's hear you play something, Hiram," Phyllis says. Hiram goes to the piano, sits down, and renders a quality version of "The Old Rugged Cross."

"God help us," Theora says.

"He just did, Theora," Phyllis says.

The parishioners gather and have a very nice service, the congregation singing two numbers with Hiram's accompaniment. Everyone thanks him for his help. As the dining room begins to empty out, Ruthie walks over and tugs on Hiram's pant leg. "Missipipi, can I watch you play the piano?"

"Sure, you can. Come on." Ruthie follows Hiram, and the two settle side by side on the piano bench. Hiram plays a short, easy ditty. "You try it now."

"I can't play, Missipipi," Ruthie says, looking up at him. She holds up her hands. "I don't have enough fingers."

Hiram holds up his hands. "How many fingers do I have?" Hiram asks.

"Ten," Ruthie says.

"How many keys are there on the piano?" Hiram asks.

"I don't know. Bunches."

"Well, I can't get to all of them, so I just have to use my ten fingers and get to as many as I can," Hiram explains. "Sooner or later, I'll get to all of them." Ruthie looks at Hiram and puts her fingers on the keys. "Just like I did — use what you got and get to as many as you can; in time, you'll get to the rest of them." Ruthie puts her fingers on some keys and giggles as she plays.

Theora has witnessed the exchange between the two and goes to her sister, who is collecting hymnals. "Phyllis, I suggest you call around and find a piano teacher. I think you're going to need one."

Hiram does manage to catch the afternoon bus back to Ft. Wood. Before he leaves, he asks Harold if he can come back the next weekend. Harold tells him, "Wait a minute, I'll be right back," and goes upstairs. When he returns, he is carrying the old valise he carried when he first came to Lake Ozark from Tulsa. He hands it to Hiram. "Here, pack a bag. We'll have a room for you."

Harry has finished his Coast Guard training and is working as a sonar technician on a vessel out of an East Coast port. The first week in October, he gets leave, comes home, marries Maxine, and takes her with him back east. It is a small ceremony, though Grant and Margaret do attend along with Maxine's parents. Harry quietly shares with his father the surprising number of intercepts his ship — and others — have had with German U-boats. Grant asks him not to tell Margaret so she won't worry "more than she already does." Harold calls with congratulations while his brother is still in Tulsa. "Why don't you put in for a transfer to Lake Ozark?" Harold suggests.

"Why, you got a U-boat problem there?" Harry asks.

"Not that I know of, but there is a small Coast Guard craft that rides around the Lake, making sure people's docks have a proper War Department permit."

"Sounds like hazardous duty," Harry says, laughing.

"It can be if some old-timer with a double-barrel decides he doesn't need a permit."

Harry laughs. "They concerned those docks will restrict shipping?"

"No, the Dam does that," Harold says.

"Take care of yourself, big brother."

"Watch your back, kid," Harold says before he hangs up.

Don Fry has been stationed at a base near Avon Park in Florida since finishing basic training. It is an officer training program required before attending flight school. He expects to be turned down for flight school due to his vision but hopes to be accepted for navigator training if his concerns come true. When he writes home, he reminds everyone that the temperature in late October in Florida is a pleasant 82 degrees, 70 degrees overnight. In a letter to Lawrence and Jessie, he tells about a weekend pass he had when he and a friend went an hour north to Winter Haven.

"We went to this tourist place called Cypress Gardens. You would have loved it, Jess. Pretty flowers and a unique tree they called a 'banyan.' They had little tour boats with electric motors that took you on a canal all through the gardens. The whole place was located on a lake, and the local kids did a water-skiing exhibition with pyramids, tricks, and stuff. The whole time, I was thinking about kids doing that at Lake of the Ozarks. Someday, maybe? When this is all over."

He doesn't become a pilot but is trained as a navigator, made a second lieutenant, and assigned to a transport crew ferrying men and equipment back and forth from near Daytona Beach to Washington, D.C. Before reporting to his duty station, he is given leave and spends most of his time in Springfield with Suzy.

"I finish up this semester, and my friend and I have put in applications to several hospitals on the East Coast," she tells Don. "The most hiring seems to be on the coasts, both of them. I decided that I had the best chance of seeing you on the East Coast."

"Oh, Suzy," Don approves. "That's perfect. When will you know? What cities?"

"D.C., primarily, but Baltimore and Norfolk...Virginia. There are Naval facilities there."

"They're all good; not far from D.C.," Don says. "When will you know?"

"Graduation at the end of January," Suzy says. "Then, internship at St. John's until I get a call. Maybe as early as late March."

"It is all going to work out," Don declares to Suzy on the last day he is home. "I know it. I can't wait to see you again."

Hiram returns to the Whitehouse on the following Saturday, October 4th, on the late morning bus from the St. Robert main gate. He is carrying Harold's valise with clothes and toiletries for an overnight stay. There is no one in the front area when he arrives, so he proceeds to the kitchen. When he opens the door, the first person he sees is Janie, who looks up and, seeing him, smiles wide.

"Hello, Mississippi. I'm so happy you came back."

"I'm glad I came back, too, and that you're here, Janie," Hiram says, smiling.

Maggie has watched this exchange with a knowing look. Hiram sees her and says, "Hello, Miss Maggie."

"Just Maggie, Hiram," she says. "I'm glad you're here; we need your help making buns for the hamburger sandwiches. Our supplier left us short this week, and we need to make about four dozen before late afternoon. You can help Janie there."

"Yes, ma'am," Hiram says. "I'll just wash my hands here first." He goes to the sink, washes his hands vigorously, and dries them. "Okay, Janie, where do I start?" he asks as he puts on an apron to protect his uniform. Janie instructs as the pair begin to mix together ingredients for the dough.

Theora enters the kitchen and immediately sees Hiram. "Oh, good, you're here, soldier. Have a room for you. Last room down the hall when you go upstairs."

"Thank you, ma'am," Hiram says. "How's your baby doing?"

"Baby's fine. Harold's fine, I'm fine. And you?"

"I'm fine."

"Will you be here tomorrow, too?" Theora asks.

"Yes, ma'am, till the afternoon bus back to the Fort," Hiram says.

"Can you play for church again? Millie and Herman are still out."

"Yes, ma'am, if you need me to."

"Can you play the Doxology?" Theora asks. "We'd like to start services with that if you can?"

"Yes, ma'am, if it's in the book. I might practice early tomorrow morning if that's okay, though."

"That's fine," Theora says. "Not too early." With that, she leaves and goes back to the dining room, where she moves two chairs together at a small table just inside and to the right of the door. She makes a sign that says "Reserved, Mississippi and friend" and places it on the table, then another, the same, and places it across the chairs. "This way, he can listen without bumping into things," she muses to herself.

In the interest of not bumping into things, Hiram asks Janie if she can dance. "Yes, some, slow dance mainly. Why?" she replies. "Can you teach me?" Hiram asks. "Maybe, why do you want to learn?" she asks. "So, I can dance with you," he says.

"Oh," Janie says, slow to register what he has said. "You want to dance with me?"

Harold walks into the kitchen, looking for Hiram. "I heard you were here, Mississippi." Harold shakes his hand. "There's a lady in the drive, got gas, and now her car won't start. You think you could take a look at it?"

Hiram looks at Maggie as if asking for permission.

"You go on. We'll be fine here."

The two men exit the kitchen and walk out to the driveway, and it doesn't take Hiram long before he finds that one of the battery cables is loose and corroded and not making contact. The problem was fixed. The lady on her way again, Harold, turns to Hiram, curious.

"Something I don't understand. Marion told me about your experience with heavy equipment. How can you handle all those pedals and controls and have trouble marching and walking?"

"Practice," Hiram explains. "I think I've been handling machinery as long as I can walk. Unlike a lot of daddies, mine was patient while he taught me. A patient man."

"As long as you want to come and help us on weekends, you'll be welcome," Harold says. "I'll pay you accordingly. You'll have a room and food."

"I don't need no pay. Army's paying me."

"Well, we'll talk about it," Harold says.

"Mr. Harold, the Fort is nice, but I miss home."

For the rest of the year, the Whitehouse became Hiram Walker's home away from home. It took some work and patience, but Janie taught him to dance, and an unexpected romance blossomed. At Thanksgiving, he joined the Robinson clan as they gathered at Bagnell. The Haages came from Kansas, one or other of the kids chanting at every moment, "We're not in Kansas anymore, Toto." Dorothy was expecting again, which was not unexpected, but much of the talk was of Theora's approaching due date. Most everyone razzed her because of her small stature: "We can roll her around the yard" or "She's as wide as she is tall." Only Hiram stuck up for her. "You be nice to Miss Theora. She's a sweet lady," and thereon endeared himself to her forever. There was some talk of potential war, and the Haage boys were especially interested in talking to Hiram and asked him many questions.

The family present at the Robinson's that day were all quite thankful for the blessings they had received and prayed for continued peace for America. In a rare moment, no one complained about the length of the prayer offered up by Bert before the meal. It was a "good day," as everyone present expressed.

That evening, after events quieted down, Bert approached Lena in private and asked her about Dorothy's next baby.

"Lena, I keep hearing those kids talking to 'Toto.' Dorothy's not planning on naming her next kid 'Toto,' is she?"

"What! Well, I sure hope not."

PART V
AND SHARE A WAR

The first Sunday morning of December, the seventh was like any other; the buses came and went on time, and newspapers arrived. More and more passengers coming through were in U.S. military uniforms and were dispersing to various bases throughout the country. In the future, those alive to experience it would talk about where they were and what they were doing when they first heard about Pearl Harbor. For every American alive on that day, the events were not simply a forever memory but something more venerable. Roosevelt called that Sunday "a date that will live in infamy." More so, the day was riveted onto every soul and could only be pried loose at death by God.

The radio was on in the Whitehouse that day as it almost always is. Though not on the outside speakers, the radio could generally be heard in most rooms of the building. Theora was upstairs lying down, a daily rest part of her routine now as her due date of mid-January approached. Hiram had just packed his bag and was in the kitchen with Maggie and Janie visiting while waiting for his afternoon bus back to Ft. Wood. Harold had just come in from getting gas for a customer and walked behind the counter to enter the sale in the cash register when he first heard the broadcast alert. "We interrupt this program to... the Japanese... Pearl Harbor. Hawaii."

Harold's initial reaction to the news alert was not unlike many others: disbelief at what he had just heard, and for a moment, he was frozen in time as the reporter continued to offer whatever details he had. "The damage to Naval and..." Theora had heard and came to the top of the stairs.

"Harold, what is happening? What did I hear?"

"It's okay, honey," Harold yelled back up to her. "Just lay back down and rest."

"No, I can't," she says as she starts down the stairs. "They attacked us. We're at war. Oh, my God, we're at war!"

Hiram comes out of the kitchen, followed by Janie and Maggie.

"Did I hear that right, Harold?" he asks.

"Yes, Mississippi, you did. The Japs attacked us."

"I can't miss that bus to the Fort," Hiram says. "They'll be canceling all leave."

"Will you be able to come back, Mississippi?" Janie says.

"I don't know what will happen, Janie. I'll let you all know."

"You take care of yourself, Hiram," Theora says, tears running down her face. Harold goes to her and holds her close. "A damn war, Harold! What if you have to go?"

"We'll manage that when that time comes," Harold says.

Later, after Hiram had left on the bus back to Fort Wood, Harold finds himself wandering around the building until Theora stops him. "Harold, please just sit down with me and talk." He walks over to the table she is sitting at in the dining room and sits briefly before suddenly rising again.

"Harold, where are you going?"

"Lon and Pauline don't have a radio," Harold says. "I need to go out there and tell them what has happened." And abruptly, he is out the front door, in his car, headed to the Stantons' shop.

Lon's first reaction when Harold tells him and Pauline about Pearl Harbor is to say simply: "We'll out-build them." Harold is quiet and doesn't respond to him as the three sit at a small round table in the back of the shop. "This country can outbuild any other on Earth. We'll build more, we'll build bigger, we'll bury them in it."

"Our manufacturing is down now, Lon," Harold says. "We've got a long way to go."

"But when we set our minds to it, look out," Lon says. Harold and Pauline both study him as he speaks. "I know how to manufacture things; I could make something the government needs right here. These people, our local people, won't all be carrying a rifle. Somebody has got to make the rifle stocks."

"What are you saying, Lon?" Pauline asks. "What do you mean?"

"I'm saying that next week, depending on what Roosevelt says tomorrow, I'm going to contact the government and see what they need to be built and let them know we can build it." Lon gets up and walks over to the back window. The view is of the lake not far off in the distance. "You know how many soldiers' footlockers could have been built just from the timber harvested from this valley when they built the lake?"

On the way back to the Whitehouse following his visit with Lon and Pauline, Harold now appears assured of something he had doubted earlier in the day. "We are going to win this war," he repeats quietly to himself as he drives.

By the time Harold arrives back at the Whitehouse, Theora has sent Maggie and Janie home and closed up as per the usual winter Sunday routine.

"Marion and Phyll and the baby are coming for dinner soon, Harold. There's plenty of leftovers in the walk-in. I'll fix you a highball."

Though not scheduled till the following morning, Marion had been put on alert since the Pearl Harbor news, along with all other U.E. Security personnel.

"They're being cautious," Marion says. "Nobody knows what to think, what to do. Reports I've heard say everybody on the West Coast is on alert. They're worried the Japs are preparing to invade there."

"Everybody is running scared, I guess," Harold says, "What kind of a world are we bringing our children into?"

The quiet conversation is interrupted by the sound of the piano across the dining room. Ruthie is sitting there tapping keys, and her slow tapping begins to make sense as the adults stop talking to listen.

"Oh... say can... you see... by the...." is the easily detected sound.

"Hiram started teaching her that little song this morning after church," Phyllis says. "She seems to learn quick." The four adults are quiet as they sit and listen to Ruthie play.

Christmas 1941 is somewhat subdued around the country, including Lake Ozark and the empty seats around family tables are indicative of the sudden travel demands. For some, the trip home may be the last for an unknown while. Hiram is able to get a brief leave and manages a bus ticket out of Rolla to Memphis, where his daddy will pick him up. He calls Harold to let him know.

"We've got a new class of recruits we just started training, and they have us on a tight schedule to get these guys ready to ship out, but my captain gave me a few days, so I headed home. I'll call when I get back to Wood. And Harold, tell Janie for me, will you?"

"I will, Mississippi. Enjoy your time at home."

Don Fry is able to get to Springfield for a few days, and Lawrence and Harvey's families gather there with him. His time home includes many hours with Suzy, though they are bittersweet. The promise of both ending up near the other on the East Coast is no longer possible. Don's new orders have him transferring along with his plane and crew to England, where they will be tasked with ferrying high-ranking officers.

Grant and Margaret stay very busy with the bar they have bought. Tom and Lena are kept busy with two young children, Bobby Sam and Teresa, and sister Ruth has married Mr. Tom Trinks. The Tulsa Pilkingtons continue to close on Sundays and Mondays, giving Margaret rest time and Grant fishing time. When they are open, they have noticed that their regular customers, most past draft age, drink more—many obviously worrying about younger brothers, nephews, and sons. Word from Harry and Maxine on the East Coast is more than business as usual, as it is now official that America is at war with the Nazis. His schedule keeps him constantly at sea, in port only briefly for resupply.

Harold and Theora's Christmas, the day spent at the Robinsons' in Bagnell, comes and goes quietly, and in mid-January, Theora gives birth to a son. The birth takes place in Dr. Attic's office in Eldon and is uneventful. The boy is named John Harold, and his father is happy, even though he is not a girl. "After all," he tells Marion, "the boy is named after me. If it was a girl, we couldn't do that."

"Well, actually, you could," Marion corrects him. "But she'll never get a date."

As for Ruthie, John's birth is just more of the same. He's nice, she tells her Aunt Theora, but he's not her sister. Her pleas to her mother are less frequent now—not that she's given up; she's more patient. Phyllis credits her time on a piano bench next to Mississippi for that.

In April, the Doolittle Raid on Tokyo produces little damage but provides a psychological boost, as it demonstrates to Japan that their home island is vulnerable. Unfortunately, the American-protected island nation of the Philippines is more vulnerable, and American Commander Douglas MacArthur is ordered by Roosevelt to retreat to Australia in February prior to the raid. In April, the Japanese began an all-out assault on the Bataan Peninsula, and by May 6th, the last of the American and Filipino troops on Corregidor surrendered to the Japanese.

Foreign civilians, including Mona and her family, are rounded up and herded into "camps." Santo Tomas, the Newland residence for the unknown future, is on the campus of the University of Manila and essentially makes the family "prisoners of war." Their treatment, initially, is not harsh — far from the horrific treatment of the surrendered Allied troops, who are force-marched to their place of internment. Many of these troops do not survive the "death march," as it is called, and those who do become "slave labor."

Mona is able to get a few letters out of the country prior to her family's internment, and she appears to portray their situation as temporary and their captors as humane. But Hannah and Jessie do not believe what she is saying. Humane people do not bomb another country for no reason. She is either overwhelmingly naïve or trying to make sure they do not worry. Jessie's repeated calls to their church offices in Springfield provide them with nothing of substance — probably simply because the church knows nothing.

It is early in the war, but the Newland family's confinement in Santo Tomas provides the first direct link of the Whitehouse family to the horrors of the conflict. There are others, indirect at this point — Don Fry, Harry Pilkington, and Corporal Hiram Walker prominent among them.

Mississippi returned from his brief Christmas visit home and is back training a battalion of combat engineers at Fort Leonard Wood. He has been able to get passes each weekend and come "home" to the Whitehouse. He and Janie, though they have never been on an actual date, are considered a "couple" and have even danced once or twice on Saturday nights, taking a break from their "chores."

Early one Sunday morning in May, coffee in hand, Hiram goes to sit with Harold on the bench out in front of the building.

"Harold, I don't know how much longer I'll get to come here."

"Why do you think that, Hiram? Something wrong with your job at the Fort?"

"No. Not that." Hiram pauses and sips his coffee. "I think they are going to ship us out as soon as we finish training our current group." Harold turns and looks at him, obvious concern on his face. "The Major, my boss, thinks our cadre is going to be given command of the battalion we're training and will ship out with the unit."

"How soon is that likely to happen?" Harold asks.

"The training cycle ends in mid-June. Soon after, I would guess."

"Have you told Janie? She is very... very fond of you, you know."

"I know. I plan on telling her as soon as I know for sure." Hiram pauses and sips his coffee again. "I was wondering..." He hesitates a moment.

Harold turns to look at him. "Yes?"

"I was wondering. If one Saturday night, Janie and I could have time off so I could take her to dinner and a movie? You know, like a date? Oh, and I would need to borrow your car."

Harold, amused, looks at his new young friend. "Well, I think we could work that out. We'll have to clear it with Theora, but I'm sure you've noticed she has been in a much better mood since she gave birth."

"Yes," Hiram giggles. "I noticed that."

Not long after word of Mona's internment, Jessie is joined at lunch at her house on Lake Road 1-A by Theora and baby Johnny. She calls it a play date with Larry, but considering he is a toddler and Johnny, a baby, there is little play taking place. She just wants to talk. Jessie has, since the beginning of the emerging relationship between Harold and Theora, come to care greatly for the younger girl. Her relationship with Harold has always been one not unlike that toward a younger brother, and the closeness between the two women grew easily out of that love.

At lunch, Jessie has a highball, and Theora turning down the offer, instead choosing iced tea.

"I don't see how you can have a drink in the middle of the day," Theora says. "It would put me to sleep the rest of the afternoon."

"Lawrence doesn't know—please don't say anything—but since word of Mona's situation, I worry a lot. I'm not sleeping well. I've found that the drink helps me to sleep when I put Larry down for his afternoon nap."

"I won't say anything, but Harold worries about you. And Mona, of course."

"Harold and Lawrence are very different men, Theora. Lawrence does not show emotion easily. He keeps it inside." She pauses and takes a drink, a deep breath. "He worries about Donnie, but you wouldn't know it."

"Well, Harold is not outwardly emotional either, as you know, Jess. But he can, and in fact, loves to joke around and laugh."

"Yes, he has always had a sense of humor," Jessie says. "But there is a lot going on inside there, too."

"There is. That is true."

"The thing is, with Lawrence, sometimes I need more, and he can't provide it."

"Have you tried talking with him?" Theora asks.

"I have. Lawrence is in his own world. His job—he is so dedicated. He's careful with money, methodically saving, thinking of new ways to earn." Theora looks at her, aware of some of what is being said.

"Please, Theora, don't misunderstand. He provides very well for his family, and I love him."

"We know you do—Harold and I both."

There is silence for a few moments, the two young women digesting their very personal conversation. And then, suddenly, Jessie looks directly at Theora.

"Theora, if something happens to me, will you raise Larry?"

Theora is, at first, stunned by Jessie's request.

"What! Jessie? Nothing is going to happen to you. Why do you say that?"

"I know nothing is going to happen, Theora. I meant, you know, just in case."

Theora looks at her friend.

"Of course I will, Jess. Of course."

The Doolittle Raid, though a needed morale boost after the devastation of Pearl Harbor, mattered little in moving the needle in America's direction. There is deep concern among the naval commanders in the Pacific theater. The American strategy is simple: is-land-hop across the Pacific, building or rebuilding airstrips until American planes can reach the mainland of Japan. Then invade.

An island already under American control and an obvious target of Japanese strategy to help reach and control Samoa and Hawaii is Midway Island. American codebreakers intercept a Japanese plan for a surprise attack on American naval forces near Midway and take the island. Boldly, knowing the details of the Japanese attack, America plans a surprise attack of its own. Four Japanese aircraft carriers and three American carriers participate. At the end of the three-day battle, all four Japanese carriers are sunk, along with a heavy cruiser. America loses a carrier and a destroyer. It is a great victory for naval and air forces and is quickly compared to England's Trafalgar battle.

To the folks at home, the Battle of Midway meant "payback" for the horrors of Pearl Harbor. The enemy carriers that were sunk, and many of the personnel that went down with them, were with the Pearl attack force. Many of the Japanese planes shot down at Midway were also there. The morale boost in America was immense as citizens listened to the news accounts and read the written accounts in the newspapers. In the Pacific theater of war, after Midway, Americans began to believe they would win.

After Pearl Harbor and America's declaration of war against Japan, the Axis powers Germany and Italy, as expected, declared war on the U.S., to which America reciprocated. In late January, the first American forces deployed to the European theater, landing in Northern Ireland, but not until late November, during Operation Torch in French North Africa, would American forces engage the enemy in battle in the European Theater.

Throughout the midwestern part of the country called Cardinal Nation, the news is good going into the summer as the "birds on the bat are sitting pretty," leading the National League. Hopes for winning the Pennant are high, and Harold makes sure the broadcast is on the outside speaker whenever the team is playing. Unusually, the Cardinals are not scheduled on Saturday, June 13th, after the news of the Midway victory. Consequently, few people are milling about in front of the Whitehouse when the afternoon bus from Fort Wood pulls in. Harold is there, having just finished with a fuel customer when Mississippi steps down off the bus.

"Well, look at you," Harold says approvingly upon seeing the young soldier. He is in his dress uniform and sporting the three stripes of a sergeant. "Do we have to salute you now?"

Hiram smiles. "I got promoted, got my own platoon now. But you don't salute sergeants."

"Well, congratulations. Janie will be impressed."

"About that. Can we have that date tonight we talked about?"

"You want to take me out?" Harold asks with a hint of Bert Robinson in his voice.

"You know what I mean, Harold — take Janie out?"

Harold laughs. "We'll manage. I bet I can get Phyllis to help out. She'll want to bring Ruthie to see you all dressed up." The two head to the door and enter the building.

"Don't you think you should ask Janie, though? What if she says no?"

Hiram looks at Harold. "What? You think she might?"

Harold chuckles again. "She's in the kitchen. Go ask her, Sergeant Walker."

He asks; Janie accepts, and Maggie reminds her she can finally wear the extra clothes she has kept in a spare room upstairs. Janie does, dresses up, Harold gives Hiram the keys, and the couple starts out the door when suddenly Hiram stops.

"I don't know where we're going. Harold, Theora, where are we going?"

"It's early yet. You have plenty of time," Theora says. "I suggest you go all the way into Jefferson City to that nice theater across from the Capitol. They show good movies there."

"Oh, Hiram, if we do that, can we have pizza?" Janie is very excited at the thought.

"What's that?" Hiram does not understand.

"Pizza. There's a place in old Munichsberg—Emma's Tap Room. They have a pizza oven. I had it once with friends."

"Piece-of-what, though?" Hiram asks, confused.

"Pizza," Janie says. He still looks confused. "Never mind. I'll show you; you'll love it."

And Janie is right—he loves it. The place is not far from the theater on High Street, and they easily make the movie on time. "That's my favorite pizza now," Hiram announces as they leave the restaurant and head to the theater.

The movie is called *That Hamilton Woman* and stars Vivien Leigh, which pleases Janie, a fan of Scarlett O'Hara. Hiram not only doesn't know who Vivien Leigh is, he doesn't know who Scarlett is either. He knows who Horatio Nelson is, as the U.S. victory at Midway has been compared to Nelson's victory at Trafalgar in newspaper accounts throughout the previous week. Although the film was released in mid-1941, there is speculation that it was quickly re-released after Midway to capitalize on current affairs. A rumor around England prior to the film's initial release was that Churchill asked for it to be made in hopes it would help rouse morale among his fellow countrymen.

On the ride home from Jefferson City, Hiram tells Janie that he expects to be shipping out soon and doesn't know where or when he will get back.

"Will you write me?" she asks.

"Every time I write my momma, I'll write you, too."

The next day, before Hiram boards the bus back to the fort, Ruthie goes to him, hugs him, and says, "Sergeant Missipipi, you look very handsome in your uniform."

"Well, thank you. Did you know you're my favorite piano student of all time?"

"I'm your only piano student."

"And the best. Ever."

Hiram tells Harold that his trainee group graduates on Tuesday and orders for the battalion could come any time after.

"I'll try to get here to say goodbye before we leave, but I don't know when."

"Just do your best, son," Harold says. "That's all anyone can ever ask from you."

That same Sunday afternoon, the Cardinals win a double-header from the Phillies, and there happens to be a number of folks milling about in front of the Whitehouse when Hiram boards the bus.

That morning at church services, Harold asks Pauline if Lon has heard anything from his inquiries to the government about manufacturing.

"He's made a lot of calls, and they keep referring him to others," Pauline says. "He's waiting for someone who promised to call him back."

"Don't let him give up," Harold says.

"Oh, he won't," Pauline assures him.

Lon isn't the only one talking to the government about work. It seems Theora and Phyllis' brother George has recently managed to secure a job in Washington as an "efficiency expert."

"A what?" older brother Clyde says, astonished when he hears. He and Pebble, along with the Pilkingtons and Claytons, are at the Robinsons' for dinner that Sunday night when Bert relays the news. "An efficiency expert? George Robinson! Oh my God, we're going to lose the war."

Clyde has received notice to report for a physical and, ahead of that, enlists in the Army in order to be able to have some control over his report date. George, who is not eligible for the draft due to a defect from birth but who wants to help, has looked to find a way to join the war effort and, in the process, soon finds he and his wife relocated to the nation's capital. Everybody but Harold laughs when Bert shares the news.

"Clyde, tell Harold the story," Theora says. "He doesn't know it."

"When we were young boys, one day, Mom was in the middle of fixing something in the kitchen," Clyde begins, chuckling to himself. "And she runs outta an ingredient and gives George the money and sends him to the store up in town to get it. What is it—a quarter, half a mile at most?" Clyde pauses and starts laughing harder. "I'll never forget it. Mom waits and waits. A long time goes by—he could have made three trips to the store and back. Finally, she sent me to go look for him. I get halfway there and find him sitting under a tree at the side of the road. I say, 'George, what the hell are you doing? Mom's worried sick.' He looks at me and says, 'I'm waiting for a car to come along so I can hitch a ride. Cars get you there a lot faster.'"

Harold laughs. "Sounds efficient to me."

On Thursday afternoon, a car pulls into the parking lot by the Whitehouse, and Mississippi, in fatigues, gets out and enters the building in somewhat of a hurry. He is carrying Harold's borrowed valise. The driver, a sergeant, also in fatigues, remains in the car.

"Harold? Theora?" There is no immediate answer to his calls, and he hurries into the kitchen, where he stops suddenly when he sees Janie and Maggie.

"Hiram? Wha…?" Janie is so surprised to see Mississippi that she can't speak. Maggie motions for him to sit down.

"I can't stay long," Hiram says as he sits. "My friend drove me over from the Fort so I could say goodbye. We're flying out tonight, my whole battalion. My first sergeant gave me a few hours so I could come and let you know. I have to be back by five." He looks at Janie and smiles as she sits across from him. "Are Harold and Theora here?"

"They're upstairs with the baby," Maggie says. "I'll get them. They will want to see you." She leaves to find the Pilkingtons, and soon, they are all gathered around the table in the kitchen when Hiram suddenly remembers his friend in the car.

"Oh my gosh, I forgot Sgt. George, in the car. Let me get him." Hiram gets up to go get his friend, remembers. "Oh, Harold, your satchel. Thanks again." Hiram hands him the valise. Harold nods, acknowledging, and Hiram goes to the car and brings his friend into the kitchen, introducing every-one. "Sgt. George—Jim—is a fellow platoon sergeant. We're in the same company. He ships tonight, too."

"Any idea where you're going?" Harold asks.

"Right now, just flying to California. That's all they tell us."

"That's a guarantee we're headed to the Pacific," Sgt. George adds. "The military is very good at protecting troop movements and deployments. They won't tell us more than that."

"You boys need something to eat? Have you eaten? I'll fix you something. Got a fresh cherry pie," Maggie, always the mother hen, says.

"No, ma'am, I'm fine. Thank you, though," Sgt. George says.

"Not so fast, Sarge," Hiram says. "You'll have a piece of that cherry pie over there, and so will I. You won't regret it. You will insult Maggie if you don't."

"Well, I certainly don't want to insult you, ma'am," Sgt. George says.

Janie, who has been mostly quiet, gets up. "I'll get it," she says.

Hiram gets up also. "I'll help you," he says.

"You promised you'd write, remember?" Janie says qui-etly as they get the pie. "You won't forget?"

"I won't forget. One to Mama, one to you."

The two soldiers enjoy their pie and coffee while the group sits and makes "small talk." A few stories are told, mostly about Mississippi, and he blushes a bit. A favorite is about Janie trying to teach Mississippi to dance. Finally, Sgt. George, looking at his watch, says to the room: "It's a quarter to four." He turns to Hiram. "Mississippi, we need to go if we're to make it by five."

The six walk out of the building to the car and exchange hugs and handshakes. When it comes to Hiram, he hesitates, and Janie walks over and stands directly in front of him. "Mississippi, you are going to kiss me goodbye, aren't you?"

Before Hiram can answer, Sgt. George interjects and says, "You know what, I better go back into the restroom before we drive back. Won't take but a minute, Mississippi."

"We'll show you where it is, Sarge," Harold says as he nods to Theora and Maggie to follow him.

With the others gone, Hiram moves closer to Janie, takes her in his arms, and kisses her. It is a long kiss, and when ended, the two stand for a time, just holding one another.

"I love you, Janie, and I'll miss you."

"I love you too, Hiram, and I already miss you."

Sgt. George comes out of the building and gets in the car, and Hiram, after another, quicker kiss, gets in the car, and it pulls out of the parking area and onto Highway 54. Janie watches it until long after it goes up and around the curve by the school road.

Theora has gone upstairs to check on baby Johnny and picks him up to hold while she looks out a front window. She is watching the young couple say goodbye. She has seen *That Hamilton Woman* and knows the history well. In her head, she rehearses Janie asking for the goodbye kiss, and suddenly, her mind is filled with the words, "Kiss me, Hardy," and she begins to cry.

When Paul and Bernie Gordon first came to Lake Ozark in 1932, they opened a small pharmacy in a building near the middle of town. Paul, being a young, licensed pharmacist, thought they would do well. As it turned out, most locals were convinced that grandma's remedies were still best for what "ailed ya," and when that didn't work, Mother Nature was a good backup. The result of all this was closing the pharmacy and taking the lease offered on the Lakeside Casino Restaurant. Consequently, Paul went from chemicals to gravies and was quite successful as a chef. When the war came along, the Army drafted him into service, running the pharmacy at the hospital at Fort Wood. They gave him the rank of Sergeant E-6, and with an assistant trained, he was able to be home most weekends.

The Saturday morning after Hiram leaves, Bernie calls Harold and Theora to tell them that Paul died during the night. "The doctor said most likely it was a heart attack, but they put on the death certificate 'natural causes.'"

People die during wartime: bullets, bombs, bayonets — lots of ways to go. That is an expected possible result of life on a battlefield. But for non-combatants, civilians, the most common end of life outside of a war zone comes with what doctors describe as "natural causes."

"What the hell is natural about a man dying of a heart attack at the age of forty-two?" Theora asks Harold.

"Nothing. Unless they do an autopsy to help them understand what happened, it's a 'natural cause.' Nine times out of ten, that means a heart attack."

Theora immediately goes to the Casino to be with her friend and mentor. Phyllis is there, and the three close friends attempt to face the change together.

"Paul seemed tired at night more than before," Bernie tells them. "I thought it was just stress from his work at the Fort. Luckily, we had recently hired an assistant chef who helped carry the load. I'll have to depend on him now."

"If I can help — wait tables, cook, anything — I'm available, Bernie," Phyllis says.

"I have a good crew now. I think we'll be okay. But thank you. I know you're there." Bernie pauses as if making a decision. "I'm going to close until after the funeral."

"That's for the best, I think," Theora says.

Bernie begins to cry softly. "I should have known something was wrong. He complained of heartburn often and lacked stamina. No energy. I should have known."

The three friends exchange looks until, finally, Bernie rises and wipes the tears from her eyes. "Well, I have a child to raise and a husband to bury. I best get on with it."

Two days later, a service is held at Phillips Funeral Home in Eldon, and Paul is transported to Tulsa for interment.

By late summer 1942, it was obvious to Harold and Theora and their employees that business was changing dramatically. No longer were Friday and Saturday the big nights for dancing and drinking; it was every night, Sunday the exception. Soldiers from Fort Leonard Wood could take leave during the week, as well as weekends and the Lake of the Ozarks was the primary destination. The Dam and Lake were sights to be admired, and the soldiers came to witness them and forget the war. Locals, too, seemed less inclined to go home at night—they wanted community. The war prompted that change, too. Something about "safety in numbers," perhaps.

This increased business activity prompted the Pilkingtons to investigate the new music machines called "jukeboxes." They couldn't afford a band every night and felt they could supplement the radio broadcasts with such a machine. Consequently, in September 1942, they purchased a Wurlitzer 950 box. It offered 24 78-rpm record choices. Its coin chute accepted nickels, dimes, and quarters, and the hope was that it would help pay for itself. However, the clientele at the Whitehouse, having gotten used to "free" music, rebelled, and it wasn't long before the coin-activated system was turned off. All you had to do was make a selection.

Only one record was a mandatory request at purchase: Artie Shaw's 1940 rendition of *Stardust*. It was for Mississippi.

Throughout America, the war made the Great Depression seemingly disappear. The draft created a labor shortage until "Rosie" started riveting. The country was building a lot of ships and planes and mechanized vehicles like tanks. Most of the factories were in or near the bigger cities to take advantage of the larger available labor pool and transportation.

In Lake Ozark, all the small businesses were hiring more help, particularly in the summer months and weekends in the spring and fall. Lake Ozark is a small town created out of the need to serve travelers to the new Dam and its resultant Lake. In 1942, small towns were the heart of America, pumping life into and through the spirit and culture of the surrounding communities. Small business is their soul. Small businesses built America. Made it what it is. Provided jobs. Filled needs. Not just in Lake Ozark but in all the communities around the Lake, jobs are being created.

To find enough help, businesses turned to high school and college students on break. At the Whitehouse, as with the other businesses, new waitresses were hired, and Harold had a couple of young boys helping with gasoline service, cleaning, and heavy lifting. Janie had advanced to the point that if Maggie needed to be away for any length of time, she could be relied on to manage the kitchen with a helper or two.

Late summer, Lon comes into the Whitehouse one morning and sits to have coffee with Harold.

"They turned me down on manufacturing anything here. But I got a call from G.E. in Kansas City, referred by the government. They want me to come there and train to manage a facility in Connecticut."

"I say that's good news, but I guess that depends on whether or not you want to go," Harold says. "Do you?"

"I want to help my country. If this is a way I can do that, then yes. I understand manufacturing."

"When will you leave?"

"The weekend," Lon answers. "They want me there on Monday."

"We'll miss you and Pauline," Harold says. "Will you keep in touch?"

"Certainly," Lon says. "I've got some work to do shutting down my shop before we go, so I best get to it." Lon gets up to go.

"Can I help?" Harold asks.

"No, no. Just winterizing everything and boarding up, and I'll be done. But thanks."

"Well, good luck. Tell Pauline we expect to hear from her." Harold takes his coffee and walks out with Lon. The two men shake hands, and Lon leaves. Harold sits on the bench to watch him go and admires Lon's deep desire to make a difference in the war. He ponders the fact that he is doing what he considers to be nothing to make a difference. Becoming a father just as the war begins has complicated his sense of responsibility. My wife and son or my country? He thinks. Do I join or wait for the draft? Which choice best serves both? Harold knows he is a strong, able-bodied young man, still in his mid-twenties, and when the time comes, they'll take him. For now, though, I'll wait, he decides.

For some time, the Federal Government has been pressuring utilities to divest themselves of assets not necessary to their primary business. Consequently, in 1942, Union Electric made the decision to begin selling their real estate around the Lake area before being legislated to do so. When the Lakeside Casino property goes on the market, Lawrence Fry, always the astute businessman, purchases it. He honors Bernie Gordon's restaurant lease and welcomes it. His primary interest is the waterfrontage available just a short walk down the hill and within a short distance of the Dam. The fact that there is also a very large public parking lot just across the street influences his decision.

Early in the fall of 1942, Fry puts in a dock below the restaurant and hires a boat and driver to take passengers on sightseeing trips on the lake. It is a trial run for what he envisions as a possible future tourist attraction for Lake Ozark. The paid boat rides are a success and operate until the cold weather starts, keeping the day visitors away. The plan is to resume the rides the following spring.

With the fall of '42 came shortages in supplies of gasoline, coffee, meat, sugar, and other commodities that had been diverted to the efforts to win the war. The changes to everyday life were significant, but considering this generation has just managed to survive a deep depression, were livable. It did, however, help Sam Overfelt to make a decision about the future of his grocery store. When he first came to Lake Ozark, he had built a house on a sizable piece of property just a few hundred feet from Lake Road 1-B. With the highway frontage of the property providing exposure, he made the decision to build small cabin units to rent to visitors. He, among others, had seen the growing need for overnight accommodations for visitors to the Lake. While still operating the grocery store with the help of his wife and son, Sam began building units one at a time over the winter of '42. His hope was to be able to eventually phase out of the grocery business, and with inventory shortages, he knew it wouldn't take long. Atteberry's, across the street, continued to operate and provide grocery service to the community as best they could.

The Cardinals managed to hang onto the National League Pennant and, on September 30, lost to the New York Yankees in game one of the World Series at Sportsman's Park in St. Louis. Harold had that and the next four games on the speaker. Four more was all it took, as the Cards won them all to win the series. The outdoor broadcasts did bring business, as Ward had predicted, but Harold was now convinced that there was no way he would retire at thirty, as Ward, tongue firmly in cheek, had also predicted. It was the Cardinals' first World Series win since 1934.

A few weeks later, in early November, the first major involvement of American troops on a large scale in the European-African theater took place. Called Operation Torch, it was an Allied invasion of French North Africa. To Jessie and Lawrence, there was concern when news broke of the campaign because their last communication from Don, though vague, still had him flying missions out of England. There had been no news since the invasion began, and the entire family was worried.

Initially, contact from Mississippi was good. Janie had received three letters, the first saying he was in southern California expecting to ship out to an unknown location soon. Those since were "chit-chat," with no definitive information provided except "Love, Hiram" at the end. There was one letter addressed to: "My Friends at the Whitehouse, %Harold Pilkington," saying many of the same things Janie had learned. He again thanked Harold and Theora and Maggie, the Claytons, and sent a special "love to Ruthie from her friend Missipipi." After reading the letter, Ruth confided to her mother that she had for a long time known how to pronounce the state Hiram came from but continued to say it her way because "Momma, I think he likes it."

Receipt of the letter from Hiram prompted Theora to put up a large bulletin board on the wall near the entrance to the dining room. At the top, she labeled the board "News from Our Absent Friends" and thumb-tacked Hiram's letter to it. Her purpose was to share information about "our collective friends" with the Whitehouse "family."

One morning in mid-December, Don's girlfriend Suzy gets off the bus from Kansas City. The bus driver retrieves her suitcase, and with it in hand, she enters the Whitehouse. Seeing Theora behind the counter, she approaches.

"You're Mrs. Pilkington, aren't you?" Suzy asks.

Theora looks up and, seeing the young girl acknowledges her.

"Yes, I am, and you are?"

"I'm Suzy Wilson, Don Fry's friend from Springfield."

"Oh, of course. I remember you," Theora says as she comes from behind the counter and hugs her. "It's so nice to see you." She pauses, realizing what her presence might mean. "Is Donnie coming? Is Donnie here?"

"No. Wish he were, but not as far as I know. I'm on my way home for Christmas and purposely took the bus that came through here, hoping to say hello. I've been working at a hospital in Kansas City."

"Come into the kitchen. Harold will want to see you." The two go into the kitchen, and Theora calls Harold, who has been stocking beer and soda. "It's Suzy, Don Fry's friend." Harold appears and, seeing Suzy, goes to her and offers to shake hands, which she ignores as she steps in to hug him.

"Suzy's on her way to Springfield for Christmas," Theora says. "Donnie's not here."

"Have you heard from him?" Harold asks. "Please, sit down." The three sit down at the round table.

"The last letter I had was dated several days before the North Africa campaign started," Suzy says. "Nothing since."

"Would you like some coffee? Or something else?" Theora asks.

"Coffee would be nice, thank you. I don't have much time. I'm on the 10:30 bus to Springfield."

"And after Christmas?" Theora asks as she gets coffee for Suzy. "Back to K.C.?"

"I've joined the Army Nursing Corps. I report to San Francisco in January."

"Ah, Suzy," Harold responds spontaneously. "Don't do that."

"They need nurses, Mr. Pilkington. I'm a nurse."

"Where will you go?" Theora asks.

"Most likely, the Pacific theater," Suzy says. "Don and I had hoped that we would be within easy travel distance from each other when this whole thing started. That's not likely to happen now. I can't just bide my time till he comes home. I need to be occupied doing something of value while we wait."

"I don't believe Lawrence and Jessie have heard any more than you," Theora says. "I wish they were here. They'll be sad they missed you."

"I plan to see Mrs. Fry while I'm home. If they come to Springfield, I'll make it a point to see them."

The visit ends when they hear the 10:30 bus pull into the driveway. As Suzy boards, Harold cannot help but yell to her, "You be careful, Suzy! Come back to us."

"I promise you!" she yells back.

Christmas of 1942 brings the first true realization of a gas shortage due to rationing. It appears that the only folks traveling much during the holiday season that year had managed to find bus or train seats, and there were a finite number of them. The Haage family, now numbering six with the recent birth of Judy, does not make it home to Bagnell because of rationing, and George and Eleanor remain in Washington. Clyde, following basic training, had been assigned to a job at a base in Alabama and remained there with Pebble. Consequently, there were empty seats around the Robinson table at Christmas dinner. Harold and Theora, and Marion and Phyllis were there with baby Johnny and Ruthie. The grace offered by Bert was even lengthier than usual, but that was okay that day as there were so many more to pray for.

"Word is we're in for a cold, wet winter for the new year coming up," Bert tells Marion and Harold while the three partake of a pre-dinner drink out on the porch. "Lot of snow melt, mixed with heavy local rain, could be coming down the Missouri and

Osage tributaries come April and May, I'm thinking."

"Flooding, you think, Bert?" Marion asks.

"Could be."

"Has Bagnell seen a lot of flooding through the years, Bert?" Harold asks.

"Well, as you know, we had a little in '41, but it didn't threaten the buildings. The worst, I've been told, was in 1915, but that was before we moved here."

"Isn't the dam supposed to help with flood control?" Harold asks.

"That's what they told us to help sell the idea to us locals," Bert says, chuckling.

"Maybe what they meant was that the flooding won't be as bad," Marion muses.

"I'm sure that's it," Bert says.

It was back to business on the 26th for Harold and Theora, as the day after Christmas was a Saturday. Maggie, Janie, and the rest of the staff were back at work, as the evening promised to be very busy. The Doerhoff Family Orchestra was booked to play, and word had gotten around. Phyllis and Jessie came to help, accompanied by baby Larry and Ruthie. Baby Johnny was there, too, and he and Larry shared a playpen under the watchful eye of the now six-year-old Ruth. Marion was on an overnight shift at the dam, having been off for Christmas, but Jay Rice and Jack Wickham were around to help Harold with any "disturbances," as he liked to call them.

At one point in the evening, the band played Stardust, and Janie excused herself and stepped out onto the back kitchen porch. She lit a cigarette, a habit she had taken up shortly after Hiram left, and stared at the lake until the song ended.

At about 9:30 p.m., an Army officer wearing an armband signifying that he is military police enters the Whitehouse and walks to the counter. Theora and Phyllis, who are standing behind it, watch him approach.

"I would like to see the owner, if I may," the officer says to them with a bit of haughtiness in his demeanor.

"I am one of the owners," Theora says in response to him. "What can I do for you?"

"I'm Colonel Barron, commander of the Military Police Battalion at Fort Leonard Wood. I am in the area making an assessment of area bars, dance halls, and businesses that offer alcoholic beverages—places our soldiers are known to frequent during their off-duty hours. I will be making a report to the commanding general at the fort as to the advisability of places that should be placed off limits to military personnel."

"I'm Theora Pilkington. This is my sister, Phyllis Clayton. My husband, Harold, and I own the business, and we do not have issues with our military customers."

"Nevertheless, ma'am, I would need to look around, if you don't mind."

"Sure, I'll show you. Follow me." Theora takes the Colonel—Lieutenant Colonel, to be precise—on a tour that includes the kitchen, the dining room, and the upstairs rooms. Coming back downstairs, she asks if there are any questions.

"Do you rent any of the rooms upstairs to soldiers and their girlfriends?" the Colonel asks.

"Colonel, as I told you when we were upstairs, there are eight rooms. One is for my chef, another for my assistant chef. My husband and I and our baby have two rooms. One is a guest room to use when my in-laws visit. And number six is storage. That leaves two vacant rooms, not in use. This is not only my business, sir, but this is my home."

Phyllis has rejoined the two since they returned from upstairs. "What my sister is saying, Colonel, is if you are looking for a whorehouse, you need to go back to St. Robert."

"I'm sorry, but I may have to recommend this establishment be made off-limits."

"I put a call into cousin Midge while you were upstairs, Theora. She should be calling back anytime. She was going to call Harry."

"Well, we'll see what the Senator has to say about this," Theora says.

"Excuse me, what do you mean, Senator?" the Colonel asks.

"Harry. Harry Truman, Senator from Missouri. Chairman of the Senate Truman Committee," Theora says. "You've heard of the Truman Committee, I'm sure?"

"Midge says she'll ask Harry to call the commanding general at the fort," Phyllis says.

"Ladies, please, I don't think that will be necessary," the Colonel, nervous now, says. "You won't have to worry about the off-limits list. Please assure Cousin Midge that the Senator needn't be bothered. Please?"

"Midge will be calling back, Colonel," Phyllis says. "I'll be happy to tell her."

"I must go now. Thank you for your cooperation, ladies. Have a good evening." The Colonel turns quickly and is soon through the door and gone.

As soon as the door closes on the Colonel, Theora turns to her sister, amused. "Cousin Midge?"

"Well, there is that second cousin on Mom's side. Up around Eldon. She has a daughter who works as a maid at the Muehlebach Hotel in KC. Harry has a senatorial office there, and sometimes, she sees him when she cleans the office. That's what Mom told me."

Phyllis pauses and takes a breath. "Her name's Midge."

"Oh, that cousin Midge."

The following Thursday was New Year's Eve, and the band was coming back, so on that night and the Saturday after, business was good at the Whitehouse. Each night had a minor disturbance, which Harold easily resolved, but for the most part, the military personnel that came to Lake Ozark were well-behaved. During the busy Saturday nights, there was usually a mix of officers and enlisted men, and should enlisted personnel start to cause trouble, an officer would remind them about their behavior. Should an officer start to get "out of line," a fellow officer, usually one of higher rank, would intervene. The system helped keep the experience of a night at the Whitehouse more pleasant for all, including Harold.

But the bar business, particularly as the Pilkingtons lived it daily, can take its toll on even young, healthy people like them. It became a topic discussed with the Claytons that Sunday, three days into 1943 when they had dinner at Clayton's apartment.

"It's hard to think of a day when this war will not be there, Phyllis, but when it's gone, we've got to find another way to make a living, Harold and I."

"I understand. Marion lives for the day we can get back in the restaurant business."

"It's what I know best. I was raised in it," Marion says. "And Phyllis has learned a great deal, too, in the last several years."

"What we envision is breakfast and lunch, and not later than seven in the evenings some days," Phyllis says. "Be home with the family in the evening."

"I think when the war is over, and we can't depend on the extra business from the Fort, we'll need to get out, too," Harold says. "In the meantime, we're trying to save as much money as possible."

"I don't want to raise Johnny in the Whitehouse," Theora says. "I want to raise him in a house."

"Those two lots on 1-A we looked at, remember?" Marion says. "I think we could buy them for a couple of hundred dollars apiece."

"And build houses?" Harold asks.

"That's the idea. We could get Bert's help. Hell, Harold, if Clyde were home, the four of us could do it in short order. Ross would help us wire them."

"Momma told me that Clyde has a two-week furlough coming up, and he and Pebble plan to be home," Phyllis tells them.

"That young Mack Brown out on 42 Highway there is doing earth-moving now. We could get him to dig the basements,"

Marion says. "There's a concrete guy — can't think of his name — in Eldon, we could get to pour the basement walls. Hell, Harold, if Mack can do two jobs at the same time, it'll be cheaper. Same with the concrete."

"Well, yeah, Marion, you're right about that. You got any figures?"

"Not yet, but I could make a few calls this week."

"I've gotten so used to waking up in the same building that I work in for so long, since 1935, I can't imagine not doing that," Harold says.

"I can," Theora says emphatically, to which Phyllis laughs heartily.

"Makes me think that a hardware store might be the retail business that I could get into," Harold says. "All this talk of building houses makes me think about all the other people going to be doing that at the same time. They're not going to want to drive into Eldon to the lumber yard every time they need a pound of nails or a few screws. That's what I need to look into."

"Well, we should have another highball before we eat to celebrate Clayton's Diner and Pilkington's Hardware Store," Phyllis says as she goes to the oven to check on her casserole.

"Make us a round, Marion."

A few weeks later, Harold and Marion make a deal on two flat, side-by-side lots on Lake Road 1-A and start to make plans to build. Before they begin, Lawrence tells Harold that the U.S. Postal Service has purchased a lot in Lake Ozark on the main road not far from the Dam. Their plan is to build a building to house the post office, with additional space on the main floor and on a walk-out basement level. The rental income from these additional spaces to the Service assures the decision to build the new post office. The small cottage next to the Whitehouse, Lawrence tells Harold, would be available to live in or buy and move to a different location. Harold tells Marion, and they put plans on hold while Harold looks into the possibility of moving the cottage.

Word has come via a letter to the Whitehouse from Virginia Quinn that Lawrence is now in the Navy. He is serving on a ship based out of Seattle, and she has moved there to be near his home port. She has joined the millions of women throughout the U.S. who are filling the factory jobs formerly held by men. She is working, she reports, on an assembly line building aircraft and doing well. Theora posts the letter on her bulletin board. Pauline writes from Connecticut to say that they are now in Bridgeport, where Lon is working in management for GE. That letter is posted, as well.

A letter to Jessie and Lawrence from Don finally comes. He says little other than he still flies out of England and shares anecdotes of life there. Jessie posts his letter on the board as well, as many locals know Donnie. There is still no word from Mona and her family in the Philippines. Jessie has repeatedly talked to the Church Administration in Springfield, but they tell her nothing because they know nothing. In contrast, there is local good news as Jo and Jay Rice welcome a daughter and name her Janice.

Harold, on a call to Tulsa, learns that Harry and Maxine have arrived for a short leave to visit both families and announce that Maxine is expecting a baby. Harold speaks to his brother to congratulate him.

"I'm surprised you figured out how that works—having a baby," Harold prods him a bit.

"It did take a while to decipher the drawings you did for me when I was young, but once I turned them right side up, it all became clear."

"Still as busy as before?" Harold asks.

"We make less and less contact now than we did. The combined efforts of the U.S. and British navies in the Atlantic have made a big difference. And the Canadians report less activity near their waters, too."

"That's good. We don't want those U-boats coming up the Osage River here."

"I'll come visit after the war, and you can pin a medal on me."

"Watch your back, kid," Harold says before hanging up.

Letters from Mississippi have become less frequent, and the last one Janie received seemed to betray a lack of his usual upbeat demeanor. A similar letter received by Harold appeared to echo Janie's. Harold tells Theora in private that "he has probably already seen too much war," and she understands but still posts his letter on the board.

Harold had talked to a company in Camdenton with experience moving houses from old Linn Creek to the new town site before the town was flooded by the lake. He has come to the decision that buying and moving the cottage is much cheaper than building a house on the new lot. With this knowledge, he and Marion move forward with digging and pouring concrete for the basements on the 1-A lots. Bert comes to help, and soon, he and Marion have a four-room house with a bathroom framed and under roof.

And then the rain came. The April showers arrived early, starting in late March, and with the spring melt, the major waterways and tributaries in the Midwest started filling up. Harold decides to put off moving the cottage until the rains have let up and the basement has had sufficient time to dry. The lots are on high ground with no threat from streams, the river, or the lake, so flooding there is not a problem. In the meantime, Marion and Bert continue to finish work inside the house, and Ross comes to wire it. It isn't long before Bert starts expressing concern about serious flooding in Bagnell.

"When's the last time you saw the floodgates at the Dam open this early in spring?" Bert asks Marion one day. "Not since they built it, I believe. And the watershed is sending even more downstream."

"What are the folks in Bagnell thinking, Bert?" Marion asks.

"They think we're going to have a flood. Folks in Tuscumbia, too. Some of the old-timers there say they've never seen so much water this early."

By the first of May, water is in the streets of Bagnell and rising. When it reaches the porch level at the Robinson house, Mr. Boots picks up Bert and Lena in his johnboat equipped with an outboard motor and takes them to the Bagnell Road turnoff at Highway 54, where Harold and Marion pick them up. Within a few days, the water moved on to 54 at that location, blocking the road to Eldon.

At the Dam, water on the lakeside has far exceeded the 660 feet above sea level full reservoir mark and soon is just four feet from the top of the Dam. The floodgates continue to send torrents of water and debris, including whole trees, into the river below. The structural engineers aren't concerned with the Dam itself; all are concerned about the power plant.

Water, with its unique ability to seek its own level, seeks it in the power plant, and the absolute priority is to not let that happen. Additional workers are hired, and soldiers are sent from Ft. Leonard Wood to help build barriers and sandbags to keep the water out and the electricity flowing. Power generation from Bagnell Dam is essential to operate the defense industry plants in St. Louis and, therefore, essential to the war effort. It is dangerous work for all involved due to the close proximity of the raging water at the base of the floodgates. Working around the clock for several days, the breach is avoided, and the power continues to flow. Finally, going into early June, there begins a very slow receding of the water flow and levels.

"Dear God, Bert, I wish the river had taken the whole place with it downstream," Lena says on first seeing her house after the floodwaters have safely receded. "Can we just tear it down and rebuild?"

"We can't afford to do that, Lena," Bert tells her. "We'll have to clean it up as best we can and fix things as best we can."

The Robinsons are not alone. With the exception of a few houses along the hillside above the town and some higher elevations above the railroad right-of-way, every building is affected by the dirty water. With Phyllis and Theora's help, Lena begins the arduous work of cleaning the floor and walls of every room. A one-story house, the water has come as high as five feet on the walls and has brought with its river mud, which is nothing more than good bottomland with water in it. When the moisture dries up, it is dirt and can be swept away, but until the moisture is completely gone, the ladies are left with mud to wipe down. With Harold and Marion's help, Bert strips the wallpaper from every room, and the drying and cleaning begin.

"No matter how clean we make these walls and floors, there will always be river inside them," Lena says to her two youngest daughters. She has just sat down on one of the cleaned porch swings. It is obvious to her daughters that she is as tired mentally as she is physically. "The only way to make it go away is to tear the wall out, and," she laughs, "that's about the same as tearing the house down."

There is no normal "back to normal" after the flood. Some don't rebuild and leave, and some new people come in thinking, "That ain't happening again for fifty years." With them are folks who put in camping spaces near the old downtown to rent to overnight fishermen. Called Camp Bagnell, the business includes a small diner, which soon has locals' full approval.

At the Lake, one early June afternoon, after the level has begun to retreat from flood concerns, a small seaplane lands out on the main channel. Taking a quick survey of the surrounding area, the pilot sees only one dock that he might tie up to and idles toward it. He is helped by the Frys' speedboat pilot as he comes to the dock below the Casino Restaurant.

"I thank you, sir," the flyer says in an English accent as he steps down from the plane and ties off. "I hope you don't mind, chap… there didn't appear to be any other landings available."

"That's alright," the boat driver says. "You don't sound like you're from anywhere, even close to here."

"I'm English but have been in Canada for many years. I've been flying fishermen and hunters into the northern territories. Terribly cold, ready for a few more months a year of warmer temps."

"Well, welcome to Lake of the Ozarks. The town you're in is called Lake Ozark."

"I thought it might be. Came by way of Iowa and took a while, petrol shortages and all. Had to avoid the major waterways, flooding, you know. Saw a story in a newspaper in Des Moines about your Dam. Thought I'd have a look."

"Things are just getting back to normal a bit," the boat driver says. "With the flooding crisis, I haven't been able to take passengers on boat rides. It wasn't allowed because of the waves it makes. Water that high, it doesn't take much to put it into basements of homes built close to the shoreline. Water at one time was only four feet from the top of the Dam."

"So, you take passengers for hire from this dock. Would it hurt your business if there was someone also offering seaplane rides over the Lake?"

The boat driver thinks about the question for a while and looks over the plane bobbing in the water near him. "Probably help draw business for both."

"So, what kind of a deal can we make?" the pilot asks.

"Oh, not me," the boat driver says. "You need to talk to Lawrence Fry. It's his land and dock. I pay him a percentage to operate here."

"How do I find this Fry chap, sir?"

"You could go to the restaurant there and call him, but you might want to walk to the post office instead."

"The post office?"

"Lawrence is the postmaster. The place is only a quarter mile up the road on the other side. He'll be there. Always is."

"Thank you for your help, old chap," the pilot says. "My name is Tommy Weber."

"John Irwin." The two shake hands. "Good luck to you."

Within a week, there is a sign at the top of the hill next to the Casino Restaurant. It reads, "Casino Pier," and under that, "speedboat rides" and "seaplane rides." On the bank below, Harvey Fry, who is a distributor of Phillips 66 products out of Eldon, mounts an above-ground gas tank with a line leading to a pump on the dock. Business is good from day one.

Harold's focus, after the flood has receded, returns to moving the cottage from the Whitehouse property to the basement foundation on 1-A. The company he has hired comes in early one morning in late June, places jacks all around and begins to raise the building slowly up from its block foundation just enough to slip a trailer with an extra-wide wheelbase beneath it. With safety vehicles in front and back, the cottage is slowly moved the three-quarter mile distance. Once at the site, the trailer is slowly backed across the basement, the trailer tires straddling each side. With the cottage in place, the rear tires are slowly deflated, and using rollers as a fulcrum, the cottage is slowly nudged from the trailer onto the foundation as the trailer is moved from beneath it.

In the next few days, plumbing and electrical hookups are done. With Bert's help, Harold adds a screen porch and a small open back porch. With a few interior jobs to be done, move-in will come later in the summer.

The Lake Ozark Christian Church had tabled any plans of building on their lot since the arrival of the war, choosing to wait. With Hiram's departure, Millicent (Millie) returned to sole possession of the piano bench during church services. Her husband, Herman, had passed from the sickness that originally took her away from it, and he was returned to Chicago for burial. Millie stayed there for a while with family, eventually returning to the Lake.

The last inventory of the Haage clan was at six with Judy's birth, and now word arrives from Dorothy that another daughter, Eleanor, has joined the family. Lena, worried about Dorothy overburdening herself, calls her.

"Don't you think it's time to stop having babies, Dorothy?" her mother asks.

"I always thought that eight would be a good number, Momma. So, in time, maybe one more."

"And that's it?" Lena asks.

"The thing is, I have two more names I wanted to use," Dorothy says. "Ann and Carol."

"For the love of God," Lena says.

"I could call her Carol Ann, I suppose."

"What if she's a boy?" Lena asks.

"Carol can be a boy's name, too. I'll call him Carol Andrew. Carol An' for short."

Lena sighs. "It's obvious you get your sense of logic from your dad."

In Lake Ozark, Ward Atterbury brings another daughter, Jerry, into the world to join her older sister Joyce, a contemporary and friend of Ruthie. And Jo and her younger sister Jude have, in recent years, welcomed two sisters and a brother to the Hoyle Atterbury clan. Shortly after, the Rices have another daughter, Judy Ann, to join sister Janice. Though not adding to the population explosion in Lake Ozark, Harry calls in late summer with news that Maxine has given birth to a daughter they have named Peggy. Harold makes a point to tell son Johnny, who doesn't understand a word he says, that he now has a Pilkington cousin. But maybe the biggest news of all mid-1943: Ira Stith gets married. Her name is Juanita, and everyone agrees that the life of a dairy farmer's wife isn't easy, so she must be a good woman.

Then, one day, not long after, bigger news arrives in a letter from the South Pacific. It is addressed to "Mississippi's Friends, %Whitehouse, Lake Ozark, Missouri." Theora is out running errands and stops to get the mail from their box at the post office. When she sees the oversized envelope, she immediately goes to the Whitehouse to find Harold. "This was in the mail," she says as she hands him the envelope. They are alone in the dining room.

"You didn't open it."

"I'm afraid of what it says."

Harold opens the envelope, and inside, in addition to a letter, is a separate sealed envelope with the name "Janie" handwritten on it. He shows it to Theora, then puts it aside and reads the main letter to her.

Dear friends of Hiram Walker,

I am so sad to tell you that Sgt. Walker was killed here this last month. Thinking our island was secure, we were working with Navy Seabees to improve the airfield, and a Jap sniper who had been hiding in the jungle shot him. Our first sergeant tracked the Jap and killed him. Hiram was a very brave soldier and died a hero. He always talked so proudly of his "family" at the Whitehouse and made me promise that if anything happened to him, to let you know. I share my deepest sympathy with you.

Hiram's friend, Sgt. James George.

"Oh, dear God, Harold, that sweet boy!" Tears are running down Theora's face as she speaks. "We have to tell Janie."

"I'll have Marylyn watch the front, and we'll tell her and Maggie at the same time," Harold says and turns to go toward the kitchen, Theora following. She wipes the tears from her eyes before entering, and Harold asks Marylin to watch the front. Maggie senses something is coming and stares at Harold.

"Janie, Maggie, sit down a minute with me." The two women sit, and Harold joins them. Theora stands just behind Harold's right shoulder, looking down to hide her face.

"We received a letter from a friend of Hiram's," Harold begins. "I have bad news." He takes a deep breath and exhales. "He was killed on an island in the Pacific recently. A sniper shot him. They killed the sniper."

Janie just looks down and stares at the table as she processes the words. It is possible that, for the first time in her life, she is being introduced to the fragility of it. "There was a note just for you inside the envelope, Janie," Harold tells the young girl as he hands her the envelope. Janie looks at the front of it for the longest time before turning and beginning to open it. As she takes out the enclosed note, a necklace with a simple, small cross falls out into her hand. She looks at it and then reads:

By now, you know of the loss of our dear friend Hiram. He talked of you all the time – about you teaching him to dance, and we would all laugh at the thought of him dancing. He loved you, I believe. He asked me one day, if anything happened to him, to get to him, take the enclosed necklace before it would be lost, and send it to you. He wore it right along with his dog tags every day. I am so sorry for the loss we all share.

Hiram's friend, Sgt. James George.

Janie slips the letter back into the envelope and puts it in the pocket of her apron. She opens the clasp of the necklace, puts it around her neck, and fastens it. Then she gets up, excuses herself, and steps out onto the back porch. She lights a cigarette and stares at the lake in the distance while she smokes.

"I feared that this day would come," Maggie says after the young girl has left the room. "Do you have any idea where he was, Harold?"

He hands her the letter. "All Sgt. George says is an island. Most of the news accounts of activity in the Pacific over the last several months have been about Guadalcanal in the Solomon Islands. Supposedly, it was secured in February, and the airstrip renamed Henderson Field. From what I read, this happens a lot. They think a place is finally secure, but there are pockets of Japs who hide out, would rather die than surrender. This son-of-a-bitch took our Mississippi with him."

Securing Guadalcanal and the Solomon Islands is considered nearly as important a success as Midway. For posterity, two US

Navy ships were later named "USS Guadalcanal," and many future American sailors will walk their proud decks. For Janie, they will serve as a reminder of a sweet boy from Mississippi she once knew.

A short time later, Theora drives to the Claytons' house on 1-A and tells Phyllis, who holds back tears, most concerned about how she will tell Ruthie, who is napping in the bedroom. "She won't understand completely; she's too young, but it will still hurt as she tries."

"Sometimes, Phyllis, I hate the Whitehouse. I hate where I live and work."

"Sometimes I hate it, too," Phyllis says. "I doubt that Mississippi will be the last boy to come through there who won't come back."

"Goddamned war!"

When Janie finally comes in off the porch, Maggie asks her if she would like to go home for a while. "You can take my car. I can manage without you for a few days."

"No. I'm fine. I'll finish preparing the potatoes to bake and stuff the mushrooms." She never talks about Hiram Walker again unless someone else first brings him up. And then, her comments are brief and to the point.

Harold, having left the kitchen and with Theora gone to see Phyllis, walks up the stairs and sits in a chair next to Johnny's cradle. The baby is sleeping, down for his afternoon nap. A father, Harold can't help wondering about Hiram's parents in Mississippi. "God, how awful it must be for them," he thinks. "Will there be a war in your future, young Johnny? Yours and little Larry's? This damn war has to be the end of it. Must be the end of it." He cries inside but fears no one will hear him.

Alone that evening, Theora and Harold talk only briefly about Mississippi. After a few moments, Harold quietly says, "Theora, I'm going to enlist."

"What?"

"I think I should enlist."

"No, you are not!" Theora insists adamantly.

"They are going to draft me any day now. I know it's coming. If I enlist, I might be able to have some control of where I go and what I do."

"You have a son. You have a business. A wife. You cannot enlist."

"I'll still have those things even if I get drafted."

"No," Theora says, disbelieving. "You're older. It will be over before they call you."

"Theora, I excelled in five sports in high school. I'm the kind they want, age be damned. Even Harvey is worried about it, and he's thirty-four."

"You will not enlist. I will divorce you if you do."

Harold pauses and looks at his wife. "No, you won't."

"No, I won't," Theora says. "I'll kill you instead."

"Then I'll enlist and let the Japs or the Nazis save you the trouble."

"The matter is settled. Go to bed."

Before news of Mississippi's passing came, Harold had arranged for two young high school boys to help move their belongings from the Whitehouse. Thus, a week later, the four began moving the Pilkingtons' belongings into the cottage on 1-A. There wasn't much to move—a chest of drawers, Johnny's cradle, some suitcases with clothes, Theora's precious cedar chest. They had purchased a new bedroom set with a mattress for the cottage, leaving the bed in place at the Whitehouse. That and a new couch for the living area are their only indulgences. The new items are delivered, but the two boys are needed to move them into the house. Theora has been able to scrounge enough excess utensils, plates, pots, and pans from the Whitehouse to stock the kitchen with the basics. After the boys are paid and have left, Theora insists Harold carry her across the threshold again.

"What! That would make the third time!" Harold protests.

"And thus, a charm," Theora says, smiling.

Phyllis, who has been helping them, turns to walk home, muttering something like, "I think I'm going to move."

Their first night in the cottage on 1-A was short, as they still had to be at the Whitehouse until late, and Harold had to be back by six a.m. Planning ahead, Harold had bought a used motor scooter from a guy in Eldon, and he used it to drive to work that first morning, leaving the car for Theora and Johnny. Weather permitting, he would use the scooter each day and appear to enjoy it, betraying remnants of youth. It made a daily trip to the post office like a tame ride at an amusement park. For some, two wheels represent freedom more than four.

But in wartime, freedom is often given up in order to fight to keep it, and so, on one trip to the post office in late September, Harold is finally confronted with that reality. Among the mail that day is a letter from the US Government's Selective Service System. Though he doesn't speak with Lawrence, the two exchange glances before Harold exits. Lawrence knows; he sorts the mail.

Back at the Whitehouse, Harold goes into the kitchen to let Maggie know he has returned. "I'll be in the dining room doing some bookwork, Maggie." Before going into the dining room, Harold, not normally a daytime drinker, nevertheless takes a beer from the small refrigerator under the front counter, walks into the dining room, and sits down, having closed the door behind him. "I can't put it off any longer," Harold thinks, and, taking a long pull on the beer, opens the envelope.

"Greetings from the President of the United States:

You are hereby ordered to appear for a pre-induction physical examination at the United States Army Hospital, Ft.

Leonard Wood, Missouri, at 9:00 a.m. on Monday, October 4, 1943…"

That was all he needed to read. That's just a week and a half away, he thinks. There's a lot to do and arrangements to make. I wonder how much time they give you between the physical and reporting for training? He sits back in his chair and drinks the beer. How am I going to tell Theora? I do not know how to do that.

Harold finishes the beer, goes, and tells Maggie he is going to his house for a bit and will be back later. As he rides home, he decides the best way is to just tell her quickly and try to move on. They need to find answers to who they can hire to help Theora with the business while he is gone.

"Johnny napping?" Harold asks Theora as he enters the house.

"What are you doing at home? I was headed that way when the baby woke up. Thirty minutes."

"Let's sit down in the kitchen. I need to talk to you."

"What's wrong?" Theora says as she sits down. "Something's wrong."

Harold sits and hands her the letter across the table. "I received a draft notice today."

Theora looks at Harold and reads the letter. "What are we going to do? I can't let you go. You have a baby… a wife. Why you?"

"Why Hiram? Why anybody?"

"You have flat feet. Tell them. They don't want people with flat feet."

Harold reaches across the table and holds Theora's hand. "Only if they cause you pain or movement issues."

"Then tell them that. Tell them you have trouble, pain."

"I can't lie, Theora. For God's sake, I was a track and gymnastics athlete in high school." He pauses and brings his other hand to hers to try to comfort her. "I can't lie."

Theora quiets somewhat and looks down at her husband's hands encircling hers. "What are we going to do?"

"Do you think Phyllis would work full-time, maybe backed up by Jessie?"

"I'm sure she could always use the extra money." She pauses and chuckles slightly. "I guess there's no way we keep from raising Ruthie, Larry, and Johnny in the Whitehouse kitchen."

"The two high school boys from this summer. We can use them on weekends and nights to handle the gas pumps and janitor issues, clean the bathrooms, heavy lifting, that sort of thing."

"With the waitresses we have now and Maggie and Janie," Theora says, "I think we'll be okay. The weekend nights will be the main concern."

"I'll talk to Jay to see if he'll work to keep the peace," Harold says. "With Jack's help, things should go alright."

Theora pats Harold's hands and gets up from the table. "Go back to work, and I'll be down as soon as Johnny wakes up."

Harold rises, goes to the door, and pauses. "Theora, I'm not going to die in this damn war. That I promise."

"I'll hold you to that," Theora says.

Early on the morning of October 4th, Harold drives Theora and baby Johnny to the Whitehouse before he heads to Ft. Leonard Wood. His mind races, though his Buick doesn't, as he maneuvers the hilly, winding two-lane road through Iberia and onto St. Robert. At the main gate, the guard tells him to "take the first left; it's the second building on the right."

Upon entering the building, he checks in and is given papers and told to keep them with him at all times. He, along with others, is then directed to a large room where each is handed a metal basket. A corporal tells the group to completely undress except for their undershorts. "Put all your clothes, including your shoes and socks, into the basket. Place the basket into an empty space in the rack behind you and close the door, lock said door, remove the key, and with the attached chain, place it around your neck where it will remain until such time as you are directed to dress again." The corporal pauses, catching his breath. "That done, move quickly to the line and fall in at the end. Keep your papers with you at all times." Harold undresses, stores his basket, and moves quickly with the others into the line. As he does, he can hear the corporal behind them begin his spiel again.

The line moves along until each examinee is asked in turn to step to a line and "cover your right eye, read the third line down. Cover your left and do the same." The examiner makes notations on Harold's paperwork and hands it back to him. At the next station, a doctor tells him to sit at an exam table. He does, and the doctor looks into his ears, eyes, and nose, takes a small metal hammer, and checks his reflexes. With his stethoscope, he listens to Harold's heart and lungs. A tongue depressor and a "cough, and again" later, the doctor glances down at Harold's papers and makes his notations. Finished, he looks up from the paper. "It says here you have flat feet. Hold your legs out straight, and let me have a look." The doctor looks closely at Harold's feet. "You have any trouble walking, standing, or running?"

"No, sir," Harold says firmly.

"How about back trouble? Your alignment looks normal."

"No, sir. No trouble."

"You enlist or draftee, son?"

"Draftee, sir."

"Well, the military takes people with flat feet unless they have complications from it," the doctor says quietly to Harold. "You sure they are not a problem? Because now is the time to say so and not later when some sergeant is yelling at you for malingering."

"I was on the track team and gymnastics and tumbling team in high school, sir," Harold says proudly.

"Cauliflower ears. Wrestler, too?"

"Yes. Sir," Harold says.

The doctor looks at him without saying a word for a moment, makes a few notations on his paperwork, and points across the room. "Go to that doctor sitting behind the desk right over there. He'll see you next. And good luck."

He does so, and the doctor behind the desk asks him to sit down, which he does. "My job is to find out if you are normal. Are you?"

"Probably not, sir, but I'll pretend I am if it will help."

"Most guys coming through here pretend they're not. You depressed? Ever have any thoughts of suicide?" the doctor asks.

"No, sir. Don't have time."

"You married? You like girls?"

"I'm married six years and have a son; he's almost two now," Harold tells the doctor. "And yes, I like girls."

"That's good. The military is not fond of guys who like guys." The doctor looks down at Harold's paperwork. "It says here you're a draftee. Not happy about that, I would assume."

"I suppose everyone has to do their part, but I have a business and a family. I'd rather not be here."

"Unfortunately, I can't do anything to change that for you," the doctor says. "I wish I could. I wish this damn war would go away."

"I understand, sir," Harold says, accepting the inevitable.

"Take your paperwork and go see the doctor at that desk near the front of the room. He'll check you out."

As Harold walks, he realizes that this appears to be the last doctor he will talk to before returning to where his clothes are located. There is that question that nags at him, and he would like an answer before he leaves. Arriving at the desk, he hands the doctor—a middle-aged man—his paperwork. "A question, sir."

The doctor doesn't look up, busily examining Harold's papers. "Ask away," he says.

"How soon after this physical before I will have to report for training?"

"Anxious to pin on your Medal of Honor, son?" the doctor responds without looking up.

"No, sir, just trying to plan ahead, sir."

"It varies," the doctor says. "Couple of weeks max, usually." He looks up from the paperwork. "So, you've got flat feet, but they're not a problem, you say?"

"They haven't ever been a problem, sir."

The doctor looks Harold over for a moment when he suddenly focuses on his left shoulder. He leans back in his chair and studies the nearly nude young man. Finally, indicating with his hand, he asks, "What's the deal with your left shoulder there?"

"I had polio when I was a child, sir," Harold answers.

The doctor stares at Harold for a long, awkward moment and then leans forward onto his desk. He picks up a rubber stamp, inks it, and stamps the top cover of Harold's paperwork. He pulls another single sheet out of the stack, stamps it, and hands it to Harold. It reads: "Denied...Medically Unqualified."

Harold stares at the paper and stutters, trying to speak... "But, I... don't understand... I..."

"Go home, young man. Go home." Harold looks up at the doctor as he reaches over beside his chair and picks up a pair of crutches. The doctor rises uneasily from his chair and places the crutches under his arms. Having risen, he exposes obvious disfigurement from his pelvis down to and including both legs. He looks at Harold. "You and me, son, we've had our war."

Harold struggles with what has just happened as he drives home from St. Robert. Somewhere within that core "male" in Harold, shame is harbored, forever docked; *he told me I was unfit… I'm not unfit.* At a certain level, he understands why the doctor said what he did. Some of the moments stayed with him: A little boy in pain, not understanding what was happening, a father's frustration, a mother's distraction. He reflects on how terrible that doctor's "war" must have been and knows how lucky he is. Part of the shame he now carries is because of the equal part relief he also harbors. It's done, over with, time to move on.

Back at the Whitehouse, Harold takes Theora upstairs to their former room to tell her what has happened. Though easily expressing her relief, she tells her husband the one thing that matters. "Harold, there is a reason that that doctor was in that position on this day." Between them, they only talk of the matter one more time — briefly — after that day.

The following day, Tuesday, October 5th, the St. Louis Cardinals take on the New York Yankees in Game 1 of the 1943 World Series, a repeat of the previous year. The National League pennant winner is led by MVP Stan Musial, who hit .357 in the regular season, and catcher Walker Cooper, the 1942 MVP, who hit .318. Cooper's brother, pitcher Mort, won 21 games during the season.

Harold tries to put the events of the previous day out of his mind by keeping himself busy — making sure the broadcast is heard both on the outside speaker and inside. The game — a 4-2 win by the Yanks in their home stadium — does bring some extra business, as does the next day's game, a 4-2 win by the Cards. But the good news ends there, as New York wins the next three and the World Series, 4-1, a repeat of the previous year, but with a different champion. Harold does his best to get caught up in the excitement of the Series, but he can't shake the memory of "that day" at Fort Wood. That, he knows, will take time.

The following Sunday, Cardinal baseball fresh on the mind of bus driver Tony Bertone. He tells Harold about the two neighborhood kids on the Hill where he lives.

"These two kids live across the street from each other, Harold, and I'm telling you, they're both going to play pro ball. They can't miss."

"You've seen them play?" Harold asks.

"Oh, yeah. I've gone over to school and watched their games. Get this, they're both catchers, but the short one — he's the better hitter — could play outfield. Listen, Branch Rickey, the Cardinals' brass, signed the older one, Garagiola, before Rickey went to the Dodgers last winter. Nobody could understand why he didn't sign the other kid."

"There's hope in the Cards' future, then? What about the other kid?"

"Speculation is Rickey knew he was going to the Dodgers and waited to sign him there. But the Yankees outsmarted him and signed the kid first."

"Well, if they're as good as you say they are, then I'll be reading about them in the St. Louis papers soon."

"Garagiola, maybe. The Yankee kid, Berra — Larry Berra — joined the Navy. Wanted to serve his country."

"That's admirable," Harold tells Tony as they walk out front.

"Or stupid," Tony says, laughing, as he boards the bus.

Harold sits on the front bench, drinking his coffee, and watches as Tony pulls out onto 54 and heads southwest. He imagines a group of young boys out on a field playing baseball, laughing, cheering, running; perhaps some future stars.

It's a pleasant scene until it dissolves involuntarily into a vision of Hiram's lifeless body lying on a Pacific Island runway. No matter how hard Harold tries to hold back, his strong body cannot keep a few tears from slipping down his cheeks.

Though they have not discussed his feelings, Theora has noticed Harold seems somewhat quieter since the day he drove to Fort Wood. She has witnessed a couple of occasions where he has been a bit curt with an employee, short-tempered — something totally out of character for him. He is not sleeping well, getting up during the night quite often. She is reluctant to talk to her husband; he just needs time, she thinks. Instead, she engages Maggie in conversation when they are alone.

"He is struggling with this draft thing," she tells Maggie. "You would think he'd be ecstatic, but no."

"Men have three brains, Theora. Some do all their thinking with the two hanging between their legs. Then there are men like Harold, cerebral, who primarily use the one up here." She points to her head. "But don't let anyone ever tell them the other two don't exist."

"This entire thing has insulted his manhood?"

"That may be the whole of it."

"He has always been so calm, cool-headed when dealing with others," Theora says. "Loves to joke."

"Give him time, Theora. He'll come out of it."

Theora decides to leave her concerns unaddressed, talking to Harold about it only if it seems to be worse or if he appears to be seriously depressed. She decides he needs a distraction and suggests they go to a movie on Sunday afternoon and then for dinner. "We can leave Johnny at Momma's; she'll love it." He agrees.

They drive to Jefferson City and see a matinee, *Casablanca*, and then have dinner at a place downtown. Business is slow this Sunday night, and they talk quietly as they dine.

"When the man gets up and leads the orchestra, and everyone sings *La Marseillaise*, I almost jumped up and sang with them," Theora says. "That's the French National Anthem."

"I know what it is, Theora," Harold says, rather bluntly.

"You don't have to be rude, Harold. I wasn't insulting your intelligence." He is quiet while he quickly adds a few drops from his flask into his soda and hides it back in his jacket pocket. "You didn't like the movie, did you?" Theora asks, finally.

"I liked it. Especially when the American saloon owner shoots the Nazi Major and the corrupt French cop, and the American saloon owner walks off into the fog to join the war effort." Harold pauses and takes a drink. "That guy Rick nobly gives up the girl he loves to do the right thing."

"Well, the girl he loves just happens to be married," Theora notes.

"That's why he's noble."

"Do you want to walk off into the fog of war and give up the girl you love?"

He gives Theora a very serious look. "I don't think war is a romantic thing."

"Oh, dear Harold...I know...I know that the physical..."

"I don't want to talk about it, Theora," Harold says abruptly, interrupting her. "It's done. Consider us fortunate."

Business that fall was good despite gas rationing, though the buses from Fort Wood brought most of the business in. Many of the soldiers who came to the lake, accompanied by wives and girlfriends, were officers or career NCOs. In most cases, they were sharing what special time they had left before the inevitable "shipping out" order came.

The first week in November, Theora sits down in the kitchen with Janie and Maggie and asks them what their plans are for Thanksgiving.

"I don't have any except to go to my folks, I guess," Janie says.

"No plans, Theora," Maggie says. "I'm not going to Wichita, and my son is not coming here. What's on your mind?"

"I haven't said anything to Harold yet, but I was thinking about us offering a free Thanksgiving meal to soldiers from the Fort and their families. Those that are in town that day. Stay open just for the afternoon, for them."

"How many folks you think that would be, that would come?" Maggie asks.

"I don't know. I don't think any other restaurants will be open. They never are, so the soldiers that are here won't have any place to eat."

"If you don't promote it anywhere but locally," Maggie says. "Post a notice out front and let the cabin camps know to tell their overnight customers. It might be reasonable."

"Won't that be expensive, Theora?" Janie asks.

"We've done very good business because of the soldiers. Most didn't ask to be stuck here. The Army sent them. We should give something back, say thanks."

"I'll be here, and you don't need to pay me," Janie says, smiling. "Free turkey dinner, and I don't have to spend the day listening to my brothers arguing."

"I might talk with Steen's up on Highway 52, maybe get some turkeys at a good price," Maggie adds, seemingly agreeing to the idea. "They're good people."

"I'm thinking turkey, mashed potatoes, gravy, rolls, cranberry sauce, tossed salad, green beans," Theora says. "You have a good pumpkin pie recipe, Maggie?"

"Got it from my mother," Maggie says proudly. "Your menu there sounds about right; it's manageable. You agree, Janie?"

"Yes, ma'am, we can do it."

"We just serve coffee and tea with dinner, no alcohol," Theora says. "Now, I have to convince Harold this is a good idea."

Not long after her conversation with the ladies in the kitchen, Theora talks to Phyllis about her plans for that day.

"Marion is off, but we've already committed to go to Red and Carrie's place," Phyllis tells her. "They eat early. Red likes to eat early, so we might get away by mid-afternoon. Come and help. I'll talk to Marion."

Next, Theora corners her husband about her idea. "What about Mag...?" Harold starts to ask but is interrupted.

"They both like the idea."

"Both?"

"Mom and Dad will come and help, too," Theora says. "Nobody's coming home to Bagnell this year."

"Marion and Phyllis?" Harold asks.

"Mid-afternoon, but they'll be here."

"Theora, how are we going to know how many to prepare for?" Harold questions. "Undercooking would be embarrassing and defeat the purpose of doing this."

"We only promote with a poster near the front counter. Ask people to sign up if they are coming. You could talk to Clark, Sam, Frank, and the others to ask their guests to sign up if they wish to come. Friday and Saturday nights before then, during the break, you make an announcement; people who want to come that day, we ask that they sign up."

"That's still no guarantee we'll get the number right."

"Then we'll overcook and sell turkey sandwiches for a week after," Theora laughs briefly. "We've made money from the soldiers being here; this is a way to say 'thanks.'"

Harold ponders for a moment and says, "Alright, we'll do it." There is a pause. Theora looks at her husband. "You know, Theora, I never once told Hiram 'thank you' for all the things he did to help around here. I just said, 'bye, be careful, stay in touch.' I wish just once I'd said, 'thank you.'"

"Well, then, on Thanksgiving Day, we'll remember him in a prayer and say 'thanks.' He'll be here, honey, and he'll hear you."

Plans for the holiday proceed well, as Theora hopes, and on that day, approximately 60 soldiers and families partake of the meal. The group includes mostly young couples, two families with small children, and a number of single GIs who happen to have the day off. Among the group, Harold notes early, is a chaplain, an Army captain, who is by himself. Harold approaches the young minister with a request.

"Captain, I'm Harold Pilkington. My wife and I own the business, and we were wondering if you would consider saying the grace before today's meal. Our only other option is my father-in-law, whose prayers are longer than the books of the Bible."

"I'll be happy to, sir. A non-denominational prayer. I'm Pat O'Conner. I'm a Catholic priest. I hope that is alright with the locals here."

Harold chuckles. "As long as it's the same God."

"The military is used to a chaplain, regardless of the minister's denomination, tending to their spiritual needs."

"How did you happen to hear about our meal and come today, Father?" Harold asks.

"Please. Call me Captain or Pat. I get more salutes as a captain than I ever did as a priest."

"Alright," Harold agrees. "Captain Pat, it is."

"A young lieutenant and his wife told me about it, so I rode over with them. I hadn't been here before. It's a beautiful place. I hope to get back again and explore."

The food is all set out on long tables to allow for a line on each side, and before starting the meal, Harold introduces Theora, Maggie, Janie, Marion, Phyllis, Ruthie, and the other staff. He pauses a moment, looks up, and says, "And thank you, Hiram, for everything," before turning to Captain Pat for the blessing.

"First, on behalf of myself and, I'm sure, all of you as well, I wish to thank Mr. and Mrs. Pilkington and their friends for this wonderful hospitality and meal. And now, a blessing, if you would care to bow your head.

God almighty, we are a gathering of souls who, regardless of our personal affiliation, today are gathered as one family of one God. We ask for your blessings today as we thank you for all your blessings to come. I stand before you today as a military man among military men engaged in a war not of our beginning but, with your guidance, a war of our ending. And note that as our founding fathers did so long ago, we remain a nation under one God with a belief in divine providence that truth and decency will win the day. Amen."

From the quiet of the room, immediately following the prayer, a young private speaks up. "Captain, for an Irishman, that was pretty well said."

With a strong brogue, the captain replies, "I thank ye kindly, young laddie." The group laughs and begins forming two lines to eat.

The day's gathering goes well, and several of the young GIs try to make conversation with Janie, who responds by showing disinterest. She is not rude, just unresponsive, and the boys decide among themselves that she has a boyfriend somewhere. Ruthie, soon to be seven, going on thirty-seven, follows her into the kitchen and out onto the back porch at one point later in the afternoon.

Janie lights a cigarette as Ruthie tugs on her skirt.

"Janie, Mississippi is alright. Momma says he is in heaven with God."

Janie glances down at her. "I know he is, Ruthie." She turns to look out at the lake in the distance. "I know."

Christmas Eve, 1943, falls on a Friday, and Harold closes the Whitehouse at 5:00 pm. The next day, the business remains closed except for Harold meeting the 7:30 bus, the only one running, and putting the daily papers in the racks. The only food offered is a cinnamon roll and coffee, and Harold closes for the rest of the day after the bus departs at 8.

The most excitement comes at dawn. Before her parents are awake, Ruthie rises, takes a quick glance at her own tree, and heads across the yard to knock on Theora and Harold's door. She wants to watch Johnny experience what she thinks of as "all the magic of Christmas." Theora convinces her that they should wait until Harold returns, which they do. Johnny is experiencing only his second Christmas and the first, where he has some idea of what is going on. Marion helps the time pass until Harold returns by making pancakes and frying bacon. When Harold returns, Marion looks at him before they sit down to eat. "I will if you will."

"Strike a blow for freedom," Harold responds as Marion goes to the icebox and takes out two bottles of beer.

"For the love of God, Marion," Phyllis mutters.

Christmas dinner is somewhat quiet, as only the Claytons and Pilkingtons gather with Bert and Lena in Bagnell. Ruthie plays with Johnny and his new toy while the adults visit. The subject of Harold's draft physical is not broached, but it is ever-present in his mind, and the rest know it. At bedtime, at home, Ruthie says her prayers as her mother tucks her in.

"Momma, how many more Christmases will we have to go through before my baby sister comes?"

Phyllis, a bit unprepared for the child's query, gives her the only answer she can think of. "I'm not sure, but I'll talk to God about it when I say my prayers tonight."

"Maybe talk to Dad, too," Ruthie says.

Phyllis, though rare, misses a beat. "Why. Yes. I will. Go to sleep now." On the way to her bedroom, Phyllis mutters something to herself about her next child not being quite so smart. "More like her dad."

By New Year's Eve, 1943, the Allies have advanced from victory in North Africa, through Sicily, and onto mainland Italy, struggling to take control of the peninsula. The Nazis, aware of the Italians' hints at a peaceful surrender, send thousands of additional troops into the country. At the White House, the one in D.C., Roosevelt has recently returned from a meeting with Churchill and Stalin, the first for the "Big Three," as they are often described. The gathering in Tehran is intended for planning the future direction of the combined war effort.

At the Whitehouse, the one in Lake Ozark plans for the big night include the popular Doerhoff Orchestra from Jefferson City. Phyllis and Jo are coming to help, though Marion has the overnight shift at the Dam, having had Thanksgiving and Christmas off. Jay, with Jack Wickham's help, will have Harold's back should it become necessary. Lawrence has agreed to run the liquor store while Jessie accepts the responsibility, with Ruthie's help, of course, of looking after the children—Larry, Johnny, and baby Janice. Lawrence had hoped his brother Harvey would be by to visit with him, but he and Vivian and the baby were at his in-laws for dinner that evening. Charley and Jean Fleetwood were in the house to dance and drink, and occasionally, Charley would wander off and sit with Lawrence, but Jean would find him. A young GI, a private, asked Jack what training he had to go through to be a professional bouncer/security guard. "I'm a graduate of the Trapp's Tavern Survival School," he tells the boy. "You get through that. You can work anywhere."

The building becomes increasingly crowded as the evening wears on, with couples and singles lining the walls and spilling out into the front room by the soda fountain. Harold knows that this can be an unlit fuse not far from the match if he doesn't limit access and, therefore, places Jack near the front door. "Let no more in and keep a count, if you can, on those that leave." He tells Theora what he has done and asks her to let him know of even the least little disturbance so he can deal with it before it has a chance to get out of hand. Theora reminds all the other waitresses to do the same.

Harold is standing just inside the dining room door, visiting with a young couple from Camdenton, John and Rosalie McCrory, regulars at the Whitehouse, when a table of soldiers gets rather loud. Harold starts to excuse himself when Jay comes by and stops him. "I'll get this one, Harold," Jay says as he walks toward the disturbance.

Four enlisted men are sitting together at a table near the center of the room. Three of them appear to be conversing quietly, while the fourth, seemingly intoxicated, is speaking loudly and with occasional curse words. Jay approaches their table, stops on the side facing the loudmouth, and kneels down so he is at their eye level. "Gentlemen, I hope you are having a good time tonight," Jay says. There is a general chorus of "yes, thanks," but not a word from the loudmouth. "Do me a favor, though—try to keep your voices down a bit so you don't disturb other guests." The three quiet GIs say "Yes, sir" and nod in agreement.

"Who the hell are you?" the mouthy one says, looking directly at Jay.

"I'm the one who is also asking you to watch your language. There are ladies present."

"Where's your uniform? You a draft dodger?" the mouthy one asks with a smirk on his face.

Jay looks directly at him as he rises. "My job is to help provide electricity to the munitions factories in St. Louis that make the bullets and bombs that you are going to use to kill Krauts and Japs." Jay looks around at the others. "Just keep it down some, boys, okay?"

"Yessir," one of the others says with sincerity as Jay turns to leave. At his back, he hears another say: "Watch it, Goose Egg, you're gonna get us thrown outta here."

Goose Egg? Jay thinks. What kind of a nickname is that? And then it hits him, the obvious—"big zero." That works. Jay chuckles.

In the kitchen, Jo corners Theora for a quiet moment. "Theora, is Harold alright? Jay says he seems somewhat tense tonight."

Not surprised at the question, Theora shrugs it off. "Oh, he's fine. He's just been a little stressed lately—business issues and all." The two ladies get what they came for and exit as Phyllis comes in.

"Momma," Ruthie says to her, "everything is fine here. Aunt Jessie is doing a very good job of looking after the babies."

"I'm so happy to hear that. You are helping her, I'm sure?"

"Yes, Momma, but I wish Daddy were here."

"Well, I do, too, but you and I will just have to dance together at midnight. How would that be?"

Ruthie lights up. "Yes, ma'am," she says.

"Ruthie, have you seen any Nazis tonight?" Maggie asks.

"Not a one, ma'am."

"That's because your father is out doing God's work tonight," Maggie tells her. "And he's very good at it."

Back in the dining room, Ira Stith gets up from his table and walks over to talk with Jay. "Any problem with them boys over there?" Ira asks, indicating Goose Egg's group.

"No. Three good kids and one mouthy one."

"Well, if you or Harold need any help, let me know."

"Now, Ira, I would not want you to get that pretty face all banged up. That new wife of yours might leave you."

Ira laughs. "You think it could get worse?"

"I don't want to take that chance. I've noticed, too, how much your dancing has improved since you got married."

"Regardless, I'll be right over there if you need me," Ira says, pointing to his table.

Jay watches Ira go and then walks over to where Harold is standing behind the front counter. "The boys at that middle table," Jay tells him. "Three of them are okay, but their buddy could be trouble later."

"Okay. How's Jack doing at the front door?"

"Fine," Jay tells him. "Got a flask tucked in his pants under his shirt. Takes a hit on it occasionally."

"I'm going to go and see how Lawrence is doing," Harold tells Jay as he walks over to the liquor store. Lawrence is immersed in a magazine, catalog, or some type of written pamphlet.

Lawrence looks up from his reading when Harold steps in. "Ever since I've been at the post office, I've taken up the hobby of stamp collecting," Lawrence says. "I get these periodicals about stamps and collecting, and I learn that way."

"Business about done for the night? You want to close?"

"It's slow now, but I don't mind sitting here. Jessie won't be ready to go home until after midnight anyway."

"Okay, it's almost eleven now." Harold pauses and looks around the front room, the fountain, and the entrance to the dining room. "You know, Lawrence, this is my ninth year in a row of being right here on New Year's Eve. It's starting to catch up to me, I think."

"It's a tough business. It wears on you. I worry that Jessie is drinking too much."

"I know she worries a lot about Mona and her family and Don, too. You want me to try to talk with her, Lawrence?"

"No, no. It'll pass. It's this damned war."

Harold hears a bit of commotion coming from the dining room and sees Theora come to the door and motion for Jay, who follows her inside the room. Harold hurries to the door as Jay reaches the disturbance. Goose and a man from another table are squared off. Jay quickly steps between them, facing Goose. "What seems to be the problem here?" Goose doesn't speak, just laughs. "You," Jay says as he points at him, "sit down."

"C'mon, sit, Goose," his friends all say. "Sit down and shut up." He finally sits down, and Jay turns to talk to the other man.

"What happened here?"

"My girlfriend and I were walking by, and this SOB grabs her and pulls her onto his lap, saying she's too pretty for me. She slaps him and jumps up, then goes to our table over there." He points to a table near the wall where his girlfriend is crying. "Then you show up before I get a chance to rearrange his face."

"If there is any rearranging done, I'll do it, okay?" Jay says. "You go join your girl." The man looks at Goose and slowly turns, walking back to his table. Harold has walked up and stands quietly on the opposite side of the table. "Now, boys, Goose, I warned you once about behavior. I believe it's time for you to go home. I want you to leave quietly."

"We'll go, sir. We apologize for our friend," one of the other men says. Another says, "Let's go, Goose."

Goose has suddenly fixed his gaze on Harold, who stands quietly, monitoring the situation. "Who the hell are you?"

"I'm the owner here and the man who is going to escort you from the building."

"You another one of them draft dodgers, coward?" Goose laughs as Harold comes around to his side of the table.

"Come on, Goose, or we're going to go back to the Fort without you," one of the companions says.

"Jay, why don't you escort these three gentlemen out of the room? I'll be along soon with Mr. Mouth here."

"Come on, gentlemen, follow me," Jay says.

"You come on too, Goose," one of his companions says as he falls in line behind Jay and starts for the door.

"So, you going to escort me out, Dodger?"

"How about you walk out to the front room with me so we don't disrupt the folks here from their fun? We can have the rest of our talk there as I escort you to the front door."

"Alright, I'm game. More room there for you to fall, coward." Harold starts to get mad. "Follow me, Goose shit, or whatever your name is." Harold heads to the door, Goose following behind. Theora has been watching all this and goes to Harold.

"Honey, keep calm now," Theora says to him. "Don't let him make you mad."

"I'm not mad, Theora," he says curtly. "Stay out of the way."

Theora goes to Phyllis' side, and the two follow Harold and Goose out of the dining room. "I'm worried, Phyllis. I've never seen Harold this way. The look in his eyes."

"He'll be alright. Theora, Jay, and Jack are right there."

"No, I mean he could hurt the other fellow."

Having reached the middle of the front room, Goose stops and faces Harold. "This is as far as I go without assistance, dodger boy."

"Harold, Jay, and I can get hold of him," Jack says, stepping toward Goose.

"No, stand back!" Harold says firmly, not taking his eyes off Goose.

Goose's three companions, very concerned, implore him to come with them without any more trouble, but he continues to ignore them. "I'm waiting for your escort, dodger boy," Goose says like he's playing a game. "You a coward?"

"You got one more chance to turn and quietly go out that door," Harold says.

"Nah, I want you to put me out that door, pussy."

"Watch your language!" Phyllis suddenly bursts out. Her sister gives her a look.

Harold takes a step toward Goose, who immediately steps in and throws a punch at Harold, who dodges it. He immediately throws two more punches at Harold, both dodged. "Stand still, you cowardly asshole," Goose says as he draws back to swing again.

Before he can bring his arm forward, Harold's right hand, backed by all the energy in his body, suddenly explodes into Goose's jaw. Goose screams with pain as he falls to the floor. Harold grabs his wrist with his left hand. "Damnit!" he says.

"Damnit." Theora goes to him.

"Harold, are you…" Harold stops her.

"Theora, wait!" He looks at Goose's companions. "Boys, you pick him up and take him to the Fort, to the base hospital. He's got a broken jaw."

"Your hand, sir," one of the companions says. "It's hurt, too. We want to pay your doctor's bill."

"Listen, you boys can best help me by getting him out of here." The three start getting Goose, who moans continually, off the floor. "If you have any trouble with the MPs or your commanding officer, have them call me. I'll vouch for you. You didn't do anything."

"Take care of your hand, Harold," Jay says. "Jack and I will finish up here."

"Everybody, please get back to work," Theora says to the employees. To the customers: "Please go back in and dance. It's only an hour to midnight."

Harold turns to go to the kitchen, still holding his right wrist. Theora follows him. In the kitchen, he picks up a bar towel, goes to the ice bin, and dips some ice onto the towel. He picks up a meat mallet, folds the towel over, and crushes the ice. "Would you fix me a drink, Jess? Double?" Harold sits down and, with his left hand, places the ice bag over his right hand and wrist. Theora sits with him and gives him a look of disapproval.

"You feel better now?"

"Not now, Theora," Harold says. "Not now."

New Year's over, 1944 ushered in, and the Whitehouse put to bed for what was left of the night. The Pilkingtons return home to the house on 1-A. After settling Johnny into his room, Theora goes to confront Harold in their small living room.

"We're going to talk now, Harold," she says quietly so as not to disturb the baby. She sits down across from him.

"Theora, I have to be up again and back to work by 6:30 in the morning. Talk can wait."

"No. We'll talk now." Harold just looks at her. It's obvious he is experiencing some pain. "Do you need more aspirin?"

"No, I'm fine."

"I've never seen you like that. Don't you think that to-gether, you, Jay, and Jack could have managed to get the guy out of the building and into their car? The other three boys were trying to help."

"Guys like that don't stay gone. They can't stand the em-barrassment. They come back. He might have hurt somebody else."

"This isn't about that. You got mad because he called you a draft dodger, a coward. That's what happened. You lost your self-control."

"Damnit, Theora, he swung at me three times."

"Harold, your manhood is intact! It always was. I can vouch for that. Get over the damn draft and move on." Harold is quiet. "First thing Monday morning, I'm taking you to El-don to see Doc Attic. I'm going to bed."

On Monday morning early, Theora, Johnny in tow, drives Harold to see Doc Attic.

"I believe your wrist is just sprained, but you broke these two metacarpal bones. We'll have to put a cast on while they heal."

"How much mobility will I have?" Harold asks.

"You can wiggle your fingers. Tickle the girls. That's about it."

"Not when I'm around," Theora says.

"How is your left hook?" the doctor asks.

"Passable."

"Use that on the bad guys for a while and let the right heal."

Harold is quiet on the drive back to the Dam until they come off the south end.

"Theora, pull off up here just past the Drexel Station. I want to show you something." Harold indicates a spot just off the highway on the lake side of the road. "Yes, right there." Theora pulls off and parks, and the couple gets out of the car.

The bare property they are looking at includes just a short, level depth from the roadway before a steep hill descends toward the lakefront, approximately 60-70 yards away.

"This lot here is available and reasonable. And not selling."

"Don't you think it's because there's no place to put a building unless you build three stories?" Theora observes.

"Exactly. The question is, could you buy the land and build three stories here cheaper than one story on a better piece of road frontage? And have the extra space to rent to help pay for it all."

"You think we should buy this?"

Harold looks at his wife. "You were right, Theora. I lost my 'footing' the other night; let that guy get to me. It wasn't just the draft. It's the Whitehouse. We've got to get out of there."

"I love you, Harold. More than anything else in the world. Other than our son, of course. You think this is the answer?"

"There's two hundred feet across here. We build a store building here. Marion builds a place for his restaurant next door. A staircase in between gives access to the next level on both sides."

"Have you shown it to Marion yet?"

"No. Just you."

"Well, let's see what he thinks."

"Okay."

In late January, Jessie's mother finally gets word through the International Red Cross that Mona and her family are alive and as well as can be expected, considering their plight. The Japanese have tightened their grip on the civilians at Santo Tomas as the war tightens its grip on them. Food rationing has begun and is a reflection of life within the civilian population on the home islands. The detainees have been able to maintain a garden and grow some food over the period they've been here, but it is not sufficient to take care of all their needs. Much of the rice crop grown on the mainland goes to feed the troops in the field. Their colonization of such places as Korea allows them the luxury of stealing the majority of the rice there and shipping it to the homeland as a supplement.

Jessie also gets more frequent news about Don, most through Mrs. Fry. He continues flying out of England, but there is no mention of where and for whom. For all the Frys, just knowing he is alright is calming. Through Don, they know that Suzy is now with the nurse corps somewhere in the Pacific. The last word he had, she was in Midway, but then the locations stopped coming, even though the letters didn't.

Harry and Maxine are still in Connecticut, and he is spending more time in port now than at sea. He is tasked with helping train new recruits in sonar and thus at home with his family more. He professes he likes it better, but the probable truth is he misses the adventure of being at sea. Maxine writes an occasional letter to their Missouri family, and Theora posts it on her board as well. She says it's for "good luck."

Harold has taken Marion down to see the lot he showed Theora.

"Well, what do you think, Marion?"

"I see your point—low land cost, put your money in the building instead. Our problem is that we're not in a position to buy now. Don't know when we will be."

"I'd buy it. All you have to do is get a building built big enough for your restaurant. You'd have a long-term lease."

"Building takes money, too."

"I know. Truth be told, we can't do it now either. But in six months, I'll be giving Lawrence his last payment on the Whitehouse. I could start looking for a buyer then, have the money."

"Look, Harold, there's something else," Marion shares. "Please don't say anything to Theora yet, 'cause I don't know if Phyllis has said anything to her. We're going to try to have another baby. I can't be taking any chances right now. I need that UE job. It pays well."

"Well, damnit, Marion. That's great! I knew someday you guys would try again. I wish you the best."

"It hasn't happened yet," Marion says, urging caution.

"Yeah, but think of all the fun you can have making it happen."

"Always looking on the bright side."

"Look, Marion, I know there is a lot to worry about — the baby and all," Harold says, serious now, "so we'll just put this on the back burner for a while."

"I don't know that we've got any other choice."

"If the property is still here when the time is right, then it's meant to be," Harold says. "If not, we'll find something else."

"Yep, Pilk, we'll find something else."

Throughout the spring of 1944, all the conversation among the populace, on the radio, and in the newspapers centers on the subject of the invasion of mainland Europe. It is not a discussion of "if" but "when." And everybody, including the Germans, knows the entry point: France. Those with family or friends training in England feel certain their next deployment will be on the road to Paris.

In April, the big news in Lake Ozark isn't the invasion — that hasn't come yet. It's the conception, as Phyllis makes known that she is expecting a baby.

"Momma," Ruthie asks after her initial excitement has mellowed, "is it a girl, a sister?"

"Darling, we won't know that until the baby is born in November. We'll have to be patient."

Ruthie, a bit exasperated, mimics her mother. "Well, for the love of God, Momma!"

Continuing the need to divest of any non-related business activities, UE sells its boat dock located between Fry's Casino dock and the Dam. They had operated a boat ride service there almost from the building of the Dam, and it is the catalyst for Lawrence Fry doing the same. The new owners, John Loc and Glenn Wood retired cops from St. Louis, name their facility Loc-Wood Boat Dock. Lawrence immediately buys a second speedboat and hires another driver, and a competition begins. Each year, regardless of the war, more and more people visit Lake Ozark to see the Dam and its resultant lake, and they want to experience it from the water or the air. Business is good at both docks.

Phyllis' pregnancy is going well, and she still occasionally helps at the Whitehouse. Ruthie tracks her like a little mother hen as if she has a vested interest in her. "Momma, you should sit down and rest now," and "Momma, maybe you shouldn't eat that," are common cautions heard. Harold's hand heals quickly, and soon, the cast is off. He is free to hit someone with it again, but Theora keeps him on a short leash. It's okay though, Harold thinks, because "I don't like having to do that. I don't want to do that again." Word does get around with the troops and locals who visit the Whitehouse to party. Getting drunk and getting disruptive could easily end unpleasantly. You don't want to "mess" with Harold.

Early on the morning of June 4, units of the U.S. Army entered the city of Rome. Early on the morning of June 6, the invasion of France begins on the coast of Normandy. Though casualties were high, the Allied troops eventually moved inland from the beach and began the difficult journey to Paris. The news is of special interest to the Frys because, as of his last letter, Don was still in England. It is unknown whether or not he is in the invasion force. Americans everywhere are excited about Rome and hopeful that our troops will be in Paris soon. The European city they wanted most to put Allied troops in was Berlin. George Patton relays through the newspapers that if you give him the tanks and enough gas, he'll be there in a couple of days. A little more gas, and he'll be in Moscow soon after. This, of course, doesn't sit well with the Russians American allies, so Ike doesn't give him the gas.

In July, Harold hands a check to Lawrence Fry for the final payment of the Pilkingtons' purchase of the Whitehouse. "Great, we can sell it now if we so choose," he says, to which Theora adds, "Wonderful, find a buyer." They talk about a sale, but both know that, at this point, they need to continue earning and saving so they will be in a better position to move forward after the war. The war, with all its horror and destruction, is there and has become responsible for America's emergence from the Depression—a positive result from payments made in blood.

Two mornings after Harold pays Lawrence, Marion walks next door to tell him and Theora about Charley Fleetwood. "Jean just called me and said Charley died this morning," he tells Harold and Theora.

"For the love of God, what happened?" Theora asks.

"Jean said he got up early and went to the kitchen, poured a cup of coffee, and sat down at the table and fell over and died. Heart attack."

"Is somebody with her?" Theora asks.

"The doctor from Tuscumbia is there. Clark and Audrey Hale. Phyllis walked down."

"Harold, I should go too," Theora says.

"Alright," Harold says, and Theora walks out the front door. "Just like Paul," Harold says to Marion. "God at random, again?"

"Suppose so," Marion says. "Natural causes."

Three days later, Charley is buried. Within the week, Jean has sold all her meager furnishings to the Hales, who will keep them in the unit for a future renter. She takes Charley's clothing to the church rummage.

"I'm leaving, girls," she tells Phyllis and Theora. "I have no family here, and I'm not close with Charley's."

Asked where she is going, she says: "I'm going to get in my car and drive west until the memories start to dim. Then I'll stop and work for a while. Take it a day at a time."

The next morning, her clothes and personal possessions loaded in her car, she does exactly that.

Mid-summer, a letter from Pauline announces that she and Lon have welcomed into the world a baby named Elizabeth Ruth. They call her Betty. Up on 1-A, late summer or thereabouts, Ross and Gladys Clayton welcome into their home a baby boy they name James, but they call him Jimmy. Down the hill and up on the point at the Cottages, a boy named James is born to the Allen family at about the same time. They call him James. A veritable "cocktail" of kids is in the mix on the first lake road from the Dam, and Ruthie hopes her momma is bringing the finishing touch. Harold and Theora continue to live next to the Claytons, with Harold commuting each day on his scooter. On many days, Theora and Phyllis get together early for coffee and talk.

"I'm going to start seeing this new young doctor in Jefferson City, Theora."

"You're not going to Dr. Attic anymore?"

"It's not that I don't believe he's a good doctor; it's that this man is a specialist, a baby doctor," Phyllis says.

"Phyllis, everything is going to be alright. The baby will be fine. Please stop worrying."

"I'm not having another baby at home or in a doctor's office. This baby will be born in St. Mary's Hospital in Jefferson City. I have an appointment to see the doctor on Tuesday."

"You want me to go with you?" Theora asks.

"No. Marion is. He insisted."

On August 25, word comes that Paris has been liberated by the Allies, and the Fry family is again encouraged that they will hear from Don soon. When a letter arrives for Lawrence and Jessie a few days later, there is no mention at all of his location, past or present. He does mention that the last he heard from Suzy was that she was on a hospital ship in the Marianas, an island group in the Pacific. Jessie wonders to herself, is it sometimes better not to know than to know?

At the Whitehouse, the relationship between Maggie and Janie has evolved into something akin to a mother-daughter bond. They talk as they work, Maggie often imploring the young girl to get out, go with friends, dance, and have fun. The girl shows little interest in doing so, and Maggie, like a mother, worries.

"Maggie, I know this sounds strange," Janie says to her one day, "but all my friends seem young to me."

"You have experienced something early in life that has matured you—more so than them, perhaps."

"Well, some of them have boyfriends in the service, a few are married, but they party all the time. Like everything is normal."

"To them, that is normal, their normal," Maggie tells her. "That's their way of coping."

"Well, it doesn't interest me."

Harold has started taking Monday mornings off and is at home on 1-A on such a day in early September when there is a knock on the door. He opens it, and standing on the front stoop is a well-dressed middle-aged woman. Though very surprised, he knows almost immediately who it is.

"Harold, I'm your mother. Virginia."

"I know who you are."

"I was going to Jefferson City and stopped to see Jessie," she continues, somewhat formally. "She told me where you live."

Theora comes into the front room, drying her hands with a kitchen towel, little Johnny following close behind. "Harold, who is it?" Seeing the woman, she instinctively knows and glances at Harold.

"This is my wife, Theora, and my son, John," Harold says to the woman who is still standing on the porch.

A very awkward moment passes between the parties until, finally, Theora speaks. "Would you like to come in?" she says and glances at Harold.

There is a pause. Virginia looks at Harold and smiles. "Yes, I'd love to," she says.

"Please, sit down," Theora says, motioning to the couch, and Virginia sits. "Would you like some coffee?"

"Yes, thank you," Virginia says. Theora rises and goes into the kitchen.

"You are going to Jeff City?" Harold asks, attempting to make conversation.

"Yes, to pick up Ginny. My daughter. Your sister. She's been visiting her boyfriend there. He's been on a short leave and takes the train out this afternoon."

Harold, who has remained standing during this brief exchange, says, "I'll help Theora with the coffee," and goes into the kitchen. Johnny remains standing across the room, studying the woman. She looks at him and pats the empty space beside her on the couch.

"Would you like to come sit with me?" she says.

The boy responds by shaking his head, "No."

"I won't bite," she says.

There is a pause, and finally, Johnny asks, "Who are you?"

Virginia's demeanor is suddenly stern as she looks back at the boy. "I'm your grandmother, and that bitch in Tulsa isn't."

The entire conversation is heard by Harold and Theora in the kitchen, and Theora reacts immediately. "Harold… no… this… I won't allow it. She has to go."

She has hardly finished when Harold reenters the living room. "Son, go in the kitchen with your mom." He hesitates. "Now," Harold says, and the boy leaves. Harold looks at his mother.

"Mother, your visit is over. It's time for you to leave now. I'll walk you to your car."

Virginia stares at him a moment and then slowly gets up and goes to the door as Harold holds it open. He follows her out and holds her car door open as she gets in. She looks at him and stutters a bit. "Harold, I don't understand."

He looks at her. "Being a mother doesn't make you a 'mom,' and being a grandmother doesn't make you a 'grandma.'" He closes her car door, turns, and walks back toward the house.

Phyllis' appointment with the new doctor in Jefferson City during the summer goes well. He is a personable young man named Julian Osman, and both Marion and Phyllis take to him from the beginning. He sets their minds at ease about the baby to come and determines the due date of mid-November. "I highly recommend him," Phyllis tells Theora afterward.

"How can you do that?" Theora asks. "He hasn't done anything yet. If you're still recommending in November, I'll take notes."

Longtime State Senator Phil Donnelly from Lebanon has been stopping by the Whitehouse off and on for a number of years. His stops are usually for lunch on Fridays as he makes his way home from the state capital in Jefferson City. It is the approximate halfway point in the drive that he takes often when the legislature is in session. This particular fall day, though, is for more than his usual cheese sandwich and coffee. As the Democrat candidate for governor in the November 1944 election, he is out campaigning. After ordering his usual, he asks Bea to see Harold, who comes from the kitchen to say hello.

"Senator," Harold says as he shakes Phil's hand. "Hope all is well with you. How's the campaign coming?"

"Doing well, we think. Could be close, but I believe we'll pull it out. The country will stick with Roosevelt, and with Truman on the ticket, I think we'll win Missouri."

"Well, Theora and I plan on voting for you," Harold says.

"Great. I appreciate that," Phil says, holding up a large poster board and laying it on the counter. "Got a campaign poster here I'd like for you to put up for me."

"About that, Senator," Harold says, appearing to choose his words carefully. "I can't do that. By putting up that poster for you or any other candidate, it implies that the Whitehouse—this business—is telling people how to vote. Some customers don't like that. Some employees don't like that. Owners of a business can vote how they want, but their business is no place to tell others what to do. I don't believe a business should be involved in politics." He pauses and takes a breath. "I hope you understand."

The senator looks at him for a moment. "Well, I don't, Harold." Phil takes the last bite of his sandwich and a long drink of his coffee. As he gets up, he reaches into his pocket, lays 35 cents on the counter, and picks up his poster. "I'm sorry you feel that way," he says and turns and walks out the front door.

Later, Harold relates the incident to Theora. "I lost a customer, I would imagine," Harold tells her.

"All customers are important," Theora says. "But 35 cents twelve times or so a year won't break us."

"Well, we live in a county full of Republicans. It could have been worse."

On November 7, 1944, Harold and Theora Pilkington go to the polls and vote for Phil Donnelly, who is narrowly elected the 41st governor of Missouri. On that same day, Roosevelt won his historic fourth term, and Missouri's Harry Truman became the vice president of the United States.

When Roosevelt ordered MacArthur to leave the Philippines early in the war, the general promised, "I shall return." On October 20, 1944, he did just that when he waded ashore on the Philippine island of Leyte. The return marked the beginning of the U.S. campaign to retake the country. For Jessie, the news was quite welcome, as it provided further hope that Mona and her family would soon be free. She tried to put aside any thoughts of the treatment they might receive at the hands of the retreating Japanese Army before their liberation. Rumors of the massacre of American prisoners of war at the hands of the Japanese had reached America. Would they treat civilian prisoners the same? No one knew, but Jessie remained hopeful that they would come home alive. She prayed a lot, aided by alcohol.

Lawrence, though one to keep his concerns to himself, betrays his inner feelings to Jessie through his demeanor. Don, his baby brother, is on his mind constantly, and he worries with his wife about Mona. Jessie knows that all of it is taking an unseen toll, and the problem only accelerates when his middle brother receives a draft notice in early October.

Harvey passes the physical and is already in training at Ft. Wood when MacArthur takes his walk onto the Leyte shore.

With the failure of British General Montgomery's plan called "Market Garden" in September, Allied forward movements were stalled. In mid-December, the Germans begin a counteroffensive that comes to be known as the "Battle of the Bulge." Allied units defend their positions heroically, hold the line, and begin to reverse the momentum by the end of December.

The month before the battle begins, on November 17, Phyllis begins her own battle of the "bulge" as she goes into labor. Marion, who has rehearsed this day in his mind many times, calmly drives her to St. Mary's Hospital, where he is welcomed by obstetrics nurse Pauline Luebbert. A few hours later, Dr. Osman performs his magic, and the baby is born. Marion's first call is to Ruthie, who is with Harold and Theora.

"Ruthie, you have a baby sister."

"Of course, Daddy! It was to be expected. God answered my prayers."

"We did an inventory," Marion says. "Ten each toes and fingers, two feet, two hands, two ears, two eyes, one nose, and one mouth."

"Belly button?"

"Yes," Marion answers. "It's part of the package."

"What are we going to name her, Daddy?"

"We are not going to name her anything. Your mother is going to name her Mary Catherine."

Within a week, Marion started calling the baby "Cookie, my little sweet Cookie." It is a name he read in the Dagwood and Blondie comic strip. The Bumsteads' daughter is named "Cookie," and Marion likes it. When it starts to catch on with others, Phyllis finally reacts.

"I can't believe you nicknamed our pretty little daughter after a snack food you read about in a comic strip!"

"Ruthie and I like it," Marion says in defense.

"For the love of God, Marion."

At Christmas, Harvey, having finished basic training, is given leave and comes home. He is scheduled to ship out for Europe on January 2 and treasures the time home. Harold and Theora offer to host a Christmas dinner at the Whitehouse for the Frys so they can concentrate on being together. Lawrence drives to Springfield and brings his mother to Lake Ozark. Bert and Lena are there as well. Bert, semi-retired, has been filling in for Harvey, managing his Phillips 66 distributorship since he has been gone, and they have much to talk about. Plans are for Bert to stay with it until Harvey returns from his deployment. Marion and Phyllis are at Red and Carrie's but plan to stop by later in the day.

Lawrence is fairly quiet for most of the day, as is his mother, reflecting their somewhat stoic demeanor. His brothers have always been more extroverted than he, though Harvey appears less so today, reflective perhaps of his imminent departure from family. Larry, Johnny, and Jane play happily in the dining room as the others talk. When the Claytons arrive in late afternoon, after everyone "oohs" and "ahs" the new baby, Ruthie plays a few Christmas songs she has learned, and the younger ones gather near her at the piano. Jessie finds occasion to slip into the kitchen at times throughout the day, and though no one remarks, it is obvious why. Before they leave to go home at the end of the day, Lawrence finds a moment with Harold alone.

"Will you talk to her, Harold? She'll listen to you," Lawrence asks him. "She loves you like a brother."

"I don't know that she will, Lawrence — listen to anyone. I can try to get her to talk to a doctor. That might be best."

"Just, please try."

"Alright, I'll try."

New Year's Eve Day, mid-afternoon, Harold is in the kitchen stocking beer and soda into the walk-in cooler. Janie is out front when a young couple comes in. The handsome young man is dressed in the uniform of a major in the U.S. Army and is escorting a very attractive young lady who appears to be 18–19 years old.

"Is Harold Pilkington here, miss?" the girl asks Janie.

"He is. I can get him for you. Who should I tell him is here?"

"Virgin… uh, Ginny. Taft. Ginny Taft, please," the girl says.

When Janie relays the message to Harold, it doesn't register immediately.

Harold shakes his head slightly. "Who?" he says.

"Ginny. Uh, Taft."

There is a brief moment, then recognition. "Ohmigod. I'll be damned." Harold goes to the sink and washes his hands, wipes them dry, and goes out of the kitchen.

"Hello?" Harold says upon seeing the couple. "I'm Harold."

Virginia puts out her hand. "I'm Virginia, your, uh, sister." Harold looks at her and, finally, awkwardly takes her hand and shakes it.

"They still call you Ginny?" Harold asks.

"I've pretty well outgrown that now," the girl says. "I mostly go by Virginia." She turns to her companion. "This is Rea Snodgrass. My fiancé."

Harold reaches out his hand, and the two shake. "Nice to meet you, Major," Harold says.

"Please," the Major says, "call me Rea."

"Why don't we go into the dining room and sit for a while. Do you have time?"

"Yes, a little," Virginia replies, and the couple follow Harold into the dining room. "We've been in Eldon, and we're on our way to Springfield and thought we would stop by and say hi."

"The last time I saw you was the summer of 1935," Harold remembers. "You were very young."

"I remember. You came by the house."

"Yes, briefly," Harold says. He looks at Rea. "Do you have family in Eldon, Rea?"

"Yes, nearby. We're thinking of settling there after we marry, and I get out of the service in the spring."

Harold is surprised at the thought that after all these years, his sister—half-sister—will be living only 12 miles away. "It is a nice town."

"I plan on opening a men's clothing store in Eldon," Rea says. "I think that the town's closeness to the Lake will be advantageous in the future. At least, that's the plan."

"I only see the area growing," Harold says. "I've got a young son; he's going to need long pants someday." He chuckles at the thought.

Rea laughs with him. "Just let me know his size; we'll stock them."

Virginia makes a move as if she is getting ready to get up. "We should be going," she says. "Mother is expecting us."

"Yes, of course," Harold says as he gets up.

"Harold, I know there are… issues… between you and Mother. I hope that we can have a relationship in spite of that. After all, you are my brother."

"That will not come between us," Harold promises. The two hug; Harold and Rea shake hands. "Let us know when you settle in at Eldon." The couple leave just as Theora comes down the stairs.

"I'll be damned," Harold stammers.

Theora overhears him. "Yes, honey, I tried talking to the Lord about that, but he wasn't listening."

"Do you know who that was?" Harold asks her. She looks at him quizzically. "That was my sister."

"Your sister?"

"Yeah, she and her fiancé are moving to Eldon in the spring."

Theora stares at Harold for a moment. He is staring at the front door. She looks at the front door. "'All the gin joints in all the towns in all the world and she' is moving to Eldon?" She pauses. "Eldon?"

"Yes, Eldon," Harold says, smiling.

Theora, serious now, looks at her husband. "I think that will be nice for you, honey." She is quite sincere. "Very nice for you."

Partiers at the Whitehouse that night are unusually composed, though midnight is still greeted with a sense of excitement, as the old year yields to time unlived. Americans are worn down by the war and hopeful 1945 will soon see the end of it. Auld Lang Syne seems to have more of a special meaning each year as war takes away old acquaintances and brings new. Sadness comes with the knowing that so many of the "auld" had been so young.

A few days after New Year's, the late morning bus from Kansas City pulls up in front of the Whitehouse, and a young staff sergeant steps off and goes to the luggage compartment to wait for the driver to retrieve his duffel bag. The soldier's left arm is resting in a sling, but with one quick motion, he snatches up the bag with his right hand and rests it on his right shoulder and follows the driver through the front door. A new waitress behind the counter, Beatrice, is serving other passengers when the sergeant reaches the counter and sets his bag down by a stool. Getting the waitress's attention, he orders coffee. When she brings it, he speaks to her.

"I'm looking for a young lady who worked here in 1942," the soldier begins. "Her name was Janie. Do you know where I might find her?"

The waitress looks at him like he's from another planet. "Uh, yeah, she's in the kitchen there," the girl says, pointing.

"Yes, that's right. She worked in the kitchen."

"No, I mean, she's in the kitchen now."

"You mean she's still here?" the soldier asks, to clarify.

"She's the assistant head chef. You want me to get her?"

"Please, if it's alright."

When Bea tells her, Janie's heart beats fast for a few moments until reality tells it to slow back down. The suddenness of hearing that a soldier was out front asking for her is beyond unexpected. She takes a moment and composes herself.

Maggie, witnessing the exchange, tries to lighten the moment. "I bet it's one of those boys that was here on Thanksgiving a few years back. Every one of those boys was smitten with you."

"Probably," Janie says and goes out of the kitchen. As soon as she comes out, steps behind the counter, and sees the soldier, she knows—and her hand instinctively touches the jewelry hanging around her neck.

"I see you got the necklace okay," Sergeant George says. "I'm glad to know that."

"Yes, thanks."

"You know me, then?"

"Yes." Janie pauses, remembering. "You were here that last day."

"Are Mr. and Mrs. Pilkington still here?" the sergeant asks.

"Yes, they still own the place. They are upstairs right now but should be down soon."

"I'd like to say hello to them."

"Do you remember Maggie? In the kitchen?"

"Oh, yes," he says, "and her cherry pie."

"Bring your coffee and come with me and say hello to her," Janie says.

"Sir, you can sit your bag here behind the counter, if you want," Bea says.

The soldier does so and follows Janie into the kitchen.

Maggie looks at him and immediately remembers. "Sgt. James George, welcome back."

"How could you remember me? That was almost three years ago. I was here only about two hours."

"I never forget a handsome soldier," Maggie says. "Especially one who loves my cherry pie."

"He already mentioned the pie, Maggie," Janie tells her.

"I see you're injured. Are you out now?" Maggie asks.

"I am. Discharged a week ago in San Francisco. Been riding the train across to Kansas City. Still wearing my uniform—makes it easier to get accommodations."

"What about your arm, James?" Janie asks. "Can I call you James?"

"James is good, or Jim. Most call me Jim." The two ladies stare at him. "Oh, the arm. I took some shrapnel from a grenade on Guam. Got evacuated, eventually to rehab in Frisco. The doctor told me to use the sling for another week. It's precautionary—I take it off when I bathe."

The kitchen door opens, and Harold and Theora come into the room. "Beatrice said we have a guest," Harold says, offering his hand to shake. "It's good to see you again, Sergeant."

James rises and takes Harold's hand. "Good to see you, sir. Ma'am."

"Beatrice said you came in off the Kansas City bus. Where are you coming from, and where are you headed?"

"I was telling them. I was discharged in San Francisco and rode the train to K.C.," James says. He pauses and looks at Janie. "I'm going to Mississippi to see Hiram's folks."

Janie sits down at the table. "You're going to Mississippi?" James sits back down across from her.

"Hiram and I became very close friends; kinda like brothers. We promised each other that if something happened, the other one would go see his family. I made a promise. I need to keep it."

Maggie breaks the sudden silence in the room. "Jim, you need more coffee, and I'm going to get you a slice of pie. Don't have cherry, but got a fresh apple." As Maggie goes about getting the pie and Janie pours coffee, Theora sits down.

"Where is your home, Jim?" Theora asks. "Where is your family?"

"Chicago. I came from there."

"Your parents?" Theora asks.

"They died in an accident when I was twelve. No other family, so I grew up in a foster home. When I turned seventeen, I left. At eighteen, I joined the Army."

"Were they not good to you, James?" Janie asks. "The foster family?"

"Oh, they were fine. They liked having me — got a check every month from my folks' estate." James laughs. "Although, they were probably relieved when I left. I was a bit of a rebel."

"So, when do you head south?" Harold asks.

"Well, I was wondering, do you have any auto dealerships nearby?"

"Eldon. Twelve miles away. There's a Ford, a Chevy, and a Buick."

"Good," James says. "I want to buy a car."

"There's not many choices right now, James," Harold tells him. "They haven't been building many cars; war and all, puts used ones at a premium."

"I just want a good, reliable automobile that I can drive to Mississippi. The train was nice. I saw some beautiful country, but I want to drive again."

Maggie senses an opening and interjects an offer. "Janie, why don't you take a few hours off? Take my car and drive Jim into Eldon. See what you can find."

Jim glances at Janie. "Oh, I don't want to be a bother."

"It's no bother," Maggie says. "Right, Janie?"

Janie looks at her, unsmiling. "No. No. No bother."

Maggie looks at Jim. "Sergeant George, you will behave yourself, or I will come find you." She points to a double-barrel shotgun lying on top of the upper cabinets, out of arm's reach. "You understand?"

He chuckles a bit and smiles at her. "Yes, ma'am."

"Sergeant, I have to run out for a bit, but if you find a car, you're not going to leave yet today, are you?" Harold asks.

"No, sir. I'll get a room for the night. Leave in the morning."

"Well, Hiram's old room is available. You're welcome to sleep there tonight."

James stammers a bit. "I, uh, Mr., uh, Harold, don't. Are you sure?"

"I have to go check on my son now, Jim," Theora says. "He's been napping, but when you get back from Eldon, I'll show you where the room is."

"We'll have dinner when you get back," Harold says.

Both Pilkingtons leave the kitchen.

"I'll get you the keys, Janie," Maggie says.

Theora tells Harold she is going to get Johnny, speak to Maggie about dinner, and go to the house.

"I'm going to go talk with Jessie while Lawrence is still at the post office," Harold says. "I'll see you at the house." He leaves on his scooter and nearly freezes on the short trip to the Frys' house just up the street from his. When Jessie opens the door, he is shivering.

"Oh my gosh, Harold," she says, seeing him. "Come in here and sit by the fireplace and get warm." He does so as she pulls up a chair across from him.

"Why don't you get another car, Harold, instead of riding that damn surfboard?"

"It is fine most of the time just to go back and forth. That's all I need."

"Theora tells me you two may sell the business later this year if the war starts to wind down."

"We're seriously thinking that," Harold says. "I'm meeting with the land agent for U.E. tomorrow about that land next to the Drexel station."

"Lawrence tells me it's been on the market for a while."

"It has," Harold acknowledges. "I'm hoping I can talk the price down a bit; get some terms."

"That steep hillside shouldn't be a problem for you," Jessie says, holding back a smile.

He notices a glass on the table next to her, half filled with what appears to be bourbon. He nods toward it. "Tea, Jess?"

"Is that why you're here?" she responds.

"I worry about you. Lawrence is worried about you. Theora… we're all worried about you."

"And I'm worried about Mona and Donnie and Harvey," she argues.

"And we're not?" Harold pauses and takes a deep breath. "Alcohol isn't going to get them home sooner, Jess."

"I know. I just need a little drink now and then. It helps with the worry."

"You know it's more than that."

"It's not." Jessie glances at her unfinished drink. "I'll try, Harold. Alright?"

Harold nods.

Larry appears in the doorway from his bedroom. He is rubbing his eyes and sees Harold and runs to him.

"Uncle Helwald!" he yells as he runs and climbs in Harold's lap. "What are you doing here?"

Harold hugs his nephew and gives him a big smile. "I came to visit you and your mom." He tickles Larry a little, and the boy giggles. "When are you and your mom coming to see your cousin Johnny at the Whitehouse again?"

Larry looks at his mother. "Momma?"

"A day this week, how's that?" she says.

"Oh, boy!" Larry says excitedly.

Harold and Jessie exchange looks. She smiles. They have known one another for a long time.

Lawrence and Jessie have received one letter from Harvey since he left on January 2, indicating he was in New York preparing to board a troop ship headed to Europe. From the beginning, his fellow soldiers tagged him with the nickname "Pops" because of his advanced age of 35. To the 18–19-year-old recruits he came in with, he was almost old enough to be their father, and they afforded him due respect. Things would be different when he got to France. The men coming in now were mostly sent to a replacement depot and assigned to an existing combat unit in need of replacements.

The men who had survived North Africa and Sicily made the walk to Rome, and those who fought from the beaches to Paris and now the Rhine had buried many friends along the way. They didn't want any more "friends," and therefore, the replacements were simply private, or in Harvey's case, Private Pops. The consensus among the vets was that it was best to keep your distance, as the new guys' lack of experience could get you killed. This was the world into which Harvey landed when he arrived at an infantry unit near the Rhine.

Word from Don remains "chatty," but his letters still lacked any significant detail, except for one mailed just after Christmas. He had written a few lines to the effect that he would be celebrating the new year in a special place on the continent, but his heart would be at the Whitehouse. Everyone at the Whitehouse guessed Paris and wanted to be there instead.

Janie returns from Eldon late afternoon, and James is not far behind, driving a used Buick. Theora gets their guest settled into a room on the second floor, two doors from Janie's room and "next to Maggie's." Business in the dining room is non-existent, January being a very slow month, so they have dinner together there.

"I see you bought a Buick," Harold says. "They're reliable cars, I think."

"Yeah, it's a '41 model. Dealer said he had just taken it in a few days ago."

"It seems odd now that I never asked him," Maggie says, "but I don't believe I know what town Hiram is from."

"It's called Clarksville," Jim says. "It's actually closer to Memphis than Jackson. I'm figuring about a ten-hour drive."

Throughout dinner, Janie is mostly quiet. She sits next to Johnny, who is posed in his highchair between her and his mom. She enjoys cutting up his meat and teasing him, and he enjoys her attention. Suddenly, a thought occurs to her, and she looks across the table at Sergeant George.

"James? You said that you and Hiram had made each other a promise."

"Yes, we did, and you want to know who he was going to go see if I didn't make it instead of him."

"Your folks were dead. You said you had no other family."

"When my folks died, they left a sizable estate that was put into trust and managed by a trustee appointed by the court." James takes a drink of his beer. "The trustee sold all the real property and turned it into cash. Per the will my parents left, the estate was kept in interest-bearing accounts until I turned 21." James pauses and laughs. "I remember that day. We were under some pretty heavy fire that day... when I turned 21."

"You never told Hiram about your family, Jim?" Theora asks.

"No." He looks down at his plate. "I didn't want him to feel bad for me. And that's what he would have done." James pauses. Everybody is quiet, sensing he is trying to compose himself. "Hiram thought family was the most important thing there was. If he wasn't talking about the folks in Clarksville, he was talking about you folks here at the Whitehouse. Oh, and he talked constantly about you, Janie." He looks at her. "I can understand why."

She blushes, gets up, walks over to the jukebox, and lights a cigarette.

"When we had to make our will before we shipped, I made him my beneficiary. If I died, the notice of my passing would go to the trustee, and he would contact the beneficiary. And then he'd know."

"He would have been mad at you, probably," Maggie says.

"No, somehow I believe he would have understood," Harold says. "That boy would have understood."

Janie punches a selection on the jukebox, and momentarily, *Stardust* begins, and everyone is quiet while the music plays.

That night, before they go to sleep, Harold reminds Theora that they have a meeting at UE the next day, late morning.

"If we can get the price down a bit, good terms, I'm ready to go ahead. What do you think, Theora?"

"I want the same as you, Honey," she says. "I'm ready, too."

"Alright, we'll do it."

"I'm going to get going with Johnny in the morning and come on down to the Whitehouse early so I can say goodbye to Jim," Theora says.

At 6:30 the next morning, Maggie is busy in the kitchen when Janie comes in dressed in street clothes. Maggie takes one look at her and instinctively knows.

"Janie? What are you up to? What are you thinking?"

"I'm going with him, Maggie."

"You're going… does he know that?"

"Not yet. I couldn't sleep. I decided I needed to do this."

"Janie, you've never been further from this county than Jefferson City. People are different."

"Good people are the same everywhere," Janie says. "I'll only talk to good people."

"What if he says no?"

"He won't," she says flatly. "Maggie, I know I'll be leaving you without help, but it's a very slow time…"

"It's not that!" Maggie sits down and points to the chair across from her, and Janie sits. "I'll get along fine." Maggie looks at the girl and begins to see the young woman she has become. "I'll worry about you."

"Ever since Hiram died, I've had this feeling of unfinished business. It's been two and a half years, and it's still there. I think if I go and stand by his grave, I'll put it all behind me finally. James is my chance to do that."

Harold is outside, just finishing with a gas customer, when Theora pulls up, and she and Johnny get out and walk inside with him.

"Jim up yet?" Theora asks.

"Not before I went outside to pump gas. He may be in the kitchen by now." Harold and Theora, with Johnny, enter the kitchen. Not seeing Jim, Harold asks about him. "I know he hasn't left; his car is in the drive."

Theora senses it first. She looks at Janie, then Maggie, who diverts her gaze back to the stove, and then at Janie, who she realizes is not dressed for work.

"Something's up. I can feel it. What's going on, Maggie?"

Maggie turns to look at Theora, then Harold. "Janie is going to Mississippi with Jim."

"She's what?!" Theora says. "You're what?"

"What does Jim say about this, and where is he?" Harold asks.

"He doesn't know yet," Maggie says.

"He doesn't know yet?" Theora says. "For the love of God." As soon as she says it, Jim George comes through the kitchen door.

"I apologize for sleeping in," Jim says. "I didn't sleep much on the train and the hospital before that. I think it finally caught up with me. I slept like a log."

Maggie hands him a cup of coffee. "Sit down, Jim. You need some breakfast."

"I already put my duffel in the car. Don't want to linger too much."

Janie sits down across from him. "I'm going with you," she says bluntly. He looks at her. What she said hasn't fully registered with him. "I'm packed. My bag's over there," she says, pointing at a bag near the kitchen door. "I'm going with you. I'll pay my share."

When it finally registers, he says, "No, you're not. That's not a good idea."

"I'm going with you, James George. You might want to get used to that fact. Now, relax, have your coffee, and eat the breakfast Maggie fixed for you."

Jim looks at Maggie and Theora. "Help me out here, ladies. This is not a good idea, right?"

"Are you sure about this, Janie?" Harold asks.

"I have to do this."

"Ladies, she is a 23-year-old grown woman," Harold says. "She has a right to make her own decisions."

"Does she have the right to make Jim's decisions too?" Theora says.

"Good luck, Jim," Maggie says, giving Jim a look as she pours more coffee for him.

Thirty minutes later, car gassed, luggage loaded, Harold slips Janie a ten-dollar bill before she gets in the passenger seat. "Buy you and Jim some meals on us, okay?" to which she whispers, "Thank you," and gets in the car. Jim George backs out and pulls onto Highway 54, heading to Camdenton and Highway 5, just as the 7:30 bus pulls in and the Whitehouse gets busy.

Later that morning, Theora leaves Johnny with Phyllis and goes with Harold to see the Union Electric land agent. The meeting goes well, and a fair price and terms are agreed to, and the Pilkingtons sign. After, they go back to the house and talk to Marion and Phyllis.

"Well, it's done, Marion," Harold says. "We got the land."

"Congrats!" Marion says. "What's the next step?"

Harold laughs. "Paying for it." They laugh with him for a moment. "Seriously, I don't see us doing anything until late this year or early next. A lot depends on this damn war."

"Everything we read in the papers and hear on the radio says the war in Europe ought to be over in a few months," Marion says.

"Tell that to the Japanese, Marion," Phyllis says.

"I hate to think what will happen if we have to invade the mainland of Japan," Theora says.

"If the amount of business we're still seeing from the Fort is any indication, this war isn't going to end soon," Harold observes.

Don Fry has just lifted off from Orly U.S. Army Air Forces field near Paris with the rest of his longtime fellow crewmen. He is in the navigator's seat, platting a course for his pilot, who is at the helm of their Douglas C-54 Skymaster. His plane is deadheading back to England on orders to be available for a turnaround with ranking passengers. Their plane's use in the European theater has primarily been to transport high-level military and civilian personnel in and out of areas of the theater as the war progressed. The ride today is smooth, and the crew speculates who their passengers for the return will be.

"Not Patton," the co-pilot says. "I hear 'ole Georgy and his tanks are up near the Rhine, heading east."

"I hope it's an experienced supply sergeant," Fry says. "That PX at Orly is always out of Luckies. Have to smoke those damn Camels. Good supply man will straighten that mess out."

"You need to give those smokes up, Lieutenant," the pilot says. "They're bad for you. They'll kill you."

"They gave me something to do to keep me out of the brothels of Paris. They go with the wine. I'll quit after the war when I'm back home with my Suzy."

"That girl is all you think about, isn't it?" the pilot says.

"She is all I think about, too," the co-pilot says, laughing.

"Hey, Red Baron, I was going to introduce you to her sister when we get home, but I just changed my mind." They all chuckle. Fry looks out his window and sees only water below and notes in his log that they are midway across the English Channel.

"You told me she doesn't have a sister," the pilot says.

"Just a brother."

And the plane explodes. Thousands of pieces of metal and men scatter wildly throughout the surrounding air and begin to fall aimlessly toward the water, the Channel swallowing them up until there is no trace they ever existed.

Janie and James remain fairly quiet for most of the first hour or so of their trip, except when they cross Route 66, heading south on Highway 5.

"The Fort's just up the road there on 66," James says. "At St. Robert. Mississippi and I transferred in together from Fort Jackson back in late '40, when the place was being built."

"I've never been there," Janie says. "Could we see it?"

"Why would you want to do that? It's a place most people just want to forget."

"I don't know."

James looks at her. She is staring out the window. "Maybe on the way back."

The Buick continues to make its way down 5 to Mansfield, across to Willow Springs on 60, then 63 South to Thayer.

"Maggie packed us some ham sandwiches and cokes if you're hungry," Janie says.

"Are you?"

"Sure, I could eat."

Just south of Thayer, James pulls into a small parking area near a creek where a few fishermen are braving moderate cold weather, the sun shining. "The sign said 'Mammoth Springs.' I'll bet that the water is cold. Hand me a couple of cokes, and I'll lay them in the water for a few minutes." James does so, and momentarily, Janie walks to meet him, carrying the sandwiches and a jar of Maggie's homemade pickles. They find a picnic table and sit down to eat.

"Darn, Janie, I didn't think to get a bottle opener."

"Me either," she says, reaching into her skirt pocket. "But Maggie did."

"Those fellas there," James says, pointing, "are fishing for trout. The water is so clear, you can see them swimming. Before we go, you should walk down and look. You can see why they call them 'rainbow' trout."

In the car and back on the road, the Buick quickly crosses the border into Arkansas. Seeing the "welcome to" sign, Janie perks up and remarks, "I've never been in Arkansas before." She hesitates for a moment. "I've never been out of Missouri before."

James laughs. "They talk funny down here. Hard to understand."

Janie looks at him. "That's what the folks from Iowa say about us in Lake Ozark." They laugh together for the first time.

The post office closes by noon on Saturdays, and on this day in mid-January, Lawrence, Jessie, and Larry meet at the Whitehouse to have lunch with the Pilkingtons.

"Weekends are busy somewhat, but the weekdays are pretty much nothing," Harold says in answer to a question from Lawrence. He looks at Jess. "Have you or your mother heard anything more about Mona, Jessie?"

"Nothing. Not a word. I've called the Church headquarters in Springfield, and they still don't know anything either."

"All I see in the newspapers is that our troops are fighting their way slowly toward Manila, but Jap resistance is heavy," Harold says.

"One day, soon, we'll get good news about them, Jess," Theora says. "Try not to worry too much."

The Whitehouse phone rings and Harold gets up to answer it. "Whitehouse, this is Harold," he says when he picks it up. A moment, and then: "Yes, ma'am, he is. Just a moment, I'll get him. Yes…" Harold places his hand over the receiver. "Lawrence, it's your mother. She sounds very upset."

Lawrence looks at him, hesitates briefly, and then hurries to the phone and takes it from Harold. "Mom?" he says into the phone. Jessie sees the expression on his face and rises from the table, slowly walking toward him.

"No, no, mom…no…" Lawrence drops the phone, and it hangs loosely from the base as he starts to walk toward the stairs to the boiler room. Suddenly, his knees buckle under him, and he goes down, recovers briefly, and continues to walk. Harold picks up the phone and motions with it to Jessie, who comes over and takes it from him. Lawrence walks down the stairs and into the boiler room, locking the door behind him. He immediately lets out a loud, long scream that is heard throughout the building; its sound waves embedded permanently into its walls. He sits on the bench there and starts to sob.

"Mom, this is Jessie. What is it?" A moment, then: "Oh, dear God! What did they tell you?" She listens for a moment more. "He's very upset. As soon as he is composed, we'll be there. Is Mrs. Parker, your neighbor, there? Good, sweet lady. Be there as soon as we can. Gotta go now." She hangs up the phone and turns to Harold and Theora. "It's Donnie. They say he is missing, presumed dead."

"What the hell happened?" Harold says.

"Not sweet, Donnie, please no," Theora utters as she starts to cry.

"His plane went down over the English Channel. There is no trace of it. The entire crew is presumed dead."

"They can't find any wreckage at all?" Harold asks.

"No trace of anything. Mom Fry has nobody to bury, she says. Nobody to say goodbye to." And she breaks down and starts to cry. Harold wraps his arms around his cousin, his "sister," and holds her close as she lets long-suppressed emotions flow.

Lawrence remains locked in the boiler room for a long time, during which both Jessie and Harold try to talk to him through the door. The sobbing finally ends, and there is quiet. After two hours, Harold goes to the door, unlocks it from the outside, and enters the room. Lawrence, still sitting on the bench, looks up.

"Lawrence, you need to go to your mom. She needs you."

Lawrence hesitates for a moment. "Tell Jessie to go home and pack a bag for us. I'll be in the bathroom."

"We'll take care of Larry," Harold says.

"Please," he says as he gets up and goes out of the room.

A few days later, there is a memorial service for Don at the family's longtime church in Springfield. Suzy, working on a hospital ship in the Pacific, gets word of Don's loss by way of a letter from her mother and sits down on her bunk and cries. After a few minutes, she wipes away the tears, puts the letter under her pillow, walks the corridor to her ward, and goes back to work. She has seen a lot of death since joining the war and is not surprised to hear of one more.

James and Janie drive until after dark and decide they should find a place to stay and wait to arrive in Clarksville the next morning. On the south side of Memphis, they pull into a cabin court, and when James requests two rooms, the male clerk looks at him with a smirk.

James gives him a serious look. "I'm with my sister. Ladies deserve their privacy." When he goes back to the car, he hands Janie a key. "Here, sis. We leave at seven."

Janie gives him a look. "We'll leave when I'm ready."

Once in Clarksville the next morning, they find the Walker residence easily after only one stop to ask for directions. The house is situated on a farmstead at the edge of town, and James notes a few pieces of heavy equipment near a barn.

"It looks exactly like Hiram described it," James says. "What say you wait in the car while I knock on the door? Just in case we're not welcome."

"You didn't tell them we were coming?"

"I thought it better not to."

"It's been two and a half years, James!"

"Just wait here."

When the front door opens, a late middle-aged man looks at James, and when asked if he is Mr. Walker, he says, "Yes, Benjamin, Ben, and you are Sgt. George."

"How did you know that?"

"Nametag on your uniform, stripes on your arm."

"I was a friend of Hiram's. I just got out."

"Yes, he wrote about you often. Please, come in."

"Sir," James points toward the Buick, "I'm not alone."

"Your wife, go bring her in."

"Mr. Walker, she's not my wife. It's Janie, Hiram's Janie."

"Oh, my God. Go get her and bring her in. I'm going to get Helen."

James brings Janie in, and after introductions, he says to Mrs. Walker: "Hiram always called you Helena and said it was a beautiful name."

"He loved it, but everybody else called me Helen, so he was about the only one who called me that. That and mom."

"I'm sure you want to go out to the cemetery, so we'll have lunch before we go," Ben says.

At lunch, Helen tells Janie that she knew it was her the minute she first saw her near the front door. "How did you know?" Janie asks.

"The necklace. I gave that to Hiram the day he left to go to service."

After lunch, Ben insists on driving to the cemetery, and James rides in the front with him. "Several months after the funeral and all, we got a letter from the Army saying Hiram had been awarded the Silver Star. Someone came out some time later and gave it to us. I told this fella, a colonel, that I'd rather have a wounded son come home carrying a Purple Heart. He saluted and left."

"Top – that's the First Sergeant – told us he recommended Hiram for the award," James says. "He deserved it."

Ben pulls his car up near the site in the cemetery and parks. The four get out and walk over to Hiram's grave. On the way to the cemetery, they had stopped to buy flowers, and Janie stoops down and lays them there. She starts to cry until she suddenly has an image of Hiram in Heaven dancing, and a smile comes to her face.

"What exactly did he do, Jim, to deserve this plot of ground?" Ben asks.

James looks at the father of his best friend for a long moment, then down at his gravestone. "We were finishing up on the airstrip on the 'Canal,' and one of Hiram's platoon was retrieving some tools we had left in the middle. Without any warning, some gunfire erupts out of the trees at the far side, and the kid takes a bullet and goes down. Top tells everybody to lay down fire into those trees. The kid is hurting and calling out for the medic, and Hiram says he's going to go get him. Top yells, 'Walker, you keep your ass where it is'… sorry, Helen, for the language… and of course he says he's going, and I tell him I'll go. I'm faster, you can't run worth a damn, and… he grabs my arm and looks me in the eye and says firmly, 'Jimbo, he's my man, my responsibility, I'll get him outta there.' He takes off running across the runway, and we all start to lay down cover fire. He never ran so good before, like 'ole Jess Owens at the Olympics. He gets to the kid, and instead of putting him on his back in a fireman's carry, he picks him up in his arms," James reaches out his arms, hands up, to remember, "and he carries the kid like a parent carrying a child. He starts running like that, and a bullet gets him in the back, and he goes down on his knees. Somehow, he gets back up and gets back to us and cover. He does the fireman's carry, and the kid takes the hit and dies. Hiram survives." James' voice is almost a stutter now as he tries to hold back tears. On the clock, it is years; in the mind, a split-second. "The kid lived. Hiram died in my arms, and just before he did, he said, 'Kiss me, Jimbo,' and I leaned down and kissed him on his forehead." He looks up at Ben and Helen. "I don't know why he did that."

Janie hears him and says firmly, "It's what heroes do."

Before they leave to return to Missouri, Ben talks to James in private. "That girl, Janie, she's sweet on you, James," he says directly.

"No, no, I don't think so. We just met. She was Hiram's girl."

"Well, Hiram's dead," Ben says bluntly. "Nobody hurts more about that than me, but you gotta move on, and she's sweet on you."

"What makes you think that, Ben?" James asks, confused about it all.

"She bosses you around, and you let her. What's more, I think you like it."

The mood around the Whitehouse for the remainder of January is predictably solemn. Many locals knew Don or knew of him and were respectful of the loss. The decision is made, right or wrong, not to tell Harvey about Don, hoping to keep his focus on his own survival. Lawrence goes back to work at the post office and immerses himself in his job, and Jessie awaits news about her sister.

James and Janie return to Lake Ozark to hear the news about Don. Janie feels bad about being gone, but Theora tells her there is nothing to be done. "That's a lot of the sadness about it, Janie, that there wasn't anything to be done. We didn't even need pallbearers."

Harold talks with James over coffee while they sit at the front counter the morning after he and Janie get back. "What are your plans now, Jim? Back to Chicago?"

"No, no. I'll never go back to Chicago," he says with a bit of distaste in his voice. "I've been thinking about Kansas City."

"You know," Harold says, "I can always find a place for you here. That is if you want to stay."

"Thanks, I very much appreciate that."

Janie comes from the kitchen carrying a coffee pot and pours more coffee for the two men. "James, get your laundry together, and I will wash it this afternoon when I do mine," Janie says. He says, "Thank you," but it is to her back as she returns through the door to the kitchen. Harold stifles a smile, witnessing the exchange.

"There were a lot of military on the train from San Francisco with me, many with visible wounds, some not so visible," James says. "A lot of them got off in K.C. I assume that they were headed out in many directions: Nebraska, Iowa, western Kansas, you know, heading home."

"And no one there will understand what they've been through?" Harold asks, more a statement.

"Only another veteran." James pauses and sips his coffee. "Harold, my parents left me a lot of money, a lot of money. I wouldn't have to work, but that's not me. I have to do something meaningful with my time, my life."

Harold nods his head in recognition of where James is going with the conversation. "You intend to help vets."

"I'm going to look into setting up a gathering place for fellow veterans to go to interact with others who share their problems. I want to speak to some of the local pastors, priests, maybe psychologists, to see if they would volunteer to help out."

"You want to do this in Kansas City?"

"It seemed like a very nice city when I came through. Nobody I talked to spoke badly about it. And it's not so big." James pauses again. He knows Harold probably has his doubts about his plans. "I don't have a college diploma, so I know many people won't take me seriously."

"I disagree, I think they will, Jim," Harold says with sincerity. "You wouldn't let that stop you anyway."

"I suppose not."

On the last Sunday in January, James leaves in his Buick to drive to Kansas City. He tells everyone he will be back the following weekend. Maggie, though she does not come right out and say it, is very relieved to have Janie back at the Whitehouse.

"We missed you here while you were gone. The trip went well?"

"Hiram's folks were very nice people, Maggie," Janie tells her. "Very kind and sweet; just what you'd expect. They treated us like we were…were family."

"What are Jim's plans now? He said he was going to Kansas City?"

"He went to investigate an idea he has to help GIs, returning veterans. He wants very much to do that. He talked a lot about it on the drive."

"What else did you talk about on the drive?" Maggie asks.

"Oh, just things."

"Is he coming back here again?" Maggie asks.

Janie looks at her. "You heard him say it. Next weekend, Maggie."

"How can you be so sure?"

"Because he's going to marry me," Janie says with certainty.

"What?" Maggie is astonished. "Do you…how…okay, the same old question: Does he know that yet? Have you told him that?"

"I'm not sure if he knows it yet," Janie says. "But I'm sure if I know it yet."

On February 3, the Santo Tomas prison camp in the Philippines is liberated by American forces with aid from Philippine guerillas. Two days later, Jessie gets word from both her mother in Tulsa and Mona's church leadership in Springfield. According to the Red Cross, they are very malnourished but expected to live. Their liberated family includes a new baby born during their internment.

The news helps to divert some of the grey clouds hanging over the Whitehouse family, and Jessie feels some relief from the concerns that are her burden, though she tries to help comfort Vivian, who constantly worries about Harvey. Other news from Tulsa is that Harry has finished his initial enlistment, and with a request from the Fire Department, he is discharged from the Coast Guard and headed home. Their big news is that Maxine is expecting a baby to join her, Harry, and baby Peggy. Harold, though he barely mentions it, is relieved that his baby brother is home safe.

In the European theater, the Allied forces have crossed the Rhine and are making their way into Germany, meeting some resistance. Harvey's unit is a leading element, and as they cross an open field, they begin taking heavy fire from artillery and small arms. Harvey's company commander calls in the coordinates for a return artillery strike and recognizes almost immediately that the shells are falling short, exploding among his own men.

Cries of "medic" fill the air all around as his men begin dropping, and the captain becomes frantic. "Cease firing! Cease fire! You're short! Cease fire!" Finally, the batteries are calm. "God. What have I done?"

"I know you gave them the right coordinates, Cap," his radio operator says. "I know you did. Look at the map. You didn't do anything wrong."

The captain looks at his radioman for a moment. "Adjust, dammit, and fire a round for effect," he says. A single round is soon seen exploding within the enemy position. "You're on it now. Take 'em out," he says into the mike. "Take care of the wounded men!" he yells to his troops.

The corpsman reaches Harvey, one of the first to fall, soon after and notes severe wounds to the right side of his face, with his right arm dangling limply by his side. "Hang on, Pops. You're gonna make it. Stay with me now. Stretcher bearers! Now!"

On Saturday afternoon, February 17, Harold is standing at the doorway to the dining room when a young man in the uniform of an Army major comes in. Harold looks closely at him as he seems familiar. The major approaches and reaches out his hand to Harold. "You're Mr. Pilkington, aren't you?"

"I am," Harold says as he shakes the man's hand.

"You may not remember me. I came to your Thanksgiving dinner in '43. You asked me to say the prayer."

"My gosh," Harold says, recognizing him. "Patrick O'Connor, now Major O'Connor, I see."

"I just returned to the States. They had me in the Pacific for a while but recently rotated me back to Ft. Wood. Drove over to see if the Lake was still here. And you and yours."

Harold laughs. "We're still here. Still trying to figure things out."

"Any luck?"

Harold chuckles. "No. What about you, Father? What are your plans?"

"I think I'll be discharged this spring. I've asked the bishop to give me a parish in the Kansas City area. My sister and her family live there."

The front door opens, and James and Janie enter. Harold turns to O'Connor. "Great, I want you to meet these folks. Guys, come here a moment." The pair walks over and joins Harold and the major. "Janie, you remember Father O'Connor from Thanksgiving two years ago?"

"Oh, yes, of course," she says. "Nice to see you again, sir." She shakes his hand. "I remember your prayer."

"This is Sergeant James George, recently retired from the Army," Harold says. "He has some plans he might want to share with you."

"Please excuse me, gentlemen, I need to get to work and help Maggie," Janie says and goes to the kitchen.

"He's getting out soon and is hoping the church will send him to K.C.," Harold shares. James perks up and shakes the major's hand. "You know where everything is, Jim. Grab a beer for the major and sit down and tell him about your plans."

The two men talk for an hour or so and promise to keep in touch. The major said he would, at his first opportunity, talk with his sister about her thoughts. As a teacher, the major says, she interacts with a lot of people who will, or do, have returning veterans in their families. The meeting between the two ends when the major excuses himself to return to the Fort.

"I've got all the masses in the morning, and I have yet to prepare, so I must get back," the major says. "Please tell Harold I'll try to stop next week. I hope to see you again, too."

Later in the evening, Janie and James are talking in the kitchen when James tells her he has decided to drive to Chicago the next day.

"I thought you weren't planning to ever go back there, James. Why now?"

"When my parents died, the trustee kept some personal items of theirs that he thought I would want someday," James explained. "They've been sitting in a bank lockbox ever since. It's time I retrieved them and brought them back with me to Kansas City."

"Will you go straight back to KC, then, from Chicago?" Janie asks.

"Yes, but I'll be back next Saturday," he says.

"Good, Maggie, and I will miss you."

Maggie, who has heard the entire exchange, laughs. "Absolutely," she says.

Vivian is informed about Harvey within a few days in a visit from a captain and a sergeant from Jefferson Barracks in St. Louis. She is extremely upset when she calls Jessie.

"I don't think I can talk to Mother Fry," Vivian says. "Will you and Lawrence do it?"

"Yes, we can. What exactly did they tell you, Vivian?"

"He has unknown injuries but is expected to live. He is being sent home on a hospital ship and will be treated in a hospital in New Jersey. As soon as he is there, I can go be with him."

"I'm going to get Lawrence, and we will drive to Eldon, and we'll talk to Mom Fry from there," Jessie says.

On the way to Eldon, Lawrence says to his wife, "This damn war better end soon, Jessie. I'm running out of brothers for it to take."

"Harvey's going to live, Lawrence. Let's just think about that."

James arrives back in Lake Ozark on Friday night, the twenty-third, and asks Janie if he can take her for a drive the next afternoon. "I want to show you something," he says. Janie works the breakfast and lunch shifts the next day before taking the afternoon off. She is due back at six for the usual Saturday night rush. At two, James, with Janie in the passenger's seat, pulls the Buick out into traffic and goes northeast across the dam and up through the cut to a hard right on Camp Road. About a half-mile down the road, he pulls to the right and behind the substation. He parks at a spot perfectly situated to see the dam and lake pictured together in the distance. It is a coolish, though sunny, late winter day. He turns in the seat to face Janie.

"This is one of my favorite spots since you first showed it to me," he says.

"I've always liked it, too," she says.

"Since I first met you, I've often thought that I would be getting to know you as Hiram's 'best man.' Seeing his folks helped me give up the guilt I carried with me since the day he died."

"Hiram would not want it any other way."

James reaches into his coat pocket and takes out a small jewelry box. "The truth is, Janie, I've fallen in love with you and want to marry you." He opens the box and takes out one of the rings. "This was my mother's engagement ring, and I want you to have it." He pauses while she looks down at it, then up at him. "Will you marry me?"

"The rings? That's why you went to Chicago." He nods. "Yes, of course, I will marry you." They kiss, and when they separate, Janie looks at him and smiles.

"We can afford a big wedding if you want," James says. "Invite everybody."

"If you don't mind, James, I don't want a big wedding. I just want my folks and my two brothers. I'll see if Maggie will stand with me as my maid of honor."

"Do you think Harold would be my best man and stand with me?"

"James, I can tell when Harold and Theora like someone, and they like you. Harold will be honored to be asked."

"I will ask him, then."

"Oh, I know," Janie suddenly says. "Marion and Phyllis and Ruthie. I want Ruthie to play 'Here Comes the Bride.'"

"Does she know it?"

"If she doesn't, she'll learn it quick enough." Janie pauses her enthusiasm for a moment, then: "It would be appropriate, before we tell anyone else, to go and talk with my parents. They haven't met you, and I haven't told them about you."

"And your brothers?"

Janie laughs. "The twins? They talk tough, but I can handle them."

Word comes from the military that Harvey has arrived at the hospital in New Jersey, and Vivian rides the train to meet him there. Soon after she arrives, she calls Jessie and Lawrence to tell them she has seen him and spent time with him.

"He has lost his right arm, but they tell him they can replace it with an artificial arm," Vivian says. "And his face on the right side needs reconstructive surgery. It has some severe wounds."

"Everybody here is praying hard for his recovery," Jessie says.

"He was in good spirits," Vivian says and starts to cry. "God, I love him so."

"Viv, you okay?" Lawrence asks.

"I told him about Donnie. It wasn't fair to Harvey not to tell him. He had a right to know."

"I think you did the right thing, Vivian," Jessie says.

"He is so sad, but I hope it will ease with time," Vivian says. "And one day, we'll be home again."

"I suppose we should be very thankful for that," Lawrence says.

The following Monday, Janie and James go to her folks' farm and have lunch with them. The twins are in their senior year in high school and not home at the time. Janie has refrained from wearing the ring until she has their blessing, which comes happily. Afterward, they go to the church in Eldon, where her family has been members for years and where she attended while growing up. The pastor agrees to marry them in what Janie describes as a small service. The event is set for Saturday, March 10, at 4:00 p.m.

"Now," she says to James, "we can go tell Maggie and Harold and Theora."

Back at the Whitehouse, Janie gathers the Pilkingtons in the kitchen with Maggie and James.

"We have something to tell you," Janie says. "James and I are getting married."

"Surprise, surprise," Maggie says, chuckling.

"Maggie! Be nice, or I won't ask you to be my maid of honor."

"I miss you already," Maggie says.

"Wonderful, I'm so happy for you," Theora says, hugging Janie.

"Congratulations, Jim, we wish you the best," Harold adds.

"When's the big day?" Theora asks.

"I told her we could afford a big wedding with all the trimmings," James says.

"We are just having a small service—my folks, my two brothers, and Maggie to stand up with me if she isn't too mad at me."

"I was wondering, Harold, if you would stand up with me?"

"Like a best man? Are you sure?" Harold asks.

"Yes, sir, I certainly am, if you would."

"What is the date?" Theora asks.

"March 10th, a Saturday at four in the afternoon," Janie says. "Christian Church in Eldon."

"That's just a week from this Saturday," Maggie says.

"Don't worry, Maggie, you won't have to wear a frilly pink bridesmaid dress," Janie tells her. "You can wear anything you like as long as it's not white."

"Janie, ask Theora about Ruthie," James says.

"Oh, yes, Theora. There's a piano in the church. Do you think Marion and Phyllis would come and let Ruthie play 'Here Comes the Bride'?"

"I bet they will and love to do it. I'll call her for you and ask her."

"Ruthie will love it. She always liked you a lot, Janie," Harold says. "We could tell."

"Harold, I want you to know I don't plan to just leave you and Maggie and Theora. We'd like to take a short jaunt after the wedding—three days, maybe—but I plan on working for a while until my job is covered. I have spent a lot of time training Bea, and I think she eventually will be good to help Maggie."

"Janie and I have talked about it, Harold. I'll go to Kansas City a few days a week, and she'll stay here and work. The place I'm staying in, KC, is just a hole-in-the-wall efficiency apartment. I need to find something else for my new bride."

"I like the sound of that…'my new bride,'" Janie says. Everyone laughs, including Maggie.

Later in the evening, alone, Theora turns to Harold, puzzled. "Did you see that coming? The marriage?"

"I wasn't totally surprised. She had him wrapped around her finger from the moment he came in that day." Harold laughs at the thought. "And he liked it."

"Well, I must say I missed it, but I like that they are a couple."

"I've been thinking, Theora. Janie wants a small wedding, but what if we hold a reception afterward here at the Whitehouse? It would be our wedding gift to them. We could invite whoever they want. Close the Whitehouse at 2:00 in the afternoon so we can go to the wedding and leave it closed the rest of the night. Hell, we'll even spend the night in our old room. The bed is still there for Johnny. I have to be here early the next morning anyway."

"It's a Saturday night, Harold. Our biggest night of the week."

"We will post a notice ahead of time that we will be closed for a private party. Word will get around. It's one night. We won't starve to death."

"Okay, we'll tell them tomorrow. See how they feel about it."

"Look, Theora, if we are going to find a buyer and sell before Fall, this may be the last chance to do something like this."

"Okay. Let's have a party!"

Janie and James agree to the reception at the Whitehouse when Harold and Theora tell them about the plan the following morning. James tries to convince Harold to let him pay the costs, but Harold insists that it is their gift to the newlyweds.

"We'll probably leave by ten or so, Harold, and drive to Jefferson City that night," James tells him. "I hope that will be alright."

"Of course, you're the groom. You can do anything you want as long as it's okay with the bride."

Plans for the wedding and reception proceed successfully as Theora dusts off Harold's only suit, and James does the same with his dress uniform, ensuring that all "fruit salad" and other insignia are in an appropriate position. Theora and Maggie go together to Jefferson City one day, and each buys a new dress: Theora's first in six months, Maggie's in ten years. Janie shops with her mother to find a dress for the wedding—simple lines, white, somewhat Victorian in style, inexpensive. James tells her whatever she wants, buy it, but she is farm-born and bred and naturally frugal. Janie, though, has saved a considerable amount from her wages over the last few years and insists on buying her mother a new dress, her first since…? Her dad insists on wearing the same suit he has worn to church on Sundays for the last thirty years, and nobody is going to talk him out of it.

Ruthie is delighted to be asked to play at the wedding and practices the music to be ready for the big day. Phyllis plans to wear a dress she already has but does take Ruth to find a new dress for the event—something that also delights her.

A couple of days before the wedding, Harold sits down with Maggie alone in the kitchen, and they reminisce about the past.

"I remember when you first came, you kept apologizing for the things you didn't know," Maggie remembers. "But you know what? I was surprised that an eighteen-year-old city kid knew as much as you did."

"There were a couple of years there when I helped take care of my baby brother. I had to learn a few things."

"You seemed to know your way around a kitchen; I remember that."

"Maggie, Theora, and I are thinking very seriously about selling the business this year—if we can find a buyer."

"I'm not surprised. I've been expecting it, and you won't have any trouble finding a buyer. You've built a very successful business here."

"We have, with your help," Harold says.

"I will stay with a new buyer if they want me long enough for a smooth transition, but I will retire soon after. I'm getting old. It's time."

"You're not old, Maggie; you're timeless."

Saturday morning, March 10th, Theora enlists Phyllis to go with her to Eldon to shop. She tells Harold that there is a shoe sale at the Eldon Shoe Store, and she needs a new pair to go with her new dress. When they return, Harold makes preparations and posts a "closed for private party" sign at the front door at exactly two in the afternoon. Jessie and Lawrence have agreed to come to the reception, Harold insisting they need positives in their life. They will watch Johnny and Baby Cookie and will bring them to the reception later, along with Larry. Maggie rides to the church with James, as Janie has stayed the night before at her parents' to avoid him on "the day." When they arrive, James and Harold hang out in the men's room, and Maggie awaits Janie and her family in the pastor's study. Marion and Phyllis have arrived at the church early as well, so Ruthie can rehearse once on the piano there.

At exactly 4:00 p.m., the pastor nods to Ruthie, who plays The Wedding March flawlessly as Janie, arm in arm with her father, walks down the aisle. A few vows, a few "I do's," a tender kiss, and a little thrown rice later, Mr. and Mrs. James George emerge. As long as everyone involved knows their "lines" and hits their "mark," it doesn't take long to get married. Then, to paraphrase Theora: "It's time to party!"

Guests at the reception are directed to enter through the door located near the front corner of the dining room. Harold has placed a sign there reading "private party entrance only." Other than the kitchen, it is the only room that is lit to discourage other business on this night. Father O'Connor is in attendance, indicative of his new friendship with James. Also, to the delight of Phyllis and Theora, Bernie Gordon comes, escorted by a gentleman she has just recently started seeing. He, like Bernie, is a single parent. His name is Gary Waters, and he has a daughter named Saundra, who is just a few years older than Kay. The Robinson sisters enjoy spending time with "ole Bern," as they like to call her, and getting to know her new beau. Jo and Jay, who have worked a few Saturday nights at the Whitehouse with Janie, also come to wish her well. Two couples of Janie's aunts and uncles come, and a few of her old friends, though many are away because of the war.

Beatrice helps Maggie and the Robinson girls set out the food in cafeteria style, and before the meal, a prayer is said. Janie's pastor is unable to attend due to a scheduled Saturday night service, so James asks the priest to say a blessing.

"People, I think — and not just Protestants — are inclined to wonder how a man of the cloth who is not married and likely to never be so can give advice to young marrieds. Well, I can't. So, I won't." A pause: the room is quiet. Then: "Except to say, James, always do what you are told and when you are told, and you will have a happy marriage. My father, the one from Ireland, taught me that." As the laughter quiets, Father O'Connor bows his head and says, "Lord, please bless this couple and all those gathered here to celebrate this new beginning. And bless this food and those who have labored to prepare it. And, Lord, especially bless our brother Harvey to get well soon and rejoin his family here. In the name of the Father, Son, and the Holy Spirit. Amen."

Toasts are given prior to the eating: Harold and Janie's father each offering one, and there are assorted others, as would be expected. But Maggie's "toast" brings tears to many, including herself.

"To my special Janie and her beau. It will seem so strange in the future not to have you by my side as we go about the day's business at this special place. How long now have we been attached at the hip? It can be counted in years. I never had a daughter, but if I did, I would want her to be just like you."

It is quiet for a few moments, a few tears visible among the gathering, until Janie speaks up and says, "Maggie, I'll be back at work next Wednesday," and tears give way to laughter.

Janie's brothers have had little time to get to know their new brother-in-law, so at the first opportunity, they corner him to ask about the military. They will soon graduate and have plans to enlist in the Marines when they turn eighteen in mid-summer.

James looks both of them directly in the eye and says, "Boys, don't do that. If you do, odds are you'll be dead by Christmas. If you have to go, join the Navy; you'll see action, but at this point, your ship will have control of any battle."

"But why not the Marines?" one of the boys asks. "They're tough; they survive."

"They are," James agrees. "But this is a different enemy than we've ever faced before. They will do anything to protect their homeland and emperor, including letting every man, woman, and child die."

"I don't understand how anyone can do that," the other boy says. "Soldiers fight, not civilians."

"I saw Japanese civilians, women with children, jump to their deaths off a cliff on Saipan rather than be captured." James pauses for a moment to see if that is comprehended. "If we have to invade the mainland of Japan, and I think we will, hundreds of thousands of American soldiers will die. And the first several waves of troops will be Marines. Join the Marines right now, and you won't be heroes; you'll be cannon fodder."

"Thanks for the encouragement, Jim," the first twin says cynically.

"I would hope that ten or so years from now, you each will be bouncing my future nephews and nieces on your knees and not rotting in a rice paddy near Tokyo."

"Thanks for talking with us about it," the second twin says.

James gets up to rejoin his bride. "I best get back to your sister before I get in trouble. I'll leave you with one thought: 'Anchors Aweigh.'"

Jessie shares with Harold and Theora that just before they came to the party, she had heard from her mother. Mona called her to tell her that she and her family were in San Francisco, being attended to at a hospital there and that when their health improved enough, they would be put on a train home. Though the news helps to provide a lift to both Lawrence and Jessie, it is evident that they both carry a lot of worry and pain, conditions that only time can heal. Their son Larry, Lawrence says, gives them a positive focus for their love. Jessie exchanges a quick look and a smile with Harold as they watch Johnny and Larry play.

Phyllis and Marion visit with Janie and her family for a while, and Marion asks where she and James are going on their honeymoon.

"Niagara Falls, I bet," Phyllis interjects.

"No, not there," Janie says.

"No, where then?" Marion asks.

"Mammoth Springs," Janie says.

"Mammoth?" Marion wonders. "It sounds bigger than Niagara."

"Oh, no, I don't think so, Marion. It's just a stream. It's on the Missouri-Arkansas border."

"One of the springs, I bet, down in the hills," Phyllis says.

"Yes, that's it," Janie says. "It's a very pretty spot. We went there before and drove on Highway 5, but James says that because we will be in Jefferson City tonight, tomorrow we'll drive on 63 straight south to get there."

"So, you've been there before?" Phyllis says.

"Yes, passed through. It was very pleasant."

"Are there cabin camps there?" Marion asks.

"Oh, I don't know," Janie says. "I guess we'll find out when we get there."

Phyllis laughs. "Our entire marriage has been like that, Janie. We found out when we got there."

"Looks like it worked out alright, though," Janie says, smiling.

Phyllis looks at Marion, pulls him close, and hugs him. "Yep, he has a 'cabin camp' in his heart."

Jay and Harold find a quiet moment together and visit over a drink. They are both avoiding their wives, who have decided to make up for all the dances they didn't have in the past because of work.

"We've sure come a long way from our Oklahoma roots, Jay," Harold says. "Civilization advances. Instead of the old 'Charleston' and the 'Black Bottom,' we now dance the 'jitterbug?'"

"Disgraceful," Jay laughs. "We Indians still dance the same way we did 500 years ago."

"Instead of cowboys and Indians shooting at one another, we've banded together to shoot at Japs and Krauts."

"Yeah, we're certainly maturing as a species," Jay says.

Harold holds up his glass; Jay raises his. Harold taps Jay's glass. "Thanks for always having my back," Harold says. Jay nods.

Father O'Conner walks up to the two old friends and excuses himself. "Sorry to interrupt, gentlemen, but it's my understanding that you two, like me, are not native Missourians."

"Jay, meet Patrick O'Connor, Major, US Army, man of the cloth." The two men shake hands. "Jay is originally from the Reservation in northeast Oklahoma and, like me, an Okie."

"Call me Pat, Jay. I am, as you can tell, an Irishman. Came here from Dublin when I was ten with my mother and sister. Posting by Uncle Sam brought me to Fort Wood."

"What is it that makes a mother uproot her family and take it so far from its home?" Jay asks. "To be so fearless?"

"My father had died in '15, and when the 'uprising' happened around Easter of 1916, my mother says we're going to America." He pauses and chuckles. "I asked 'why,' she said 'there's nothin' here, lad,' and we left."

"Most American Indian tribes were nomadic prior to the white man's arrival, but that pretty much ended with the reservations," Jay says.

"I asked my mother how we could leave Ireland; it was our home, and she says: 'Ireland is our past, and the past should be left where we lived it.'"

"Any news of you getting a Kansas City parish?" Harold asks.

"Yes, I think so. I'm due to be discharged next month, and word from the Bishop is that I'm in line to get a church in one of the small towns near the city."

"Well, we'll all be Missourians then," Harold says. "Right now, Theora is giving me one of her 'come here and Show-Me looks,' so I'd best go see what she wants."

"Harold," Theora instructs, "James and Janie have changed into their traveling clothes and are getting ready to leave. Janie is going to throw her bouquet for the girls to catch."

"Well, gather them up, and Marion and I will make sure no one escapes," Harold says.

"Alright, girls, group up!" Theora yells. "Janie is going to throw the bouquet now." All the young, single girls gather. "You, too, Maggie, get in there," Theora demands.

"Wait!" Marion yells. "Bernie's not in there. Bernie, get in there."

"You heard the man, Bern," Harold tells her. "Get in there."

Bernie reluctantly gets up and stands near the back of the group. Just as Janie turns her back and throws the bouquet, Bernie lifts her hands, palms up in front of her in a shrugging gesture, turns to Harold as if to say, "Why am I here?" and the tipped bouquet lands in her arms.

"Oh, my God!" Theora exclaims, laughing.

Phyllis joins her in laughing. "For the love of God, Bern!"

Goodbye, hugs and handshakes completed, more rice thrown. Harold unlocks the front door of the Whitehouse. The newlyweds depart through it as a gentle breeze from the building's air drifts away with them into the future.

As the party begins to wind down, Theora goes to Harold and asks him to come with her into the kitchen for a moment, which he dutifully does.

"Honey, step out onto the porch with me for a minute," Theora says. "There's something I want to tell you."

Harold follows her out onto the back porch. "A bit chilly but dry," he says. "Not too bad, though. Moon's out; you can see the water." He offers Theora a cigarette, but she shakes her head "no." He lights one. "Can I have a sip of your drink?" he asks.

"You won't like it," she says as she hands it to him. He takes a sip and wrinkles his nose.

"Tonic water? What happened to 'let's have a party'?"

"I went to see Dr. Attic in Eldon this morning."

"Dr. Attic? Are you alright? Why the doctor?"

"He said that I'm pregnant. I'm going to have a baby." She pauses, looking Harold in the eyes. "We are going to have a baby."

"I thought you went to get shoes. That's what you said."

"I bought a pair." Theora holds up her foot. "You like them?"

"Sure, they're great." Harold takes his wife in his arms. "Maybe a girl this time," he says. "I'd like to have a daughter."

"I'll tell God what you said, Honey," Theora says to him.

"I love you, Theora Robinson."

"I love you too, Harold Pilkington."

They kiss and embrace for the longest time, illuminated by the light of the moon. For a moment, it looked as if the moon had winked, but it was probably just a small bird passing quickly by.

EPILOGUE

LAKE OZARK, MISSOURI
EARLY MARCH 1945

It is Sunday morning, March 11. My father rises quietly from the bed, trying not to awaken Mother, and proceeds down the hall to shower and dress. As he passes the door to our room, he sees Mother sitting on the edge of the bed. "I'm going down," he says quietly so as not to wake Johnny. Mother smiles a 'good morning' to him. "Take your time," he says in return. Father goes down the stairs and into the kitchen, where Maggie has already prepared coffee and is frying ham.

"I thought you were going to sleep in and let Bea do that, Maggie?" Father says.

"I woke up early. Couldn't go back to sleep, so I decided to get up and come down."

"I didn't see Bea out front?"

"She is out there. Was talking about picking up in the dining room, but not much left to do with everybody pitching in last night to help."

"They sure did, didn't they?" Father says.

"Coffee's perked, Harold. Have some fresh gravy soon. Biscuits going in the oven in five," she says.

"Smell's good," he says as he pours himself a cup of coffee. "I'll open up and meet the bus," Father tells her.

At 7:00 a.m., Father unlocks the front door and walks out, sitting on the bench just outside the front door, waiting for the bus. The early bus out of St. Louis is always on time, with 7:30 arrival and 8:00 departure. Or at least, it is on Sundays when Anthony Bertone is driving.

He thinks back to the night before. All the joy of the evening helped to drown out the pain and sadness of recent years. The consensus is the war in Europe will soon be over, but Japan, it appears, is determined to fight to the end. God help us to keep that from happening, Father prays silently.

Oh, yes, the baby, Father reminds himself. I haven't forgotten. I'm going to be a dad again. He smiles. Theora surprising me like that. Maybe a daughter this time… more important, a healthy baby. This makes it even more urgent to sell and move on. My God, I've been in this building since I was eighteen years old. Theora, too; seems like we grew up here. I don't want my children to grow up here.

When he first came to Lake Ozark, there were so few residents; not really a town yet. There was a new building, the School of the Osage, as important an anchor as any. Marion, the Moores, Phyllis, Theora, and Jo and her family were here, but the town was a name only, as yet undefined. Together with others from out of town, Jay Rice, the Frys, the Gordons, and the Jameses among them, they invented a community. Among the anchors to hold people here was this building… the one they called the "Whitehouse," a place not to be owned but used.

Father is reminded of an anonymous quote he read in a book in high school. He is only now realizing why it stuck with him, but it did:

"Nothing is ours to keep for ourselves. Money, talent, time, whatever it may be that we possess, is only ours to use. This is the great law written everywhere."

We've seen a depression and a war, Father contemplates with some amazement, and most of us aren't even thirty yet; Bernie, the Frys, barely late thirties. And I'm going to be a father again.

Father looks down at his watch. It is 7:27. He glances down the highway toward the dam and sees the bus at the far end coming his way. Tony pulls the bus into the driveway and stops exactly at 7:30, opens the bus door, and announces to the passengers that they "have 30 minutes, the food's great here, and we leave promptly at 8:00." Father watches as the few passengers step down. He counts eight, including a young man in Army uniform who walks with a limp, a cane helping him along. The soldier glances at Father briefly as he enters the building. Tony retrieves a bundle from the overhead rack and comes off the bus.

"Here's some St. Louis papers for the racks, Harold, I'll take the rest inside," Tony says as he hands off some of the papers.

"Thanks, Tony," Father says as he loads the racks and returns to sit, drinking his coffee. Bruce James pulls into the driveway, gets out, and gets copies of the St. Louis papers.

"Morning, Harold," he says. "Be back later for church. See you then."

"Morning, Bruce." Harold watches Bruce as he gets back in his car to leave. Harold reflects on the rumors that Bruce is expected to be appointed the next Superintendent of Bagnell Dam, perhaps as early as this year. He always stays in touch with what's happening in St. Louis, habitually reading the papers, Harold notes. Smart man, he thinks. Harold appears oblivious to all else, it seems when momentarily he looks up and sees the young soldier with the cane standing, looking down at him.

"You mind if I sit down with you?" the soldier, a sergeant, asks.

"No, not at all," Father says. "Sit down."

"I asked the little lady inside, the pretty one with the freckles if I could buy my cup," the soldier says, holding up his coffee cup. "Take along as a souvenir of your place here."

"And what did she say?" Father asks.

"She said I was the first to ever ask such a question and, after all I'd been through, if that was the one thing I wanted, she'd just give it to me. I left her a tip."

"That was my wife. Theora. I'll tell her you called her pretty," Father says.

"I know. I recognized her from before," the soldier says.

Father looks at the sergeant curiously. "Why," he asks, "would you want a souvenir of this place, Sergeant?"

The soldier looks directly at Father and says: "You don't recognize me, do you?"

Father looks at the young man and slowly shakes his head. "No, I can't place you," Father says. "I'm sorry."

"I was here with three of my buddies from Ft. Wood on New Year's Eve '43. I got drunk and was causing trouble. The night ended with you breaking your hand while breaking my jaw," the soldier relates, smiling.

Father looks at the soldier for a brief moment and then, suddenly: "Goose Egg! Oh, my God. Goose Egg. You back to get revenge, gonna hit me with that coffee cup?"

"No, sir," the soldier says, laughing lightly. "You see, I kind of look back at that night as the moment that saved my life. You probably saved my life."

Father does not understand the sergeant. He only remembers how angry he got that night, something he regretted and knew was uncharacteristic of him. "I apologize for that night; I should have handled it better. I could have handled it better. I hit you. I was angry. I should not have hit you."

"My buddies took me to the base hospital when we got back, and after my jaw was sufficiently healed, I got put in the brig for a month," the sergeant continues. "By the time I got out, my buddies, my unit, were headed to Europe. I didn't ship with them. I had to start basic training all over again." The soldier looks down at his leg for a moment and readjusts his posture on the bench. "80% of my original unit died on Omaha Beach on D-Day, including two of my buddies. The third friend was taken out by a sniper before the unit got to Paris. Before they shipped, they told me they had been back and inquired about you. How you had polio and all, turned down for the draft."

Father looks out at the street. "Still, I was out of line. Shouldn't have hit you."

"No, sir. You see, sir, by the time I got to France, the only fighting going on in Paris was over a bottle of wine or a girl. I only saw limited action until Market Garden. Took shrapnel from a grenade early in that mess." The soldier pats his leg. "Tore my leg up pretty good, and they brought me out. Eventually got to Jersey, where I've been rehabbing since. Heading home now. I'm convinced I wouldn't be if it hadn't been for that night." He pauses, glances over at the bus, and then back to Father as he holds up his cup. "This coffee cup will remind me of that."

"Where is your home, Sergeant?" Father asks. "What do you call home?"

"Stillwater, Oklahoma. You heard of it?"

"Oh, yeah," Father says. "I'm a Tulsa man myself. Born and bred. Out there at A&M, you got some great wrestlers. Art Griffith's boys."

"I've heard. I was a rodeo guy myself. Gonna give it a try again when I get better."

"Where'd that nickname, Goose Egg, come from?" Father asks.

"For a long time after I started rodeoing, I hadn't had a win, and they kidded me about the big zeros I kept putting up," the soldier explains. "Wasn't long 'til that became 'goose egg.' The name followed me into the Army."

The passengers have begun coming out and reloading, followed by Tony, who speaks to Father as he walks to the bus. "Heading out, Harold. See you next trip." And to the soldier: "How about you, Sarge, you ready to go?"

"Yes, sir, right behind you," he says, then turns to Father and reaches out his hand to shake. "Tulsa, I hope you and that pretty lady with the freckles have a very happy life."

Father shakes the young man's hand. "You, too, cowboy, you, too," he says. The sergeant reenters the bus, sits, and Tony pulls out onto the highway. Father glances at his watch and smiles. It is 8:00 A.M.

Father reenters the Whitehouse and goes back into the kitchen. Johnny is sitting in his high chair, eating a biscuit with gravy. Maggie is watching him as she cleans up. "Wouldn't eat the ham," Maggie says. "Wanted bacon. 'Kwispy bacon, Maggie,' he says to me. 'Kwispy bacon.' And I fixed it."

"Good morning, Johnny. Eat good now," Father says as he kisses the top of my brother's head. "Tell Maggie 'thank you,' Johnny. Okay?" The boy, his mouth full, nods. Father refills his cup with coffee and goes out of the kitchen. "Bea, have you seen Theora?" Father asks the waitress, who stands behind the counter.

"In the dining room, I believe, Harold," the girl says. Father walks to the door, looks in, and sees Theora standing across the room in front of the jukebox.

"Theora?" Father says.

Mother looks up and, seeing him, says, "Honey, come here a minute, would you?" It is not a question. A brief male "what now" passes through his thoughts as he walks across the room to her. Mother looks up from the jukebox and turns to him.

"I've been thinking about maybe we should wait to sell the business until after the first of the year. January."

"Why the change of mind?" Father asks.

"The baby is due in early October, and I think it would be nice if this child were like the others. Like Ruthie, Larry, Johnny, and Cookie… born a child of the Whitehouse family."

Father looks at her and repeats, "A child of the Whitehouse family." He ponders the thought for a moment, then says, "If that's what you want. One more Christmas and New Year here can't hurt, I suppose." He laughs.

Theora turns to the jukebox and punches a selection. "Dance with me," she says.

Father looks at her. "Theora, it's 8:15 A.M."

"Honey, dance with me. Put down your cup and dance with me." Reluctantly, Father sets his cup on top of the jukebox and takes Mother into his arms just as the sounds of *Blue Moon* fill the air with requited love.

Father kisses Mother, and they dance as the band plays, and… the matter is settled.

And that is how I became a child born a member of the Whitehouse family.

Way back then... when we all were young.

ACKNOWLEDGEMENTS

First of all, to niece Terri Davis, who, in the fall of 2022, said to me, "Tim, you should write a book," thanks?! As that desire had been smoldering for many years without action, she had lit the fuse. The White House Hotel is the result of that "flare-up."

To the three people in my world who would understand the folks who populated the "Whitehouse" – Ruth Clayton Phillips, Cookie Clayton Thelen, and Judy Haage Rentschler – your advice and consent of the manuscript were more than invaluable in writing this book. In the text, I managed to mention every grandchild of Bert and Lena Robinson, including, in a circuitous way and unborn at that point, the youngest, Carol Ann Deveney. That's appropriate, as she is the "cherry on the top" of a wonderful family. Thank you, and love you all!

To Jim Pilkington, my late cousin and friend – who, in myriad conversations over the years about Tulsa days, fueled the manuscript – I wish you were here to read it. Perhaps your grandson will approve.

Jill and Jason Luebbering, niece and nephew, who have experience in publishing (Jill wrote a great book, "aNNA'S hELP"), were very valuable in helping me understand the complex process. Thanks, guys!*

Dear friends, Sharon and John Bertone, humored me through many meals and "happy hours" as I talked about the book in progress, read the manuscript, and offered valuable insights. Thanks, kids.

I would be remiss if I did not mention my in-laws, Bill and Verna Luebbert, and Lynn and Norbert (deceased) Luebbering. They have managed to also indulge me over many years – 52 and counting. I can only imagine it wasn't easy.

Special thanks to Roni De Jong who provided a vintage post-card on which the cover artwork is based. She discovered the postcard in the collection of her now deceased father, Henry Heldstab.

In my author's note, I mentioned that I was not a historian. Others have done that better than I ever could. That said, I would recommend all the history books about the lake area by the late Dwight Weaver and Donna Shockley Carrender's excellent history of the School of the Osage. Great reads! For more detailed information on the history of Miller and Camden Counties, I recommend their respective historical societies.

To successfully detail the importance of my wife, Carole, and my daughter, Christina, in the process of completing this book is impossible. The book simply would not exist without their almost daily indulgence in my efforts. They are "long-suffering" and thus should be "long loved." So be it.

**That is not a misprint; actual title, great read!*

ABOUT THE AUTHOR

Tim Pilkington was born and raised in Lake Ozark, Missouri and is a graduate of the School of the Osage High School. He has a BA degree from Drury University and an MA from the University of Iowa. He is the author of The Cricket's Song, a two-act play about a family in Bagnell during the construction of Bagnell Dam. He has written two unproduced screenplays, one of which, Driftwood, he is currently adapting into a novel. Tim lives in Florida with his wife Carole. They have one daughter, Christina, a chamber executive in-central Florida. The White House Hotel is his first novel.